S0-AEZ-416

# UNFORGETTABLE

*Titles by Alison Kent*

UNDENIABLE

UNBREAKABLE

UNFORGETTABLE

# UNFORGETTABLE

## Alison Kent

HEAT | NEW YORK

**THE BERKLEY PUBLISHING GROUP**
**Published by the Penguin Group**
**Penguin Group (USA) Inc.**
**375 Hudson Street, New York, New York 10014, USA**

USA | Canada | UK | Ireland | Australia | New Zealand | India | South Africa | China

Penguin Books Ltd., Registered Offices: 80 Strand, London WC2R 0RL, England
For more information about the Penguin Group, visit penguin.com.

This book is an original publication of The Berkley Publishing Group.

Copyright © 2013 by Alison Kent.
Excerpt from "The Gunslinger's Heiress" copyright © 2013 by Alison Kent.
All rights reserved. No part of this book may be reproduced, scanned, or distributed in any printed or
electronic form without permission. Please do not participate in or encourage piracy of copyrighted
materials in violation of the author's rights. Purchase only authorized editions.

HEAT and the HEAT design are trademarks of Penguin Group (USA) Inc.

Library of Congress Cataloging-in-Publication Data

Kent, Alison.
Unforgettable / Alison Kent.—Heat trade paperback edition.
pages   cm
ISBN 978-0-425-26413-3
1. Man-woman relationships—Fiction.   2. Texas—Fiction.   I. Title.
PS3561.E5155U54   2013
813'.54—dc23
2013002897

PUBLISHING HISTORY
Heat trade paperback edition / August 2013

PRINTED IN THE UNITED STATES OF AMERICA

10   9   8   7   6   5   4   3   2   1

Cover photograph by Claudio Marinesco.
Cover design by Sarah Oberrender.

This is a work of fiction. Names, characters, places, and incidents either are the product
of the author's imagination or are used fictitiously, and any resemblance to actual persons,
living or dead, business establishments, events, or locales is entirely coincidental.
The publisher does not have any control over and does not assume any responsibility for
author or third-party websites or their content.

# ONE

"I'M NOT WEARING a costume," Boone Mitchell said, staring at his sister and the Dalton Gang member she'd tamed. Boone was the last of the hell-raising trio still standing, and he had no plans to fall—especially if falling meant wearing *O Brother, Where Art Thou?* black-and-white prison stripes the way Casper Jayne was doing now.

"It's a costume party," Faith said. "Of course you are." Her own getup consisted of boots, a hat, and a cropped denim vest and matching miniskirt, both with leather tassels and brass hardware. She also had a star pinned to what little fabric there was covering her chest. And what looked like a real gun hanging from a belt at her hip.

"I'm not wearing a costume," he repeated, glancing from one of the ridiculously garbed two to the other. *Calf nuts on a cracker.* He'd thought he was ready to settle down, but if this is what relationships did to men . . .

"Sorry, dude," Casper said, his arms out as he tested the length of plastic chain between the matching black shackles binding his good wrist to the one in the medical brace. "The woman's the boss."

"Not on my ranch," Boone grumbled, leaning against the sink in the kitchen of the house Casper and Faith shared—a kitchen that would easily hold four of the one Boone cooked in for no one but himself since Casper and Dax Campbell, the third of the three partners in the Dalton Ranch, had abandoned him. The fact that they'd done so for women . . .

"It's an Old West theme so just go as a cowboy," Faith said, as she crossed to where he was trying to stay out of the way. She had a length of black fabric in her hands and a look in her eyes that bode no good. She reached up to tie it around his head, adjusting the holes he was supposed to be able to see out of, but couldn't, catching his hair in the knot and swatting away his hand when he tried to free the strands. "I'm not finished."

As far as he was concerned, she was. He had no idea why he'd agreed to stop by the Mulberry Street house on his way from Lasko Ranch Supply back to the ranch, especially when he'd known this would be the outcome. Faith had been reminding him of the charity masquerade party for weeks. She'd bought him one of the pricey benefactor tickets when she'd bought hers and Casper's, even though he'd told her she was wasting the cash.

"There," she said, stepping back with her hands at her hips to take him in. "Perfect. Or it will be as soon as you put your hat back on."

He slapped his hat against his thigh, raising a cloud of dust that had his sister grimacing and waving her hands. "What? I've been working."

Faith scrunched up her nose. "Maybe you should shower first, change clothes."

"Clean clothes means a trip to the ranch. And if I go home, I'm staying."

"You could wear something of Casper's."

"Uh-uh," Casper was quick to put in. "I don't have enough shirts that I can afford losing any to his shoulders."

"You would if you'd let me buy them," Faith said, then turned to Boone. "You'll have to go dirty then."

"Or I could just not go."

"You're going." She tapped a finger to her chin and considered him. "But you need spurs or chaps or something."

"The spurs and the chaps are at home, and if I go home—"

"Yeah, yeah. You're not coming back. I guess this will have to do."

"You want me to go as a cowboy, *this* is what you get."

"Wait. I've got an idea," Casper said, turning to bound up the stairs, the plastic ball and chain fastened around his ankle thumping behind him.

Boone looked from the man he was having a hard time recognizing to his sister, whom he'd never seen so happy. "Ball and chain, huh?"

"It's a good life," she said, her smile dreamy. It was a new look for her. A good look for her. "You should find someone to tie you up. At least once in a while."

"I've got 'once in a while' covered. And she doesn't make me run around wearing zebra pj's."

Faith huffed. "I'm not *making* Casper do anything. I just told him if he wore that, then I'd wear this," she said, and held up her hands like some *The Price Is Right* model.

"Are Mom and Dad going to be there? Because you wearing that"—he gave her a quick once-over because she *was* his sister and he preferred not to look—"is going to have Mom gathering napkins from the tables to make you a serape."

"Momma and Daddy are in Houston until late Sunday night. Texans football this weekend." She tugged on the bottom of her vest that left her midriff bare. "Besides, if you think my outfit's going to raise eyebrows, you should see what Arwen's wearing. Dax is going to be shooting eye daggers at anyone who looks at her wrong. Assuming he lets her out of the house."

Now, the Dax part of that equation would be worth seeing. But Boone wouldn't be looking at Arwen just like he didn't look at Faith. Arwen belonged to his partner in the Dalton Ranch, making her family, too. "Doubt he'll have much choice, the party being at the Hellcat Saloon and Arwen being hostess."

"Well, he'll have to get over it. Having her place chosen to host the library's fund-raiser is a huge coup. Kendall was afraid the committee would vote down the suggestion and we'd end up at the country club where everything would cost twice as much."

"Kendall?"

"Kendall Sheppard. She owns the bookstore? You danced with her at the folks' anniversary party? She's on the library board."

"Right." One of the few eligible single women in Crow Hill, and a friend of his sister's. Meaning he crossed paths with her often enough to make Faith's matchmaking obvious. He just wasn't too good with names. "I guess that means she'll be there tonight."

"She will. As will Lizzie Nathan and Everly Grant and Nina Summerlin. You'll have a great time."

Before he could tell her his idea of a great time would have all four women in his bed, not on a dance floor, preferably at the same time, Casper clattered his way back into the kitchen. "Here," he said, handing Boone a leather gun belt. And a gun. "Buckle this on, and with the Zorro mask, you're set."

Boone spun the old Colt's cylinder looking for bullets, happy to find he wouldn't accidentally be shooting anyone, or his own foot. "Like two eyeholes in a black scarf is going to fool anyone?"

"The point isn't to fool anyone," Faith said, tying on her own mask that was a lacy-looking metal cutout and didn't hide much of her face at all. "The point is to have fun. To dance and drink and flirt and pretend for a few hours that you're someone else."

That was just stupid. "I like who I am. I don't want to pretend I'm someone else."

"Then don't. Just dance and drink and flirt."

"I don't want to—"

"Just drink. Jesus, Boone. You can do that, can't you?"

"Sure he can. Especially with all that drinking going toward a good cause." Casper pulled a long strip of drink tickets out of Faith's top, tore off half of them, and gave them to Boone. "Sheriff here's made of money. She can buy more."

Boone folded the tickets and stuffed them into his pocket while Casper stuffed his back between Faith's breasts. She slapped at his hand, took care of the tickets herself, then handed him a plain black mask that Boone supposed was prison-issue to go with the stripes. Casper snapped it into place, rolling his eyes as Faith lifted his hair to hide the elastic, yelping when she pulled too hard.

Seeing the two together had Boone smiling. And after all the years he'd spent enforcing the Dalton Gang's no-sisters rule to keep them apart. Still, the time had needed to be right, and the sixteen years he, Casper, and Dax had spent away from Crow

Hill before returning to take on the ranch they'd inherited had given both Faith and Casper a chance to get their act together. It had been a lot of years, but it had been worth it.

"Wow, y'all look great," came a voice from the doorway that led into the house's main hall.

"Hey, Clay," Boone said to the fifteen-year-old boy Casper was in the process of adopting. "You and Kevin up to holding down the fort? Because say the word and I'll grab a pizza from the Flying Pie and we can hang out and watch all the Bruce Willis movies you want."

"Kevin and I got it covered," Clay said, reaching down to pat his scruffy mutt who was the size of a few of the calves Boone had moved from the Braff pasture this morning. "And I think tonight's going to be *Star Wars*. And then bed by eleven since it's a school night," he added, getting a nod from Casper.

"See?" Faith waved Boone and Casper toward the door where Clay was standing. "Clay and Kevin have it covered. Let's go."

Boone jammed his hat on and followed the sheriff and her prisoner to the front of the house where his truck was parked on the street. He'd drink up the tickets Casper had given him, doing his part for literacy, and hope like hell he didn't end the night wearing prison stripes. Or worse.

Dragging home his own ball and chain.

"DO YOU KNOW how amazingly hot you look?" Everly Grant asked of Arwen Poole, whose already impressive chest had been corseted into a rack that almost had Everly drooling. She pushed her bonnet off her head, letting it hang down her back by the ribbon tied at her throat. "And what amazingly drab lives schoolmarms must've lived in the Old West? No wonder we were all spinsters. We can't get a cowboy to look at us sideways wearing this plain muslin crap."

"But you make an adorable schoolmarm," Arwen said, reaching beneath the bar for a deep margarita glass and exposing even more of her cleavage. How she kept those things from popping out of her barmaid's white blouse . . . "No doubt there's some rancher out there looking to be taught a thing or two. And you're just the teacher to do it."

Picking at the buttons fastening the bodice of her ankle-length dress, Everly glanced down at her chest, which left absolutely everything to the imagination, and gave her a full, unobstructed view of her lap where she sat on a Hellcat Saloon barstool. It was hopeless. *She* was hopeless. "Let's see. Amazingly hot versus adorable. The only rancher I'm liable to attract is one looking to have calf nuts fried to a crackly crunch for dinner."

Arwen screwed up her face and made a *yuck* motion with her tongue as she filled the glass from the margarita machine. "I don't know about that. I'm pretty sure I saw Boone Mitchell giving you the eye."

Boone Mitchell. Everly shivered. He would making putting an end to her four years of abstinence worth the wait. "Yeah, no doubt coming up with a reason to head in the opposite direction should I get close."

"Everly! Stop it. You're gorgeous and everyone here knows it." Arwen twisted the top off a bottle of Dos Equis and up-ended it into the slush of the frozen margarita via the hook on the side of the glass. "There's nothing wrong with making a man wonder what he'll find beneath your clothes if he's lucky enough to get you out of them."

"At this rate, no one will be finding out anything." And for a very long four years, that had been exactly what she'd wanted. No leading anyone on. No inadvertent flirtation. No accidentally attracting a man who might think she was willing to take whatever he thought she had coming once they were in bed. She was done being a victim. "But that's okay. I'm supposed to be on the clock."

"That's right. You're covering the event for the paper." Arwen signaled over Everly's head for one of the saloon's servers, pushing the "beer-rita" toward Luck Summerlin as she approached. "This is for Bubba Taylor. Get his tickets first," she said before turning back to Everly. "Want one? Working girls drink on the house."

Working girls, though of a different sort than Arwen meant, also got all the action. Everly would definitely rethink her costume next time. "Sure, but just the margarita. I don't need the beer. One drink will have to do me tonight."

"Coming up," Arwen said, reaching for a smaller glass this time. "Having to stay sober at a party's hardly fair, and I say that from a lot of personal experience."

"It's a good cause. I just hope the story raises more awareness about the cuts to the library's funding. I know Kendall's got a selection of books she's lending out at the bookstore, but that puts her in a bind." Everly reached for the margarita Arwen slid toward her, stirred it with her straw. "Roma Orleans is pretty much handling the entire library herself, and she can't keep it open but a few hours a week."

"I know. Faith said Clay's been volunteering both there and at the bookstore, shelving returns, cleaning toilets, whatever needs to be done. And he spends almost all of his allowance on new books to help Kendall out. She said he's read all the Jack Reacher and Harry Hole books, and has started in on Lucas Davenport."

Blood and guts and violence, yet the boy was the sweetest thing ever. "That kid is something else."

"Tell me about it." Arwen leaned across the bar to wipe a spill. "Dax pays him to come over after school and cook dinner a couple nights a week. He makes a double batch of whatever it is, giving us another two meals of the leftovers. The rest of the time we eat here. I'm totally off the hook for cooking."

"And you like it."

"I do." Arwen nodded, and laughed. "I had no idea I hated to cook as much as I do until Dax moved in, and I felt like I needed to make more of an effort at feeding him than bringing home burgers or ribs."

"Oh, please. I'd eat here every night if I could. I eat here too often as it is. And anyway"—Everly was a big believer in household members sharing household duties, even if her ex had held the opposite view—"he can cook just as easily as you can. It's not like he's the only one working dawn to dusk."

"I know, but he's out in the heat. And he drives a half hour to the ranch and a half hour back."

"Well, at least you're not having to stay till the wee hours anymore. How's Luck working out as manager?"

"She's not."

"What?" Everly asked once she'd pulled her straw from her mouth and swallowed.

"I decided to give Myna Goss the position. Her husband's only home a night or two a week, and she enjoys staying busy. Luck's just too flighty" Arwen said with a wave of one hand. "She's great with the customers, and can watch the place in a pinch, but I just feel better having Myna close up the nights I'm home with Dax. I want to enjoy him, not worry about what's going on over here. It's getting tough to find quality time lately, what with the schedule he's having to keep."

"I'll bet Faith's happy Casper's done with breaking horses," Everly said, reaching again for her drink.

"Yeah, well, until Casper's hand gets put back together, he's done with a lot of what he used to do."

Everly had heard gossip about Casper needing surgery, and Arwen's tone left no doubt as to her feelings about his recent reckless behavior. "I wondered about that, how he was faring. Is that making things harder for Boone and Dax?"

"They've got Diego Cruz on full-time now. I think Faith's helping out with his salary, though I can't say for sure. Her way of covering Casper's part of his partnership deal with the other two, I imagine. And that with her having quit the bank."

"You girls are awesome," Everly said, blowing out an envious sigh. "Doing for your men like that."

"With all they do for us? I can't imagine *not* doing for them." Arwen replaced the damp napkin beneath Everly's drink. "Well, for Dax. Casper's all Faith's. I love him as a friend, but he's way too much for me to handle."

Everly looked down, toyed with the stem of her glass. She'd never had what her friends had. In fact, she'd had such an opposite experience with her one and only serious relationship that she'd sworn off men for years, wondering if she'd ever want to risk her heart again. Or risk her emotions, her body, her mind.

"Ev? You okay?"

"I'm fine," she said, clearing her throat. "I'm just so happy for you and Faith. And I feel like a fifth wheel these days at lunch. I may have to start eating at the store with Kendall," she said, laughing at the look on Arwen's face.

"I wish Kendall could afford to take an hour once a week and come eat with us." Then she lifted a scolding finger. "And if you even think about not showing up tomorrow, I'm going to come to the paper and hunt you down."

"Yes, ma'am. I'll be here," she said, loving that her move to Crow Hill had brought her such very good friends—a bit of a surprise in such a small town, one populated primarily with crusty retirees and equally crusty landowners running ever-dwindling herds of cattle. She followed the other woman's gaze, Arwen turning to take in Boone Mitchell as he approached.

"Arwen. Everly." He nodded to both of them, neither their masks nor his fooling anyone. In fact, Everly hadn't seen a mask tonight that did. A good lead-in to her story perhaps . . . *Even their masks couldn't hide the identities of the generous library patrons determined to make up for the county's recent funding cuts brought on by the region's economic blight.*

"Hey, Boone," Arwen said, one eyebrow arched. "You ride in tonight on a horse?"

"Almost," he said, reaching for the designer beer she handed him. "Blame Faith. She wouldn't take no for an answer, and I don't fit in Casper's clothes."

"Uh, I'm not even going to ask," Arwen said, laughing and tearing off his drink ticket when he offered her the long strip. She nodded toward his bounty. "Thanks for the donation."

"This is Faith, too. I can't afford a pot to piss in," he said, then looked from one woman to the other. "Sorry about that. I'm not used to having to watch what comes out of my mouth since I'm usually talking to cows."

Arwen reached out to pat his free hand where it rested on the bar. "You're in character. Don't apologize."

He pulled his hand from beneath hers and jerked off his hat, tugging off his black silk mask, then settling his hat back in place. "Criminy but that thing was making it impossible to breathe."

And now Everly was the one who couldn't catch her breath. She'd known Faith in college, but had never met the other woman's brother until he'd returned to Crow Hill several months ago. She had seen him in passing, at a distance, in a group where she was usually engaged in conversation while he hugged the edge of the room and scowled.

Up close, he was intimidating. His size, his bearing, his swagger and attitude, and all the things that made him male. She watched his throat work as he swallowed, the sheen of dried sweat there, the beard stubble dark on his chin and jaw, watched him backhand his wrist across his mouth when done, his gaze catching hers and burning.

She smiled, feeling awkward, and reached for her drink, holding the glass in one hand, fingering her straw with the other. He made her nervous, but it was a nervousness drawn from deep in her belly, a nervousness not of fear or of dread but of unexpected desire.

It had been so long since she'd felt that sort of primal pull that she closed her eyes and let it consume her, giving in and imagining Boone's powerful body bare between her legs. Which probably wasn't the smartest thing to be thinking, because she could feel his heat radiating at her side, and smell the earthy musk of his skin, and oh, but she loved the tingling at her nape, and the tightening of her breasts, and the tickles of pleasure making her wet.

Arwen picked that moment to break into Everly's longing. "Do you need another drink before I get back to work? Boone, another beer?"

"I'm good," he said, and Everly nodded the same.

"Okay, then. You two have fun," the other woman said as she headed through the swinging doors into the saloon's kitchen, leaving Everly and Boone to deal with the silence enveloping their tiny little space in the very large room.

Her hands twisted together in her schoolmarm lap, Everly

raised her gaze to Boone's. His longneck was back at his mouth, his eyes still bright as his gaze held hers. She didn't think he was drunk. At least not too. And she had nothing against drinking. What she did have was too much experience with the liberties taken by those who couldn't help but let alcohol win.

She took a deep breath, looking for something to say, but before she found anything that wouldn't get them into trouble, Boone did that for her by asking, "Would you like to dance?"

# TWO

"SURE," SHE SAID, looking down at her skirt before looking back at him, her eyes big and brown, with lashes like a calf's, or bristles on a broom, or a paintbrush. "But only if you promise not to step on this ridiculous dress."

"It's not ridiculous," he said, leaving his beer on the bar and offering her his hand. He liked her dress. Liked the buttons straining to hold the front of it closed. He wanted to pop them open, to get rid of her bra, to bury his face between her tits and taste her. She squeezed her fingers around his and he wondered how his calluses felt against her palm, if she'd mind them scraping down her belly. "It's just long."

"Ridiculously long," she said as he spun her into his arms, her steps kept short by the length of the skirt. She slid her hand from his biceps to his shoulder and held him tight. "I had it in the closet—don't ask—and thought since I was working tonight, it would be more appropriate than . . ."

"What Arwen's wearing?" he asked, though he'd done his best not to notice the other woman's assets too closely. He couldn't deny that he'd like to see Everly in the same getup, her tits straining against the laces tying them in place.

She nodded. "Or what your sister's got on, though having Casper or Dax hovering might drive me insane."

No hovering. He'd remember that. "What did you mean, you're working tonight?"

Her laughter punched him in the middle of his chest. "Well, I'm not a working girl, if that's what you're asking, though the dress should've been a giveaway."

"That's not what I—"

"I know," she said before he could get out the rest of his apology. "I tend to babble when I'm nervous."

"Are you nervous?" he asked, wondering if he was doing something wrong, or if he was doing everything right. He liked the idea that he might be. "Do I make you nervous?"

"It's complicated." Her hand at his shoulder slid to his neck. Her fingers toyed with the ends of his hair. "Just know I don't mind that you do."

He wasn't sure what to say to that, but since she wasn't letting nerves keep her from pressing against him, he moved his hand farther down her back to the swell of her bottom and kept it there, pushing against her when his touch brought up the corner of her mouth. "So. You work at the *Reporter*?"

"I do," she said with a nod. "I've been there about four years."

"Yeah, that's right. You knew Faith at school."

Another nod. "Finance track for her, journalism for me." She stopped as if considering how much she should say, and he figured she probably knew about the trouble Faith ran into while there. But she seemed to shake it off, getting back to his question. "It's not quite as challenging, or as exhausting, as my previous job, but it keeps me busy. Keeps me entertained. Lots of human interest news 'round these here parts."

Her exaggerated drawl had him chuckling. "What did you do before?"

"I worked at KXAN in Austin."

"Yeah? That's pretty big stuff."

"Maybe. But I like it here, not being recognized everywhere I go. Not being recognized for being on TV, I mean," she amended. "Because everyone knows everyone else 'round these here parts."

He was having trouble getting a read on her. She liked it here, so was she laughing at herself? He didn't think she was making fun of small-town life. Not smart to be shitting where one ate. "You're right. Everyone does. Made it kinda dicey when the boys and I came back. Never knew who we'd run into that might still be holding a grudge."

"Did you get a lot of that?"

"Less than I thought," he said, though he couldn't speak for Casper or Dax with much authority. He was still waiting for the Big One to land in his lap with the stink of a fresh cow pie. And if he were a bettin' man, he'd lay odds the shit would arrive courtesy of Les Upton. "Guess time does heal all wounds."

She dropped her gaze from his, looked out at the crowd without seeming to really see anyone. And then she finally said, "Some wounds," leaving Boone to figure he'd scratched open a raw spot.

He slid his low-riding hand up to the small of her back, not wanting to take advantage. "Sorry 'bout that. Didn't mean to cause you any upset there."

"You didn't," she said, wetting her lips as she returned her attention to him. "We all have them, I guess."

"Wounds? Yeah, I imagine so."

"And you didn't have to move your hand."

"Okay," he said, and put it back, squeezing just a little and feeling a jolt in his balls when she smiled.

They finished out the dance without saying anything more. Boone caught his sister's gaze a couple of times, but ignored the look she was giving him. He couldn't decipher it anyway. He'd had one too many beers for doing any deciphering. Besides, his dancing with one of her friends was his business—and Everly's—not Faith's. And besides again, she'd been the one to make the suggestion back at the house.

Still, he couldn't stop himself from thinking his sister had something on her mind, and that something was related to Everly, and it was something he needed to know, most likely dealing with her wounds. 'Course, it could just be that Faith didn't like seeing his hand on Everly's ass, but that sure as hell wasn't her place to decide.

All too soon the song ended, couples separating, clapping, some making their way back to their tables or to the bar, others staying where they were and waiting for the band to strike up again. Everly stepped out of his arms, kinda reluctantly, he thought, as if maybe she wasn't sure he wanted her there. Except he couldn't really imagine her thinking that. Not with the way her nipples had gone hard when she'd told him she didn't mind his fondling.

"Thanks for the dance," he said, wanting to stick around for another, but needing a break before he reached for the hem of her skirt and ripped the fabric to her waist. That was the beer talking. The beer and having her close.

But it was a thought he couldn't deny having. And it didn't stop there. He kept on thinking of where things might go once the dress was out of the way and he could get to her skin. He had a feeling he would love the taste of her skin.

She reached up then, brushed back some of her long blond hair escaping from the bun thing she'd wound it into on the back of her head. "Thank you for taking pity on me."

He frowned. She had to be kidding. "What makes you say that?"

"You're the first man to ask me without a wife or a girl-friend suggesting it."

"I think you've got that wrong." In fact, he knew she did. She might've danced with some married guys, and a few who were attached, but she'd danced with others, too, and none of it out of pity. Appreciation was more like it.

She was fun. She wasn't on the make. She didn't give a guy a complex over his two left feet, or give him reason to feel she'd rather not have his hands on her. That part was, in his case anyway, just the opposite. "You're a great partner."

"Well, thank you for that. I'm going to sit at the bar now and make the notes I should've been making all this time. Maybe talk to some contributors, get some sound bites. You know. Work stuff," she said, fiddling with the bow of the silly hat hanging down her back.

"I'll walk you on over, then I'm heading out. Morning for us rancher types comes early 'round these here parts."

She laughed, and he placed his hand at her back and crossed the room at her side, both of them saying hello to friends who spoke, neither of them stopping for more conversation.

At the bar, he let her go, and she climbed onto a stool, pull-ing a small spiral notebook and pen from a pocket in her dress. She clicked the end of the pen, flipped open the notebook's red cover, jotted down the time and the date. She was ready to get to work and he was hanging around for no reason.

Unless liking her was a good enough one. He thought it was, but he still needed to go. "Good night then. Good luck with your story. I'll, uh, see you soon, I guess."

"Good night Boone, and thank you." She clicked her pen off, clicked her pen on, then lifted her gaze to meet his, her eyes broadcasting a similar frustration to the one clawing a hole in his gut. "And I hope you do. Because I'd really like that."


MAKING HER WAY out of the Hellcat Saloon, Everly wasn't surprised that Arwen had been wrong and she'd been one hundred percent right. Her innocent schoolmarm costume had warded off any and all sexual advances, and most of the nonsexual ones, too. She'd danced with Casper and Dax, and told herself they weren't pity dances, but she was hard to believe.

She'd danced with Josh Lasko, who belonged to Dax's sister, Darcy. They'd had a wonderful time talking about how he'd built out the attic of his family's feed store into a loft. She had a thing for interior design. But just a thing. No degree. No experience other than outfitting every place she'd ever lived, from her childhood bedroom to the house she now owned in Crow Hill.

She'd danced with Greg Barrett, the Campbell siblings' half brother, and his sculpted male-model cheekbones, but there'd been nary a spark. She'd danced with others, too . . . the owner of the local animal shelter, the area's go-to veterinarian, Coleman Medical Center's chief of staff. Okay. She'd danced a lot more than she'd realized.

All the single men on that list were well employed, age appropriate, and drool worthy. But her appreciation for each had been purely aesthetic. There'd been no heat simmering between their bodies when close, no palms dampening, no nipples growing hard. She hadn't thought about binding any of them to her headboard and climbing on top.

Hmm. Maybe her post-Toby shields still weren't ready to come down, she mused, taking off across the asphalt parking lot, the mid-October night still warm. Except that wouldn't explain wanting to crawl out of her own skin and into Boone Mitchell's when she'd danced with him.

Those thoughts . . . Whoa. Kinky and raw and utterly delicious. And having one hand on his shoulder, her breasts crushed to his chest, his belt buckle catching on the fabric of her dress, had only led to others. Ones even more kinky, and so utterly raw her body responded deliciously at the memory.

Voices murmuring just ahead had her slowing her steps, the hair at her nape standing on end as she stopped. A male voice, and a female voice, more deep grunts and silly giggles than anything. Obviously she needed to change direction or risk interrupting someone's dalliance. Not that she was averse to watching. She rather enjoyed watching—something she'd had no opportunity to do since moving, with Faith's help, to Crow Hill.

And if that day hadn't nearly turned her into a basket case . . . The two of them throwing her clothes and shoes, belts, scarves, and purses into big black trash bags, using one carry-on for her jewelry and makeup and toiletries, another for all the appliances she needed to style the vanity that was her hair. Then had come her electronics and their web of cords and chargers she'd never thought she'd untangle.

But that was it. She'd left the few pieces of furniture she'd picked out to complement Toby's decor. She'd left all the kitchen gadgets she'd added to his collection, even her beloved espresso machine. She'd left mementos from high school and college and her alphabetical vacations; so far she'd made it up to the Es . . . Ecuador, Egypt, Estonia, Ethiopia. She'd had to leave her piano—she hated leaving her piano—but she had taken the framed photos of family and friends she'd lovingly displayed on top.

Four years later, those were all still in boxes. Unpacking them meant seeing Toby's face, his nose red from Africa's sun, his lips blue from the biting cold in the Andes. Seeing Toby's face would bring to mind his hands, and his hands would bring to mind her bruises. And those would bring to mind his tears, and his apologies, and the smell of alcohol on his breath, and then the blame.

She'd blamed herself for staying.

He'd blamed her for making him hurt her when she stayed.

The sound of a loud female moan snapped her back to the present. Her head popped up and she caught the other woman's eye. It was Luck Summerlin, trapped between the bed of an extended-cab dualie and the body of Boone Mitchell. Her stomach fell, her heart fell harder. What felt like jealousy started to rise and she tamped it down. What Boone did—and with whom, even if that whom was Luck—was none of her business. So what if he'd had *her* on the verge of moaning not twenty minutes ago.

Walking again, and more hurriedly this time, she tucked her gaze away, focusing on her keys and on getting to her SUV without tripping over her schoolmarm hem. She had no claim on Boone. All they'd done was dance. He was free to do whatever he wanted with anyone who was willing. And as everyone in Crow Hill knew, Luck Summerlin was the definition of willing, much to her father Royce's red-faced chagrin.

For some reason, that made her feel a little bit better. Stupid, she knew, but Boone hooking up with Luck wasn't what it would be if he were out here with Kendall Sheppard, for example. Not that Kendall would be caught dead engaging in such a public display of raunchy affection. Because that's all this was, Everly acknowledged, her SUV at the end of the long row in her sights. Boone was drunk, Luck was open for business, and Everly was making too much out of his hand squeezing her ass while they'd danced.

She clicked the unlock button on her key fob, watched her taillights flash. If she'd been smart, she wouldn't have said a word when he'd moved it away. But she'd been hungry for the contact. It had been wonderful, his large hand heavy against her, warm and possessive. And it had been safe. They'd been in the middle of the dance floor, surrounded by friends, and in Boone's case family. It wasn't like Boone touching her was going to lead to anything rough.

That didn't explain why she would trade places with Luck Summerlin in a heartbeat. Why she wanted to turn around and do just that. She wouldn't, of course. She couldn't. And her libido, waking up after a very long and purposeful abstinence, would have to understand.

But just as she was opening her door, a big body moved in to loom over her, and a big hand came down on the SUV's roof in a smack. She jumped, feinted to her left and away, then caught a whiff of sweat and horse to go with the beer, and realized the only danger she was in was being crushed beneath him if he passed out and fell.

"You leaving already?" Boone asked, his words less slurred than she would've expected from someone who'd downed as many drinks as he had after delivering her back to the bar. But then he was a pretty big guy. And, slurred words or not, he was more than pretty drunk.

"I am. I need to type up my notes while they're fresh in my mind." Then, hating herself for doing so, she asked, "What happened to Luck?"

"Who?"

Everly rolled her eyes. "The woman you had pinned against your truck. The woman whose spread legs you were grinding between."

"Don't remember."

"You don't remember what you were doing five minutes ago?"

"I'm not even sure I remember my name."

Was he teasing? Or serious? "Do you want me to remind you? Or would you rather work it out for yourself?"

"My name is Boone Mitchell, and I'm thinking I don't need to be driving back to the ranch."

And thank goodness he *was* thinking that. It would be easier than taking away his keys and getting slugged in the process.

"You got an extra bed?"

She had one bed. Her bed. And no man had hung his hat on her headboard since she'd moved into her house in Crow Hill. This one might be the first, though in his condition he'd be sleeping there alone. "I've got a sofa."

"I don't fit on most sofas."

"I do. You can have the bed."

"But I can't have you?"

"With the number of beers you've had? I doubt you can have anyone."

He laughed, a low rumbling sound that had her curling her toes. And clenching muscles south of her belly. "One beer. A dozen beers. That's never been a problem. But since you said no . . ."

She liked that he hadn't overlooked that part. "The offer of the bed is still open."

"Okay then. Let's go home."

Ignoring the tug in her tummy at his choice of words, she opened the door to the backseat. Boone crawled in, grumbling about tiny square holes and big round pegs, and collapsed. She shut the door, locking him in, and slid behind the wheel, hoping, as she did, that he didn't mind sleeping right where he was.

Getting him out of the SUV would never be as easy as it had been getting him in.

# THREE

BOONE WOKE TO the smell of coffee. And bacon. And real
butter on toast. No. The smell of pancakes. And maple
syrup. And maybe even scrambled eggs. Stomach grumbling, he opened his eyes to the realization that he had no idea
where he was. And that meant he had no idea who was cooking
the breakfast his gut was aching to down.

A ceiling fan spun overhead, but it was a shiny black enamel
and definitely not the dusty unbalanced number in his bedroom at the ranch. And he was pretty sure it didn't belong to
Luck Summerlin because, as his brain found a gear and engaged, he remembered her skedaddling with a shriek last night
'bout the same time he'd unzipped his pants.

He also remembered a schoolteacher in a bonnet, and when
he tucked an arm beneath his head to raise it off the pillow, he
saw the same bonnet hanging from the room's doorknob. He

also got a whiff of himself. Criminy, but he needed a shower. He'd gone straight . . . somewhere without having one last night.

A costume party. A fund-raiser. With Faith and Casper. And Luck Summerlin, who'd promised to treat him right, then left him hanging. But that still didn't explain where he was now. Or who had taken him to bed with him smelling like a horse, because the woman was a saint. Or a crazy. If it was a woman doing the cooking, and not some dude. Though the bonnet told him that was so.

He pushed up to his elbows, let the rush of blood to his head settle, then tossed back the sheet and swung his legs over the side of the bed. His bare legs. His bare feet. His bare balls still heavy and telling him all he'd done in the bed was sleep. Huh. That was unexpected. Or not, he mused, standing and hit again with his stink, which was followed by his stomach turning beer-flavored flips.

A shower first. Breakfast would have to wait. A quick look around the room done up in black and white and yellow and red showed him two doors, one closed, most likely a closet, the other open and dark, but not so that he couldn't tell it was a bathroom. He rounded the bed, switched on the light inside, stepped into the tub, and closed the clear curtain dotted with red and black spots. Hot water was beating him in the face before he even took time to pee.

Finally he turned his back to the spray, shook his hair like a dog, and opened his eyes. Nope, not a clue. He'd never seen this tub before. The enclosure was tiled in the same red, white, yellow, and black he'd woke up to. The bottles of body and hair soaps had labels with fancy names not found on the shelves at Nathan's. He squirted a pool of shampoo into his palm, scrubbed the grit of yesterday's hours spent on horseback from his hair, then used some sweet-smelling gel to wash his pits and his crotch.

The worst of the ripeness gone, he took a bit more time to lather up the rest of his body, lingering between his legs and hefting his uncomfortably heavy balls in one hand. Whoever he'd come home with had tucked him in, but certainly hadn't offered a hand—or a mouth—where he most needed it. Not her fault. He'd been so out of it he didn't even recall having fallen into bed.

He pulled at his cock, his palm slick as he cupped it over the head, tugging with each pass, and he was nearly cattle-prod hard when he thought again of the bonnet he'd seen hanging on the bedroom door. He stroked harder, thought harder, his cock going harder when he pictured the dress that matched the bonnet, and the buttons straining to hold the top of it closed over a gorgeous set of tits.

The tits he remembered. The tits got him going. Reaching again for the gel, he squeezed a puddle into his palm, frothing it up beneath the stream of hot water slamming against his back. And then he closed his eyes, pictured the buttons popping open, one then another, baring mounds of creamy flesh.

He stroked again, tugging down on his root, and gave the head a good rubbing, sliding his hand behind his balls and rubbing there, too, reaching back to toy with his ass, slipping his finger inside to the first knuckle, and grinding against it before withdrawing and getting back to the image of those tits.

The nipples, tight like ripe cherries, popped free; and he groaned, feeling them against his tongue as his cock jumped, as his balls drew tight to his body. He imagined sucking on them, rolling them between his fingers, biting down until she moaned. Those moans had him pulling harder, rubbing harder, his cock lifting up to meet the downward pressure of his hand.

The thought of straddling those tits, lubing the valley between and fucking them, holding them together like a tight, hot cunt, aiming his big third eye at the O of her mouth, did him in. He reared back, grimacing. The shower beat against the top of his head. His cum spurted against the tiled wall until he was spent. His legs ached, his balls ached, his cock softened in his hand to hang against his thigh.

The picture of those tits still in his mind's eye, he cleaned up the mess and rinsed, then shut off the water, jerking open the shower curtain only to find he wasn't alone. Everly Grant stood in the bathroom door—a door he'd left open. A door from which she could have easily watched his very personal show. Thinking about her doing so had his balls rumbling again.

"That answers that question," he said, reaching for one of the towels folded on the shelf above the toilet.

"What question is that?" she asked, her face blank of any reaction at all.

*Interesting.* "You're not Luck Summerlin."

"I think you scared her off trying to stick your tongue down her throat," she said, her gaze going from his face to his cock, then slowly back.

"Silly girl," he said, feeling another twitch firing off down below and wrapping himself as best he could in the towel. He didn't want to scare her, too. What he wanted to do was fuck her and her magnificent tits. "Thanks for the use of the bed. I'll strip the sheets for you. Doubt you'll want to be sleeping on those tonight."

She reached for the door to pull it closed, giving him, he guessed, the privacy he didn't need to dry off. "I'll strip the sheets. You go eat breakfast. It's on the table."

"And my clothes?"

"On the back of one of the chairs. All clean."

A saint. He'd been right. "Thanks. I'm pretty much about to pass out from starvation."

A heartbeat of tension passed between them. He felt it in his throat when he swallowed. Saw it in hers when her tongue flicked out to wet her lips. She caught one edge of the lower with her teeth before saying, "I've got a feeling starvation's not what's got you weak in the knees." And then she closed the door.

He wasn't sure whether to laugh; or whip off his towel, whip off her clothes, and whip them both into a lather as he rode her. In the end, he didn't laugh, or do any whipping. But he did promise himself he'd be taking that ride.

And soon.


Finished with switching out the fitted sheet, Everly smoothed the top one into place, trying to erase from her mind the picture of Boone in her bed. It was a queen, and she usually slept on the right. That left room for whatever book she fell asleep reading, or her extra pillows, or her laptop and story notes spread out on the other side. She slept with work many nights, and never disturbed so much as a pencil.

It would be hard to share a bed with Boone Mitchell and not . . . be disturbed.

They'd danced together, so his size wasn't a surprise. Except it was when he was naked and sprawled across her mattress, two pillows bunched up in his arms, a foot hanging off the side of the bed, his tight bare ass begging, at the very least, to be slapped. If not slapped, then bitten, and licked, which she'd found herself wanting to do.

Straightening the bound edge of the sheet, she breathed deeply, smelling fabric softener and little more. He'd left nothing of himself in her room, and she thought she might miss the part of him that didn't smell like livestock. It had been so long since she'd slept with a man. That quiet intimacy, even more than making love, was something she hadn't thought she'd miss, but she did, and terribly so.

She liked that he'd come to the fund-raiser as himself, straight from the back of a horse. No one who hadn't danced with him would've noticed his earthy scent, and she didn't remember him dancing with anyone else but Lizzie Nathan. Luck Summerlin had certainly had no issue with the aroma rising from his skin and his clothes. But then Luck Summerlin would put up with most anything to have men other women wanted. At least until it came time to deliver on the promises she'd made.

Everly punched up her pillows, then punched them again. She felt consumed with . . . envy, which made no sense. She had no claim on Boone. All she'd done was get him to a safe place to sleep. And undress him. And tuck him in. And grow wet with the strongest rush of longing she'd known in years. It was proximity; that was all. She would've felt the same for any man she'd stripped out of his clothes. *All of his clothes.*

He'd helped with his boots, and his hat was still in her SUV's backseat, but she'd done the rest, and getting him out of his briefs . . . wow. His penis, even soft, was thick and long, the veins beautifully distended, the head a perfect mushroom crown she'd been unable to resist touching. She'd wanted to take him into her mouth, to tongue him and tease him and feel him harden. She wanted that now, and couldn't wait for him to finish breakfast and get out of her house.

Especially having seen him naked and sober and fresh from the shower, the skin of his body lighter than that of his arms and his neck. A cowboy's tan. His legs covered with hair the same dark brown as that cushioning his penis, as that thick in his armpits, as that matted wet in the center of his chest.

And especially having stood in the open doorway of the bathroom and watched him give himself the pleasure she could've given him last night if she'd been willing to go to bed with a drunk. She hadn't been. A case of "been there done that" way too often and never *ever* going to do it again. Boone wasn't her ex. She knew that. But that knowledge didn't change any of what had happened in her past to bring her to Crow Hill.

"What do I owe you?"

She hadn't heard him behind her, and she squeezed her eyes shut, buried her face in the throw pillow she held, then placed it on the bed. She plumped it, too, made sure it was just right, made sure *she* was just right, before turning around. "I'm sorry, what?"

He was clean and beautiful, his hair damp, his face sporting a day's beard since she hadn't offered him a razor. The clothes he'd worn last night now smelled of her laundry soap, like he smelled of her bath gel. Except he didn't. On his skin, the grassy, green scent brought to mind the wide-open spaces, not the cool mountain meadows the label evoked.

"This is the best bed and breakfast I've ever stayed in." He took a step into the room. Took another. "I want to pay you for the night."

Her room seemed much smaller than it had just moments ago. "You paid me by not driving drunk. I didn't have to worry about who you might run off the road."

"Would you have worried?" A dark brow went up.

"Of course. Faith's my friend," she said with a dismissive wave of one hand. "You're her brother."

"But you wouldn't have worried just because it was me." This time it was the corner of his mouth that lifted.

"Yes, I'd have worried." She crossed her arms, rubbed her hands up and down them, swallowed hard. "I like you."

"Good. Because I like you. And I'd like to give you something in exchange for your hospitality."

Oh, what she wanted him to give her. She reached for another of the throw pillows she'd tossed in a pile to the floor, plumping it, smoothing it, waiting until she'd positioned it exactly before saying, "That's not necessary."

"Then at least let me thank you," he said, and the air tightened around them.

She could hardly find enough of it to breathe. The things she was thinking, the places her mind was going . . . "You just did."

He chuckled softly. "I'd like to thank you with something more than just words. Let me buy you supper."

"That would be nice." But it wasn't what she wanted. She knew exactly what she wanted. It was time. She was ready. And what better man than Boone Mitchell to help her forget the past? "On one condition."

"What's that?"

"You stay sober." Because that was the only way this would happen. "And we come back here after."

His pulse jumped in the vein at his temple. "For a nightcap? Coffee?"

Her pulse jumped between her legs. "I was thinking dessert."

"Dessert." He walked deeper into the room, and he smelled of maple syrup, and her stomach tumbled.

She nodded. If they were going to do this, she would have

to make sure she didn't get hurt. Not physically. Not emotionally. It would be an affair of bodies only, no strings, no attachments. "Dessert."

"Are you talking pie?" Another step. "Cake?" Another step. "Ice cream sundaes? I like ice cream sundaes."

"I'm talking me," she said, her voice steady, confident, her nerves not.

"You."

She reached for the last pillow, squeezing it with shaking fingers. The thing was, to get what she wanted, she couldn't worry every time he reached toward her, lifted his hand, made an innocent move. She had to be able to relax. To know she wasn't in danger of any kind. "If you're into dessert, that is. You may just like supper—"

"I'm into dessert. But I don't see any reason to wait." Another step, and he was standing so close she had to lift her chin to meet his gaze. "Why not have it after breakfast?"

"Breakfast."

He nodded. "Breakfast."

"Now?" Her entire body bloomed with heat.

He gave a single nod. "Sheets are clean. I'm clean." He reached for his wallet, tossed two foil packets to her bedside table, then popped the snaps of his shirt, leaving it on, the two sides parting to show off a strip of shadowed skin.

The skin she'd touched when tucking him in, pulling the sheet up to cover him, dragging her nails through the wedge of hair on his chest, wanting to drag them elsewhere. She wondered if he remembered her touching the ridge of his penis where the head met the shaft. He'd been so hard, and so very soft.

There were so many ways she wanted to touch him. "Just

so you know, I am on the pill and I'm clean, but you might want to hear me out before getting undressed. I do have . . . conditions."

"I'm listening."

"No one, absolutely no one knows about this."

"Okay. Next."

"I'm on top," she said, and his hand went to his belt buckle. "I'm in charge," she added, and he shrugged out of his shirt, lowered his zipper, rubbed his thumb across the bulbous head of his cock covered by his white cotton briefs.

"Anything else?" he asked, still rubbing and making her wet.

She touched her lips with her tongue and nodded, then walked into her closet where she kicked off the leopard print stilettos she wore with skinny brown pants and a lacy ecru tunic, and came back with the handful of scarves that would guarantee her safety and the orgasms she was aching for.

"Wrists and ankles. Yours. Tied to the bed."

# FOUR

NEVER AGAIN WOULD Boone take a schoolteacher at face value. The woman wanted to tie him to her bed. He'd done a lot of tying in his day, cows, calves, a horse or two. Dax to the grill of the flatbed when the other man had pissed him off. But he didn't think he'd ever been the one tied up.

Should be a thing a man remembered, but there'd been a lot of years go by, and when the women had been in short supply, the beer had been plentiful. It could've happened, but somehow he didn't think it had. And he was happy about that because *this woman* he would never forget.

He shucked off his shorts and his jeans, hooked a finger in one sock and then the other, tugging them off and standing buck naked in front of her. A smile came over her face then, one he couldn't give a name to, but he held out his wrists anyway, ready to be bound. Ready to be fucked within an inch of his life. And that wasn't even a question. He could see it in her eyes. A curious, needy hunger that had his cock going thick.

"On the bed," she said, her voice reedy, nearly breathless. "On your back."

He walked close to her, brushed the fabric covering her hip with his that was bare, felt her shiver before he moved away to roll into the center of the bed. He lay there spread-eagle, waiting. It wasn't exactly the most comfortable position he'd ever been in, the goods on display like the dessert she'd wanted and her tongue slicking her mouth, but he wasn't about to complain.

The bulk of his cock rested against his thigh as he stretched out his arms, turning to watch her circle the bed. She knotted one end of a scarf around each of his wrists, the other around the largest spindle of the headboard's black iron frame. She did the same with his ankles, binding them to the footboard.

He tested each bond once she'd moved to the next; she wasn't kidding about wanting him bound. He might've been able to slip the knots, but it felt more like the harder he tugged, the tighter they drew, and he didn't want to test his theory and cut off his circulation. Plus, the fact that she'd roped him first and not made doing so part of the sex play told him a lot.

For some reason, she was keeping her distance, walking from corner to corner, making sure he couldn't get loose. He tried not to let it get to him, that distance. He was here to get blown or laid or whatever she had on her mind. The fact that he wouldn't get to touch her didn't matter, he told himself, as long as she'd be touching him—though he hated not getting to fuck her tits. That thought had his cock stirring, lifting from his thigh, going just hard enough to cause him to suck in a breath he then had to slowly let go.

She liked the sound. He could see it in her face where she stood at the foot of the bed. She'd already gotten rid of her shoes, and was now starting in on her blouse, a long, sleeveless number with a lot of buttons down the front. Judging by this outfit and last night's, she seemed to like buttons. He like them, too, and eventually would get his turn. He had to believe that. He couldn't imagine this would be the only time they'd get naked, or that she'd want him tied up the next. If she did, well, that's when they'd have to do some discussing of turnabout and fair play.

For now, he'd content himself with watching the show. And it *was* a show, one he would've gladly paid to see: the buttons coming undone, her tits swelling out of the lacy bra she wore, her nipples like dark juicy centers in the sheer cups. The long blond waves of her hair fell around her shoulders. Her lips parted. Her tongue peeked from between. Her eyelids grew heavy over her big black pupils.

She kept the blouse where it was as she reached back to unzip her pants, pulling them down her hips and leaving her bottom half wearing only a thong. It was the same creamy color as her bra, which was the same creamy color as her blouse, and all of it was pretty close to the same creamy color as her skin. He wondered how creamy her pussy was, how soon he would get to find out.

Because surely he would get to find out. Surely she wasn't doing all of this just to make him sweat. If he hadn't been so long without having his cock seen to, he might've insisted on supper before dessert, giving them a little more time to get acquainted, but he was pretty sure they were on the same page. He'd been pretty sure of that while they'd danced last night. He'd been damn sure of it when he'd caught her watching him cleaning his rifle in the shower. Then he stopped worrying and got back to enjoying, because her blouse was falling off her arms to the floor.

She might as well have been naked, what little good her underthings did, but he wanted her out of them; and she, wanting the same thing, was getting there, reaching back to take care of her bra, then slipping off the scrap of fabric serving as panties. Both pieces were gone when she straightened. And when she did, so did his cock, bobbing up as a drop of clear fluid beaded on the tip.

She studied him, her head canted a bit to the side, then cupped both breasts, reaching up to twist and pinch her nipples, shuddering as she did, shuddering again as she slid her hands down her stomach to her bare pussy and spread open her lips, toying with her clit before fingering herself. Before fucking herself, gasping as she pushed into her cunt and pulled out.

He tugged against the scarves, tugged hard, bruising both wrists in the process. He wanted to finger her. He wanted to fuck her. He wanted that cunt and that ass and those tits. A growl came rumbling up his throat and he didn't even try to stop it, howling when it reached his mouth because he couldn't keep it in.

Raising his head, he gave it a jerk as he said, "Turn around," his cock jerking, too.

She did, offering him a look at her very fine ass, and then she bent over, offering him a look at a whole lot more, her hair falling like a curtain as she glanced at him, as she slid her middle finger into her mouth, then reached between her legs and slid it into her cunt. She fucked herself, spread herself open, showed him every bit of herself he was dying to see. Dying to stick his tongue in. Dying to bury his cock in.

He wanted her on his face so he could breathe her and taste

her and lap her up till she came. But she was on the floor, and he was on the bed, and there was a good six feet of space between them. And damn but her pussy was gorgeous. A deep dark pink, and so wet he couldn't think of anything but the heat of her lube coating his shaft as she took him deep and ground down.

She came to the foot of the bed then, her tits smaller than he'd expected, but perfect and unbound, and climbed onto the mattress between his legs. She knelt there, looking down at his cock. As he watched, her eyes darkened, and she licked her lips before parting them.

If there'd been any room left in his cock for more blood, it was gone now. He didn't think he'd ever been this hard. And damn if he wasn't getting pissed that his hands weren't free to hold his shaft, to guide her head. But it was too late for that, and her lips were closing around him, and *calf nuts on a cracker* the woman knew what to do with her tongue.

With her lips tight beneath the ridge of his head, she toyed with the seam, with the slit, with the skin pulled tight, until he couldn't help himself and he bucked up into her mouth. She lifted with him, anticipating, following him down again and never letting go. She sucked him, ringing the fingers of one hand beneath her mouth to squeeze, sliding to the base of his shaft and back. The fingers of the other found their way between his legs, holding his balls, rolling them, before sliding into the shadows and parts unknown.

He started to object, but closed his eyes instead, and left her to go where she wanted. That seemed to be into his ass, and he squirmed against her finger there as her other hand stroked him but good. He clenched his abs, trying to hold back the sounds coming up out of his gut, but he grunted and groaned, then he gave up. He hadn't had a woman take him over like this in, well, probably never, and since he liked hearing he was doing things right, he imagined she might enjoy the same.

What he wasn't sure she was going to enjoy was him unloading in her mouth, and that was going to happen real soon if she didn't let up and give him a minute to stanch the flow. And it seemed she came to the same realization at just about the same time because she pulled off in one long slow suck, then climbed up his body, dragging her wet pussy up his chest to his face, holding on to the headboard and lowering herself to his mouth.

He did this a lot better when he had use of his hands as well as his tongue, but she knew her own mind, and who was he to say no? He might not be wearing prison stripes, but she had him jailed just the same. He had to say, he didn't much mind. There was something about a woman knowing what she wanted, and doing whatever it took to get it. Even if that meant tying a man up and riding his face.

He blew a stream of air down the seam of her lips, then lifted his head to part them with his tongue. She slid along the tip, back and forth, putting him where she wanted him. He flicked over her clit, short, sweet butterfly touches until she couldn't take it anymore and ordered him to give it to her, "Harder."

He pushed the flat of his tongue against her, then held the tip there like he would his cock. It was rod stiff as he licked her hard, dragging her clit upward, then letting it go to pop down. Her tits bounced as she moved, and that had him wanting to buck his hips upward again, but he stayed where he was, using his tongue and his lips, licking and sucking, and finally catching her clit with his teeth.

She laughed, then slid her fingers down between her legs, rubbing places he wanted to rub but couldn't reach with his mouth. Her upper arms pushed her tits together, and the tips pouted and begged. His mouth was watering, his cock leaking, and all he could smell was cunt. She was juicy and fresh and he wanted to eat her, but her eyes were closed, her mouth open. She was lost in getting herself off.

He felt it when she came, her whole body going tight then shuddering, melting over him, her limbs first, then her torso as she collapsed on his. His cock stood at attention against the crack of her ass, and he waited for her to realize he was there, flexing so that he bobbed against her. Moments later, she giggled, then groaned, scooting down his body and holding his eyes while she rolled on his condom.

He wanted to grab his cock, swipe the head through the folds of her pussy, spread her moisture and find her entrance and push home. But he couldn't hold anything. And he had to trust she wasn't going to make him regret letting her have her way.

She put him at ease then, doing exactly what he'd wanted to do, wrapping her fingers around his shaft and positioning him, lowering her body just enough to take the head of his cock inside and hold him there. She moved her hands to his shoulders, bracing her weight and drawing in a deep breath as she pushed her way down. All the way down. Embedding him to the hilt.

She didn't give him a chance to groan, to close his eyes and savor the sensation of being gloved: the compression, the heat, the rush of blood thickening his already thick cock. She brought her mouth down to cover his, sliding her tongue between his lips as she began to ride. Up and down, up and down, grinding in a mean figure eight until it took everything he had not to blow.

Fuck it. Why was he waiting? He'd given her what she'd

asked for. It was his turn now, and he took it. Surging up into her, pumping with his hips, setting the rhythm he wanted, and kissing her all the while. She was the one to pull away, to gasp, to toss back her head and cry out as she came for the second time. Her long blond hair tumbled down her back, and goddamn but he wanted to wrap the waves around his wrists instead of the scarves.

He watched her until he couldn't watch anymore, closing his eyes as his own release burst free, his cum shooting in such powerful spurts he felt as if his guts were being mangled. He clenched hard and bore down, filling her until he couldn't move, until she couldn't move, the both of them nearly shaking with the violence of what had just passed between them.

It was a long time before she rolled from on top of his body, stretching from where she lay at his side to release his left hand, holding his wrist and rubbing the skin with her thumbs. It felt so good, the way she touched him, the way her tits dragged across his chest when she untied his right and did the same.

After that, he sat up to release his ankles, then lay back down, wrapping both of his arms around her and holding her close, feeling her heart beat against his chest. Feeling his heart tumble, and take a really bad, really long and damn dangerous fall into a place it had no business going.

# FIVE

A T A KNOCK on her office door later that morning, Everly looked up to see her boss, Whitey Simmons, editor in chief of the *Crow Hill Reporter*. Whitey was also editor of the sports section and the business section.

Everly covered human interest and local happenings. Clark Howard took care of classifieds and advertising, while Cicely Warren worked part-time to handle the occasional letter to the editor or opinion piece, and the obits. And that was it. The entire *Reporter* staff.

Whitey walked farther into Everly's office, which did have a door but was barely large enough for her desk, her chair, and the long visitors' bench beneath the window that faced the newsroom. That was where Clark and Cicely shared opposite sides of a cubicle. Since her first day here, Everly had thought the space would be better served by gutting her office and Whitey's and giving them cubicles as well.

But her boss would never go for it. He liked the illusion of power that having a door gave him, when all he did behind it when closed was nap. "I was beginning to wonder if you were going to make it in this morning, Grant."

Everly had been wondering the same thing. She leaned back in her chair, crossed her legs, felt the pull of long-unused muscles and skin scraped raw by Boone Mitchell's beard. "Late night with the fund-raiser. But I've got my notes and I'll have the story on your desk before lunch."

"You got a final tally on the cabbage raised?"

*Cabbage. Lordy.* "No, but I've got checking with Kendall on my schedule. She'll have an estimate at least."

Whitey gave her a nod. "Once you're done with that, I've got a new assignment for you."

Good. She needed something to get her mind off the fact that Boone Mitchell had washed his own dishes before he'd come back to her bedroom and taken off his clothes. That he'd put away the syrup. Put away the butter. Rinsed out the coffeepot and dumped the grounds. What man did all of that?

Or had she just always known the wrong men? "What's up?"

"A human interest piece. I'm thinking three issues at least. Big spread. Lots of photos."

What in Crow Hill could be worth that many column inches? "What's the topic?"

"The Dalton Gang."

*Gulp.* This couldn't be good for her newfound sex life. "The Dalton Gang? Why?"

Whitey propped a hip on the corner of her desk. That forced him to turn at an awkward angle to see her. "Everyone's been talking about their return to Crow Hill, but it's been what?

Four months now? Five? And there's been nary a hint of scandal from the past popping up the way folks figured would happen."

Intrigued in spite of her apprehension, she asked, "And you think something should have popped up by now?"

But Whitey was off in his own world. "Dax Campbell shacks up with Arwen Poole and finds out he has a half brother—"

"That's hardly scandalous—"

"Casper Jayne owns a piece of Crow Hill history free and clear, and is adopting a teenage kid—"

"That's not scandalous either—"

"And Boone Mitchell's coming up clean as a whistle when everyone knows he got in more trouble than the others back in the day."

She hadn't known that. *She* hadn't known that at all. She knew what it felt like to hold him in her mouth, to straddle him, to ride him to an orgasm she would never forget. She knew she was in trouble because of that. *So* much trouble because of that.

But she hadn't known he'd left trouble of another sort in his wake. Looked like she needed to go digging in the *Reporter*'s archives. "You're talking about their personal lives. Those things aren't anyone else's business."

"They're everyone's business. That's what news is."

He was right, but still she heard herself arguing. "That's gossip. That's speculation. That's—"

"It's what people want of their celebrities. Look at TMZ."

So the Dalton Gang were celebrities? And Whitey wanted them exposed? "They're ranchers—"

"They're rancher celebrities then. However you slice it, Crow Hill wants to know all about where the three have been, what they've been doing, what it's been like to come back to a town that sent them running. And"—Whitey held up a finger—"what they were running from."

That wasn't exactly the story Everly had heard from parties close to the three about their departure. But if that's what everyone in town was thinking, and saying, such a feature might not be a bad idea. She could dispel the rumors and tell the truth, though she doubted that's what Whitey had in mind.

Problem was, how impartial a story could she write with the things she now knew about Boone?—not that any of those particular facts would make it into a profile, but her bias was there, and might show, and she didn't want anyone knowing what she'd done. If anything, her time with Toby had taught her to keep her private life private.

"Well, Grant? You think you can get me something on Crow Hill's three bad boys? Say, we start with Dax Campbell. Talk to his sister . . . She married that Lasko kid, right? And to his old man, if you can get into the mansion on the hill where he's been holed up since his heart attack. Maybe you can find out what happened to his mother since no one else seems to be able to."

Everly put down her foot. "I'll do the human interest story. But I won't do it from the Jerry-Springer-dysfunctional-family angle. And it makes much more sense to start with Boone Mitchell. He was the last to leave, the first to come back. His family's still here, all of them respectable members of the community. Readers will more readily identify with him than with the other two."

Whitey's heavy brow came down as he thought. "You're saying give them what they know, draw them in, make them comfortable, then introduce the more exotic."

"I wouldn't call Dax or Casper 'exotic.' But yes. Serials work best with cliffhangers, and escalating drama, to bring readers back for more." Plus, she wanted to find out about Boone's hell-raising past now, not later, after she'd profiled the other two.

"I like the way you think, Grant." Her boss waved the fat pen he held between two fingers and chewed on in lieu of a cigar. "I knew putting you on the payroll was the right thing to do."

As if he'd had any other applicants willing to take what he called pay. He'd been lucky to get her, and he knew it. And he hadn't asked questions, which for Whitey was hard to believe.

She waved him on as he left her office, and promised to get back to him in a day or two with thoughts on an approach for the Dalton Gang piece. In the meantime, the fund-raiser story was waiting, and the keys clicked as her fingers flew.

> *Even their masks couldn't hide the identities of the generous library patrons determined to make up for the county's recent funding cuts brought on by the region's economic blight.*

Not that getting back to the fund-raiser story could keep her mind off her morning with Boone. Every time she shifted in her chair, she felt a part of him somewhere, and since he'd let her have her way with her scarves and watched without complaint, she'd let him have his when his eyes had asked for seconds.

> *Thanks to arrangements made by library board member Kendall Sheppard, owner of Sheppard's*

*Books, ticket holders were treated to authentic Western swing music played by local resident Mac Banyon's band, the L'Amours.*

He'd rolled her over after untying his ankles, covering her body with his, spreading her legs, sliding his hard cock deep. It hadn't taken him five minutes to recover. She didn't think he'd even gone soft. And though she'd had absolutely no reason to be fearful, she'd been unable to help the nerves that had come over her, waiting for him to get rough.

*With the dining room of Arwen Poole's Hellcat Saloon cleared of its tables, attendees, dressed in costumes befitting the Old West theme, enjoyed an evening of good food and plentiful drinks, their boots scooting in lively Texas two-steps across the floor.*

Boone Mitchell was a big man, tall and broad and brick solid. Where Dax and Casper were both lean, their sculpted muscles tight, their builds rangy, Boone had the shoulders of a mountain man, the arms, too, as if he spent his days swinging an ax to fell trees. Or excavating slabs of granite. A picture due as much to his stony silence as the size of his arms and his hands.

*As of this writing, donations totaling $5445 have been made. Those wishing to contribute can contact Shelly Taylor at the First National Bank: staylor@ crowhillfnb.com.*

And oh, his hands. His fingers. When he'd used his knee to spread her thighs, then pushed two fingers inside . . . She swore it was like being filled with a cock. Except not Boone's cock. Because his was sized in direct proportion to the rest of his body. And size did matter. No matter the assurances to men that it didn't, all women knew that to be the truth. And speaking of women . . .

She finished the first draft of the story, sending a quick email to Whitey that she had to run out but would have the final version to him no later than two. It wasn't like the *Reporter's* deadlines didn't have plenty of wiggle room. The problem was the wiggling she was doing in her chair. She needed something, or someone, to help get her mind off Boone.

And she had the perfect two someones in mind.

"Nice party last night," Dax said, riding up and sidestepping Flash to a stop beside Boone as he and Casper climbed down from the cab of the flatbed. The three had finished the morning's most pressing chores and were ready for lunch.

Suffering a half-booze, half-sex hangover, Boone and his bad mood didn't have the patience for Dax and his good one. Especially since Boone had lunch duty this week, meaning the other two would get in some siesta time while he panfried stew meat for sandwiches. "What you remember of it, you mean."

"What's not to remember?" Dax and his horse backed up to give Boone the room he was motioning for. If he couldn't get to the house to cook, no one would be having lunch. "Beer. More beer. Boobs. More boobs."

"Better have been Arwen's boobs you were looking at," Casper said. "Not Faith's."

Dax spun around, Flash's hooves stirring the dirt of the ranch yard into a choking dust. "Of course I was looking at Arwen. But you saying you didn't get a look at Kendall Sheppard in that feathery saloon-gal getup with her skirt rucked up around her garters? Or Lizzie Nathan decked out in that nearly see-through lace thing like she'd come straight from a brothel?"

"Can't say I did," Casper said. "The sheriff kept me on a tight leash last night. And kept my drink tickets in her cleavage. If there were boobs there other than hers, I couldn't tell you."

"Enough." *Calf nuts on a cracker.* Talking about tits was going to have Boone turning around and heading back to town and dragging Everly out of her office to bed. Or at least to the cab of his truck. Where he'd drag her out of that long, lacy top she'd worn to work and suck on her nipples until she screamed.

Damn but the woman could scream. "We need to be thinking about making it to the end of the year without going completely broke. Not talking about tits. Especially when one of the pairs belongs to my sister."

Dax leaned against his saddle horn while the other two set about unloading the truck. "Looking at tits is the spoonful of sugar that makes the medicine of being broke go down."

"What, are you Mary fucking Poppins now?" Boone grumbled, pulling on his gloves.

"Better than being Oscar the Grouch, or whoever you are." Dax slid from Flash's back and led the horse toward the barn.

Casper followed, his hands full of the tools he and Boone had been using to restring a downed section of fence. Boone reached for what was left of the spool of barbed wire, and brought up the rear. He tossed the load beneath the shelves of tools and other hardware that sat just inside the door, then pulled his hat from his head and dried his forehead in the crook of his elbow.

He looked from Dax, where the other man was pulling the saddle from Flash's back, to Casper, who was loading a new spool of staples into the fencing gun. He couldn't believe he was asking this, but it was on his mind and would bug him until he got it off. "What do either of you know about Everly Grant?"

"Arwen's friend? The reporter?" When Boone nodded, Dax shrugged. "Not much, really. Seems nice. Knows how to dance. But that's it for me."

"Faith went to school with her at UT," Casper said. "Surprised you didn't know that."

"I did know that," Boone said.

Casper looked over as if Boone was wasting his time. "Then why not ask Faith what she knows?"

"Thought I'd ask you two *boobs* first."

This time the other man's look was withering. "She was a newsreader in Austin. On one of the major networks. Came to work on the *Crow Hill Reporter* about four years ago."

"I know all of that, too."

"Sounds like a hell of a downward career move to me," Dax said.

"Yeah, I think there's a story there, but it's not one Faith's shared," Casper said, using the barrel of the gun to count the boxes of staples left on the shelf.

Boone had been thinking the same thing since Everly had told him. Moving from a major network in Austin to the *Crow Hill Reporter* didn't make a whole lot of sense. Either Everly had wanted out of Austin, or had wanted in to Crow Hill, and Boone couldn't see but one of those situations being the case.

"Why the interest in Everly?" Casper asked. "Especially since you know everything we do."

"No reason," Boone said, and shrugged. "She said she was covering the fund-raiser for the *Reporter*. Just made me curious and all."

At that, Dax coughed a mumbled *bullshit* into his hand.

"What was that?"

"Maybe you're curious because she had to bring you back to the saloon to pick up your truck this morning."

Shit. "Who told you that?"

"I live with Arwen, dude. Her cottage is right there on the same block."

Boone shoved his hat back on his head. "You were already saddled up when I got here. You couldn't have seen who might've brought me back for my truck."

"I didn't," Dax said, leading Flash into his stall. "But I did see her load your drunk ass into her SUV last night. And since your truck was still there when I was pouring my coffee . . ."

Busted. "I don't even remember that happening. I woke up and smelled pancakes and coffee, and had no clue whose bed I was in. Alone," he hurried to add before the other two started in. "I slept there. She slept on the couch. She went to work. I came here." So what if he left out all the stuff in between involving clean sheets and silk scarves?

"You thinking of hitting that?"

He glared at Dax. "If I was thinking of doing anything, I wouldn't call it 'hitting.' And I damn sure wouldn't tell you."

"I had to put up with you giving me hell about Arwen. I figure turnabout is fair play."

*Turnabout* and *fair play*. The same words that had gone through Boone's mind this morning while watching Everly strip. "I never gave you hell about Arwen."

"You gave me hell about Faith."

"Faith's my sister," Boone said to Casper. "And you were the worst possible match I could see her making."

"That *could* better be past tense, bro," Casper said, clicking the fencing gun's trigger. "Otherwise I'm gonna have to staple your balls to your thigh."

Boone felt his balls drawing tight at the sound. "Yeah, well, you keep doing reckless shit like putting your hand through truck windows, I might change my mind. We're already short on money, short on supplies, short on time to do what needs to get done. And now we're short half a man. Faith may be willing to put up with you being stupid, but I'm not. Don't let it happen again."

Casper straightened. "Are you threatening me?"

"It is what it is," Boone said, his ire rising. "The two of you are showing up later and later each morning, and half the time there's still a shitload of work to be done when you call it a day."

"I'm thinking what's wrong here, more than me and Casper getting laid regularly," Dax said, "is that you're not."

"Fuck that. And fuck you. This isn't about who's getting laid. It's about who's putting in more time on the ranch. Who's shouldering more of the workload. Who cares the most whether or not we save Tess and Dave's ranch."

"Uh-uh. Don't even start in with that shit," Dax said, latching the stall door before heading for the tack room. "You're not the only one who cares about saving what Tess and Dave left us."

"Well it's sure feeling like it these days. Like you've both found the life you want with your ladies, and the ranch is taking a backseat."

"Family always comes first, Boone," Casper said, finally putting the fencing gun where it belonged, and Boone breathing easier because of it. "You being the only one here to grow up in a functioning family should know that."

And maybe that was it. He was still thinking of his boys as family, and they'd both moved on. Dax was making his own life with Arwen, and Casper was doing the same with Faith and with Clay. All of that left Boone the one with extra time and nothing to do. Why that was suddenly giving him hell when he'd been fine being on his own up till now . . .

"I'm gonna head to the house, scrounge up lunch. Should be done in about fifteen," he said, slapping his gloves against his thigh before shoving them in his back pocket.

"Boone, wait," Dax called from behind him, but he was in no frame of mind to spill more of his guts. All he'd wanted was to see what the other two might know about Everly. Not find out he wasn't imagining the winds of change blowing over the ranch and the life he'd returned to.

Whether the Dalton Gang survived the storm remained to be seen.

# SIX

"THE FUND-RAISER WAS amazing," Faith said, sliding into the chair at the corner table she shared weekly with Everly and Arwen for lunch. "I'm so glad Kendall convinced the rest of the library's board members to hold it here."

"It was an Old West masquerade ball." Arwen reached for her tea glass and sipped, giving Faith a shrug. "The saloon made the most sense. Though Kendall getting the board to vote on the theme before booking the venue helped."

"It also made sense because the country club would've cost more, leaving less for the library." Faith signaled their server for her usual French fries and Coke. "I would've *loved* to have used the Mulberry Street house, but it's such a pain, hauling food and drinks across town, and Casper grumbling the entire time about his personal space being invaded."

"It's called catering, Faith. We hauled the food and drinks

for your parents' anniversary party. We could've done it again. But, yeah. It was easier this way," Arwen said, picking a cucumber slice from her salad and biting it in half. "Oh, did I tell you . . ."

Holding a wedge of her club sandwich in both hands as she chewed on the bite she'd taken, Everly let the rest of what the other women were saying slide in one ear and out the other. She wasn't really hungry, but it was either keep her mouth full of food or risk blurting out something about her morning with Boone.

She wanted to tell them everything. She'd loved watching Faith fall for Casper and Arwen for Dax. But Boone was Faith's brother, and she could hardly talk about his body, or his hands, or how he kissed, when the other woman had known him since she was in diapers.

And besides. Everly wasn't falling for Boone. They'd had sex. She'd like to have it again, but who knew if that would happen.

So, yeah. Her thinking lunch with the girls would get her mind off her morning hadn't turned out like she'd hoped, because no matter the talk of the library and the house on Mulberry Street and last night's fund-raiser, her mind was on the scarves she'd never again be able to wear as accessories.

"Everly?"

"Hmm?" She looked up at her table mates. Both women were staring as if she'd been talking with her mouth full. Which she hoped wasn't the case, considering her thoughts of the last few minutes.

"You've been staring off into space since I got here," Faith said.

"I had a busy morning," she said, sitting straight as she returned her sandwich half to her plate. She needed to tell them.

Their men were involved. And talking about it would at least keep her from blurting out the truth about what she'd done with Boone. "Whitey gave me a new assignment earlier. A human interest story."

"Yeah?" Faith asked, stirring her straw through her ice. "Someone in Crow Hill that interesting?"

"Three someones, actually." *And . . . here we go.* "He wants me to do a profile on the Dalton Gang."

"What?" That question, loud enough to turn heads, came from Faith.

"Why?" And that one, less loud than it was sharp, came from Arwen.

Everly picked up her sandwich again. "He said their return has been the talk of the town for months, so it's time to give readers something more than speculation." Whitey hadn't said any of that, of course. But she wasn't about to tell her two friends her boss wanted her to dig for dirt on the three men. All who were friends of her friends, if not more.

"What sort of slant are you giving the story?" Arwen asked, going where Everly had feared.

She shook her head. "I haven't decided. I mean, I just got the assignment. But I do think Crow Hill needs to see the men as they are now, and stop expecting the sort of trouble they caused as boys."

Faith's order of French fries arrived then, and she reached across the table for the ketchup, saying, "I'm not sure I like this idea," as she squirted a pool on her plate.

"It's for the *Reporter*, Faith. Not the *National Enquirer*. And it's me doing the story. I think you know me. Both of you," she added, turning to Arwen.

"I do," Faith said. "But there's a lot you don't know about Casper. I'm sure it's the same for Dax."

Arwen nodded. "I'm with Faith on this. The past needs to stay in the past."

Everly wanted to stab herself with her knife for saying yes to Whitey in the first place. Except this was her livelihood, and these women her friends. They should know better than to suspect whatever it was they were suspecting. "C'mon, y'all. I'm not going to do a hatchet job here. I'm a damn good writer, if I do say so myself. I know there are two sides to every story."

"I think that's part of the problem," Arwen said, poking at her salad with her fork.

Faith concurred with a nod as she jabbed a French fry. "You've got to know there are a lot of folks out there just waiting to drag the boys through all their old crap, and leave them there to wallow."

"Which is why I'm the best person to write the story. I'm not digging for dirt. I'm only looking for the truth."

"Some of their truth *is* dirt," Faith said.

Arwen nodded down at her salad. "She's right."

But before Everly could respond, Faith went on. "So if you run across it, because that's going to happen, Ev, and you know it will, are you going to print it? The dirt?"

Everly took a moment to chew a bite of sandwich and find an answer they all three could live with, but especially Faith. An answer that wouldn't feel like a betrayal of the friendship that had saved Everly's life. "If it's something of interest, yes, but only if I have the full story."

"Even full stories can end up making the boys look bad."

Frustration began to knot in her midsection. She wanted her friends' support. She wanted their involvement, their input. She didn't want what was her job to come between them. "Do y'all not have things in your past you wish weren't there?"

"Of course, but our pasts aren't going to print under the guise of human interest," Faith said.

"Details from mine did," Everly replied, which Faith knew well. "Without all the facts and beneath a much bigger microscope than the *Reporter*."

"And look what happened. The speculation about those things drove you out of Austin."

"The events drove me out. Not the speculation." Though the questioning looks and hushed whispers from friends and coworkers hadn't helped. Neither had the private asides from family members who felt it their duty to remind her they'd never understood what she saw in Toby and had disapproved of him from day one.

"Wait a second," Arwen said, holding up one hand. "Events in Austin? Is this something you'd like to share? Because if not, that's fine, but know I'm lost here."

Everly had never spoken of what had brought her to Crow Hill to anyone besides Faith. But since she was asking them to understand her putting their men in an unwanted spotlight, and Arwen was a friend and deserved to know . . .

Looking from one woman to the other, she took a deep breath and said, "My ex was abusive. Most of it was emotional, but it was still abuse. It wasn't until our relationship was ending that it turned physical."

Arwen's eyes had gone wide, but before she could speak, Faith added, "And because Everly was on network TV in Austin, her face was easily recognized when she went to the ER to be stitched up."

"Oh, God, sweetie." Arwen reached across the table, squeezed Everly's wrist. "I had no idea. Did he hurt you badly?"

Her stomach churning, Everly tried to shrug off the question.

But Faith let her off the hook and answered for her. "Badly enough that she left Austin and came here."

"I've always wondered why anyone would choose to live in Crow Hill, but this . . ." Arwen squeezed again before letting go. "I never imagined. I'm so, so sorry."

Trusting her voice not to break, Everly picked a strip of bacon from her sandwich and pressed forward. "I knew what he was doing, long before he struck out. And I knew not to let him get to me. But telling myself I wouldn't fall for his begging and crying, didn't work. I went back."

"Even after he hit you?" Arwen asked.

"No. Well, yes. But only once," she said as she tore the bacon into ribbons. "The first time he used his belt. I stepped toward him as he swung it."

Arwen looked to Faith, then back and said, "And you blamed yourself for getting in the way."

Everly nodded. "Just that time. The next he used his fist."

"Did you call the cops?"

"She did. And she called me," Faith said. "I helped her pack up and move. Though I wouldn't exactly call what we did that day *packing*."

The bacon was in a pile now, so Everly started in on the bread, pinching off pieces of toasted crust. "I had several friends on the APD. Two of them came by while Faith and I grabbed what I needed. I didn't take anything of Toby's. Or anything we'd bought as a couple. And thank goodness we'd kept our money separate. Wardrobe, makeup, jewelry, toiletries, electronics . . . That was it. I replaced everything else. Well, almost everything else," she added wryly. "My house doesn't have room for a piano."

Faith turned to Arwen. "You should've seen the baby grand she left."

"I had no idea you played."

"I haven't for a while," she said, feeling a hint of a smile at the thought of shopping for a small upright, then cleaning her hands on her napkin. "Anyway. That's my story. And it's the best 'been there done that' case I can make for telling that of the Dalton Gang. Unlike some news outlets, I actually know the meaning of being fair and balanced."

Her companions quietly let that settle, Arwen finally saying, "There's a piano at the ranch house, you know. It belonged to Tess. I'm not even sure she played. Or how long it's been sitting there."

Oh, good. They were moving on. "No. I didn't know," she said, picking up the half of her sandwich she hadn't mangled. "But now I'm itching to get my hands on it."

At that, a sly grin pulled at Arwen's mouth. "The way you and Boone were looking at each other while dancing last night, I thought maybe you'd be itching to get your hands on him."

Everly looked quickly to Faith, who was frowning, then down at the mess on her plate. If only Arwen knew . . . "I haven't been with anyone since Austin. I've dated, but I've always come home alone. Last night though . . ."

"Did you?" Arwen asked. "Come home alone? Or did Boone come with?"

"I'm pretty sure I saw him leave with Luck Summerlin," Faith said, still frowning, leaving Everly to wonder if his sister had a problem with her seeing Boone, or Boone seeing her, or both.

Arwen shook her head. "Luck came scurrying back inside a few minutes later."

"I ran across the two of them in the parking lot," Everly said. "Right about the time all her moaned *yes*es became squealed *no*s."

"Ah, yes. That would be our Luck, so to speak."

Everly grinned. "Boone saw me getting into my car and came over. He was pretty drunk. So I drove him home."

"To the ranch?" Faith asked. "Or to your home?"

"Mine," she said, still unable to get a read on the other woman. "He spent the night in my bed. I slept on the couch. And I washed his clothes and made him breakfast before he ever woke up."

"Then he left?"

Everly nodded, then lied. "I drove him here to get his truck, and I went to work. I'm assuming he went to the ranch."

"Does he know about the story? For the paper," Faith said, waving her hand. "Not Austin. And thank you for not letting him behind the wheel."

"You're welcome," she said, the ice she had yet to understand beginning to thaw. "And, no. You two are the only ones I've told about the story. I didn't get the assignment until an hour ago."

"But you're going to talk to Boone."

"It would only be two-thirds of a story if I didn't," she said, looking from Boone's sister to Arwen who asked, "Who else are you going to talk to?"

"Like I said. Families. Friends."

"Enemies?"

"I'll talk to whoever I need to. I want as much information as I can get."

"Okay then. I'll make you a list."

"Of Dax's enemies?"

"Of people I think you should start with. And you can take what they give you and go from there."

She didn't need a list. She knew how to dig for source material, where to look for buried secrets, how to unearth the past.

But she also knew not to look a gift horse in the mouth. "Thank you. I appreciate it. And if you want, I can start by talking to you."

Arwen stuck out her tongue. "I was afraid of that."

When she turned to Faith, she got a roll of the other woman's eyes for her trouble. "Yeah, yeah. I'll pencil you in. And make sure Casper does, too."

"Excellent," she said, rubbing her hands together with an abundance of glee, the first she'd felt since Whitey had dropped the story into her lap. "I love it when a plan comes together."

# SEVEN

EVERLY DIDN'T WORK on Saturdays, but was quite sure Boone did. Ranchers, she'd learned since leaving the city for cattle country, kept incredibly long hours. To make their living off the land, they had no choice. They didn't sit at a desk, in an air-conditioned office, electronics the tools of their trade. They were at the mercy of Mother Nature, using brute strength and cunning to beat the bitch at her game.

All of that made getting in touch with the rancher she needed to talk to difficult. Thanks to Faith, she had the number to the house's landline, but either he didn't carry his cell when riding the range, or there was no service out there with the prairie dogs and rattlesnakes and cows. That left her stuck having to call the house until he answered, or leaving a message and hoping he was the one who got it instead of Casper or Dax.

Boone needed to hear about her assignment ASAP. Especially since Faith and Arwen would, by now, have told their men about it—Everlys' fault for feeling compelled to share, an anomaly she still hadn't worked out. It wasn't like she'd told friends and family members of other story subjects what was coming. But this one arriving on the heels of having Boone in her bed . . .

She sighed, second-guessing yesterday. Maybe she shouldn't have mentioned the story to her girlfriends at all, and instead cornered all three members of the Dalton Gang at once, slamming them with a hard-hitting interrogation the way Whitey wanted—even if he hadn't spelled it out in so many words. She'd known him four years. He didn't have to.

Scoops. Exclusives. Bombshells. She was supposed to drop explosive questions into her interviews, giving no advance warning, then watch the shrapnel fly. It was her job to knock the three members of the Dalton Gang off balance, to bleed their secrets onto the page. Collateral damage was nothing. No details were off-limits, no matter how revealing, how hurtful.

Her arms crossed on her kitchen table, her chin braced on her stacked hands, she stared unblinking at the cordless handset of her house phone. It stood on end between the bottle of CapRock Roussanne she'd just opened and the glass of the same she'd just poured. She hated what passed for news these days: the sensationalism, the exposés, the absolute lack of respect for privacy as long as the story was served.

Even before the last straw with Toby, which had cast an unwanted limelight on her, she'd decided she was done with anything that smacked of tabloid journalism. That sort of reporting had its place: selling papers, gaining viewers, giving a public hungry for celebrity news what they wanted. But having her own life pried into had shown her what happened on the other side of the camera or pen.

She wouldn't do that to the Dalton Gang. She wouldn't have done it even before yesterday morning with Boone. Not to say yesterday morning wasn't going to make keeping the story impersonal a challenge, but at least she didn't have to worry about his feelings, or hers, since their encounter had been purely sexual, no emotions involved, no promises given, no future plans made.

Still, she did have her assignment, and spending Saturday night home alone drinking wine was not going to get it done. She'd just picked up her phone to dial again, staring at the dark display, when the screen lit up and it rang. Boone's number, but he wouldn't know who he was calling.

"Hello?"

She answered, then listened to him grumble and curse in the background while her voice registered. "I've got fourteen missed calls from your number. I was about to tear whoever'd been harassing me with hang-ups a new one."

She cringed. Hard to blame him. "Sorry. I didn't want to leave a message. I kept hoping I'd catch you."

"You've been calling the house off and on all afternoon. Why would you expect to catch me here?"

"Because I'm an ignorant city slicker who thought you might take off early on Saturday?"

He snorted. "You might be a city slicker, but you're not ignorant, and you've lived in Crow Hill long enough to know weekends mean nothing to ranchers."

He had her there. "I should've left a message. I just wasn't sure you'd get it."

"Now that's a legitimate cause for concern because I'm not always one to check."

Hearing him drawl out the words *legitimate cause* brought a smile to her face, and she pulled her wineglass closer. "What made you check now?"

"I always look at the incoming log in case my dad's called. He never leaves a message either." He paused, and she heard the banging of cabinet doors, the clanging of pots and pans, cutlery. "Why do you people do that? Or not do that, I guess, is the question."

"Usually, I do." She ran the flat of her index finger over the base of her glass. "But like I said, I wanted to catch you and didn't want to sweat out the wait, wondering if you'd gotten the message." She paused, picked up her glass, took a sip. "Or if you'd call me back."

Another snort hit her ear. Then an even louder banging sound as if he'd slammed a skillet onto the stove. "You thought after yesterday morning I wouldn't call you back?"

Eyes closed, she remembered the scruff of his beard on her skin and shivered. "When I called, I wasn't even thinking about yesterday."

"I haven't stopped thinking about yesterday." His voice slid over her, silky and smooth and warm.

Her heart thumped hard, and then a second time, but she held back admitting how often he'd been on her mind. "I actually called because of work."

"Work can wait. Tell me about the scarves."

"What?" she asked, her heart tumbling and turning the word breathless.

"Tell me about the scarves." It was a demand, not a question, and the skin at her nape tingled.

She closed her eyes, swallowed. She supposed his curiosity shouldn't surprise her. "What about them?"

"Well, I sure as hell don't want to know where you bought them or how much they cost."

That had her smiling again. "And here I was all set to give you shopping advice."

"I want to know why you made me keep my hands to myself for so long."

An explanation that would take too much time to go into; it had been stressful enough telling her girlfriends about her ex. Telling Boone the full story would add levels no amount of wine would help relieve, and so she glossed over the truth. "I like getting what I want. The scarves make sure I will."

"You're talking orgasms," he said, and when she stayed silent, added, "You could've just asked."

It had happened before, a man promising to show her heaven, then making the trip alone. "Until the fund-raiser, we'd hardly spoken two words to each other. I didn't know what you'd say."

"I'm a guy. That should've been enough of a clue."

"Some guys want things to go their way."

"Some guys are selfish pricks, but I get it. I could've been one." More banging of dishes. "Now you know I'm not. At least most of the time."

Really. He made it so easy to smile. "So, the reason I called—"

"Fourteen times," he cut in to say.

"The reason I called fourteen times was to ask if we could get together for an interview."

"An interview?" he asked after his silence had her swallowing half the wine in her glass.

"For the paper. I've been assigned a human interest story on the return of the Dalton Gang to Crow Hill."

He grunted. "Not sure the type of interest humans around here have in the Dalton Gang is fit for the *Reporter* to print. Not sure it's the type the boys and I want printed."

That sounded a lot like a rehash of Arwen's and Faith's argument. She gave Boone the same response she'd given them.

"Whitey wants a story. Who would you rather have write it? Whitey, me, Clark Howard, or Cicely Warren? Because it's going to be one of the four of us. And my bias is going to be a little bit different from theirs."

"Well, that's a given," he said, then added a quick, "Hang a sec," returning after the kitchen faucet came on and went off. "Dax once cut donuts in Clark's front yard after he told him to stay away from his daughter, so he's no fan. And Cicely's hardly any better. She propositioned Casper when he was sixteen."

"What?" Everly asked, nearly spilling the refill of wine she was pouring.

"He told her he'd rather take it up the ass from one of Rooster Hart's Charolais bulls than let her get hold of his dick."

That had her sputtering. "Cicely's got to be twenty years older than Casper."

"And probably just as much of a degenerate now as she was then."

Everly was never going to be able to look at Cicely Warren with a straight face again. "And Whitey? Did one of you ruin his yard or his daughter's reputation? Because if he came on to you, I do not want to know."

This time it was Boone laughing, a low rumbling growl that slid into the pit of Everly's stomach. "Not that I can recall. But Whitey will want to sell as many copies as he can, so he'd be the worst choice. He'd make what dirt he can find sound even dirtier."

Except she wasn't sure anything could sound dirtier than Cicely Warren soliciting a teenage Casper Jayne. But she only knew the middle-aged, and unfortunately unattractive, woman now. She hadn't known her then.

She hadn't known any of the story's players then. It was

very possible what she found out about Boone might change what was so far her good opinion of him.

The thought did not thrill her. "Does it worry you?"

"What?"

"That I might find out some things you'd rather I not?"

"Whatever's out there is in the past and can't be undone. I figure you've got some skeletons of your own you might prefer I not know about."

"I do," she said, glad to see they were on the same page, and supposing she should brace for her skeletons lifting a hand from the grave.

"I guess we're even then. Ask me what you will."

"Thank you."

"No need," he said, the sound of food sizzling reaching her ears with the words. "Just making sure you get your info from the horse's mouth rather than just horses' asses."

She flicked a nail over the wine bottle's label. "Do you think Casper and Dax will be as accommodating?"

"No, but I'm happy to come along when you talk to them, keep them from giving you too hard of a time."

She'd never had a hero in her corner before, and her heart soared. Too bad she was going to put him on public display now that he was there. "I'll be fine. I'd rather talk to them without a buffer."

"The offer's there. If you should need me. Or just a buffer."

He was a nice man. "Who's going to keep *you* from giving me too hard of a time?"

"No one. Because I'm pretty sure hard is the way you like it."

And she was pretty sure she'd like it any way he wanted to give it to her. "I'll see you Monday then?"

"Make it noon. I have to stop for lunch anyway. I'll meet you at the house."

"Will the others be there?" She didn't want to arrive prepared for one man if she'd have the chance to talk to all three.

"They're going to a cattle auction. We'll have the place to ourselves."

Just her, and Boone, and all those wide-open spaces. She took a deep breath, and a long swallow of wine. "You're not going?"

"I'm not a fan of spending more of the ranch's money than we have to."

Interesting. "So they're buying? Not selling?"

"The only thing we have that's worth selling is, according to Darcy anyhow, some antiques that belonged to Tess."

"Are you going to sell them?" she asked, sensing a hesitance in his voice.

"We may have to. We did lease rights on a few acres for an oil well going in now."

"That's exciting." Wasn't it? Black gold. Texas tea.

"It boosted us over a bad hump. But we've got a lot more humps and no more guaranteed boosts. Unless we sell the antiques."

"Why is that a question?" she asked, frowning.

"Selling them? Because they were Tess's."

"But they're yours now."

"Doesn't matter."

"Don't you think she'd want you to get what use out of them you could? Even if that use is the cash selling them brings you?"

"Still seems wrong. And disrespectful somehow." He went silent then, the sounds of dishes and utensils and the refrigerator door opening reaching her ears. "But we're about out of options."

"The Daltons meant a lot to you, didn't they?"

"They meant everything. Listen, my food's ready here and I'm starving, so why don't I tell you about them on Monday?"

"Okay. I'll see you then," she said, barely stopping herself from adding *I can't wait*.

Because it was the truth. She couldn't.

# EIGHT

EVEN MORE THAN he'd missed his boys the sixteen years he'd spent away from Crow Hill, Boone had missed his mother's cooking, especially her Sunday pot roast. Knowing it was in the oven at home, carrots buried in the juices beneath it, sometimes potatoes, too—though he preferred his mashed—had made sitting through Pastor Cuellar's sermon the worst hour of each week.

Things were better now that his Sunday mornings were spent working, and the only time he saw Pastor Cuellar was if they happened to pass in the aisle at Drury Hardware. The pastor took no salary, and used his family money to keep the First Baptist Church building in good repair. Since Boone was the only one of the Dalton Gang still living on the ranch, keeping that house the same fell to him.

Unfortunately, he didn't have the Cuellar fortune. Or even much of the money he himself had made while working as a hand in New Mexico. And as little cash as he had to spend on home maintenance, he had even less time. Meaning he really needed to head back and use the rest of the day to do something about the back porch steps, now that one of the boards on the bottom one had split clean in two.

And it wouldn't hurt for him to run the mower over the grass growing up through the weeds in the yard. Would make the place look less like it belonged to the neighborhoods in Southwest Crow Hill and more like the homestead Tess had taken so much pride in. 'Course Tess had been gifted with a green thumb, growing okra and corn and squash and tomatoes every year, and keeping the beds in the front of the house filled with flowers she coaxed to blossom no matter the heat.

But before he left town to do either of those things, he needed some answers from the woman beside him.

Standing next to his sister in front of the sink in their parents' home, drying the clean dishes she handed him, Boone thought back to the time he'd spent with Everly on Friday, and all the things about her he didn't know. Things he wanted to. Things that he hoped would put the rest into some perspective. Because as it stood, he couldn't figure out much of what made her tick. Except the sex. And the scarves.

"Do you miss the bank at all?" he asked, thinking he could get at the answers he needed by going in through a side door rather than barging in through the front.

"I miss seeing the people I worked with, and the customers. I don't miss giving bad news to clients." Faith rinsed another plate and slid it into his towel-covered hand. "And I don't miss pantyhose and pumps. I don't miss those *at* all."

It was strange seeing his sister around town in knee pants or capris or whatever they were called, and frilly summer blouses, even T-shirts, instead of the suits she'd worn to the bank for years. "You're not bored? Not having something to do all day?"

"I have a lot to do all day. I just do it at the house, not at the bank." She reached for the sprayer, aimed the water at a spot of dried potato. The food went down the disposal before she dunked the plate in the sink of soap bubbles. Why she didn't just use the dishwasher instead of putting herself through this every week . . . "You'll have to come by and see what I've done to the third floor."

That had been the floor where Casper's bedroom had been. The one, Boone had learned from a much more vulnerable Faith than this one, where the other man, as a kid, had stuffed balls of newspaper into holes in the ceiling to keep spiders from dropping down onto his bed. "Thought you might be sealing it off."

"You thought wrong. I'm gutting the floor and turning it into a home theater for Clay and Casper and all their movies. And for Clay's video games. It's going to be amazing."

Now the nightmares would be on big screens instead of in Casper's head. "Good for you. I like that you still look out for him. Casper. I think he'll need that the rest of his life."

"I like it, too. And I think so, too." She used her sponge like a weapon against the gravy burned on the bottom of a saucepan. "Though it's not the same sort of looking out our folks did when he was in school."

"I don't need to hear about your sex life."

"I'm not talking about sex. Jesus, Boone. Relationships are more than sex. You, better than any man I know, should get that."

Because of the example their parents had set. Because they'd stuck together through all the hell he and his sister had put them through. "You're good for him. You've made him a good home."

"Doing that's a lot more fun, and much more satisfying, than handling the ranch's accounts, and telling you no every time you need money."

"So you don't miss it at all?"

Frowning, she looked over, blowing a wisp of hair away from the corner of her mouth. "Why are you asking me about missing the bank?"

"No reason," he said, grabbing for the plate she hadn't finished rinsing.

She held tight, even with wet hands. "Yes reason. Usually after Sunday supper you're parked in front of the TV watching football with Daddy and Casper and Clay."

Today he'd sent his mother in his place. She loved football more than he did anyway, even if he'd played all four years of high school. And she loved having a fifteen-year-old nearly adopted grandson to spoil. Clay had no idea how lucky he was. Except he did.

"Fine." He didn't have time for subterfuge anyway. He had chores and animals waiting. "I want to know about Everly Grant. Why she's here. In Crow Hill."

"Everly is why you're asking me about the bank?" she asked as she got back to the dishes.

"I talked to her at the fund-raiser. We danced. That's all." But it wasn't all, and with this being his sister, by the end of this conversation, she'd know it, too. "I'm curious."

"You're curious because you didn't learn anything when you spent the night in her bed?"

*Calf nuts on a cracker.* Women. "She tell you that?"

Faith nodded. "Friday at lunch. Said you were drunk, she drove you home, she slept on the couch."

"That's pretty much what happened." And since it looked like that was all Everly had said, he wasn't saying anything more. "Tell me about her."

"Not much to tell," she said, starting in on the silverware. "We were in school together. She came to visit a few years ago, loved it, and got the job at the *Reporter*."

"That's a bunch of crap. No one in their right mind chooses to live in Crow Hill."

"You did. Dax and Casper did."

"That's different. We grew up here. We inherited the ranch. We had a reason."

She thought a minute, then argued. "I chose to live here. Arwen chose to live here. She could've left anytime."

"Not the same. You both grew up here, too. You came back because of the folks." And because of things she'd been through they didn't talk about. "Name me one other person who lives here on purpose. Someone who didn't grow up here. Someone who didn't take over their folks' business, like Josh Lasko or Lizzie Nathan. Everyone we know was born here and stayed. Except Everly."

"Greg Barrett."

"He doesn't count. He's related to the Campbells."

She took another thoughtful break to scrub a really long carving knife. "Kendall Sheppard. She didn't come for a job. She's not related to anyone. She didn't grow up here. She moved here and opened her own business."

He hadn't thought of Kendall Sheppard, though her opening a bookstore in a place like Crow Hill also didn't make a lot of sense. "She doesn't count either."

"Why?"

"Just answer me."

"Why?"

Did everything have to be such a big deal? "Because I want to know what the hell Everly's doing living here."

"Why does it matter . . . ? Wait," she said, turning to him, giving him that look he hated. That know-it-all, little-sister-got-something-on-her-big-brother look. "She didn't sleep on the couch, did she?"

"Yeah. She did," he said, and left it at that.

"Then what's going on here? What aren't you telling me?"

He jerked the knife out of her hand to dry it. "She kept my drunk ass from driving. That's all."

"I've never known your drunk ass to drive. You always sleep it off in your truck."

He did, but hadn't thought it necessary to tell Everly that. "Help me out here, Faith. I want to know what I'm up against."

"You mean besides what you've already been up against?" she asked, one dark brow rising.

"Not funny."

"Oh, it's funny. Funny in the same way you tried to keep me and Casper apart."

"That was in high school."

She sputtered. "Are you saying you didn't invoke the no-sisters rule once you three were back on the ranch?"

"Only because I wasn't sure if Casper was serious. But this isn't the same. Everly and I are just . . ."

"Just what, Boone?" She turned to him, shoved a soapy fist to her hip before realizing what she'd done. "Crap," she said, grabbing his towel and drying the blouse she'd worn to church. "What are you and Everly exactly? Because she's my friend—"

"And I'm your brother—"

"—and I don't want her to get hurt."

"I'm not—"

"Uh-uh. Save it. You won't know if you're going to hurt her until it's too late. And she's been hurt enough."

That's what he'd been afraid of. "So, I shouldn't see her again."

"You don't think not seeing her again won't hurt her?

"Criminy, Faith. Do I or don't I?"

"That's up to you," she said, turning back to the dishes with a shrug. "Just make sure you do the right thing."

As long as the right thing was drowning himself in the sink? "Well, she's coming out to the ranch tomorrow so I'll have to see her then."

"The ranch? Why would she come to the ranch?"

"An interview, or some bullshit. Her editor wants her to do a human interest story on the Dalton Gang coming back to Crow Hill."

"Oh, yeah. She mentioned the assignment at lunch on Friday. Strange the paper would want to do something now. You've all been back for months."

"Don't look at me. All I know is that I'm first up, then she'll want to talk to Dax and Casper."

"Hmm."

The idea of Faith trying to rein in Casper, or of Arwen doing the same to Dax, made him laugh. He didn't have to be reined. He knew how to keep his mouth shut. And Faith knew that better than anyone. "I won't bug her about it if you tell me what she's really doing here."

"Everly being here is Everly's business. If you want to know what happened, you'll have to get the story from her."

"So something did happen."

"Something always *happens*, Boone. Dave and Tess dying

brought you back here. Dax and Casper, too. I came back because of, well, everything that happened at school. Arwen stayed because of what happened with her father. It's called life. And if Everly decides to make you a part of hers, then I imagine she'll tell you everything you need to know. Until then . . ." She made a zipping motion across her lips, threw the imaginary key into the dishwater.

Boone rolled his eyes, then stuck his hand in the sink and went fishing. Faith laughed so loud and so hard, Casper came running from the other room, followed by Clay and their folks.

With their audience looking on, Faith wrapped her arms around Boone's neck and hugged him, smacking a big kiss on his cheek, before pulling the stopper out of the sink and letting the answers he wanted go down the drain.

# NINE

On Monday, Everly steered her luxury hybrid SUV into the main yard of the Dalton Ranch precisely at noon. When she'd called Boone Saturday evening, she'd been glad he'd suggested the time. She had no idea what kind of schedule he kept—other than its demanding a whole lot of very long hours—and hadn't wanted their interview to get in the way of his work.

Work, she'd learned, for most men was sacred. Or if not sacred, then more important than anything a woman might need, especially if that need required any of their precious time. Though, granted, she'd come to that way of thinking based on what she'd been through with Toby. Dinners had been planned around his comings and goings, vacations arranged when he knew he'd have a lighter-than-usual workload, though because the idea appealed to the attention seeker in him, he'd embraced the alphabetical trips she'd started the summer after high school, though he'd insisted they start over at A.

Even sex had been slotted in when he was ready, never mind that she had a headache or the cramps, that she had to be up early and needed to get to sleep. That she was too wrapped up with a story to clear her mind and reach orgasm—and God help her if she dared try to fake her way through. For some reason, Toby measured his prowess, and the state of their relationship, based on how hard she came.

She supposed it wasn't fair to use him as a benchmark. Unlike her ex, her father had been completely unselfish, devoted to his family, a true head of household, seeing to the needs of those with whose care he'd been charged. But he'd also been fond of putting his foot down, having the last word, the final say. And many times simply because doing so worked with his vision of what was acceptable. Or because doing so was convenient for him. And she'd hated that. Hated it.

Surely there was a middle ground. And logically, she knew there was. She'd seen it in Dax and Casper, the way they were with their women. Both men were completely full of themselves, but not for one minute did they consider their desires ahead of their partners'. Boone had been equally thoughtful of her, but most of their time together had been spent having sex, and it would take more than orgasms at his hands to really know him. Still, a man was never as vulnerable as when naked . . .

Pushing that thought and others that were equally unproductive from her mind, she grabbed her purse and stepped from her SUV, dropping her keys down inside. Shading her eyes as she looked for Boone, she realized she could probably have left them in the ignition. There was no one around, as far as she could see, leaving her unsure where she'd find him. The house sat to her left, a corral or pen in front of her, the barn and a second corral or pen to her right. For her article, she'd have to get the terminology correct.

She'd also have to get it correct because it mattered. If she and Boone were going to explore this . . . whatever it was between them, she wanted to pay attention to his life. And that had nothing to do with her past. It was just who she was. Curious as well as exacting, and granted, maybe a little bit of a compulsive perfectionist. But those traits had served her well as she dug for the meat of her stories. Though—*oh my*—what she'd like to dig for now . . .

Boone was walking toward her from the barn, wearing boots and jeans and a blue plaid shirt left untucked. One gloved hand gripped the stock of a very long rifle. His purposeful stride ate up the ground and stirred trails of dust in his wake. His hat brim was pulled low, and a bandanna fluttered from his back pocket. She imagined the body beneath his clothing, his cut abs, his huge biceps, the silky wedge of his chest hair, his thick cock resting beneath the denim against his thigh.

A shudder ran through her, and she had to remind herself she wasn't here for more of what they'd shared Friday morning. Not that she wouldn't love a repeat, but this was his house, not hers; with his bedroom, not hers; and his bed, not hers. She had too many . . . rules, she wanted to say, when she had to admit they were hang-ups. The fact that she'd broken her promise to herself, to take things slow with the next man she decided to sleep with, was already causing her grief.

She could not afford to be tempted by the external trappings: the beautiful body, the face she wanted to frame in her camera's viewfinder, the light finding his cheekbones, the slope of his nose, his lips that were amazingly soft despite the abuse they took from the elements, the sun and the wind and the dry, dry heat.

Neither could she be tempted by the sex. No matter how delicious. She could enjoy it, and she would, but she could not allow it to mean more than the good time it was. That was the bottom line. Bodies only. No emotions. No attachments. No connections. No expectations of more. Though watching him approach, she knew in the deepest part of herself, sticking to her bottom line was going to be a battle.

Slowing only long enough to lay the gun in the bed of his truck, he continued toward her, tugging off his gloves and tossing them into an empty wheelbarrow as he passed. Her stomach clenched. Her thighs trembled. If she hadn't known him, she would've run. He was that intimidating. That . . . She didn't want to say *frightening* because she wasn't scared. Except a part of her was. The part fighting that bottom-line battle. That had sworn to never give up her heart.

He reached her then, took her by the hand, pulled her across the yard, up the back porch steps, and into the kitchen. Once there, his hat sailing from his hand to the table, he continued to hold on, tugging her behind him toward the house's staircase, climbing a lot faster than she could without scrambling. She was breathless when they reached the second floor, but Boone wasn't winded at all, and she knew what she was feeling was anticipation. Wondering what he had in store. Wondering what he would do if she asked him to let her go.

When he led her to an open door, a carelessly made bed in the room behind, she tested her theory, slipping her hand from his before crossing the threshold. He stopped and looked back. His eyes were hooded and dark, his pupils wide, his jaw taut and straining. His chest rose and fell rapidly, and the faded denim beneath his belt buckle strained to contain him. His wanting her was obvious.

What she was waiting for was his insistence that she wanted this as much as he did, the pressure to acquiesce, the demands that she owed him; that this was his right, that she could give or he would take. That she had no say in this matter, or in any other.

Instead, he said the only words she needed to hear. "It's up to you."

She stepped into the room and closed the door, leaning against it. "Is this where you want to do the interview?"

"This is where I want to fuck you. The interview can wait."

"There *will* be an interview," she said, reaching for the buttons down the ruffled front of her sleeveless crêpe de chine blouse.

"Stop," he said, coming toward her and taking hold of her hands, pinning them against the door near her shoulders. His gaze held hers, and she wondered if he could see how hard her heart was beating, if he saw any of her past fears flash in her eyes. "I wanted to unbutton your dress when we danced. I wanted to unbutton your top when you had me tied to your bed. If I don't get to unbutton you this time . . ."

His gaze dropped from hers to her breasts that rose and fell as she struggled to draw a normal breath. It was impossible, breathing normally, with the way he was looking at her, with the want in his eyes, with lust beating a sharp tempo in the hollow of his throat. The skin of his neck, prickly with a day's worth of beard, was sweaty, and no doubt salty, and baked by the sun. She rose up on her tiptoes, opened her mouth there, and drew her tongue in a line to his chin.

He groaned, his head falling back on his shoulders. "I don't even want to know what that tasted like."

"It tasted like you," she told him when he looked back to her. "Like hard work and hard muscles and hard sex."

"You do like your sex hard, don't you?" he asked, a brow lifting, one corner of his mouth lifting, too.

"I like you hard."

He still held her hands, and he pulled them both to the fly of his jeans. "Then I've got what you like."

She wrapped her fingers around his bulk and squeezed, his whole body shuddering, hers shuddering, too. "But it's not where I want it."

"Oh, it will be," he said, the words deep and rough and visceral. "Just as soon as I get you out of those pants."

Her gaze snagged by his, she slid her palm down his length to cup the bulb of his head. "What about my buttons?"

His breath hissed out, a sharp push between his teeth. "I'll get to those later. This needs taking care of first. And this time, I give the orders."

"Orders?" she asked, feeling a jolt of something rich and raw, but not frightening. Not frightening at all.

"Hands and knees. Yours. On the bed."

She took a step back, her hands going to the zipper of her skinny black pants. She lowered it, the raspy sound like a groan in the air, and kicked out of her Louboutin red-soled stilettos. Still wearing her blouse, she peeled her pants down her legs, rolled her panties off, too, her top swaying around her hips when she straightened and covering her to mid-thigh.

Boone shook his head, popping open all the snaps of his shirt in one hard tug. "Woman, don't even move."

Her heart fluttered in her chest, a butterfly, a hummingbird. A wasp ready to sting. "What happened to my hands and my knees on your bed?"

"I'm taking an extended lunch hour. We've got time," he

said, tugging off his boots, shucking down his jeans and shorts, his cock rod hard as he freed it.

It took all the willpower she had not to reach for him, to stroke him and fondle him and bend to take him into her mouth. She remembered his taste, the feel of him, the skin covering his taut shaft, that of a different texture stretched over the crown.

He was so beautifully male, his muscles defined, his skin sleek, his body hair having never known a razor or wax. She liked that most of all. That he looked like a man, not what haute couture had decided made for a pleasing male form, one smooth body nearly indistinguishable from the next.

When he came to her then, she held on to his biceps and looked up. He looked down, searching, asking something she didn't understand, arguing with himself as if he wasn't sure this was really what she wanted. After all, she'd come here for work, to ask him questions, not to strip out of her clothes because he had fucking on his mind.

And that made her smile. Because her mind was filled with the same. The smells of heated skin, the sounds of flesh slapping flesh, the taste of salt and bitter cum. Shivering. Eyes gone dark.

Her smile assuaged him, and he knelt in front of her, lifting her blouse to expose her pussy, leaning in to kiss her belly just above her bare lips. She curled her toes against the gritty hardwood floor, a tremor crawling the length of her spine and vibrating in the small of her back. Then vibrating deeper when he parted her lips with the tip of his tongue, sliding down to lap, then up to push on her clit, staying there, playing, flicking back and forth with the pressure he'd learned she loved.

He'd told her not to move, but she was all in, and she wanted as much say as he'd claimed. So while he held her hips, his fingers gouging her, his thumbs rubbing the skin of her inner thighs, she made quick work of her buttons, letting her blouse fall to the floor behind her and reaching back for the clasp of her bra. Before she could shake free of the clinging cups, Boone's hands were there, his fingertips grazing her areolas hidden behind lace the color of eggshells.

The circles of skin pebbled. Her nipples pebbled, too, tightening beneath his touch, then beneath his mouth as he pulled away her bra, tossed it . . . somewhere, tongued her and sucked her and caught her between his teeth. She threaded her fingers into his hair and tugged. "Don't stop."

He didn't, cupping her breasts in his palms and pushing them together, moving from one side to the other. She couldn't stand it anymore. She used her hold to guide his face back between her legs. He laughed as he settled his mouth over her pussy, pushing apart her thighs to slide a finger deep. She gasped, groaned, and he crooked it to rub against the sensitive pillow just inside her opening, a grating sort of scratch that sent her soaring.

His tongue slid low, dipping into her entrance when he pulled his one finger free, sliding back up through her inner lips when he pushed back in with two. She raked her fingernails over his scalp, and he laughed again, a growling, guttural sound, his teeth catching lightly at her clit and scraping over it before he sucked her into his mouth. The pressure was too much. She lifted up onto her toes and let go, shuddering, tugging at his hair as she came.

Sensation rushed her like a wave, knocking into her and nearly taking her off her feet. Boone wrapped an arm around her waist and held her, finishing her off before moving up her body, drawing the flat of his tongue up her midsection until he'd reached her throat, then her mouth. And then he kissed her, his lips demanding, his teeth sharp, his tongue finding and mating with hers.

When he dipped to lift her, she grabbed his shoulders for purchase, holding on while he carried her to the bed. There, he rolled the both of them to the center, sheathing himself with a condom before covering her. His big body made her feel fragile and small. She pulled her knees along his hips, and he settled between her thighs, reaching down to guide his cock into place, a smile tugging at the corners of his mouth when he did.

"Does this mean you're happy?" she asked, running a finger over his lips and into his dimple hidden by beard stubble.

He turned his head to bite at the heel of her palm. "I was just thinking this is a hell of a way to spend a lunch hour."

She couldn't disagree. And as he pushed into her, filling her, joining their bodies fully, she hooked her heels in the small of his back for the ride. He rocked against her slowly, his elbows above her shoulders on either side of her head, his fingers toying with her hair where it fell across his pillow, no doubt in a messy splay of waves that would soon be tangles—and she couldn't be bothered to care.

How could she when her body was buried beneath his, the mattress soft beneath her, the sheets smelling of Boone and Boone smelling of the wide-open spaces? He pushed in and pulled out, buried his face in the crook of her neck, grunted against her skin and bit down. A tingling sensation, like an electric buzz beneath her skin, raised the hair on her arms, at her nape, and coursed through her limbs until even her fingertips prickled from the powerful surge.

They'd been in bed for only minutes, yet she was ready to come for the second time. She wanted to wait, to draw out all of what she was feeling, to let it take her over, pull her under, consume her, but Boone chose that minute to increase his speed, and the strength of his thrusts sent her over. She cried out, pushing up against him as he shoved her down, quaking on top of her, grinding against her, the base of his cock like a steel rod shoved hard to her clit.

He groaned, a long, gut-wrenching sound that vibrated through his whole body. She felt it in his chest, crushing hers, in his belly, where his hair sparked friction against her skin as he writhed, in the short ragged bursts of air blowing furnace hot on her neck. She finished as he did, both of them sighing out long, exhausted breaths, both of them laughing softly.

She came down from an incredible high, rubbing circles along his spine, loving the resiliency of his skin, the muscles beneath, the way he shimmied under her hands. It was magical, making a big man like Boone Mitchell react to her touch, and one so simple after the near violence of the intimacy they'd just shared. Yet it was a violence she'd invited, and engaged in, and wanted more of, because this was Boone; and he was giving, not taking, not demanding, not hurting. It was a heady thing to feel no fear.

But it would also be nice to be able to move, she thought, smiling privately, before pushing at his shoulder and rolling him away. "What happened to hands and knees?"

"Eventually. But not today. Because after this, I'm going to be doing good to walk out of the house and finish all the work on tap for the afternoon."

She turned to her side, her hands together on her pillow, her chin on top. "I hope you're not blaming me for your weak knees."

"Actually, I am. I heard you drive up, and came out of the barn ready to answer your questions—" He stopped, his eyes closing, his long lashes dark against his cheeks before he looked at her again.

But he didn't say anything more. Just stared at her, his gaze sleepy and searching, and so she pressed, asking, "What changed your mind?"

"You," he said, that gravel in his voice again. "You were standing there, your face to the sun, the wind blowing your hair and your top . . ." He went on, his voice dropping. "You were standing there, in the dirt, in those spiky heels without worrying that you might get 'em dusty, or step in a hole and go down, but like the ranch was where you belonged. That was unexpected. And that's what changed my mind."

She swallowed his words like bad medicine, staring at him, not knowing what to say because she didn't want to hear that. She really did not want to hear that. She did not belong, not here or to him. She'd spent four years putting herself back together, and Boone's return to Crow Hill was not going to derail her.

Yet when she looked at him, the longing in his expression fierce and raw, it nearly killed her not to acknowledge the admission he'd made, and to instead blithely say, "Believe it or not, I know how to look where I'm going." She moved just enough to drop a quick kiss to his lips. "And I've been wearing heels almost every day for the last ten years of my life."

"Guess you don't buy them in Crow Hill," he said, his tone resigned, the light in his eyes gone.

She'd done that, disappointed him, but it couldn't be helped. "You guessed right."

"You got any boots?"

She twisted her mouth to the side. "No, actually, but I'm thinking it's time I buy a pair."

"I'm thinking so, too." He propped up his head with an arm tucked beneath. "Can't take you horseback riding in heels."

"You're taking me horseback riding?"

"Thought I'd take you out to see my oil well."

"Boone Mitchell." She shifted up onto one elbow, pushed a fall of hair from her face. "Are you trying to impress me with your assets?"

"Thought that's what I just did," he said, reaching out to tweak a nipple.

She gave him a withering look. "You still owe me an interview, you know."

"Hmm."

"What?" she asked, slapping his hand, feeling the pop reverberate where he held her pinched tight. "You thought you could distract me with sex?"

"Something like that."

"Uh-uh. Not happening. Though I think we're going to have to conduct this interview in a public place."

"Must be hell not being able to keep your hands to yourself."

*That* she wasn't going to dignify with a response. Even if truer words had never been spoken. Not that she was the only one with the problem, she mused, reaching down to lift his hand from her breast. "Could you get away for supper tonight? At the Rainsong Cafe in Fever Tree?"

"Should be able to."

"Do you want me to come by and pick you up?"

"And risk never making it to supper?"

Good thing one of them was thinking straight. "Then I'll meet you there. What time?"

"Make it eight," he said, covering her for a gorgeously smothering kiss that tasted of heat and sweat and salt; that had her melting beneath him, breathless, desperate, then rolling off the mattress and leaving her there as he walked naked out of the room.

She scampered out of the bed and into her bra and panties,

zipping her pants, stepping into her shoes, and rushing down the hall for the staircase. By the time she reached her SUV, she'd only managed a half dozen of her blouse's buttons, but they were the ones that would keep her from getting arrested, and that was fine.

What wasn't fine was the way watching his bare ass as he'd sauntered away had her never wanting to leave. Had her, in fact, wanting to spend the rest of the day with him, on horseback, or in the barn while he did . . . whatever it was that he did. Had her wanting to belong.

If she'd been compelled to do any of that for her story, that would've been fine. But she'd wanted to do it because she enjoyed his company. He made her laugh. He made her curious— about his work, about his family, about the things he loved, the things he hated, his dreams for this broken-down ranch.

And that was skating too close to the emotional involvement she'd sworn to avoid. Not even for Boone Mitchell would she step into that trap.

# TEN

As much as he hated leaving the ranch at the end of a day, Boone meant what he'd said to Everly. He'd never be able to answer her questions if they were alone in the house. Their being alone would have him dragging her up the stairs to his bed. She could ask him what she wanted to know while there, but he'd have a hard time answering with his blood in another part of his body than his brain. And he was pretty sure she'd have a hard time taking notes with her hands busy elsewhere.

As it was, he mused, dragging his saddle and blanket from Sunshine's back, he wasn't exactly thrilled about this interview business, no matter his sounding all grown-up when he'd agreed to let her question him. He got that she was just doing her job. He also got that having her be the one to tell the Dalton Gang's story would keep it from turning into some sort of literary lynch mob. Everly at least would be fair, he was sure of that, even with the less-than-positive parts of his past. He just hoped in all her digging she didn't come across sins he'd forgotten committing.

They had to be out there. He was certain they were. But he'd been away from Crow Hill almost as long as he'd lived here. Hard to recall everything a man did as a boy, especially a teen boy fascinated with his own dick. And everything in high school had been about his dick. Unless it had been about beer. Combine the two and they made for a volatile combination. They also made for a lot of forgettin' going on.

Mostly, though, he was worried about her running across the real trouble he'd got into with Les Upton. Granted, Les had caused the trouble . . . for his daughter, for his wife. For Boone. But Boone and his favorite part of his body had not been innocent in that night's debacle.

If he and Everly were to get serious, he'd tell her about it. It was something he'd want her to know. But he would not open up that vein for her newspaper story even should she ask. Those facts had seen enough print back in the day.

"You want to come to town?" Dax asked, coming out of the tack room and stopping at Sunshine's stall. Casper had already headed home, the two returning later than expected from the auction. "Arwen's working tonight so I'm eating at the saloon. Happy to buy you a burger and a beer."

Boone had kinda forgotten the other man was still here and huffed in response. "Happy since she owns the place and you buying means no money changing hands, you mean."

Dax shrugged. "What can I say. It's one of the perks of the relationship. The second best, I'm thinking."

"Sharing her bed being the first."

"I don't think so." Dax pushed up on his hat brim before draping his arms over the stall door, moving one foot to the bottom rung, moving it away when it creaked in protest. If they didn't get a break soon, this barn was going to fall down around them before they could afford to build a new one. "I'd have to put that second, move eating at the saloon down to third. First has to be just knowing she's there."

That had Boone thinking back to what Faith had said about Casper, and relationships being so much more than sex. It wasn't something he didn't know, and he'd found himself often wishing he had a woman waiting at home at the end of the day. But until Everly, he hadn't thought about one specifically beyond having her in his bed. And his thoughts were only traveling along those lines *because* she'd been there.

Criminy but this mating shit was complicated.

"So?" Dax asked again. "Supper?"

He shook his head. "I'm eating in Fever Tree. At the Rainsong Cafe."

"What the hell for?"

"None of your business."

"So you've got a date."

"I'm meeting Everly Grant. But it's not a date."

"Well, damn, son. Good for you. Now you asking us about her the other day makes sense."

"She's a nice girl."

"Nothing wrong with nice girls. Nothing wrong with naughty girls either."

"Whether she's naughty or not, this is just supper," he said, slipping off Sunshine's bridle. "She's going to want to be talking to you, too."

"Why would she want to talk to me?"

"She's doing a piece for the paper on the Dalton Gang."

"Right." He drew out the word, ended it with a huff, reached up to rub a hand over his forehead. "Arwen said something about that, but why the hell she'd want to write about us . . ."

"Because her editor asked her to, I guess. I just figured it was better to answer her questions than to have her go asking around about us."

"Good thinking," Dax said. "Heading off the vultures at the pass."

That sent him back to something he'd been thinking about. "Don't you find it strange that we haven't been called out by anyone from back in the day?"

"Well, it's not like we were criminals, exactly. Or felons anyway. I figure we all engaged in some borderline behavior. And maybe if the sheriff had been more on the ball we would've done some time. Bad enough having to sleep off all those drunks in a jail cell."

A few of Boone's escapades had been more than borderline. And his folks had pulled more than a few strings, called in more than a few favors to keep him on the outside. He'd locked away most of those crimes, but he'd brought out a few of them over the years, not quite sure what he'd been thinking when he'd shot up the back side of Lasko's feed store, or left shovelfuls of cow shit to decorate the base of the high school's hurricane statue.

And then there was the Upton family, and everything that had gone wrong there. Lucinda had split a long time ago, and he hadn't seen Penny since coming home. He didn't know if she was still here. He couldn't imagine any reason she would be. He was pretty sure he'd seen Les in his wrecker a few times. But just the wrecker. No wreck, like carrion, drawing him.

Dax was still talking. "Most of what I remember involved

daughters of fathers who didn't have much of a sense of humor. I think Casper got in deep shit a time or two. Mostly I recall the hell we raised together. Like the time we loaded up ol' Harris Bell's prize bull in the back of Dave's trailer and hauled that rank motherfucker to Len Tunstall's slaughterhouse."

Lucky for them, Len Tunstall recognized the Longhorn and called Harris Bell to come pick him up, or else there would've been some expensive steaks hitting somebody's grill. "I think the thing that got me in the most trouble with my folks was slashing Pastor Cuellar's tires at two a.m. Sunday morning so he couldn't make the drive to church."

"Huh, yeah. Who would've thought he'd ride to First Baptist on horseback?"

The memory had Boone grinning. "I saw him when he got there. His suit coat was flapping behind him like some wild west gunslinger's. And boy was he giving me the evil eye. Of the pastor variety."

"Your fault for not being too sick to get up and go to church."

"More like I had parents who wouldn't let me get away with faking it."

"I always thought Casper and I lucked out by not having our folks up in all our business. But you were the lucky one, dude. I just didn't realize it at the time."

Lucky wasn't even the half of it, yet he'd screwed that pooch so many times it was amazing he hadn't ended up in boot camp. "Hard to feel lucky when your parents drive you to school, and then stay because they both work there."

"Guess it does kinda take Big Brother to the extreme. But everyone loved your folks."

"Not sure that made it any better. Half the time I wasn't

sure if kids trying to make friends were more interested in scoring points with the coach. Or getting off the counselor's shit list."

"Or if they were after your sister."

"Some of that, too."

"I figure sooner or later something from back then will show up and raise more hell than we ever did. But I'm sure not going to go out of my way looking for it."

"No need to go looking. More of a need to be ready."

"Shit. Who's ever ready for their past to blow up in their face?"

Boone had a feeling Dax was right. He could hang out at the ranch, spend twenty out of twenty-four hours a day working, avoid town as much as he could, save for Sunday supper with the folks. It would never be enough. If his crimes were going to come packing for a showdown, there was little he could do to stop it.

"Speaking of crimes blowing up, you hear anything from Penny Upton since you got back?"

Boone found himself smiling, though not at the question. This was why he and Dax had been such good friends. Always on the same wavelength. Often reading each other's minds. "That was her father's crime. Not mine. I was just the unlucky bastard who Les caught with his pants down. Could've been half a dozen other guys."

"It was more than your pants being down. It was your dick being—"

"Yeah, yeah. I know where my dick was. Just happy I got out of there with it. The way Les was swinging, I wasn't sure fortune was going to be on my side."

Dax bit off a nasty curse. "Sure wasn't on Lucinda's. Even

with you stepping between her face and her old man's fists, she took a brutal beating."

"Penny's wasn't much better. If the sheriff hadn't gotten there when he did, I'm not sure Les wouldn't have killed the both of them. And me, too."

"So?" Dax asked. "Have you seen her?"

"Penny?" Boone shook his head. "Haven't even heard if she's still living in Crow Hill, but then I don't get out much. Kinda hard to imagine she'd stay. She wouldn't have had a lot of reason to. Especially with her father having come back here after his incarceration. Though why the hell he did that . . ."

"A father who tried to beat her to death, and very nearly did kill her mother." Another bunch of spewed cusswords. "Wonder where Lucinda ended up."

"Far, far away is my guess."

"Well, hate to say it, but this time I'm happy you took one for the team and it wasn't the whole gang who found out what Les Upton was capable of." Dax pushed off the stall, resettled his hat. "I'd thought about taking Penny for a ride a lot of times, but am damn glad that never came to pass."

"I bet you are," Boone said without admitting that was one fuck he'd take back if he could.

"I'm gonna head on to town," Dax said with a slap to the stall's slats. "See if I can talk Arwen into taking a dinner break instead of making me eat by myself."

"Suck it up, man. I eat by myself most every night, and it hasn't killed me yet."

"Just keep the eyes in the back of your head open. Make sure Les Upton doesn't try to finish what he started."

"You don't have to tell me," Boone said, pulling out his

pocketknife and the apple he'd grabbed earlier from the fridge, and slicing off a hunk for Sunshine as Dax left. Then slicing off a hunk for himself, hoping it would hold him until he could get to the restaurant.

He was goddamn starving.

# ELEVEN

"I'M STUFFED," EVERLY said, pushing away her plate and half-eaten New York strip. The Rainsong Cafe was known for nearly family-sized servings, and that included their steaks. "If I had a dog, I'd take the rest of this home."

"I have two dogs," Boone said. "Three when Clay brings Kevin over. I'll be happy to take it."

The man was incredibly transparent. And exceptionally breathtaking tonight, his long hair brushed back from his face, the ends catching in his collar. He smelled like soap and fresh air, and he made her hungry. "Why do I think the dogs will never see it?"

"Because they won't," he said, gesturing toward her plate with his fork. "I can eat that for breakfast tomorrow with a couple of tortillas and eggs."

"Then you're welcome to it," she said, wondering how close to true the rumors ran that the Dalton Ranch was verging on bankruptcy. She hated thinking this man, so honorable and so proud, might be going without things he needed—food, fuel, equipment, clothing. Making do with the barest necessities, spending on only what was essential, rich with land and the freedom of working for himself, but living below what amounted to poverty level.

She wiped her napkin over her mouth, then laid it on the edge of her plate. "This is my treat, by the way. A business expense. Since it seems the only way we'll ever get this interview done is for me to ask you my questions in public."

He grunted at that, though it had been his idea. "You didn't ask me much of anything tonight."

She hadn't, even though she'd learned a lot about him by enjoying his conversation and his company. "I guess that means we'll have to do this again."

His gaze came up from his plate to meet hers. "Your expense account have pockets that deep?"

She laughed, toyed with her napkin's selvage. "I don't think Whitey even looks at what I turn in."

That earned her another grunt. "That's because he doesn't want to rock the boat. He knows he's lucky to have a big city pro on his staff of amateurs."

"I wouldn't call them 'amateurs.' Everyone there does their job well." Smoothing her fingers over wrinkles in the napkin, she thought about the last four years. "It's just a different mindset. What counts as breaking news has a local flavor. Like Henry Lasko retiring and giving the feed store to Darcy and Josh. There's less interest in what's going on in Hollywood, or Washington, except as it affects beef and oil. If the residents want to know about the monetary crisis in Greece, for example, or the unemployment rate in Iceland, they'll get that from the national news."

He held up a finger, finished chewing before he spoke. "But if they want to know which Dalton Gang member used the back side of Lasko's for shotgun practice, they'll look in the archived pages of the *Reporter*."

"Exactly." She waited a handful of seconds, filing away that bit of Dalton Gang history, then asked, "So? Who *did* shoot up the back side of the feed store?"

His laugh was boisterous and full of secrets and like tires on gravel. "That'll cost you another dinner. Unless one of the boys spills first."

*The boys.* All three of the men used the term. As did Arwen and Faith. She wasn't sure if it spoke to the connection they'd made as young teens, or the Peter Pan attitude they often displayed. "Here's what I find most interesting, and this after living here four years and going to school with Faith, and hearing about your escapades to the point where I couldn't wait to meet all of you."

"That so?" he asked, his dark brows lifting, and the sweep of his lashes made even darker by the contrast of his starched white shirt.

"Yeah," she said, nodding, then going on before the look in his eyes had her losing her train of thought. "Your three backgrounds are so disparate, yet none of that played into your friendship."

"Why would it?" he asked, getting back to his food as she crossed her legs and watched him.

She enjoyed watching him. His purposeful economy of movement. His thoughtful use of the space around him. The flex of his muscles that brought to mind the ones she couldn't see. His thighs. His pectorals. His abs that tightened into sharp relief when he came.

She closed her eyes, breathed away her arousal, looked at him again. "Dax came from one of the most influential families in Crow Hill, but had next to nothing in the way of parenting, or so I've gathered from what others have said. Casper had no money at all, and no parenting either, except what he got from your folks. You had the most all-American, middle-class upbringing of the three of you."

"What does that have to do with anything?"

"No one would ever guess, from how close you are, that you didn't grow up next door to each other on the same block. But take the gang out of Crow Hill, and it's less likely you'd have run in the same circles, even if you'd all gone to the same school."

"You forget we all played football. And we all worked for Tess and Dave. We're different in as many ways as we're similar. Trust me."

"Yes, but weren't you friends even before all of that? The football and the ranching?"

"Dax and I were. We started kindergarten together. Casper didn't move here until seventh grade, but he fit right in."

"Because of football?"

"Because he was a misfit." He gave her a loose shrug. "We all were in our own way."

Now she was really curious. "I get Casper. I even get Dax. But you?"

"Don't let the all-American, middle-class upbringing fool you," he said, his grin twisted.

She thought back to what Whitey had said when he'd assigned her the story. That of the three Dalton Gang members, Boone had been in more trouble than the others. And she was weighing her options for questioning him about the specifics when he reached across the table for her hand.

"What's this scar?" he asked, holding her by the wrist and rubbing his thumb along the line of white flesh lighter than the skin of her inner arm and the width of a belt buckle's prong.

She knew that because it had been the prong from Toby's belt buckle that had split open her skin. He'd been sitting on her chest, his cock in her mouth, her wrists and ankles bound much like she'd bound Boone's, only Toby had preferred leather to silk. And he'd been angry because he'd been unable to come while she sucked him. Her fault, of course. She hadn't used her tongue in exactly the way he'd liked, going too slow when he'd wanted fast, speeding up when he'd wanted her to slow down.

While she'd been rubbing the circulation back into her wrists after he'd released her, having jacked off all over her face, he'd reached for the belt on the floor. She'd been lucky he'd waited until then, swinging when she could defend herself rather than whipping her while she was flat on her back and bound. She suppressed a shudder at the thought of the damage he could've done. And his attack had come out of nowhere, unprovoked, unwarranted.

No. She refused to dwell there. She'd made it out of that night with only a single scar to show for it. She didn't count the ones she couldn't see.

But she wasn't going to say any of that to Boone. "I slipped on a melted ice cube and fell in my kitchen several years ago. I reached for the stove but grabbed the door. It came open and I hit the edge when I went down."

"Stitches?"

"A few, yeah."

"That must've hurt."

"It did." But not as much as Toby's tears in her palm as he'd wrapped a towel around the gash before driving her to the ER. He'd tossed the belt, a very expensive Jack Spade, in their condo's Dumpster on the way to the car. As if the symbolic gesture might actually mean something. "But being recognized in the ER was even more annoying."

"How so?"

"It's not always easy, living life under a microscope." And what a hypocrite she was, complaining about the limelight when she was about to flip the switch and shine it on him.

"I can relate to that, though not in the same way. No one in a small town has any expectation of privacy." He leaned his left forearm on the table's edge, gestured with his hand. "You know everyone. You look out for everyone. It's just how it is 'round these here parts."

She smiled as she thought back to the night they'd danced. "I don't mind being recognized here, though I'm not sure why exactly. It was just different in the city. The face people saw on TV was not the same face that showed up in the ER at midnight."

"Did that bother you? Being seen without your war paint?"

She laughed. If he only knew. "That's more accurate of a description than you might believe. But to answer your question, no. It didn't bother me to be seen. It bothered me that because I didn't want to answer questions about what had happened, I was called a bitch, or worse, when all I wanted was to live my personal life off camera. How I managed to fall in my kitchen and cut my arm on the sharp edge of the stove was nobody's business but mine."

Who was she kidding? The story was ridiculous. Even hearing herself repeat it to Boone had her wanting to roll her eyes. Toby had been the one to come up with the explanation for her injury. She hadn't known what to say when the doctor had asked her what happened. She'd been so close to blurting out the truth, certain the staff already expected abuse. And then she did the very thing she'd sworn she wouldn't do. Helped Toby cover it up and get away with it.

"Is that what made you move here? You finally got fed up?"

"In a way, yes," she said, comfortable with that part of her reality. "There was a tipping point. And I finally tipped."

"I've been wondering about that, why you'd give up a position on air in Austin to work for the *Reporter.* Can't imagine Simmons over there can pay you close to what you must've been making."

"He can't. But the cost of living here's a lot less. My house was a steal. And I didn't need a new wardrobe for work."

"You sold your place in Austin?"

She looked down at her plate. "It was my ex's place. We dated a year. We lived together for two."

He didn't say anything to that, just took his knife to his rib eye, forking up one bite then slicing off another as he chewed. She twisted her hands together in her lap, glad she'd already finished eating, because her appetite was long gone. Thinking about Toby did that. Talking about him, even without mentioning his name or his crimes and fetishes, meant she wouldn't be getting it back.

She hated that she'd let him intrude. Boone's question had been curious, innocent. He hadn't been prying into the disaster her relationship had been. He couldn't have known she'd lived in Toby's condo, couldn't have known that was where she'd suffered most of her injuries, there in the privacy of her own home, at the hands of the only man who'd ever told her he loved her. He hadn't. If he'd loved anyone, he'd loved himself, but she wasn't even sure about that.

*Enough,* she told herself, and tossed back her hair. She refused to give any importance to her past and risk having Boone ask more questions. So far she'd gotten off light. She was thirty-two years old. It wasn't hard to believe she'd had a serious relationship, even though she'd been fairly naive when she and Toby hooked up.

Probably too naive, she'd thought more than once since leaving. Someone with more experience might've seen signs she'd missed. Looking back from this distance, it was easy to see her inability to do so was the result of a childhood she'd thought perfect, never realizing how overly sheltered she'd been.

But none of what she'd revealed would raise any red flags. And tonight, that was all that mattered.

While Boone finished mopping up his bloody steak juice with his Texas toast, Everly signaled to their server for a to-go box for her steak. The young man returned minutes later with a Rainsong carryout bag, along with their check. Everly reached for it, but Boone was quicker than she was.

"This was supposed to be a business expense," she reminded him. "My business expense."

"Uh-huh," he said, glancing at the check, then leaning to the side to dig for his wallet. "One of these days when we actually talk business, you can pay. In the meantime, it's on me."

She would've suggested someplace less pricey if she'd thought Boone would insist on paying. "At least split it with me."

He laid bills to cover the total plus the tip inside the check folder, handing it to the server as he walked by. "Keep the change."

"Thank you, sir. Ma'am. You two enjoy the rest of your evening."

"Are we done here?" Boone asked, once they were alone.

"As long as you tell me we're okay."

"Why wouldn't we be okay?"

"Because you haven't said anything since I told you about my ex."

He shrugged. "That's just me not liking to think about another man having his hands on you."

If he only knew. "I'm thirty-two years old, Boone. I had a whole different life before moving here."

"I know."

"Just like you had a whole different life while you were away."

"I know."

"Then what about my having an ex is bothering you?" She let the words hang there, a sort of a question, wondering what he was thinking and why. Wondering most of all where she fit in, and how she felt about it when she wasn't supposed to be feeling. Just having fun.

"It's not bothering me. Okay. It is bothering me. But that's because I'm lousy at sharing."

That made her laugh. "You are a funny man, Boone Mitchell. How, exactly, have we been sharing anything with my ex?"

"We haven't been," he said, lechery tugging at his mouth. "But I'm just caveman enough to want to have been your first."

She wasn't sure what to say to that, so she stayed silent. But she couldn't help thinking they weren't on the same page at all, and didn't know why she'd assumed otherwise. She'd been a long time without a man. And she hadn't gone into this affair with much thought.

But that's all it was. An affair. Purely sexual. She knew that. He needed to know that. But she also wanted to understand why his wishing he was her first had sent such a strange jolt of longing through her uninvolved heart.

"So, *now* are we done here?" he asked, and she nodded, adding a "Sure" that didn't sound very sure at all.

She scooted her chair back, but before she got all the way out of it, Boone was there to help her. She didn't need his help. She was perfectly capable of getting up from her seat on her own. But she liked having him there behind her, liked his hand at her back, his manners. The Coach and Mrs. Mitchell had done a good job with this one. And, she imagined, the influence of the Daltons had a lot to do with the man Boone had become.

If she'd had any interest at all in a relationship, she could see herself falling for Boone. It would be an easy trip to make, and a short one, at that. But she knew what she wanted, so having this conversation with herself was totally unnecessary. And the brush of Boone's hip against hers meant nothing.

As they left the restaurant and started across the parking lot, Everly looked up to see Darcy and Josh Lasko headed their way, and welcomed the distraction. Boone guided her toward them, his steps and hers slowing.

"Hey you two," Darcy said, giving them each a kiss on the cheek.

"Darcy." Boone returned her kiss, held out his hand for her husband. "Josh."

"Good to see the both of you." Finished with Boone, Josh gave Everly a hug even though she'd extended her hand for him to shake. "Food tonight as good as always?"

"It was, yes," Everly said. "I tried to save room for dessert, but only made it through half my steak before I had to stop."

Boone held up the white paper bag he carried. "And because of that, I get to have steak with my eggs for breakfast."

Darcy leaned against her husband and smiled. "I had no idea how late it was until Josh asked if I planned to stop working to eat. Then I realized I was starving. And he was nice enough to suggest a night out."

"How're you liking lawyering for yourself?" Boone asked.

"I'm liking it a lot. A whole lot. I'm able to keep my caseload to a manageable level—"

"Don't believe her," Josh cut in to say.

Darcy hooked her arm through his and rested her head on his shoulder. "He's only saying that because he never saw what I went through working for The Campbell."

Everly smiled. She didn't know another couple in all of Crow Hill who fit together as perfectly as these two. "Sounds like things worked out beautifully for both of you."

"They did that," Josh replied, covering Darcy's hand with his. "They did that."

"Listen," Darcy said, turning to Boone to ask, "did Dax ever say anything to you about Nora Stokes being interested in some of Tess's old furniture?"

Boone gave it some thought. "He mentioned you saying you were pretty sure we had some valuable pieces. I don't recall him bringing Nora into it."

"Typical Dax. I told him months ago. I'm kinda surprised Nora hasn't brought it up again. She said the old buffet in the living room could be worth a couple thousand dollars, and the sideboard in the kitchen even more."

"Thousand? As in . . . thousand?"

"As in several thousand," she said to Boone, turning to Everly to explain. "When I was staying at the house during the summer, I started going through the Daltons' things. Dax didn't want to talk about selling any of it. But that was then," she said and looked back to Boone. "Right after y'all had lost them. Maybe now you three might want to listen to what she has to say?"

"Yeah. I'll give her a call. Thanks for mentioning it."

"Oh, one more thing," Darcy said, stopping again after she

and Josh had started moving toward the door. "I think I saw Les Upton's wrecker parked out front on the shoulder when we pulled in."

"Shit. All right. Thanks."

"You'll give me a call if you need a restraining order?" she asked, her concern snagging Everly's attention.

"Yeah, that's not going to happen."

"Okay, but let me know if I can help."

"Thanks, Darcy," he said, then looked at Josh. "You two enjoy your supper."

Everly waited for an explanation, but when Boone said nothing, she pushed to get one. "Who's Les Upton?"

"A blast from my past," he said with a snort.

So he *had* been involved in some sort of scandal. One Darcy thought might require a restraining order all these years later. Interesting. "Someone you went to school with?"

"I went to school with his daughter," he said, his hand low on her hip guiding her toward her car.

"Went to school with . . . and went to bed with?" Because having known the man's daughter in school wouldn't be reason enough for behavior Darcy thought legally worrisome.

"It was a long time ago. I went to bed with a lot of girls."

But there was more to the story of this particular one. "Boone?"

He was busy scanning the road in front of the restaurant. "I don't see him, but I'm going to follow you home just to be sure."

"Wait a minute," she said, pulling away from his hand, her heart suddenly pounding. "To be sure of what? That I make it without getting run off the road?"

"No. Nothing like that." But he still wasn't looking at her.

She grabbed for his arm and made him. "Is he dangerous?"

He reached up, ran a thumb over one eyebrow. "He's a nuisance is all."

"Then why are you going to follow me home?"

"I want to make sure you get there safely."

"Safely? Dammit, Boone," she said, her heart having moved into her throat to choke her. "What's going on? What have you gotten me into?"

"I haven't gotten you into anything," he said, biting off a curse as he looked down at her. "Upton's been pissed at me for sixteen years. I've been wondering how long it would take him to crawl out of the woodwork and into my face."

"You think he might follow me to get back at you?"

"I doubt it."

"But if he does? Then what? Do I need a . . . gun?" She was not going to be a victim again. Not Toby's directly. Not Boone's secondhand.

"No, Everly. You don't need a gun," he said, opening her SUV's door. "Just wait for me before you leave."

"Fine," she said, sliding into her seat and reaching for her door to shut it, but Boone held on, waiting for her to look up. "What?"

"Don't be mad."

Mad? He thought she was mad? Try furious. Also try scared to death. And then try furious again. "I just want to go home."

He waited a long several seconds before asking, "Alone?"

She'd been looking forward to another night with him in her bed. But now . . . "That's probably for the best."

He glanced away, muttered a low, "Shit," under his breath, the word less about his not getting laid than the reasons for it.

Whipping off his hat, he stepped into the V of her open door. "Nothing's going to happen to you. Les isn't dangerous. He might want to scare you because it's a way to get to me, and

I'm sorry for that. And I'll do everything I can to keep him from having the chance. But he's not a threat."

"Then why did Darcy mention a restraining order?"

"That's just Darcy being Darcy."

"I'm not sure that's good enough."

"It's all I can do."

"You could've mentioned this before now. I don't like stepping into someone else's shit pile because I don't know it's there."

"We just talked about this the other day. Everyone's got unknowns in their past. Even you, I reckon."

"Not any that might cause trouble for you," she said, though she wondered if Toby had really given up trying to ruin her life.

Boone dropped his gaze to his hat where he worried his way around the brim. "The boys and I raised a lot of hell in the past. None of that's a secret, and seeing as how you hang with my sister and Arwen, I'm pretty sure you were aware of what you were getting into when you asked me to stay for dessert."

She was beginning to wonder if that hadn't been a horrible mistake. Was this her lot in life? Being attracted to men who meant trouble? Even, in Boone's case, inadvertently? And if that was the truth, what did it say about her? "I didn't know I'd be getting into this."

"You haven't gotten into anything. And there's no reason to think you will."

"That's why you're following me home? For no reason?"

"Can we talk about this when we get there? And just go?"

She was shaking her head before she even realized she was going to say no. "I don't think so. If you want to follow me, that's fine, but we're done talking for tonight."

"Everly—"

"Later, Boone. I just want to go." Avoiding his gaze, she took hold of her door, leaving him no choice but to get out of her way. He helped her shut it, then circled the rear of the SUV on his way to his truck parked on her passenger side.

She turned her key and backed out of her spot, waiting to pull out of the parking lot as he'd asked. She wasn't stupid. She wasn't going to rush home ahead of him just to prove she didn't need his protection when she very well might.

And that was the problem here. She'd come to Crow Hill to get away from a man with a violent nature. Why in the world would she get involved with one who might bring more of the same into her life?

# TWELVE

OVER THE LAST two days, Everly had spent way too much time looking over her shoulder. She hated the feeling of being watched, especially when no one was watching her. She hadn't seen hide nor hair of Les Upton, or his tow truck anyway, since she'd never met the man and had no idea what he looked like. Neither had she seen hide nor hair of Boone. And she hated that even more because she'd thought he might've been keeping an eye on her, making sure she was safe.

He could've been there, she supposed, looking out for her, but really, such a thought was ridiculous. He was at the ranch, working as he should be, and she had no call for alarm because Upton wasn't a threat. Still, she'd wanted Boone to be there. She'd wanted to catch a glimpse of him. His dark eyes, his dark hair, the muscles in his forearms that made her think of thick marine ropes. But her wanting that was not because she might be in danger.

Two days now she'd gone without seeing him, and she missed him more than she should have, and in ways that made no sense in the scheme of a purely sexual relationship. She wanted to hear him laugh, that deep gravelly rumble that tickled her to her core. She wanted to smell his sun-warmed skin. And she wanted to see his eyes soften when he talked about Sundays spent with his family.

And, yes, she enjoyed him in bed, but didn't need him for sexual pleasure, though the orgasms he gave her were so much more fun than the ones she gave herself. There was something about the hair on a man's body, the scrape of it against her skin, and his weight as he pressed her down and possessed her.

Obviously, however, she must need him for something, or her heart wouldn't have thumped in her chest like a kick drum when, realizing she was no longer alone, she looked up to see him—and not Whitey—blocking her office door.

His shoulders filled the open space from side to side, his hat brushed the frame when he ducked and stepped through. His hips were stout, his thighs thick, his legs long. The heels of his boots were worn, but still gave him two extra inches of height. He was imposing, a broad, towering figure and impossible to ignore—not to mention impossible to miss.

"What are you doing here?" she asked, pushing up out of her chair and pulling him all the way into her office before Whitey got wind of his presence, though that ship had no doubt already sailed.

She shut the door behind him, then closed the blinds on her window that faced the newsroom. She couldn't have her boss knowing she and Boone were involved. Not when she was supposed to be writing what amounted to an exposé on the man. Though considering the circulation numbers of the *Crow Hill Reporter*, the extra hint of scandal provided by news of their affair might actually be good for sales.

"I was in town," he said, moving out of her way as she pushed by to shutter the blinds facing the sidewalk on Main Street. "Thought I'd see if I could buy you lunch."

She peeked between two of the slats but didn't see anyone taking undo notice of her office or her visitor. Or of Boone's truck—sporting a capital *D* hooked over a capital *T* that was the Dalton ranch brand—parked out front. "As much as I would love to, it's probably best if we don't."

"Why's that?"

"You're the subject of a story," she said, finally turning to him and crossing her arms. "I can't be fraternizing."

The roll of Boone's eyes said she was two days too late. "That shit may fly in Austin, but not here. No one's going to care what we do together as long as they get to read about the sins of my past."

He was right, of course. So why was she hesitating when she was so glad to see him, and actually very hungry? "I don't know—"

"Tell you what," he said, his arms crossed, too. "Ask me some questions while we eat. I'll see if I can't come up with some juice for your story to make it worth your time."

"And my money?" she asked, because lunch with a story subject in the middle of the day would get back to Whitey, and if she didn't turn it in as an expense . . .

He nodded. "Hellcat Saloon okay? Or are we keeping this on the down low?"

"The interview, or the . . . involvement?"

"*I* was talking about the first," he said, opening her door and tugging down the brim of his hat as he ushered her out. "But I'm thinking *we* need to talk about the second."

"That might be a good idea." Considering how much of the talking they'd done together so far had been words not fit for print. "And we need to talk about Les Upton, too."

"Hold on," he said, reaching for her arm and pulling her to a stop before she'd taken more than two steps into the newsroom. "Has he been harassing you?"

"I haven't seen him, no," she said, raking back the hair falling into her eyes, giving up on hiding his visit. "Or I haven't seen his wrecker, since that's the only way I'd recognize him."

Boone gave a jerk of his head toward her desk. "You can access the paper's archives on your machine, yes?"

She looked from his face to her surprisingly sophisticated monitor where, in a window hidden behind that of another program, she'd already done some looking into his past. What she hadn't done was decide how fair and balanced her story would be after so thoroughly invading his privacy. "Yes, of course, why?"

"C'mon," he said, motioning her back inside. "Sixteen years ago. The dirt's all there, and a photo. He'll have aged, but I imagine Google can give you a newer one."

"Boone, it doesn't matter—"

"It does matter. It matters to me. I want you to know what he looks like. He won't always be driving his wrecker." He was insisting, even though the other man wasn't supposed to be a problem.

"Fine," she said, tossing her bag to the bench next to the door and returning to her chair. "You know, I've lived here four years and haven't even heard of Les Upton. The only mechanic I know is Skeet Bandy."

"Upton's garage is closer to Luling. Or it was last I knew. I haven't had call to head up that way since moving back."

Interesting that he wasn't worried for his own safety. Only hers. "I thought the advice was to keep your enemies closer than friends."

"I don't think of him as an enemy. I don't think of him at all."

"He obviously still thinks about you. And Darcy considers him enough of one to ask about a restraining order."

He stood there, his hands now at his hips, his gaze boring into hers. "Upton is my business. Not Darcy's."

"And not mine."

"Criminy," he muttered, and pulled off his hat. "I would've told you the whole story eventually. I just didn't think you needed to hear it yet."

"Why not?"

"I was a teenager and it was ugly, and I don't want you using it to judge me now." He worried his hat brim, frowning, shaking his head as if arguing with himself. "But since Darcy put it out there, I'd rather you hear it from me and not someone you interview who might twist it up."

"Except I'm not hearing it from you," she reminded him.

He gestured toward her screen with his hat before settling it back in place. "Just read it. We'll talk about it over lunch."

"Are you going to wait? While I do?"

He nodded. "Then I'm going to drive you to the saloon. I don't want to be sitting there and not have you show."

Because after she finished reading, she might change her mind about lunch. That's what he was saying. And that's what made up her mind.

She got to her feet, grabbed her hobo bag from the bench. "Let's go eat. You tell me what happened. I'll read the story when I get back."

"Okay then," he said, falling into step behind her. "My truck's out front."

She said nothing else as they left the building, Boone seeing her into her seat at the curb outside. The ride from the *Reporter* to the saloon took less than five minutes, a typical trip length to anywhere in downtown Crow Hill. Strangely enough, she loved it.

She'd lived her whole life in Austin. Gone to school in Austin. Worked at one of Austin's television stations. She was a city girl through and through, yet glancing across the cab of the truck, she had no trouble understanding the appeal of living in a home on the range.

And that made no sense at all. She barely knew the man behind the wheel. But the thoughts she was having had little to do with sex and everything to do with who and what he was. Honorable, loyal, industrious, humble. Honest. Above all, honest.

The man Toby had never been.

He glanced her way as he put on his turn signal, caught her taking him in. "What?"

"You know my house isn't but another two minutes away. We could have lunch there." She bit at the corner of her lip, holding in the moan tickling the back of her throat. "Maybe dessert."

He canceled the turn signal and returned his attention to the road, moving his foot to the accelerator from the brake. Two minutes later, and without another word, he was turning onto Pineycreek Avenue, then pulling to a stop in her driveway so hard her shoulder strap popped her against the seat. He shut off the truck, but left the keys in the ignition.

His hat brim was pulled low on his forehead when he looked

at her. "I know what we're doing here, but I want you to tell me anyway."

Where to start? So many thoughts had been swirling through her head since Monday at the Rainsong Cafe. She didn't know what to say to him except that she wanted him fiercely. "I like that you want me to know about your past. I like how up-front you are. About everything."

"Why wouldn't I be?" he asked, and seemed genuinely confused. "I've got a lot of stuff I could hide, but what's the point? Especially with you being a reporter and all."

No. That wasn't what she'd meant. "You're honest with everyone. It has nothing to do with me. It's about you being a good guy. And I like that."

One wrist draped over the steering wheel, he stared through the windshield, grimacing as if his being good was a myth. "I won't say I'm not ashamed of things I've done. I've got more than enough shame. And I'd do over a whole lot of stuff if I could. But since I can't, facing and dealing with whatever, or whoever, comes my way is all I've got."

"Like Les Upton."

He turned his head, his gaze piercing, searching, making sure he had her attention before he asked, "You want to talk about Les now? Here?"

Contradictory to what she'd said earlier, she didn't want to talk about Les at all. But she felt that of all the things Boone had in his past, this was the one that perhaps haunted him most, and because of that, she nodded.

"Okay. Like I told you, I went to school with his daughter." When she arched a brow, his mouth pulled into a smirk. "And I went to bed with his daughter. Penny. Lots of guys went to bed with Penny. She kinda reminds me of Luck Summerlin in that way, except Luck comes from all kinds of money, and doesn't put out as much as she teases about doing so."

"Penny did put out, but didn't come from money."

He nodded, reached up and rubbed at his eyes with one hand. "Her mom, Lucinda, she was a stunner. She'd been a cheerleader in high school, good grades, came from a decent family, was pretty popular from what I understand. How she ended up with Les . . ."

"I can probably fill in those blanks," she said, thinking of her upbringing and the first time she'd met Toby.

"Is it some kind of girl thing?" he asked, frowning as he glanced over.

A thing for some girls, anyway. "Was Les a bad boy? From the wrong side of the tracks, or from an abusive home? Did he drive a hot car and smoke and drink and act like he didn't give a shit about getting in trouble?"

"Sounds like you're describing Casper Jayne. Except he had my folks, my family, and then he had the Daltons in his corner. I doubt Les ever had anyone. Except Lucinda."

"How long did that last? Her being in his corner?"

"Penny was eighteen when her mom split for good, so that long at least. Though I have a feeling the corner thing was over with the first time Les hit her."

An icy chill rose the hair on Everly's arms. "Hit his wife? Or his daughter?"

"I know he hit his wife, but I wouldn't doubt Penny took a few punches over the years. And learned from them." He shook his head as if reliving a memory and not liking it much. "She knew how to fight back. I saw it happen."

"When was that?" she asked, not sure she wanted to know.

"The night Les came home and caught me with my dick in his daughter."

Crude, but she got the point. His relationship with Penny hadn't been more than sex. "That must've been unpleasant."

"For Lucinda more than anyone," he said with a snort. "She'd come home first. Stood there in Penny's open door and watched us fuck."

"Seriously?" she asked, disbelief like a fist slamming into her.

"Oh, yeah. I about shit a brick when I saw her there." He barked out a harsh laugh. "Penny told me just to ignore her, and went back to grinding."

Everly cringed, swallowing hard as she imagined Boone's panic. "What happened?"

"Nothing. At least not then. Lucinda shook her head, rolled her eyes, and left. And, yeah, I know this because I was watching her until she moved out of the door, wondering what she was going to do. I heard the refrigerator open, heard her pop the top on a beer, heard her pull a chair out from under the table, and flick her cigarette lighter. Smelled the smoke."

"And what was Penny doing while you were listening to all this?"

"Oh, I was still fucking her. But only my dick was in it. My head was wondering what kind of shit Lucinda was pulling, because I just knew things weren't going to end well."

"And they didn't."

"Nope," he said, finally thumbing the button to release his seatbelt and scraping both hands down his face. "That's when Les came home. Their house was pretty small. You walked in the front door and you could see straight to the kitchen. And Penny's room opened up off the living room."

Everly easily pictured the whole tableau—mother, father, daughter, and the Dalton Gang hell-raiser in the middle of it all. "So when Les walked in the front, he could see his wife sitting at the table with a beer and a cigarette, and see your bare ass in his daughter's bed."

"That's about the size of it." He wrapped his fingers around his steering wheel, twisted his hand back and forth. "He didn't know who to go after first. He just stood there while I scrambled back into my pants, hoping I'd get them zipped before he took a knife to my dick."

Her chest ached from her jackhammer heart. "Jesus, Boone."

"He went after Lucinda. His fists. His belt. A rolling pin. It was marble," he added, and Everly gasped, then nearly vomited when her stomach began to roil. "Penny was screaming the whole time, still naked, crying at her dad to stop, beating on him until he turned and started beating on her. Lucinda wasn't making a sound. After I got my pants on, I took off for the kitchen, yelling at Penny to call 9-1-1 and tangling with Les.

"He caught me in the jaw with the rolling pin, but I ducked and it glanced off instead of breaking my face. I smashed a blender into his head. He came back with a chair. After that, we just used our fists. It took the sheriff forever to get there. Lucinda was unconscious. Les had heard the sirens and was long gone. Penny was sitting on the kitchen floor sobbing, bleeding from a gash on her forehead, the phone in one hand, smoothing back Lucinda's hair with the other. I had to manhandle her to get her to put on her clothes."

At that, Everly started shaking, her hands first, then the whole upper half of her body. Her eyes were wide open, and she was looking at Boone, but all she could see was Toby. His fists. His belt. There had never been a rolling pin, but she didn't doubt if she'd stayed there would've been that, or worse. A blender or a knife or a chair.

Her voice scratched her throat on the way out. "What happened to Lucinda?"

"She spent a week in the hospital. Les, it turned out, hadn't gone far. The sheriff found him in the back room of his shop, blood still on his hands."

"Did he go to prison?"

"For battery, yeah, though not the attempted murder he deserved. I had to give a statement. My folks had to come to get me, so they heard the whole thing. It was probably the worst experience of my life. For weeks after, I spent more time at the Daltons' ranch than I ever had. I needed to keep busy, and Dave always had something I could do."

"And you?" She swallowed, tasted bile. "How badly were you hurt?"

"Bruises. A few cuts. Nothing that needed stitches like Penny's.

Tears were spilling down her cheeks when she pressed the fingers of one hand to her mouth. "Boone. I'm so sorry."

"Don't be. It was a long time ago."

"Still—"

"It was a wake-up call I needed, but it's over and done with, and I'm fine. But now you see why I didn't want you to hear this from someone else. It's bad enough that you had to hear it at all." He reached for her free hand, then suddenly frowned. "Criminy, Ev. Your fingers feel like ice cubes."

She let him take both of her hands to rub between his, unable to tell him what she was thinking, the memories of flinching away from Toby, of the second trip to the ER that had put an end to his intimidation and to their relationship. That had put an end to the life in Austin she'd loved.

"C'mon." He tugged her toward him. "Let's go in. Get you some hot tea or something."

Hot tea. Something she needed. Not the sex they'd come here for. He helped her across the cab and out the driver's door, and she leaned into his big body when he wrapped her close with one arm.

She stayed tucked against him as they walked up the driveway, as she unlocked the kitchen door and they went inside. Once there, she felt capable of drawing a full breath for the first time since he'd begun his story.

And she thought she was going to be okay until he looked at her, his eyes shadowed by the brim of his hat, and said, "Tea first, but his time, no scarves."

# THIRTEEN

"IS THAT AN order or a request?" She stared at him, her skin blanched of color, her voice as flat as the pastures that spread from the ranch house and barn to the horizon.

Boone wanted to kick his own ass even more than he wanted to get his hands on her, and he wanted them all over her, everywhere. He wanted her flat on her back, begging beneath him. He wanted her on her knees begging, too. But something was wrong, and he wanted first to know what it was, because her being okay was all that mattered.

He held out his arms. "Neither one. It was my very bad attempt to lighten the mood. C'mere."

Exhaling fully, she did, shutting her eyes before she buried her face in his chest. Her arms went around his waist, then she pressed her wrists between his shoulder blades, her fists at the base of his neck holding him, as if she couldn't bear his leaving.

He thought back to the truck, how cold her fingers had been. How wide and frightened her eyes. Her reaction hadn't been just to his story, no matter his description of that night. She'd been remembering something else. He was certain of it. Maybe the something Faith had mentioned. The something Everly hadn't told him about, keeping him at a distance—the same way she'd done with the scarves.

Even now she was trembling, her whole body aligned with his and shaking. And her shaking was getting to him. He wasn't about to bed her when she was this upset. He just wished he knew what had gone wrong. Yeah. Because all he'd done was give her the grisly details of a man nearly beating his family to death . . .

The pit of his stomach started gnawing, and he tightened his arms around her. "Everly?"

"Hmm?"

"Is this about Lucinda taking that beating? Because as bad as it was, it was a long time ago. Last I knew, she'd recovered and moved on. Les, I don't give a shit about. And I imagine Penny's okay, too."

She lifted her head. "And you? Are you okay?"

Her concern was for him? "About what happened that night? Yeah. Why?"

"It didn't stick with you?"

"Well, sure. Stuff like that does. But I don't think about it much. Once in a while, maybe," he said, his hands sliding down her back. "Like when I drive past their old house, or see a tow truck. It'll come back then."

She dropped her gaze to his shirt front. "I don't know if I could be that strong."

"It's not about being strong. It's more knowing nothing about that night can be changed. It's accepting that and letting it settle and putting it away. Doesn't do a bit of good to dwell on what's done with. A man could go crazy, doing that," he said, pushing down thoughts of what might be going on in her mind. "And I try not to borrow more crazy than I have to."

But she surprised him with a tender smile, saying, "Listen to you, going all cowboy-philosopher."

"I'm not *that* deep," he said, watching something in her eyes flare to life. Her fingertips weren't cold anymore where she'd tucked them inside his shirt collar. Her body wasn't shaking beneath his hands. She was thinking about how things were between them in bed. He knew it.

He was thinking about those things, too, but it still wasn't time. "Are you going to be okay? With my baggage?"

She threaded the fingers of one hand into his hair. "I'll just add it to the weight of my own."

"Yours heavy?"

"It's . . . not light," she said, screwing up her nose in a grimace.

"I've been wondering ever since Faith told me . . ." *Calf nuts on a cracker.* "Shit."

Her hands slipped from his neck to her sides and she took a step back, pushing a fall of hair from her face as she lifted her chin. "Faith told you what?"

"Something happened. Those were her words. Nothing more," he said, gripping the back of the closest of her kitchen chairs and leaning against it. "No details about what it was. Just . . . something happened."

She took a few seconds to let that sink in, then circled the table and asked, "Why were you and your sister talking about my past?"

"I asked her why you came here. She said if I wanted to know, I needed to ask you." He remembered more, bowed his head and told her. "She said you'd been hurt enough. And that I'd better not hurt you because you were her friend."

More seconds ticked by, a slow sort of death knell. "And when did you and your sister have this conversation?"

"Sunday. At my folks. We were washing dishes after supper—"

"*You* were washing dishes?"

Her question had him looking up again, and frowning. "Faith was washing. I was drying. What?" he asked when she started shaking her head, adding another, "What?" when she gave a disbelieving sort of snort.

She moved one hand to mirror his on the back of a chair. "You cleaned up the other morning after breakfast."

"Why wouldn't I?"

"You're kidding, right? This is more of your trying to impress me with your assets?"

It wasn't either of those things, and he wasn't sure why she thought it was. "You cooked. I cleaned. That's the way my momma taught me it worked."

This time, the smile that came to her mouth seemed almost ready to stay. "I really need to get to know your momma."

Now he was curious. "How can you have lived here for four years, been friends with Faith, gone to school with Faith, and not know my momma?"

"I met her and your dad at their anniversary party, but only briefly. I . . . don't get out much. Except for work. And lunch each week with the girls. And even that took a lot of persuasion by Faith."

"How come?"

She shrugged, then pulled down all kinds of shutters over the teasing of moments before. "Like Faith said. Something happened. I came here to forget about it. Or at least to get over

it. That meant sticking close to home where I knew I'd be safe."
She took a deep breath, blew it out. "And . . . I didn't mean to
say that."

He was glad she had, because now everything was making
sense, his putting her in the path of Les Upton, her needing that
first time to hold him down with scarves. "When Faith said
you'd been hurt, I didn't know she meant physically." Which is
why Everly had gone ice-cold when he'd told her about Les
beating Lucinda.

Again, she brushed back her hair. "I'd rather not talk about
this."

He got that, he supposed. He didn't exactly like talking
about his past. And he hadn't talked about all of it. Just enough
for her to realize he was pretty much an open book. He didn't
see much of a need not to be. And he'd respect her wishes.

But down the road, he'd want to know. And if this thing
between them got real, he'd expect her to tell him. Just like he'd
expect her to want to hear all of his truths—the good and the
bad. Hard to build a lifetime of trust without a solid founda-
tion. Until then, well, he *had* promised her lunch.

"What've you got in your fridge?" he asked as he turned to
open the door.

"So you cook as well as clean?"

"I'm not Clay. Or Arwen's Myna Goss. But I do okay." And
anyone could manage grilled cheese.

She pulled out a chair and sat, letting him rummage. "I
guess living alone on the ranch means you've had to learn."

"I learned a long time ago," he said, finding bread in the
box on her countertop. "But living alone on the ranch means if
I want supper, I have to cook it. If I happen to be in town when
I get hungry, and happen to have the cash, I'll stop off at
Arwen's, or the Blackbird Diner."

"Or treat a friend to a wonderful steak dinner at the Rain-song Cafe?"

Was that what they were? Friends? "That, too. Though less often. I don't get to Fever Tree much."

"Well, if we ever get there again together, I will be paying for dinner. That was way too pricey a meal for a struggling rancher to cover."

"If I wasn't able to cover it, I wouldn't have agreed to go," he said, pulling out Jarlsberg, Cheddar, Gouda, and Parmesan. He left the goat, the blue, and the Brie. "You like a little cheese to go with your wine?"

"I do," she said with a laugh. "I have bread, cheese, and fruit for dinner at least a couple times a week. I'd say I'm low maintenance when it comes to food—"

"Except you didn't get all of these at Nathan's, so your maintenance meant a trip out of town. For cheese," he added, giving her a look over his shoulder.

"I went out of town for more than cheese," she said with a laugh, "But yes. I picked up my favorites, along with a case of wine, when I was in Austin last week."

"You go back often?"

"Only when I'm in the mood for new shoes."

He wasn't sure if she was teasing. Rather than ask, he went looking for a cheese grater. "I've seen your closet, you know."

"You've seen the closet in my bedroom."

"You got scarves in the other ones, too?" he asked, still not looking at her, his heart beating a little harder, his pulse racing a little faster.

She took longer than he'd thought she would to respond. "Did the scarves bother you?"

"Did they keep me from enjoying being with you? No."

"But?"

He found a bread knife and a cutting board, started slicing her loaf of French. "I wondered that morning why you tying me up wasn't part of the fun. Why you needed me bound before you even touched me."

"I told you—"

"I know what you told me. That you were guaranteeing your own good time. But now that I know about you being hurt, it's got me wondering . . ." He didn't need to finish the sentence. He didn't want to finish the sentence. She'd made it clear the subject of whatever had happened to her was off-limits. But she'd also made it clear that whatever had happened had her feeling less than safe.

Had tying him up been some sort of bulletproof vest?

"That's not exactly true," she finally said, her voice behind him tiny and soft.

"Which part?" he asked, as he turned on the fire beneath the skillet he'd found, because it wasn't like he hadn't felt the knots against his skin for hours after.

"I did touch you. Before you were bound."

They'd danced. She'd helped him into the backseat of her car. She'd most likely had to help him out and into her house. So, yeah. She'd touched him . . . And that's when it hit him like a horse's hoof to the gut that she wasn't talking about any of those situations.

He finished slicing through the bread, crumbs scattering on the cutting board, and laid down the knife. Then he turned to look at her, leaning back against the counter. "You took off my clothes."

She nodded. "You don't remember any of it, do you?"

He could lie, but doing so would serve no purpose beyond masking his chagrin that he'd gotten falling-down drunk on his sister's dime. "Not a goddamn thing."

"I thought I was going to have to leave you in the car," she said, her gaze cast down, her finger following patterns in the table's wooden top. "You were snoring before I ever pulled into the driveway."

"The saloon's like six, seven blocks from here."

"You were snoring before we ever got out of the parking lot."

"Dadgum. That was some good beer Arwen was slinging." But that wasn't the part of that night he was interested in revisiting. "Did you wake me up, or just roll me out of the car and through the house?"

"I don't know if you actually woke up, but you did walk in pretty much under your own steam."

He crossed his arms over his chest, crossed his feet at the ankles. "And then you took off my clothes."

Her throat worked when she swallowed, when she returned her gaze to the pattern in the table's pine. "I didn't want you leaving bits and pieces of your ranch all over my house. I got you to take off your boots in the laundry room. Then decided it was as good a place as any to leave the rest of your things."

He'd found his keys and his wallet on her kitchen table when he'd gone in for breakfast the next morning. And his clothes, all of his clothes, had been freshly washed and dried, and waiting on the chair like she'd said. "The rest of my things. Including my drawers."

"You'd had them on all day. I thought while I was washing . . ." That was all she said, but she shrugged, leaving him to think how personal a thing it was to have a woman dealing with a man's day-old drawers.

"You put me to bed naked."

"I did."

"And that's when you touched me."

"It was."

"So, tell me about this touching," he said, his balls tightening, his cock thickening. "What type of liberties did you take?"

A smile pulled at the corners of her mouth. "Not as many as I did later. But enough."

"You touched my manly business."

Her gaze came up then, and a tiny desperate laugh escaped her mouth. "You're beautiful."

"Me? Or—"

"All of you."

"So . . ."

"It was just before you turned over onto your stomach. You'd fallen onto the bed. One leg on, one leg off, your arms spread wide. And your . . . penis . . . It was . . . loose, like your . . . balls. All of it relaxed and just laying there. I ran my fingertip around the ridge of the head. That was all. But since I didn't have your permission, I apologize for invading your privacy."

"You molested me."

"Yes. I did," she said, frowning, as if she hadn't thought about it that way before. "I shouldn't have, but we'd been so close while dancing, and I didn't think you'd mind."

He didn't. He just wished he'd been awake for it all. "So when you offered me dessert after breakfast, you knew exactly what you'd be getting."

"I knew what I'd be getting when you took off your clothes in the laundry room. And I had a pretty good idea on the dance floor. But, yes. You made me . . . hungry."

"Hungry. Huh." He rubbed at the back of his neck. "I'm guessing you don't mean in the grilled cheese sandwich sort of way."

"Not really," she said, her voice breaking, the rasp of desire strumming his nerves. "And anyway, if you wanted to wait . . . they're a lot better when they're hot." She nodded toward the skillet that was smoking. "Grilled cheese sandwiches."

He reached over, turned off the fire, scooted it off the grate, then went for her where she still sat at the table, grabbing her hand, pulling her down the hallway to the bedroom where they'd been headed all along.

She took care of her clothes while he got out of his. He liked undressing her, liked a lot having her undress him, but some things just wouldn't wait, and this was one of them. He needed her, and now. Her feeling the same way put a powerful spin on the urge that was sucking him in like a twister.

They were naked in seconds, his boots giving him the most trouble and putting him behind. That gave her a couple of moments to watch, and her watching had his dick swelling as he shucked out of his shorts, crawling with her onto the bed where he swore he was sheathed and inside of her before they were all the way there.

And then he was on top of her, slamming into her, his fists on the mattresses above her shoulders, his elbows locked as he pounded. His eyes were closed, and he knew she was with him, but he was all about his cock and nothing else mattered as his mind held tight to the picture of her touching him while he slept.

He grunted, he groaned, he shoved into her, bouncing the both of them so hard Everly finally cried out, "Boone!" and brought him back. He slowed then, stopped, opened his eyes and looked down to see hers wide with fear.

She wasn't aroused. She wasn't having a good time, and could he blame her? He was rutting on her like some kind of goddamn pig. *Calf nuts on a motherfucking cracker.*

What in the hell was wrong with him? "Sorry. I'm sorry. I didn't mean—"

She brought up her hand and pressed her fingers to his lips, and he lowered his body and brought his forehead flush to hers, resting there, calming there, waiting there until she told him it was okay to move, to speak. To apologize for being a pig.

Her heart beat like horse hooves pounding the prairie from her chest to his, rattling him to the core. He'd done this to her, scared the shit outta her, wanted her so badly he hadn't stopped to think about what he was doing. He hadn't stopped to think about anything. All he'd done was take her.

Once his heart was no longer galloping, and he could feel that her pulse had slowed, too, he lifted his head, brushed back her hair, and looked into her eyes, his searching, desperate, hoping to see that he hadn't hurt her. More than anything, he couldn't stand the idea that he might've hurt her.

"Are you okay?" he finally asked, his voice a whisper.

"Yes, I'm fine. I just wanted to make sure you didn't forget about me."

That wasn't what he'd heard when she'd cried out his name. "I'm not about to forget about you. Ever. But that's not what's going on here."

"Boone—"

"Everly," he said before she could try and convince the both of them he'd been imagining her fear, rolling over and pulling her on top of him. "I'm sorry. You started talking about touching me and I pretty much lost my mind. It won't happen again. Trust me."

"I do trust you," she said, and this time she was the one brushing his hair from his face. "I do."

"But you were afraid I was going to hurt you. I did hurt you—"

"You didn't—"

"But I scared you. I could tell by the sound of your voice.

And by the look in your eyes. You can't trust me if I scare you."

She stared down at him, pressing her lips together before taking a deep breath and saying, "Do we need to talk about this now? When you're . . . filling me up so beautifully? Couldn't we finish this first?"

His cock wanted to do just that. Or it did until the rest of him got in on the act, realizing how precarious her hold on her emotions really was. "Why don't we finish this another time? I don't want—"

"Shh," she said, covering his whole mouth with the cup of her hand. "I do want. Yes, we'll talk, but this first. I don't want to leave you like this."

Uh-uh. He wasn't going to have her doing this because of any discomfort he might be in. He shook his head on the pillow, dislodged her hand. "I can take care of myself. As you well know."

"I do know," she said, leaning down to brush her lips over his. "I can take care of myself, too. But it's a lot more fun when you do it."

They were talking about sex, getting each other off and nothing more, even though minutes ago the near violence of his lechery had reached the emotions she'd been trying to kept out of their bed. If that was all she wanted from him, his cock, a good fucking, he could give her exactly that—and remind himself there was nothing else between them at the same time.

Except he wasn't that guy. And that wasn't at all what *he* wanted, though until just this moment he hadn't realized that sex with this woman would end up not being enough. Oh, he'd take it. And he'd have fun. But he needed her to know he wasn't here just for her pussy. As much as he'd come back to Crow

Hill for the ranch, he'd come to settle down. It was time. He was ready.

And as he moved again to cover her, he thought maybe it was time for her, too. For some reason that thought had him growing even harder, determined to give her more pleasure than she'd ever had. He rocked against her slowly, pulled out slowly, took his time pushing back in, repeated the process until she squirmed beneath him, pressing him to hurry, begging him to make her come.

Coming was the easy part. They both knew that. What he wanted now was to give her something more, something bigger. Something she would remember when she thought about him later. Something she could look back on if it turned out they weren't looking for the same thing.

Threading his fingers into her hair and holding her head in his hands, he looked down into her eyes, stopping the motion of his body anytime she closed them. He could tell by the tightness in her jaw that she hated it, but when he used his eyes to ask her to trust him, she did, relaxing beneath him, her breath beginning to puff against his cheek in short hot bursts that felt like steam.

He reached down with one hand, pulled her knee high along his side, riding more closely against her, as close as he could get without climbing completely inside. Her softness tempted him because his life was hard, and it was so easy to forget all of that when she gave him this.

He lost himself in her, forgot the weight of the morning, the work left waiting to take up the rest of his day. He forgot about having gas in only one tank of his truck, about the fridge at home and its single stick of butter, its last three eggs, about the new hole in the sole of his best pair of boots.

Nothing existed but the woman beneath him, her hair spread out like waves of corn silk and wheat, her eyelashes as long as Sunshine's. This was what he'd thought about when he'd started thinking it was time to come home. And he was going to do his damnedest to keep his history from screwing things up.

# FOURTEEN

THE NEXT MORNING, Boone slid into the Blackbird Diner's corner booth, nodding at Teri Gregor when she lifted a coffeepot to ask if he wanted a cup. The early rush had thinned, meaning the coffee would be fresh, and not a lot of people would be stopping to shoot the shit. Exactly what he'd been hoping for.

He was here for a reason. And that reason didn't have anything to do with revisiting the crimes he'd committed in high school and taking a lot of heat for his past.

He'd been wondering when those transgressions would come back to bite him in the ass. Hell, he and Dax had talked about it just the other day. He wasn't surprised it was Les Upton's teeth clamping down, but he'd never expected Everly would get caught in the middle of that particular piece of ugly.

And he sure hadn't been eager to tell her all that had come to pass that night, but with Les prowling, it couldn't be helped.

She deserved to know, even if before he'd left Crow Hill, and after graduating from high school, things with the Uptons had been settled. Or so he'd thought.

Les, apparently, thought otherwise. Though what he was expecting from Boone after all these years wasn't exactly clear. Les was the one who'd stirred things to the point of involving the law, not Boone. Les was the one who'd tried to take his wife's head off with a rolling pin, not Boone.

Les was the one who'd come through the door, not liked the scene he'd walked into, and used it as an excuse to loose a festering rage. Boone might've helped set that off by banging his girl, but Penny had been eighteen and old enough to decide rights and wrongs for herself.

Why the attempt at intimidation now? Unless Les ending up broken and alone, a convicted felon, a local pariah, had left him steeped in hurt needing an outlet, and that outlet needing to be Boone.

There'd been no sign of the other man Monday night as Boone had followed Everly home from Fever Tree. He'd waited in front of her house while she'd parked and gone inside, his truck idling, his farewell no more than a wave when he'd hoped to end the evening tying her to her bed.

Her return wave had seemed hesitant, as if she were reconsidering having him stay. But she'd shut the door, her front porch light remaining on, the one above her garage and kitchen entrance coming on, too. Instead of leaving, he'd circled the block, shutting off his headlights as he'd rolled to a stop farther down Pineycreek, idling there for twenty minutes while watching to see if Les was going to show.

Les hadn't shown, and Boone would've stayed longer if Clark Howard hadn't come out with his shotgun to run him off. And no doubt that story had circulated the next morning in this very place, ordered up with coffee and eggs by the diner's regulars.

Fortunately, things had gotten back on track yesterday, and damn if that hadn't been the best grilled cheese of his life, but he had to admit that earlier in the week he'd been doubtful. Nothing anyone did in Crow Hill went without notice. And he hated having put Everly in the spotlight when the hurt of her past had her preferring a quiet sort of life.

Still, it was no different for anyone else. Didn't matter if that anyone was a member of the Dalton Gang, the local high school football coach or guidance counselor, a retired loan officer from the First National Bank. Boone's entire family had spent time under the microscope the residents used to judge who fit in and who didn't.

The Mitchells hadn't been a part of the town since its founding, the way the Campbells had. They'd moved here for his father's coaching job when he'd been three and Faith one. His mother hadn't gone back to work until they were both in elementary school, making Crow Hill the only home either of them had known.

Yet they still got the third degree—him for his long-ago hell-raising ways, and his sister, most recently, for leaving her banking position to take up with Casper Jayne. Here they were, he mused, bringing his mug to his mouth, pillars of the community, yet still thought of as fresh blood by those who'd been here since God was a pup.

Faith had been right to remind him, in her roundabout way, of all the things their parents had gone through, and how dealing with the heartache he and his sister had caused had tightened their bond. It had been because of their folks that the two of them had turned out as well as they had. And they had turned out well, Faith having more to show for her years and education, though he hadn't done too badly.

Now that he was back with dreams of settling down, it would be nice if he had something of worth to offer a woman. The ranch was a fucked-up mess, but apparently was sitting on a mighty nice oil prospect. And then there were the antiques Tess Dalton had used every day, as if she'd bought the furniture at Drury Hardware instead of it coming down to her from the generations of her family.

Hard to believe he and the boys had been walking right past the kind of money that would make a difference in the running of things. Even harder to think about actually selling the pieces Tess had so dearly loved. As dire straits as she'd been in before passing, even she had preferred leasing grazing land to Henry Lasko over parting with the antiques.

He'd have to see what Nora had to say, then go to the boys with her offer. He wasn't making this decision on his own. He might be the only one living on the ranch, the one these days with the most at stake as far as their shared possessions, but that didn't mean he could dispose of anything without their say.

"Boone Mitchell," Nora said, cutting into his reverie as she stopped at his side, the gray bob of her hair swinging to a stop, too, her eyes above her tiny reading glasses twinkling. "Finally. I didn't think I'd ever get one of you boys to talk to me."

Boone pulled off his hat and stood, accepting her warm hug and returning it. "Mornin' Mrs. Stokes."

"Sit. Sit. And call me Nora," she said, letting him go to slip into the seat opposite. "You're not in high school anymore, and as much as I appreciate the Coach instilling manners in you, 'Mrs. Stokes' makes me feel about a hundred years old, and I've got another forty to go before I get there."

"Let me heat that up for you, Boone," Teri said, arriving to top off his mug, then leaning down to kiss her mother's cheek. "You want a cup, Momma?"

"I'd love a cup of hot Lipton, sugar. If you don't mind." She looked from Teri back to Boone. "Switching from iced to hot tea is a sure way to get the weather to cool off. Or so I try to convince myself every year, when autumn arrives and it still feels like summer."

Boone smiled, and Teri rubbed her mother's shoulder before saying, "Be right back with it."

Nora watched her daughter walk away, then laced her hands in front of her on the table and leaned toward Boone. "How *are* your parents, Boone? I guess they're plenty happy to have you home again."

"Yes, ma'am. So they say. And it's nice to be back for my momma's Sunday pot roast."

"Oh, I can't remember the last time Gavin and I ate supper after church with your folks. I'm going to have to invite us over real soon," she said, laughing.

Boone laughed, too. "Momma's cooking's one of my favorite things about being back."

"You'll have to try and get to church with them one morning. Your mother would love that."

"Yes ma'am," he said, knowing she spoke the truth, knowing, too, he wasn't much of the churchgoing sort. "I'll do my best."

"I know you will," she said, reaching across the table and squeezing his hand. "Now, are you able to talk to me about the antiques Tess left to you boys? Or do I need to wait till Casper and Dax can join us?"

"You can talk to me, but I will need to run things by them before agreeing to anything." He wrapped his hand around his mug, frowned down into the brew. "Though with me being the only one living at the ranch anymore, I'm going on the idea that I've got more say with these things than they do."

"Then I'll let you work out all of the particulars with the others." She sat back as Teri returned with her tea. "I just want to tell you what you've got in that house, because I don't think you know. Tess kept her private business private when it came to those precious possessions."

She certainly had that. Neither Tess nor Dave had treated the furniture like anything special at all. "What I don't get, if these antiques are as valuable as you say, is why she didn't sell them herself, use the money for what she needed instead of making a deal to lease grazing land to Henry Lasko."

"Well, now, that I can't speak to with any authority, but my guess would be that she'd come to the end of her life and knew they might be worth more to you boys. That you could sell them as you needed to, or hold on to them for later should the economy turn around."

Which it hadn't, and was beginning to look like it wouldn't in Boone's lifetime. Maybe Tess had been prescient after all, giving him and the boys a bit of a safety net. Of course if not for Darcy pointing it out, none of them would've known they were sitting on what to them was a possible fortune.

Once Nora had fixed her tea to her liking, she spent the next fifteen minutes describing the pieces of furniture he lived with daily. The pieces he didn't think twice about when walking by, except to remember watering down the liquor bottles Dave kept in the sideboard, the same sideboard where Tess filed clipped recipes she rarely used, rustling up old favorites instead.

The memories made it hard to think about getting rid of

anything that had belonged to the older couple. But if he was going to make the ranch his home, and come hell or high water that's what he wanted to do, turning the house into a shrine to Tess and Dave didn't make a lot of sense.

Sure, he'd always see them there, caught off guard by the picture of Tess in the kitchen, standing at the stove frying up chicken legs, or sitting at the table patching Dave's shirts. Dave reading his paper in the living room, the old TV that didn't pick up but two channels on rabbit ears flashing in green, red, and blue against his white hair.

But he needed to make new memories, his own memories with his own family, though whether or not that would ever happen was up for grabs. Hell, he couldn't even find time to sit down with Everly for the interview he'd promised her. Finding a woman, raising kids . . . He'd had to back-burner both of those things almost the minute he'd hit town and realized the truth of his shared inheritance.

Except he couldn't deny that for the last week he'd been imagining Everly in the role of the woman to give him his family. No, that wasn't right. He'd been thinking she was the woman he wanted to make a family with. There was something about her—her totally inappropriate footwear and impractical buttons aside—that made it easy to see her rounding up their brood. He was thinking four, at least, maybe six—

"Boone? Have you heard anything I've been saying?"

He blinked up at Nora. "Yeah, sorry. Just letting some of those numbers sink in."

"Once they have, and I can't imagine it will take long, I think you'll see the worth in letting me set up this auction. I've mentioned the pieces to several people, and there is a lot of interest, let me tell you."

But Boone only caught half of that because through the window behind Nora's head, he caught something a whole lot more pressing than her take on selling his furniture.

"Would you excuse me for a moment?" he asked, but he didn't wait for an answer, bolting from his seat and to the diner's front door. He pushed out into the morning's climbing heat just in time to see the tail end of Les Upton's tow truck cruise by, the blinker stuttering as the wrecker slowed then turned toward downtown Crow Hill.

It was a coincidence, he was certain, the other man showing up in the same part of town at the same time of day as Boone himself. Except it was hard to accept it as such since the chance of his being here at all was as slim as a half of a toothpick.

# FIFTEEN

PARKING IN THE main yard of the ranch house, in the same spot she'd chosen when she'd come for Monday's interview, Everly waited for the dust stirred up by her tires to settle before opening her door. The October evening was still warm, though not uncomfortable, the sun setting sooner these days than it had just a week ago.

Autumn was her favorite time of year. The arrival of the cooler air, the crisp early mornings, the short evenings spent enjoying the sunset and the arrival of the dusky chill, one holiday after another leading into the new year.

Granted, the holiday season in Crow Hill was a far cry from those she'd spent in Austin, but she loved the cookie exchanges, and the garland hung on the town's streetlamps, the colorful lights adorning the windows of the local businesses, the popcorn balls and homemade fudge dropped at the office by advertisers and friends.

Exiting her SUV, she lifted a hand to shade her eyes, looking beyond the corral into the far pastures, their ragged fences like stitches quilting them together, the whole cloth vanishing into the distance like a sea of spun gold. She took a deep breath, blew it out slowly. Oh, but Boone must love the view from here.

What would it be like to wake up as light first broke over the horizon, turning the grass in the fields the colors of thick cream and buttered toast? To spend the day in the elements, skin baked by the heat, lips parched by the dry breeze, hair turned to straw by the sun?

To come home, to sit on the back porch and nurse a beer or a glass of wine, watching the sky, so blue throughout the day, going pink and orange and purple as night fell, as the stars appeared on the stretch of canvas the color of ink?

And . . . wow, she mused, laughing to herself, leaning against the front of her vehicle and soaking in the scenery and the absolute peace it evoked. That had certainly come out of nowhere. She was a journalist, not a poet, and she was certainly not the philosopher she'd seen in Boone. And, to boot, she was a city girl at heart. She'd only come to Crow Hill because Faith had made the suggestion.

Faith had also been the one to convince Whitey his personnel budget would be well served by new blood, a fresh perspective, and Everly's experience. And that made Faith's questioning of her intentions for the Dalton Gang story sting a bit. Faith should know better. Everly hadn't grown up here. She had nothing to prove, no wrongs to right, no revenge to mete out in print.

After four years, Crow Hill felt like home as much as Austin ever had. And that surprised her. Oh, she still stuck out—driving a luxury hybrid SUV, wearing labels other than Wrangler and Tony Lama, doing much of her shopping online because she couldn't find the brands she wanted in town. But she couldn't remember the last time she'd thought it was time to leave.

Crow Hill was a close-knit community, family-owned ranches, family-run businesses. Her own family had long ago scattered across the Lone Star State. Missing them was made easier by friends who gave her life an abundance of riches, who were there when she needed them, always.

She wouldn't want to stay here alone, however, and that had nothing to do with Boone; they'd only just started seeing each other, and she'd never believed in love at first sight. But from what she'd learned of him over the last week, he was the type of man she would want to spend her life with.

There would be hardships, of course. Making a living off the land never came without them. And she knew from her girlfriends what the three members of the Dalton Gang faced daily, the struggles they worked to overcome. Struggles made worse by their lack of money.

All of it was a viciously unrelenting cycle—raising stock, feeding stock, selling stock at a loss, yet *having* to sell to afford to raise and feed the next season's calves, which depending on beef prices and the whims of Mother Nature, might have to be sold for even less in order to do it again.

Snagging a twist of hair and tucking it behind her ear, she wondered what it had been like here for Tess Dalton, no children of her own, the three Dalton Gang boys coming into her life as teens, her days spent at Dave's side, or seeing to the homestead to free him from having to take care of those chores as well.

Could Everly do that? Be a rancher's wife? Work dawn to dusk, see her husband doing the same, wondering each and every day whether the next would be easier, bringing good news or just more grief? Neither Faith nor Arwen had ever lived on a ranch. Their men were the ranchers, but Casper and Dax both left the job *at* the job when they went home at the end of the day.

Boone did not. He lived in the Dalton house and was rarely off the property. When he did leave, it was still work that most often brought him to town—though lately it had been her. And that had her feeling as guilty as it had her feeling, well, special.

What, besides taking him into her bed, had she done to deserve his attention? How had she managed to snag his affections? Why was he taking time for her? Surely he'd made arrangements for sex elsewhere, ones that didn't involve any local women who might want more than his—

"What're you doing here?" Boone's voice broke into her reverie, derailing her rather disturbing musings and startling her as he approached from the direction of the barn. His tone broadcast his surprise, the smile breaking across his face declaring his happiness that she'd decided to visit.

"Enjoying the view and the evening," she said, feeling a thrilling rush at his reaction, then adding as he drew near, "And waiting for you." She watched his eyes flash as he walked, his nostrils flare as he reached her. And then he was there, looping an arm around her neck and bringing her close for a kiss.

It was a sweet kiss, a tender kiss, his mouth tasting of salt and a day spent in the sun, his lips dry as he pressed them to hers, lingering, though not as long as either of them would've liked. But oh, what a welcome. As if he'd been waiting all day to see her. As if she were his reason for coming home.

How easy it would be to get used this . . . this . . . joy. Utter joy. His at finding her waiting. Hers at being what he wanted, what he needed, at giving him what no other woman could because she was meant to be his.

And, good grief, what a ridiculous train of thought to be traveling, just because his kiss had her bones melting and her heart swelling in the cavern of her chest.

He was slow to pull away, asking as he did, "What did I do to get so lucky?"

Stepping out of his embrace, she circled the SUV, reaching into the backseat to bring out the picnic basket she'd packed. "I brought you supper."

"Yeah?" His grin grew at least two sizes. "I'm just about hungry enough to eat a side of rhino."

She opened the top and peered inside, fighting a grin of her own. "Well, I've got grapes. Dried cherries and apricots. A baguette. Gruyere and Camembert and Danish blue cheese. And a bottle of CapRock Roussanne."

He screwed up his face. "Then what you meant is that you brought *you* supper."

His disappointment made her surprise that much better. "I also have a double brisket platter with all the fixin's *and* a whole pecan pie from the Hellcat Saloon. It's not quite a side of rhino, but . . ."

"Now that's what I'm talking about." He reached around her and grabbed the big basket. "C'mon. Let's go in."

Hooking her arm through his when he offered, she fell into step beside him, wishing they could spread out a blanket in the closest pasture and share their meal as the day fell away. "I felt bad after lunch took the turn it did yesterday. Not the . . . part where we ended up in bed. But the stuff before. When we were talking. *And* the decided lack of anything filling to eat."

"Nothing there to feel bad about," he said, frowning as he

looked down at her. "Man *can* live by grilled cheese alone if he has to. I should know."

"You didn't eat much," she said, feeling even worse about that.

"You didn't eat much either. Of your lunch anyway."

She stopped, squeezing her thighs together as she looked around the ranch yard. "Could we eat out here? Do you have a table? Or we could let down the tailgate of your truck?"

He laughed, a big loud guffaw that made its way up from his chest to spill from his mouth. "Afraid if we go inside I'll want dessert first?"

"Actually, I'm more afraid I will," she said, the admission fluttering in her belly.

"Then your wish is my command," he said, leading her to the far side of the house where an old picnic table sat beneath the huge spreading oak that shaded the structure. He started to set the basket on top, then stopped. The surface was covered with dried acorns and bird droppings and cicada shells, and looked like it hadn't been used in a decade or more. "Well this wasn't such a good idea."

"Hang on a second," she said, opening the basket and pulling out the blue and green plaid blanket packed on top. She shook it out and covered the table, realizing too late the benches were just as filthy. Of course if not for her heels . . .

"Here, help me up," she said, bracing a hand on his shoulder as she stepped onto the bench that was worn but still solid, then turned to sit on the table. Boone did the same at the other end, leaving the basket of food between them. "Perfect."

"If your idea of perfect is you being down there, me being over here. But since I'm about to keel over from lack of rhino," he said, setting her bread and grapes on a plate on the table, "I guess it'll do."

She pulled out the bottle of wine and two glasses. "I read once that Michael Phelps burned something like ten thousand calories a day while training."

"Not sure I've ever had ten thousand calories' worth of food in the house, but I could probably give him a run. Eating. Not in the pool. Never got in much swimming time."

"You weren't born in Crow Hill, right?" she asked, handing him the corkscrew when he reached for it. "I seem to remember Faith saying your family moved here when you were kids."

"We did. We were. We came here for my dad's job at the high school." He pulled down on the corkscrew arms, worked the cork free, and poured her a glass, pouring himself one as well instead of heading to the house for a beer. "Been coaching for about thirty years. Mom waited until Faith and I were both old enough to enroll, then went to work at the middle school. She moved to the high school the same year I did. They've both been there long enough that they're as much an institution as the bronzed hurricane in the school's courtyard."

"Is that what that is? A hurricane?"

He snorted, found a fork and the pie. "Looks like a big turd, if you ask me."

"Was that what you thought when you played football?"

"I did."

"I'm guessing you didn't make your feelings known to the sculptor. Or to your coach."

"The Coach got to hear me make fun of it over the dinner table for years." He said it around a big bite of pie, then set aside the dessert and found the aluminum to-go pan of brisket.

"How did that go over?" she asked, pinching a grape from the cluster, a gust of wind lifting her hair from her neck.

"I think he held the same opinion, but wasn't about to say so. He just stared me down anytime I opened my mouth about it. And then I closed my mouth, and waited until I could come out here and laugh about it with Dave. He didn't work for the school, so he didn't mind that particular disrespect."

"But he minded others."

"Oh, yeah. As laid-back as he was, Dave was not an easy man to work for."

"Really," she said, because nothing could've surprised her more. The three Dalton Gang members had done nothing but sing the other man's praises. "I've never heard anyone else say that about him."

"Did you ever meet him?" he asked, digging a spoon into a container of *charro* beans. "He was still alive when you moved here I think."

"He was. But, no. I didn't meet him. I did see him in passing. And he was always scowling. But I see that a lot on you rancher types." Another grape, then she tore off a hunk of bread, and found a knife to spread the cheese. "I figured it was all that time spent squinting into the sun."

"Part of it, yeah, but I think Dave did that on purpose. He was a gentle kind of guy, I'd guess you'd say. Didn't like raising his voice. The scowl probably helped when he wanted things done a certain way."

"His way?"

He nodded as he moved to the potato salad. "It was always a way that made sense. I never stopped to wonder if another way or method might be better. I guess that's why I had so much trouble after Casper and Dax left."

"What kind of trouble?"

"They both took off not long after graduation. Pretty much back-to-back, leaving me the only one who knew Dave's routine, his preferences, his rules, if you will. He brought in some hands, but they didn't like taking orders from a seventeen-year-old who'd only been ranching part-time for a little over three years."

She reached for an apricot slice. "Was it hard after they left? Dax and Casper?"

"On the ranch? Or just in general?"

"Both."

"Is this going into your story?" he asked, his eyes finding hers over the pan of brisket he'd returned to.

"Some of it might," she said, popping the fruit into her mouth. "I'll have to rely on my memory. My notebook and my digital recorder are both in the SUV."

He snorted. "I'd say you were really letting your hair down tonight, except here you are with the buttons and the shoes."

She straightened her legs, turned her feet this way and that. "Until you tell me to come with boots and jeans for that horse-back ride, you'll get me as me."

"I never did ask if you could ride." He stopped, taking in her skinny black pants and long sleeveless swing top. "A horse, I mean. Can you ride a horse?"

"I've ridden before," she said, reaching for her wine before she reached for him, because that's what the look in his eyes had her wanting to do. "It's been a while, but I guess it's like a bicycle? Or . . . riding other things after a long hiatus? It kinda all comes back."

"About that." He swallowed more potato salad, downed half the wine in his glass like it was water. "Would've been hard pressed to tell you were out of practice. If that's what you're saying here."

She nodded, leaned down to dust off the bright fuchsia toes of her Prada pumps. "Until the other morning, it had been a while."

"How long is 'a while'?" he asked and stopped chewing.

"Four years."

He blinked, blinked again. "So . . . all the time you've been in Crow Hill—"

"Celibate as a nun," she said, meeting his gaze over the rim of her wineglass.

"Why didn't you come see me sooner?" he asked, his expression awash in disbelief.

She smiled at that. "Sooner, I wasn't ready to come see you. Or anyone. And you haven't been back that long for me to come see."

"What happened?"

"You danced with me."

"I know that part of what happened. I was asking about what happened to make you close up shop."

Those weren't things she was ready to talk about. Not in any kind of detail. And not with him. "I had just ended the relationship I told you about. I wasn't ready to get involved in another."

"But now you are."

Was that where they were headed? Into a relationship? Was that what all her earlier thinking about living here had been? Was that what he wanted?

She started to tell him she wasn't averse to things between them becoming something more, but she held off, biting back a truth it surprised her to acknowledge. She needed time to come to grips with what she was feeling.

With the fact that she *was* feeling. In the meantime . . .

She gave a noncommittal shrug and sipped at her wine, then. desperate for a change of subject, asked, "Was leaving hard because your family was here? Or hard because you were abandoning Tess and Dave?"

"A whole lot of both," he responded after a long pause. "But it got to the point that I just couldn't stay."

"Faith missed you a lot, when you were gone. When she found out you'd be coming back for the ranch . . . She wore this smile for weeks. It was like a kid finding out Santa Claus was real after all."

He grunted. "Too bad I couldn't have put that smile on her face by coming home for her and the folks instead of for an inheritance."

"You can't think that way."

"I can. And I do. I visited during the holidays every year, but it's pretty shitty to say you don't want to move back, and then do it because someone left you a ranch." He poured more wine, for him, for her, drank his, then grabbed a handful of her grapes. "I'd told myself when I left that I was never going to live here again. Except for my family, everything that had made Crow Hill home was gone. The boys. Then Dave passed. Finally Tess. There wasn't anything left. Nothing."

Her reporter's antennae were twitching, and she wanted to know what he'd skated over, what he'd left out; but she knew to get what she wanted, she had to keep quiet, to let him talk while she listened.

"I hadn't even known I wanted to cowboy until the folks sent us to work here. I didn't want to go to college. I had the grades. Had killer SAT scores. Hell, I even got recruited by some smaller schools' football programs. If I hadn't sabotaged a blow-off economics class I took my senior year, I could've gone to any school I wanted."

That didn't surprise her. He was a very smart man. What did surprise her was that he would throw away such a gift. "Why didn't you want to go?"

"School bored the shit outta me," he said, putting the top back on the brisket and crimping it closed. "I knew Casper wasn't going, and things had already gone south for Dax with his old man. Dave didn't pay enough to call those wages a living, so even if the boys could've stuck out their family shit, they needed more money than they could get working here. So did I."

"I can't imagine he wouldn't have understood that. Dave, I mean."

"He did. I still felt like a dick for walking out on him." He closed up the potatoes, beans and pie, finished off his wine. "Can you stick around for a while? Let me go in and get cleaned up? It's a nice night. Be great to sit out back with someone besides myself and my beer cooler."

"Sure," she said, waving a hand over their picnic. "I'll pack this up. You go on in."

"Thank you. This was great. Really great."

"I'm glad you liked it."

She swore he started to say something more, but then he dropped another kiss on her mouth and headed toward the house, leaving her to wonder if her coming out here had sent him the wrong message.

Then wondering what message she'd wanted to send, besides being neighborly and bringing supper to a friend, because even she wasn't buying that one anymore.

# SIXTEEN

WHILE BOONE SHOWERED upstairs, Everly stayed put on the first floor. The only other visit she'd made here she'd spent in Boone's bedroom, and he'd hurried her up the stairs, leaving her no time to take in her surroundings. Now that she had time, she could see what he meant about the state of things.

*Old* was the first word that came to mind. *Worn* was the second. Paint, floor tiles, blinds, appliances. All were in need of an upgrade.

The place was more cluttered than dirty, though the kitchen floor could use a mop, the windows a swipe of Windex. There were dishes in the sink, but they'd been rinsed, and the stove surface was smeared with hastily wiped-away grease.

She wondered as she walked through if the kitchen sideboard was one of Tess's antiques. It was covered with a clutter of paper and tools and shop rags as if it had been picked up for ten bucks at yard sale.

Remembering Arwen telling her about Tess having a piano, she headed for the living room. The old upright sat against an interior wall, a four-legged adjustable stool in front of it. She sat, spun, smiling as she rose to the height she needed, screwing up her face as she played a series of scales and realized how out of tune the instrument was. And how stiff her hands were.

Still, it was lovely to run her fingers over the keys, and she settled on a rusty rendition of Scott Joplin's "Maple Leaf Rag," laughing each time she slipped up and the notes rang sour. Not that anyone would be able to tell, she thought, considering barely half the keys produced the sound they were supposed to.

Boone came into the room as she finished the song, wearing only his socks with his clean clothes, and his steps lighter because of it. "I didn't know you played," he said after she'd stopped and swiveled the stool to face him.

She caught the scent of his soap and shampoo, and wondered for no reason that made sense how many other women knew what he smelled like fresh from the shower, his hair brushed back, the ends snagged in his collar, his face razored clean. Why seeing him like this seemed so intimate . . .

She tightened her core around the longing coiling inside her, a longing that wasn't about having him, but being with him, sharing moments like this one, so simple, so uncomplicated, drawing them incredibly, powerfully close. "It's been a while since I have. I left my piano in Austin when I moved."

She didn't want to think about what had happened to it. If Toby had pushed it off the balcony and watched it explode, then burned what was left in the street. Or if he'd just taken an ax to it in the middle of the living room.

Whatever he'd done, she didn't have a doubt that it was gone forever. Same with her beloved espresso machine. She needed to buy another. Four years, and she'd yet to replace it. She didn't know why when she'd started every morning of those years in that condo with a double shot. Maybe that was the reason . . .

"Must be like riding a bike," Boone said, bracing an elbow on the top of the old upright. "Doesn't sound like the time away has hurt you any."

Riding a bike. Piano playing. Sex. "It comes back. I'm kinda rusty, but not as bad as I'd thought."

"You take lessons as a kid?"

She nodded. "Mostly against my will."

He laughed. "Why's that?"

"I was way too busy taking dance and gymnastics. Who wants to sit and practice piano when floor routines and *Swan Lake* are waiting?"

"So you liked dance."

"I loved dance. I hated having to quit."

"Why did you?"

"I hit puberty. My build was all wrong. I was short, and sort of . . . hippy. But I made a great cheerleader. And the gymnastics helped with that. Of course, with cheerleading comes football, and as you know, with football comes boys, and gymnastics went the way of dance." She raised an index finger. "But I didn't quit cheerleading, proving I do have it in me to stick with some things."

"Things that you're built for."

"Something like that, though not just physically. I know this sounds . . . I don't know. Too privileged, maybe. Or entitled. But I want to like what I'm doing. Not do it because it's

expected of me. Or because it's proper. I don't mind being improper if I'm having fun. And if I'm not bored. I hate being
bored."

She gave a self-conscious laugh, pushed a fall of hair away
from her face instead of hiding behind it, which is what she
wanted to do. Why was she telling him all of this? "That must
sound terribly shallow. And selfish. And it's neither one. Not
really."

"Nothing wrong with liking what you're doing," he said,
his gaze traveling the length of the eighty-eight keys. "I like the
hell out of ranching. I'd like it a lot better if it wasn't such a lost
cause, but at least I'll go down with a smile on my face."

"It's not that bad, is it?"

"It's that bad." He moved to sit on the edge of the couch,
his elbows on his knees as he looked up at her. "Do you like
the paper? Working there? Because I can't imagine having
Whitey Simmons for a boss. He taught my Sunday school class
one year, and I swear I fell asleep every week listening to him
drone. I think I was grounded for almost all of fifth grade."

That made her laugh. "He's probably the easiest boss I've
ever had. And this is definitely the easiest job." Another laugh,
this one self-deprecating. "Crow Hill has been good to me.
And good *for* me. I like my life here. Not just because my job's
easy, or because my boss isn't hounding me twenty-four seven.
It's more that nothing's ever . . . unexpected. Except you." She
held on to the piano, swiveled back and forth on the stool.
"You were definitely unexpected."

"I'm going to take that as a good thing," he said, a dark
brow arching.

"It *is* a good thing," she said, meaning it more than he could
possibly realize. In the last week, her outlook on so many
things had changed in ways she would never have imagined,

and all because this man had come into her life. "I like that I met you."

"I like it, too."

Silence fell between them then, as if they were both struggling with what *liking* meant. As if neither one of them wanted to be the first to define it, or to change the subject until they understood its import and weight. Until they knew how close they were to crossing the line from liking to something more.

But her nerves finally got the best of her and she moved, the stool squeaking as she shifted. "I should probably get home."

It was the first thing that came to mind, though she'd been waiting for him to ask her to stay. After lunch yesterday, she needed to know if the fear his roughness had dislodged from inside of her had him changing his mind.

Or if he was feeling as torn and confused as she was. They were supposed to be having an affair, not doing all this strange soul baring.

"You don't have to," he said, alternately fisting and spreading his fingers. "But I can understand why you might want to."

He'd switched on the lamp in the corner and the light bathed one side of his face, leaving the other in eerie shadow. "I don't know that you do."

"You haven't been with anyone in the four years you've lived here. Obviously there's a reason for that. Then you choose me, and I ride you like you're a bronc that needs breaking." He lifted his head, his gaze searching hers. "I think you were already broken, and I made things worse."

"You startled me, yes. But it wasn't about making things worse. Or about breaking me. It was quite the opposite, in fact." And she was still dealing with that.

He snorted, shook his head. His mouth pulled sideways. "I left out of your place yesterday thinking you might fall to pieces after I was gone. I've been worrying about it ever since, so what you're saying isn't helping me understand what went wrong. Because something went wrong, didn't it?"

"Not really, no. It was just another moment I hadn't expected, because I liked that you were rough," she said, heat rising up her neck to flush her cheeks. "It surprised me that you were, and surprised me that I did. But I never thought you'd hurt me, or that I wasn't safe with you through the whole thing."

"You make it sound like a rubber-glove exam," he said. "Except for the liking it part."

That caught her so off guard, she burst out laughing. "Thank you. I needed that. God, did I need that."

"I could go all cowboy-philosopher on you again and tell you laughter makes the best medicine, but I'd rather you tell me about the fear."

"Maybe someday."

"But not now."

She shook her head. "Supper was wonderful, the company, the food. I don't want to lose this . . . feeling."

"And what feeling is that?" he asked, his tone concerned.

She did what she could to set him at ease. "Happy. Relaxed. Comfortable. You're making me want to stay here."

"Good. Because that's what I was aiming for."

"I just don't know if it's a good idea." The last thing she wanted to do was lead him on. "I've got a rather . . . complicated past."

He laced his hands behind his head and leaned back, slouching against the cushions, his knees spread wide. "I'm a big boy, Everly. In case you've missed that one of the times you've seen me with my clothes off."

"It's not about you, you know. My . . . hang-ups," she said, even that admission causing the pit of her stomach to burn.

"Yeah, I'm figuring it's about the ex in Austin. And I'm also figuring he's the reason you're living in this shit hole and wasting your time with Whitey Simmons."

Frowning, she asked, "Is that what you think? That I'm wasting my time?"

He sat forward again, frowned again, worked his hands in and out of fists again. "You had a pretty high-profile career before coming here. Made a lot of connections over the years. Connections you could've parlayed into another high-profile position. Maybe in another big city. You're smart. Ambitious. Talented. Gorgeous. But instead of doing that, you're hiding out in a tiny little office working with Clark Howard and Cicely Warren and Whitey Simmons.

"You can't use your connections here. You can't use but bits and pieces of your talent. Now, if you'd moved here to take the waters, or whatever, that would be one of those horses of different colors. So in that regard, yeah. You working for the *Crow Hill Reporter* is a big fat waste of something. Could be it's not time at all. Could be something insignificant. Or could be something big enough to swallow you whole."

He stopped, and his words hung in the room around them, a smoke ring hovering before dissipating, the smell lingering long after. The funny thing was, he was right. At least when it came to her connections and her talent. She could be doing so much more with her time. But she didn't *want* to be doing more. And that was what she was only coming to understand.

Admittedly, the job with Whitey was supposed to have been a stopgap, getting her over the emotional hump after Toby. Yet four years later, she could hardly remember what about her on-air position, her social circles, her speaking and emceeing engagements made the stress of maintaining that lifestyle worth it.

What she did know was that tonight wasn't for scrolling through the choices she'd made and assigning reasons why. Nothing in the past could be changed. Besides, Boone and the sunset were waiting. Later, she could examine her life.

She gave him a smile and signaled a time-out. They could get back to this later. After his words had set. "Didn't you say something about the back porch and a beer cooler?"

He stood, offered her his hand. "I did, though it won't hurt my feelings if you'd rather stick to wine. And I say that mostly because I think I'm about out of beer."

The chair on the back porch was actually an old metal glider, once green to match the house's shutters, now as peeled as the shutters were faded. The rounded seashell back was warm when she sat, and Boone pulled a beer from the cooler after pouring her another glass of wine.

He joined her then, draping an arm across her shoulders and bringing her close as the glider moved back and forth, pushed into service by his stocking feet. Everly tucked hers into the seat beside her, slipping her shoes off and setting them on the porch, before leaning against him.

She drank her wine. He drank his beer. Bing and Bob lay in the dirt with their snouts resting on their paws, their eyes darting. The sun spilled a palette of colors across the pasture, the barn throwing a long, cool shadow toward the house.

Relaxed, Everly didn't want to think about Austin or Toby or her job with Whitey Simmons, or why she'd yet to replace her espresso machine.

All she wanted to do was sit here, with Boone, and never move again.

# SEVENTEEN

THE ONLY TIME Everly had been inside Casper's house on Mulberry Street was for Faith's parents' thirty-fifth anniversary party. It had been a wonderful night, the place newly renovated, empty of furniture save for rented folding tables and chairs. The decorations had been simple—hurricane lanterns in bowls of aromatic cedar and mesquite, and tiny white Christmas lights strung in what had seemed like miles and miles of decorative greenery.

Now, a month later, the entire house was furnished, and all at Faith's hand. That had Everly smiling because Faith had studied business and finance, yet Everly had always known the other woman wouldn't be happy for long at Crow Hill's First National Bank. This house and its gorgeous interior proved where her true talents lay. And the best part was that Faith had not only found her calling when she'd found her man, she'd found herself in the process.

Walking through the front door into the hallway that bi-
sected the first of the three floors, Everly breathed deeply of the
scents of old and new wood. "When is *Architectural Digest*
going to feature Crow House?"

"No time soon," Faith said, closing the front door behind
her. "Nor will any other publication, though I can't say I
mind."

"Why not?"

"Why won't we get a magazine feature?" Faith shook her
head. "We didn't apply to register the house as a historical
landmark. And we didn't stay period authentic with the reno-
vations. We did what we wanted. We'll be lucky to get a mention in *Texas Monthly*, though Casper doesn't want the house
mentioned anywhere."

"Why not?"

"He's got this idea that hordes of visitors will stop by with
cameras and wanting tours."

"I can see that going over well. Casper opening his home to
strangers."

"Hey now," said the man in question, stepping out of the
library where Clay sprawled in a recliner, his dog sprawled on
the floor at his feet, watching something with a lot of explo-
sions on a big-screen TV. "Here I am, opening it to you."

Everly bit her tongue and let Faith answer. "Everly is not a
stranger and you know it."

"Not to you maybe."

"And not to you either," Faith said, punching him in the
shoulder before turning to Everly to add, "He's just being
grumpy because I told him he had to talk to you."

Everly bit back a grin as she watched him rub the sting from
Faith's playful blow. "I promise it'll be totally painless. Or at
least mostly painless."

"Well, c'mon then," he said, gesturing with the hand around which he still wore a brace, giving his woman an eye. "Let's sit in the kitchen. Faith says it's not comfortable, but it's where she keeps my food and drink, and I think I'll be needing a hefty dose of the latter."

"He's not the only one," Faith mumbled as she walked beside Everly behind him. "And don't worry. I'm leaving. I'm taking Clay to Sheppard's Books to stock some new titles for Kendall. And I'm taking along a bottle of the CapRock Roussanne from your housewarming gift."

"Mmm. Wine. Good stuff that wine."

"Oh, yeah," Faith said, wrapping an arm around Everly's shoulders, the two of them giggling like they'd already downed a whole bottle as they followed Casper to the kitchen. Once there, Everly climbed onto a stool at the center island while Faith pulled a glass from the rack hanging above the kitchen's stainless steel wine cooler. From there, she selected two bottles, one for Everly and one to take with her.

She handed Casper the corkscrew while she packed her tote with her bottle, her corkscrew, glasses for two, and cheese and grapes from the fridge. When Casper frowned, she pecked him on the cheek and said, "Girls' night out," then stepped back and called down the hallway, "Clay! Let's go!"

"Don't you be driving home," Casper told her, nodding toward the bottle in her tote.

"I've got Clay and his new hardship license. And it's one bottle of wine for Kendall and I to share. We may not even go through the whole thing. I'll be fine."

"Yeah. Letting a barely fifteen-year-old behind the wheel. That makes me feel so much better."

"The license was your idea, sweetie. And he drives out to the ranch by himself all the time."

"That's different."

"Right. Because it's a thirty-minute instead of a three-minute trip."

"Yeah, yeah. Just go. Have fun. Be safe."

"I will. I love you."

"I love you, too," he said, grabbing her around the waist and pulling her to him for a kiss that was not a peck on the cheek, and left Everly wanting Boone.

Clay came clambering into the kitchen then, grabbing Faith's keys off the counter before anyone had a chance to object. "I'm driving, right?"

"You're driving. I'm drinking." Faith ruffled his hair, though he was almost taller than her, and she had quite a reach. "But not so much that I won't be able to keep an eye on the speedometer."

"C'mon, Mother Faith. I don't speed." He leaned down, nuzzled his face to that of his dog. "You be good, Kevin. You stay with Father Casper. I'll be back soon."

Faith hooked her tote over her shoulder, pushing Clay toward the front door when he straightened. "Let's go, driver."

"Yes, ma'am," he said, and bounded down the hall to the door.

Everly couldn't stop grinning. "Mother Faith? Father Casper?"

"It's his fifteen-year-old idea of a joke," Faith said with a roll of her eyes, giving Casper one last kiss, and Everly one last hug. "You two behave."

And then she was gone, Everly and Casper alone, the big house an echo of noises around them. Casper reached for the wine bottle and filled her glass, his eyes on his task as he asked, "Where do you want to start?"

*At the beginning,* she thought to say, then decided Casper

wasn't the Dalton Gang member to be flip with. He was the one with the abusive background, the one no one had ever thought to see settled down and settled well. Yet here he was, father-to-be of a fifteen-year-old, husband-to-be of one of her oldest friends.

He owned a showpiece of a house built over a century ago by one of the town's founding fathers, Zebulon Crow. And he owned part of a ranch bequeathed to him and the others by one of the best-loved couples to ever call Crow Hill home.

He'd come a long way. He'd established himself as a responsible and productive community member. She wanted her story to show that. She wanted to tell the residents of Crow Hill about the real Casper Jayne—not focus on the hell he'd raised as a teen.

"Faith said you moved to Crow Hill around sixth or seventh grade?"

"Seventh. Met the boys the first day of football practice," he said, grabbing a beer from the refrigerator and screwing off the top with his good hand. "Well, *my* first day," he added, climbing onto the stool across from hers. "They'd been having two-a-days since early August. It took Mrs. Mitchell to convince me to try out for the team. She was still over at the middle school then. Moved to the high school the same year we did. We had her watching our grades and the Coach watching to make sure we didn't show our asses."

"That worked out pretty well," she said, knowing how influential Boone's parents had been in Casper's life, too.

"For the Mitchells, maybe," he said, the longneck cradled between his good hand and his bad. "I'd been used to doing pretty much what I wanted with no one giving me a second look. Now all of a sudden I couldn't so much as take a piss without one of them wanting to test it."

"For drugs?" she asked, surprised. "Or . . . that was an exaggeration, wasn't it?"

"Yeah, but not much of one. The Mitchells were not about to let their kids, and me and Dax by extension, turn out to be anything but well-adjusted members of society," he said, then brought the beer to his mouth.

"Looks like they did a good job."

He cocked his head, cocked a brow. "Hard to believe, really, since it was all Boone's fault we got into so much trouble. He was the biggest hell-raiser of the three of us."

Again Whitey's words came back to haunt her. And now having heard the story of Les Upton . . . "Boone? Really?"

Casper laughed, a gruff grating sound that was filled with more evil than humor. "Don't let the boy fool you. He hasn't always been the nice guy he is now. Hell, I'm not even sure the nice guy now bit isn't an act."

"What makes you say that?" she asked, reaching for her wine and downing a long swallow.

"We all left a lot of messes behind when we split, so none of us were looking forward to the shit we knew would hit the fan when we got here." He lifted his bottle again. "Boone being a nice guy, well, who knows how much that's helped keep the vultures at bay."

"You're saying this Boone that everyone sees around town is not the Boone you and Dax work the ranch with every day?"

He shook his head, swallowed. "No, he's the same. He's just a lot . . . quieter, I guess. We've all tried to stay out of sight, but Boone's done the best job at keeping his head down. And he's had less blowback."

She found Casper's assessment intriguing. "Because of his doing that? Rather than the status his family has in Crow Hill? Or maybe the pranks he pulled—"

"Pranks," he said with a snort. "Guess you could call some of that shit 'pranks.' Like him and Dax loading up Harris Bell's prize longhorn bull and hauling it to Len Tunstall's slaughterhouse."

"He told me about that," she said, the admission earning her a nod.

"I think that was the one that had the big man's folks sending him to the Daltons. Unless it was his shooting up the back of Lasko's."

And that answered that. "They must've meant a lot to you. The Daltons. For you to come back knowing you could face a lot of backlash."

"We wouldn't have been able to come back if not for Tess and Dave, and I don't mean their willing us the ranch." He stared at the label on his beer, frowning and rubbing a thumb across the raised print. "They weren't the ones who straightened us out, you know, even though that's what everyone thinks. They're the ones who gave us what we needed to straighten out ourselves. I've always wondered if the Mitchells knew that would happen when they laid down the law."

"To you and Dax, too?"

"Yep. All for one, one for all. They basically told us if we wanted to spend any more time in their home, we'd help Boone give Tess and Dave a hand."

Interesting. "Some kids might've balked at orders from a friend's parents."

The sound he made was as much chuckle as snort. "Those kids have never had Catherine Mitchell's pot roast."

She really needed to try this pot roast. "Did you stay in touch over the years? You and Dax and Boone? You rode bulls professionally, right?"

"I did, and we didn't." He finished off his beer, rocked the bottle side to side on the island. "Rodeo means one night in one town, the next in another. Sometimes a state away. Sometimes more. I hit Albuquerque one year when Boone was cowboying nearby. Turns out he'd planned to come to the show, not even knowing I was there, but work got in the way."

"Ships passing in the night."

"Something like that. Seeing them again once we were all back"—he shook his head, smiled at the memory— "that was one of the best days of my life for sure."

"Tell me about it," she said, scratching the word *reunion* in her notebook.

"Boone was already here. He was the first one to come home. And he may have already told you this, but he'd been back pretty regularly, family holidays and all."

He had, so she nodded, and that seemed to give Casper a reason to frown. "What's the deal with you and Boone anyway?"

The question came out of the blue and she looked at him sharply. "What do you mean?"

"You just taking him for a ride, or what?"

"My being with Boone isn't any of your business," she said, looking down and drawing three sharp lines on the page of her notebook. Then drawing two more.

"He's my friend. I don't want him getting hurt, or being used, or whatever's going on here," he said, hopping down for another beer, tossing the bottle top at the trash. It bounced off, hit the floor, rattled to a stop.

"Again, my business is not your concern."

"And, again. It fucking well is," he said, then held her gaze as he drank.

"We're done here," she said, her eyes on her notebook as she closed it, as she clicked off her pen, as she stored both in her oversized hobo. No story was worth having her personal life brought into the mix. "If I need anything else, I'll let Faith know."

"You do that. Just don't be messin' with Boone."

She jumped from her stool, circled the island to where he sat, got as far in his face as she possibly could. "Do *not* tell me what to do. You have no say in my life. And I'm pretty sure the only say you have in Boone's concerns the ranch."

He said nothing, so she went on. "You have your life in town now. You have Faith and you have Clay. Boone is alone out there. He eats alone. He sleeps alone. He may spend his days working with you and Dax, but a lot of that time he's also alone. So do *not* talk to me about what I do with Boone. It is none of your goddamn business."

"Yee-haw," he yelled, cocking back on his stool. "That, my dear Ms. Grant, is what I wanted to see. Some passion that's not about what he puts between your legs."

"Casper!" At Faith's gasp, both Casper and Everly turned. "What in the world is going on here? I thought this was an interview, not an inquisition."

Everly took a deep breath. "It's my fault—"

"I doubt that," Faith said, interrupting before Everly got out the rest of what she'd been going to say. "Casper? Explanation, please?"

"Where's Clay?"

"He's still at the bookstore. Kendall was busy, so I'm going back to get him at ten. Now, what's going on here?"

"I'm just looking out for your brother," he said, lifting his bottle to drink.

Faith grabbed it from his hand. "Boone? What's he got to

do with . . . Oh," she said, having got a look at the color heating Everly's face. She turned back to Casper. "And you have a problem with this, why?"

"I don't want to see the big man get hurt."

"Oh, cry me the Colorado River. You three cause each other more grief than any relationships with women ever could." She looked at Everly again. "Did you get what you needed for your story?"

"I got some. I could use more."

"And you'll have it," she said, and Casper groaned behind her. She reached back without looking and jabbed him in the chest. "I'll set it up. And I'll stick around to make sure this one behaves."

Everly looked over Faith's shoulder to where Casper sat pouting like a little boy who'd crossed a line. Or a man who knew he had a lot of groveling ahead of him.

And that made Everly smile.

# EIGHTEEN

BOONE WAS PARKED outside Everly's house when she pulled into her driveway. He knew she'd been talking to Casper. Knew that because he'd seen Clay with Faith on Main Street as the boy had parked Casper's truck in front of Sheppard's Books. He'd stopped to say hi as they'd climbed down, learned that Everly was at the house on Mulberry Street for Casper's interview.

What he didn't know was why he'd had to hear that from someone other than Everly. Granted, they hadn't made plans for tonight. They hadn't been making plans much at all. Except for his interview that had turned into sex for lunch in his bedroom, and supper at the Rainsong Cafe.

The rest of their time together had been spontaneous. His showing up at the paper to take her to lunch, grilling cheese sandwiches in her kitchen after exhausting them both in her bed. Her bringing a picnic out to the ranch last night, playing his piano, sitting with him while the sun went down.

They'd been doing a lot of eating. And they'd been doing a lot of talking, though he still couldn't believe he'd spilled his guts about his past with Les Upton a couple of days ago. Their winding up in bed following that tale had been a hell of a thing, one that had stayed with him long after.

This whole Upton business was getting out of hand. Darcy seeing him parked on the road between Crow Hill and Fever Tree was no big deal. The man owned a wrecker service, and there was a bend there that too many people took too fast. Les knew where he'd find the most wrecks, just like Ned Orleans knew his speed trap there would help him meet the county's ticket quota that he swore was an urban legend.

That's all it was. A coincidence. Les out doing what he called a job, and Darcy unfortunately spotting him. Boone seeing him outside the Blackbird Diner, that was no more suspicious, even though explaining to Nora Stokes why he'd shot out of there had required some storytelling his folks would not have liked.

Climbing down from his truck as Everly left her SUV, he headed up the driveway toward her, arriving at her kitchen door to find her fighting the lock with her key. "Need some help?"

"I've got it," she bit off, biting again with an annoyed, "What are you doing here?"

"Waiting for you. You know, like the other night you waited for me." Though maybe he shouldn't have. She didn't like hovering, or anything unexpected. Except for him. She had said she liked him. "I figured once you finished with Casper, you'd be coming back here."

"You knew I was with Casper?"

"I saw Faith in town."

"And you've been here how long?"

She finally got the key in the lock. He watched as she fought to turn it. "Since then."

"Why didn't you come over to Casper's?"

"I didn't want to get in the way."

"So you decided to sit out here?"

"I can go," he said, taking a step in reverse. He was obviously in the way of something, and he could be in his own way at home without getting lip about it.

"You don't have to go," she said, waving a hand as the door pushed open. "Just . . . come in."

He followed her inside, tossed his hat to the table, and crossed the room in case she preferred he keep his distance. And thinking that left him wondering if he shouldn't just go. "How was Casper's interview?"

"Fine."

She cut into the word so sharply he knew it hadn't gone fine at all. Meaning more than likely it wasn't his showing up unannounced that had set her off. "Everly?"

"What?" She stood with her back to him, staring into her refrigerator, as if she'd find a way to avoid his question behind the cheese and the wine.

"How did Casper's interview go?"

"I said *fine*," she repeated with a snap as she straightened, turned, and shoved her hands into her hair.

He crossed his arms, leaned a shoulder on the frame of her kitchen door. "You won't mind if I don't exactly believe you."

"Believe what you want," she said, letting her hair fall and slamming the fridge.

Yeah . . . this wasn't about her being annoyed at him for showing up unannounced. He'd bet, well, the ranch on it.

"What did he say? Because I know Casper. And if you're react-ing like this—"

"Like what?" she asked, her brown eyes popping.

"Really?" He arched a brow. "You're going to make me put it into words?"

"You might as well. It's not like I haven't been called a bitch before."

He wanted to beat the shit outta himself for going there. "You haven't been called one by me. And you won't be. I figure if you've got a burr up your butt, Casper put it there."

"You could say that," she said, then blew out a long slow breath.

He moved toward the table, pulled a chair out from be-neath. "Then come sit down and tell me about it."

She took a couple of steps toward him then stopped. "I'm not sure I want to."

"Why's that?"

She shook her head, let it fall back on her shoulders. "Be-cause things went south when talk turned to you. And I jumped all over Casper because of it."

Okay. This needed a lot more explanation. "Why did you talk about me during your interview with Casper?"

"I didn't. Or I didn't until he basically asked me what my intentions were toward you."

*Calf nuts on a cracker.* "Criminy."

She looked at him then, her head canted to the side. "Your partner is afraid that I'm taking you for a ride."

That would've been funny if Boone hadn't stuck his nose in Casper's relationship. "I guess he doesn't understand that I like that you are."

"Is that what you think? That I'm . . . using you for sex?"

Wait a minute. Wasn't she the one who'd made a point to tell him she had hang-ups and didn't want anything more? "You and I are having a really good time together. And that good time includes a lot of really good sex. But none of that is any of Casper's business. And I'll remind him of that in the morning."

"Don't do that," she said—no, she whined.

*Women.* "But you just said—"

"I didn't say for you to go try and fix anything for me." Still whining. He waited for her to stomp her foot, thinking that would fit here. "I just told you what he said because I needed to get it off my chest."

"Me reminding him of what's his business and what's not is just as much about me as you. He's my brother-in-law as well as my business partner. And he needs a reminder."

She blew out an exhausted breath. "I don't want him thinking I came tattling to you so you'd go out and beat him up or whatever."

*Casper Jayne could use a beating.* "What's wrong with running to me?"

"I'm an adult. I can take care of myself."

"No one said you can't. But it's okay to lean a little bit. To ask for help."

"Yes, but not for something like this."

"Like what?" he asked, because he needed to be sure what she was saying.

"Like Casper . . . hurting my feelings," she said, mumbling the last words and turning away.

Is that what this was? She'd let Casper get to her? "C'mere," he said, circling the table and reaching for her.

She dropped her gaze to the floor, scuffed the toe of another very expensive shoe against the tiles. "I'm being dumb."

"No you're not. You're being honest," he said, hooking an arm around her neck and bringing her close. "I like that."

"I don't know why," she said, and pouted. "It's really pretty pathetic."

"Hey, you," he said, brushing the pad of his thumb over a speck of loose makeup at the corner of her eye. "There's nothing pathetic about standing up for yourself."

"But over something so insignificant—"

"It's important to you," he said, stepping back and nudging up her chin. "That makes it significant."

"You're just saying that because you're hoping to get laid."

"I am hoping to get laid." The smell of dew on grass rose from her hair and he breathed deep. "But I'm saying that because it's true. I don't like hearing you rag on yourself for something that hurt. Even if it seems like something small."

She shrugged. "I'll get over it."

"You don't need to get over it. Own it. And then let me make you feel better."

He leaned down, brushed his lips over hers once, twice, waited for her to relax and join him here in the moment, to leave her confrontation with Casper behind. It took her longer than he'd thought it might, yet he didn't push, he just kissed her, moving his mouth along her jaw to her ear, nuzzling his cheek to hers, his chin against her neck, his beard rough.

She shivered, once, twice, and reached for his hand, bringing it up to cover her breast. "Feel that?"

He nodded, skated the flat of his palm over her hard nipple, his cock twitching.

"Your beard does that every time. The way it scratches."

"Then I promise never to shave before seeing you. If you like it that much."

"I do. It tickles, but it's so much more. Like you're scraping every one of my nerve endings. And when you're between my legs . . ."

"I've wondered about that. If it hurts. I'm pretty sure I wouldn't want to feel it rubbing against my business."

"You never know. You might love it."

He wouldn't, but no need to press the point. He liked her skin, her face, her lips and mouth and tongue. He liked soft and wet and insistent, and she gave him everything, gave him all of it. Gave him so much pleasure he doubted she knew. "I'd much rather have *you* rubbing against me."

She reached down to fondle the bulge in his jeans. "Like this?"

The sound that came out of his mouth was a soft moan. The one rumbling up from his gut was not soft at all. "Do it again," he said, and she squeezed and he moaned, and she squeezed even longer this time, her mouth seeking out his, her tongue finding his, her body melting into his, charming, lustful, a mix of so many tenors and tones he was drunk with it.

"Should we take this to the bedroom?" he asked, his lips at her ear.

"I don't want to move," she told him, moving anyway, her thighs on his, her fingertips in his hair. She stepped into him fully, crushing her breasts to his chest, lifting up onto her tiptoes to reach places her three-inch heels didn't.

He could've stayed where he was for hours, except for the fact that he couldn't get to her the way he wanted, and so he bent his knees, cupped the backs of her thighs, and picked her up. Her legs went around his waist and on his way from the kitchen to the living room, her shoes fell, one then the other, leaving him with her skinny blue pants and a host of buttons holding her blouse in place.

She giggled as she kissed his neck, one arm hooked around it, the other massaging tiny circles on his scalp and making it hard to walk. He reached the living room, found the couch and

backed up to it, falling down and taking her with him to straddle his lap.

"We probably shouldn't be doing this," she said, her arms
still around his neck as he started in on her buttons.

He was frowning when he asked, "Why not?"

"The riding thing. Me on your lap. I don't want to prove
Casper right."

"Fuck Casper. And fuck your buttons."

She looked down to his hands, back up to his eyes. Hers
blazed. "It's an old blouse."

"That so," he said, thinking what it would sound like to
send two dozen tiny crystal buttons flying across her hardwood floor. "Still looks like someone could get some good use
from it."

"You could be that someone."

"Yeah?"

He placed a finger in the hollow of her throat, ran it down
the long line of buttons. She shivered when he crossed the valley between her breasts, shivered again when he dipped into
her belly button. Her last shiver came when he reached the end
of the line, the final button, the hem of the long blouse falling
to a V between her spread legs.

He toyed with the button there, holding it with his index
finger and rolling it side to side against her mound. She closed
her eyes, let her head fall back. A shudder ran through her, and
he watched it happen . . . watched her throat work, her nipples draw tight, her chest rise and fall as she tried to breathe.
He was having just as much trouble breathing, and it was all
because of seeing her, feeling her, the changes in her body as
she readied to take him.

He was ready to take her. Lust felt like fingers dragging over
the skin of his thighs, like teeth nipping along the trail of hair

down the center of his stomach. Like lips squeezing the head of his cock. Like a tongue pushing up between his balls. All that, and he hadn't even touched her. Just her damn button, playing it like he would her clit, and against her clit, making her writhe in his lap.

With his free hand, he reached between her legs, drawing the long side of his fingers up the seam of her pants and that of her pussy's lips. She was hot and damp and he pushed up into her, moving back and forth, flicking over what parts of her he could feel through the cloth.

She shoved her fingers into his hair and tugged, pulling his head back so he had to look up at her. "Take off my clothes. All of them. I want to be naked with you."

"You sure about the blouse being old."

"It is, but I wouldn't care if it wasn't."

"And the rest?"

"Take them off. Ruin them if you have to. Then ruin me. And hurry."

Criminy, but he didn't know what to say. He knew what she was asking for, but he didn't know what was driving her need. He wanted to take the time to care, but he couldn't. Not with the way she was looking at him, a heated expectation, a powerful need. And not after telling him just yesterday that she'd liked it when he'd lost control the last time they were in bed.

He gripped the hem of her blouse beneath the last button, gripped it hard, ground his jaw, and tore. The buttons scattered as he'd expected, pinging and clattering and bouncing across the living room, disappearing under furniture, hitting walls, rolling. He'd have to remember to look where he was stepping when he got up, but for now, nothing mattered except getting her out of her clothes.

Her chest was rising and falling when she shrugged off her

top. It fell to the floor behind her, and he pulled her toward him, reaching for the hooks of her bra as he buried his face in her tits. He breathed her in, flowers and grasses and woodsy streams, and sex. Hot skin and anticipation and serious liquid lust.

She pulled her arms free from her straps, found his head, and held him while he moved from one side to the other, tonguing her nipples, biting down, sucking her into his mouth. Working at the zipper of her pants while doing that, frustration rising as quickly as his cock. *Ruin* the only word that came to mind.

He yanked at both sides of the fabric, and the zipper tore away, creating a gap between her body and her pants. He slid one hand down over her ass, finding his way around to her hip, and inside her thong, and to the lips of her pussy and her clit. She squirmed to the side, making room for him between her legs, and he pushed a finger into her, and she ground down against him, gasping, her hands on his shoulders as she tossed back her head and moaned.

It wasn't enough, this partial touching of her, and he pulled free of her pussy and dug in his pocket for his knife. When she saw what he was doing, her eyes went wide, and her whole body went still. She held her bottom lip between her teeth, raised her arms to the top of her head and the pile she'd made of her hair, her tits bouncing in front of him.

He held her pants away from her stomach and used the tip of the blade to nick a spot he then split a bit further. Done with the knife, he grabbed tight and tore, rending the front of her pants from the waist to the crotch. He didn't need any help ripping the fabric of her thong out of the way. That left her wearing rags on both legs, the rest of her body bare.

"Make me come," she said, her mouth finding his, her

tongue mating with his, his fingers finding her cunt and pushing deep. She kissed him, held his face with both hands, licking and stroking while he fingered her. Two fingers. Three. His
thumb on her clit, rolling the nub, his free hand twisting her
nipple as she rode his hand and groaned.

Her skin was flushed and salty, her pussy wet and tight. Her
mouth was hungry. His mouth was hungry. His cock bound by
his clothes and straining. He needed to be inside her, to pound
away this infernal need gripping him by the balls.

He pulled his mouth from hers and moved to her tits, sucking one nipple, then the other, both his hands now between her
legs, his fingers fucking her and rubbing her, pressing and
pinching and helping her climb. She clawed at his shoulders,
grinding down, tightening.

He felt her muscles contract seconds before she cried out
and let go, shuddering, collapsing, her naked body beautiful,
her pleasure nearly killing him. Easing his hands from her
body, he wrapped one arm around her and swiveled, tumbling
her to the couch. Then he stood only long enough to shove his
jeans to his knees before he covered her where she waited.

Cock in hand, he found her tight hole and pushed in. All the
way in. He left nothing of himself behind. None of himself
bare of her. With his face buried in the tangle of hair at her
neck, he breathed her in, finally moving when he couldn't *not*
move, when her fingers began to trip up and down his spine.

He rolled his hips slowly, feeling her, all of her, his cock
slick with her cream. And hot. So fucking hot. The heat got to
him. The suction of her cunt. Milking him. Skin on skin. Slick
and swollen and like a band squeezing him from the base of his
shaft to the skin of the head as he stroked.

He was done. All in and done. He shoved into her, lifted his
head and his upper body, his abs contracting, cum shooting in

bursts like gunshots triggered from the base of his spine. And then it hit him.

For the first time in sixteen years, the first time since the night he'd sworn his dick would never touch a pussy unsheathed, he hadn't used a condom.

He was fucked in so many ways he didn't know what to do.

# NINETEEN

"KNOCK, KNOCK," FAITH said, her knuckles rapping on Everly's open door. "Got a minute?"

Everly looked back at her screen. It was Saturday. Her day off. Her day to do whatever she wanted, even if that meant nothing but drinking wine on her back porch and reading a book. Instead, she'd come into the office because all she'd been doing at home was pacing and staying mad, at herself and at Casper, and thinking Boone had ruined her. Just like she'd asked. Her clothes. Her body. Possibly her heart.

At least at the office she had work to keep her mind off all of those things. Or so had been the plan. "Not if it's about Casper."

"It's about Casper," Faith said, coming in anyway, having obviously seen Everly's SUV in the rear lot.

"Leave the door open," Everly said, before Faith shut it all the way. And then it hit her how she sounded. It wasn't even her being defensive. It was her being rude. It was her being the bitch Boone had refused to call her. What in the world was wrong with her? "I'm sorry. I didn't mean to bark."

"Ev, listen to me. I don't want you to think twice about anything he said, or take it to heart, because it was just Casper being Casper and blowing off steam. Now," she said, stopping to take a deep breath. "Can you take off the rest of the day and let me buy you a drink or five?"

Five sounded good. She liked the number five. And she liked no-nonsense Faith because she made it impossible to stay mad. "Only if we drink someplace where we won't have to worry about getting home after."

"Like my place? Or your place? Or Arwen's?"

"I vote for Kendall's store."

"Perfect. When I was there last night with Clay, Kendall mentioned having nothing on tonight's calendar. I'll make sure she's okay with all of us descending on the store. And I'll call Arwen and tell her to meet us."

"That gives me time to wrap up here." Not that she had anything to wrap up. She'd been shopping at Amazon. Not working. "I'll meet you there in . . . twenty minutes?"

"Make it thirty. I'll run by the house and grab a blender, and I should have plenty of margarita mix in the freezer. I'll see if Arwen can supply the booze."

"And maybe nachos?"

"Sounds like a party to me."

Faith flounced out of the office, looking happier than Everly had ever seen her. Whether that newfound joy was the result of the other woman's relationship with Casper, or finally walking away from a career she'd never wanted, Everly didn't know.

What she did know was that she wanted to feel that care-free, her past in the past and not bouncing up when she wasn't looking to mess with what was a pretty perfect present. Would Faith have found herself without first finding Casper? Or were the two events dependent on each other?

And was Everly missing out on something equally life changing by keeping her affair with Boone emotion free?

She'd sworn when leaving Austin she would never be a victim again, and being with Boone, she hadn't once gotten the sense she was anything but cherished. That she was important to him. That he wanted to be with her and do for her because he enjoyed her.

Even early in her relationship with Toby, she hadn't felt as important to him as she already felt to Boone. She wasn't particularly proud of what that said of her choice to stay with Toby as long as she had, but dwelling on it only made her miserable.

She was damn tired of letting Toby make her miserable.

Pushing aside thoughts that were hurting more than helping, she shut down her computer and packed up her things, ready for a night on the town—or at least a night in the bookstore's comfy reading room with her friends. Locking up and leaving her SUV parked behind the newspaper office, she set off to walk the few short blocks through downtown, loving the peace and quiet.

At the far end of Main Street she could see the flash of red taillights as vehicles braked to pull into the Hellcat Saloon. It would be the same behind her, she knew; though the Blackbird Diner was smaller and closed earlier, it would still be full, as would the Dairy Barn out near the high school.

Saturday night in ranching country was a far cry from what she'd known in Austin, she mused, stopping at the corner as a tow truck cruised Main Street in front of her. Camino's, the only real bar in town, was more of a beer joint and pool hall, and from what she'd been able to tell, it did less business than

Arwen's. There were no clubs for dancing, no lounges for wine or cigars, no sofa rooms for casual hookups.

Having drinks with her girlfriends at Kendall's store was the closest thing to a girls' night out she could get in Crow Hill. And she didn't mind at all. In fact, she could probably live the rest of her life and never miss the lights or the noise or the crush of bodies Saturday nights brought to Austin's 6th Street.

She glanced the other direction, checking for traffic, then looked back and went completely still. A shiver ran through her as she realized what she'd just seen—and whom the tow truck belonged to. It was too far away now to make out the driver, but even from this distance the sign across the back window clearly said *Upton's Garage.*

Was this a coincidence? His driving by while she was walking to Kendall's? He couldn't have known where she was going; she hadn't known until a half hour ago. Had he been circling the block, stalking her, waiting for her to leave the *Reporter*'s office? Surely not. What reason would he have to harass her?

Hurrying across the street to the alley behind the buildings, she ran as fast as her stupid shoes would allow to the bookstore's back door. Kendall answered her frantic knock and drew her into a hug, then stepped free to close the door. Faith stood at the back room's counter, assembling her blender and lining up glasses.

"Is Arwen going to make it?" Everly asked as she crossed to the corner bathroom, needing a moment to catch her breath, though pretending what she needed was a mirror to straighten her blouse and her hair. "Her parking lot looks like she's got a full house." *Deep breath. Deep breath. Deep breath.*

"She said she'd be down soon," Faith called in answer. "She's got extra staff on for the evening so didn't think she'd have a problem getting away."

And yet months ago, before Dax had come into Arwen's life, Everly mused, leaning forward to clear away a smear of mascara, the other woman wouldn't have left the saloon in the hands of anyone else on a Saturday night. Talk about the changes a man could make in a girl's life . . .

"I'm so glad y'all were in the mood to do this," Kendall said. "I was not looking forward to going upstairs to spend another Saturday night alone. It sucks being single in a town where the only meat market really is a meat market."

"You know," Faith said, glancing over her shoulder as Everly switched off the bathroom light, "I think tonight would be the perfect night for you to tell us what in the world made you open a bookstore in Crow Hill. Because really. Crow Hill?"

Kendall laughed. "It's not that big a deal. I'm happy to tell you. I'm surprised I *haven't* told you."

"I'm surprised, too, but wait for Arwen. She'll want to hear the story."

"If you're expecting a tale of intrigue and deceit, you're going to be sorely disappointed."

"Someone's been reading too many of her own books," Faith said to Everly in an aside, as a knock on the back door sounded.

Everly jumped. Faith frowned. Kendall looked from one to the other then went to open it, quickly relieving Arwen of one of the boxes she held. "Thank you. I should've just made two trips instead of trying to get everything inside in one."

Lifting the box to her face, Kendall breathed deep of the spicy aromas. "I don't know what this is, but I want it now. I'm starving."

"It's the makings for nachos. Faith placed the order. And this," she said, setting the other box on the floor and coming up with two bottles. "Tequila and ice for four."

Faith grabbed one and went to work mixing drinks, while Everly laid out four plates on the countertop, and Kendall did the same with the food. Minutes later, all four women were laughing their way through the nacho assembly line.

Balancing plates and glasses, and Faith the pitcher of margaritas, they left the private back room for the public reading area—a large square in one corner of the store lit by low-burning lamps on end tables piled high with books. The fringed shades cast a golden glow over the hardwood floor and the braided rag rug centered in the circle of sofas and chairs.

Arwen and Everly claimed the two ends of one sofa. Kendall curled up in a huge wingback chair. Faith stretched out on a wickedly plush chaise lounge. They spent the next two hours discussing everything under the sun—Everly's shoes, and Faith's plans for Casper's home-theater room, and Arwen's new kitchen table ordered from a furniture builder in Hope Springs, and Kendall's decision to open a store in Crow Hill.

Halfway through their second batch of margaritas, with the plates of nachos decimated, Arwen tucked her feet beneath her and turned into the corner of the sofa to face Everly. "Darcy mentioned to Dax that Les Upton's been causing Boone some grief."

"What?" Faith's gaze swung from Arwen to Everly. "Is that right?"

Everly shrugged, thinking it interesting that they all turned to her when she and Boone weren't an official couple. "Darcy saw his tow truck a couple weeks back. He was parked off the road outside the Rainsong Cafe. But he was gone by the time Boone and I left, so if he's been giving Boone grief, I'm not aware."

"Someone needs to burn down his garage, run him out of town."

Arwen gasped. "Faith!"

"Oh, I'm not going to do it." Faith fluttered a hand. "Or even pay someone to do it, though on this side of two pitchers of drinks, doing so sounds like a very good idea."

"I saw him earlier," Everly said, and all three women turned to look at her, grilling her with shouted *what*s and *when*s and *what did you do*s. "When I was walking over from the paper. His truck was on Main Street. I was waiting at the corner to cross the street, and he drove by."

"Did he say anything?" Arwen asked.

"What did *you* say?" Faith asked.

"I didn't do or say anything," she said with a shrug, glancing at Kendall whose eyelids kept drifting closed. "He was already past when I realized it was a truck from his garage. And I don't even know if he was driving."

"I can't believe he's still in business," Arwen said. "And he would've been driving. He doesn't employ anyone else anymore."

"I can't believe he didn't get a shiv to the throat in prison," Faith said. "After what he put his family and my brother through, he deserved it."

Arwen slid from the couch to the floor and reached for the pitcher to refill her glass. "Did you ever hear what happened to Lucinda and Penny?"

Faith was the one to answer. "I think Lucinda went to stay with relatives after she was released from the hospital. I imagine Penny went with her. I thought I'd heard she'd come back to town, but that was a while ago, and if she did, I haven't seen her."

Everly wasn't sure why she found that interesting, but she made a mental note to find out what Penny had been up to, and if it might hurt Boone. Though why the other woman would want to cause him trouble all these years later . . . "I think I've had too much to drink."

"And I'm pretty sure there's no such thing," Kendall said, joining Arwen, prone on the floor.

There was when her thoughts were going crazy places. "Then maybe I should have one more margarita," she said, upending the rest of the pitcher into her glass. "In case you're right."

"She's right," Faith said, and that was that.

BOONE HAD JUST stepped into the ranch house kitchen Saturday night when the phone rang. Thinking it might be Everly, he grabbed it without looking at the display and said, "My place or yours?"

"Thanks for the offer, but I'm gonna be sticking close to the house tonight."

"Casper. What's up?" And how the hell was he already back in town?

"You got anything going on tonight?"

"Since you turned down my offer, not a thing but feeding my face and a shower," he said, staring at the lone stick of butter occupying the space in his fridge. Tomorrow, after Sunday supper, he had to buy groceries.

"Why don't you skip the food and come to town?"

*Criminy.* Gas money did not grow on trees. "I don't want—"

"Dax is on his way. We'll be at Sheppard's Books."

Boone shook his head, trying to make sense out of Casper's lack. "I don't need anything to read—"

"Everly's here. Drunk off her ass along with Kendall, Arwen, and Faith."

Boone straightened, slamming his head into the freezer door that had magically come open. "What the hell?"

"They had some kind of girlfriend drink-along or something.

Must've killed a pitcher of margaritas apiece, judging by the tequila empties. The reading room at the back of the store looks like, well, some kind of brothel. Who knows what madness went on here, though I'm goddamn sorry I missed it."

Rubbing at the back of his head, Boone couldn't decide between laughing and groaning and wishing he'd been there to see it all, too. Get a few glasses of wine into Everly, and the woman was saying yes even before he got out his requests. Switch her favorite drink for Faith's favorite tequila . . . "Give me thirty minutes."

"She ain't going anywhere. None of 'em are. I'm thinking of setting up cameras and my own YouTube channel in case they stir. And you can probably make a meal out of the leftover Mexican food in the back room."

"Thirty, I said." His stomach grumbling, he slammed down the phone, wishing he could skip the shower, but the dried cow shit soaked through the knees of his jeans made that impossible.

Dax was with Casper at the bookstore by the time Boone arrived. 'Course Dax only had a few blocks to travel, while Boone had a trip—one he'd be making in reverse with Everly. He didn't want to leave her at her place alone, and he had work in the morning.

Casper had gotten inside by using Clay's key. The kid did some part-time work for Kendall, leaving Boone to wonder if the boy would be the one to clean up this mess, because wow. Whatever had gone on here, a lot of spleens had been vented. Though what these four women all had to be riled up about . . .

Yeah, that would most likely be men.

He looked down at Everly where she lay on her stomach, stretched out on a sofa, one hand holding an empty glass above her head, one knee tucked close. Her hair spilled across her back, and her shoes that had cost more than he had in the bank were stuck between the sofa's arm and a cushion. Through it all, she was smiling.

That smiled grabbed his gut and his groin and twisted. "We just gonna stand around until they wake up, or what?"

"Only if you still want to be standing here come lunchtime tomorrow," Casper said, hunkering next to the lounge where Faith lay passed out and tucking her hair behind her ear.

"What about Kendall?" Dax asked, nodding toward the floor where she and Arwen were spooning like hot lesbians in love. "She's got an apartment upstairs, I think Arwen said. Should we take her up there, or let her sleep it off here, or what?"

"I'd feel better not leaving her alone," Boone said. "Even if this is where she lives."

Casper was nodding as he thought. "We've got plenty of room and aspirin at the house. One of you help me get her in the truck, then Clay can help me get her out."

"Sounds like a plan," Dax said, squatting to scoop Arwen off the floor. She flopped against him, and he used a knee to adjust her while he found his balance.

Casper took care of Faith, while Boone saw to Kendall, laying her in Casper's backseat before going back for Everly. He got her into his front seat, then made another trip to the store. Dax returned, too, and looked around the room. "We just gonna leave all this?"

"I'm not stopping to clean," Boone said, though he did grab the box with the tortilla chips and containers of beans, guacamole, and *queso*.

"Faith can damn well give Clay a bonus to take care of it," Casper said from the doorway. "Let's get outta here."

Nodding, Boone shut off the lights as Casper locked up, heading for his truck and Everly. Before he could climb in, he had to move her out of his seat. And once he was settled, she curled up against him, her head falling back, her eyes fluttering open.

"Hi," she said, her hand sliding across his chest, her fingers toying with his snaps. "I've been waiting for you all my life."

"That so?" Would've been nice to be able to believe her, but he knew well the voice of booze. "Looks to me like you didn't wait for much of anything tonight."

"I waited for Faith to come get me from the paper before I started drinking. And I waited for Arwen to bring the nachos and tequila before I started drinking."

Yeah. Hard to do much drinking without any drink. "So this is Arwen's fault?"

"Faith brought the blender. Arwen brought the ice. Kendall and I brought a great big margarita thirst. Usually I drink wine. Have I told you how much I love wine?"

"No," he said, rolling his eyes. "How much do you love wine?"

"I love wine like God loved Abraham. That much, is how much I love it." She looped her arms around his neck and hung there, swaying, her head coming up long enough for her to say, "But not as much as I love you."

The fact that she was drunk as a skunk didn't stop the words from punching a hole in his chest. Her rubbing against him as he drove deepened the hole. The reality that he'd been her first in four years, and she'd been his first with no condom in sixteen, well, he was going to need time to process where exactly the hole was going, because he didn't like this feeling of falling with no bottom to stop him.

"Where's your SUV?" he asked, as they left Crow Hill's city

limits to be swallowed up by the wide-open spaces' pitch-black night.

"It's at the paper."

"Faith give you a ride to the bookstore?"

"I walked over. Oh," she said, popping up. "I saw Les Upton."

"When did you see Les Upton?" he asked, because he was pretty sure she was mixing up reality with Margaritaville.

"Before I walked over. No. I mean, while I was walking over. He drove by on Main Street. I saw his truck. It said Upton's Garage on the back window. I wonder if he knows his turn signal is messed up. It's all fluttery and stuttery, like it can't decide if it really wants to work or is just playing at it."

*Motherfucker.* That sounded like a pretty damn specific sighting, complete with drunken mechanical commentary. Especially since he'd seen the same truck recently and knew that blinker.

Suddenly he was really glad he was taking her back to the ranch, and that she wasn't spending the night at home alone, no matter all her lights and her locks meant to keep danger at bay.

# TWENTY

"**B**OONE?" EVERLY SAID, pushing up onto her elbows in his bed. "What am I doing here?"

From the stuffed side chair where he sat pulling on his boots, he said, "Sleeping off one of the best drunks I've ever seen."

"Feels like one of the worst," she said, dropping back to the pillows.

"Best. Worst." He stood, shaking the legs of his jeans into place. "Pretty much the same thing when it comes to a drunk."

She groaned, pressing the heels of her hands into both eye sockets. "I don't have your experience, so I'll have to take your word for it."

He reached for the glass of water and the two aspirin he'd left for her on the nightstand. Then he sat beside her and propped her up. "Here. These may not help, but they won't hurt. And finish the water. All of it."

"I'm not sure I can keep it down," she said, taking the pills from between his thumb and forefingers, the glass from his hand.

"Then throw it up. There's always more where that came from."

He thought she tried to give him an evil eye, but couldn't tell because her whole face had scrunched up against the sunlight streaming in through his window. It was nearly ten. He'd been up before dawn, leaving her a note before riding out to take care of what chores couldn't wait till Monday.

Most could, but there was always something pressing. And he'd needed some space to get over the memory of her drunkenly admitting she loved him.

"I've gotta be at my folks' for Sunday supper in a couple of hours. You're welcome to come along, or you can stay here, or I can drop you by your place. Just let me know."

"Do you want me to come with you? To Sunday . . . supper?" she asked, and he could almost hear her stomach roiling at the thought of food. "Will Faith be there?"

"I'd love for you to, but maybe another Sunday would be better. And yeah. She will," he said, taking the empty glass from her hand.

"Another Sunday probably would," she said, resting her cheek on her updrawn knees, her bra strap falling over her shoulder. "But I don't have plans for today, and if Faith can be stoically hungover, then so can I."

"C'mon then." He stood, tossed back the sheet and blanket, and reached for her hand. "I'll take you home, help you shower, and if you're not feeling any better, I'll head over alone."

She swallowed, her throat working against the words as much as the water and aspirin as she swung her legs over the side of the bed. "I don't like you being alone."

"I don't like it either," he said, giving voice to the truth for the first time. "It's been nice this last week having you around, having someone to talk to who's not a cow or a horse or Casper or Dax. Having someone to sleep with, and I don't just mean the sex."

"Did you sleep here last night? With me?" she asked, fixing her fallen bra strap. "I'm so embarrassed that I have to ask."

"I did, but nothing happened. I did have to nudge you over a couple of times."

"God." She grimaced, pushing her hair from her face. "Was I touching you again?"

That brought the first smile of the morning to his face. "You were snoring."

She gasped. "What? I do not snore."

"Oh, yes. You do. Big time."

"Now I want to cry," she said, sniffling. "It's too soon in this relationship for you to see me at my worst."

She'd said *relationship*. He wondered if she even realized it, or if it had been a slip. "Hey, first night we spent under the same roof, I was drunk off my ass. Figure it makes us even. Except for the touching part."

"I still can't believe I told you about that," she said, and cringed.

"That you told me, or that you touched me."

"Told you."

"So the touching me . . ."

Her gaze came up to meet his, all liquid and sober and soft. "It's not hard at all to believe I did that."

Her admission took up all the space between them, growing into something big and living and grabbing him by the throat. He'd been doing fine up till now. He hadn't thought much at all about getting her home last night, getting her undressed, sleeping with her, breathing her skin and her hair. Or about her tucking her hands between his legs because she'd been cold and said he was warm.

Now all he could think about was getting out of this room before the heat consuming him led to something she wasn't up for.

"How about you get dressed. Your pants and blouse, all buttons intact, are on the back of the chair here. Your shoes underneath on the floor. I'll meet you downstairs," he said, and she nodded. "Good. Do that, and we'll go."

For most of the drive from the ranch to Crow Hill, Everly slept, her legs crooked beneath her, the crocheted throw from his bedroom chair covering her, her body curled into his side. He drove with one hand, his other arm draped around her. It was all he could do to keep his eyes on the road and off her, how small she was on the truck seat next to him, how her hair fell like waves of wheat and prairie grass, and smelled like air filled with early morning sun.

*Calf nuts on a cracker.* What was he doing, paying attention to the way she smelled, and getting all poetic about it? She was a good time, the best time he'd had in forever, but he'd seen her house, her wardrobe. Her damn buttons and shoes. She belonged on a ranch about as much as he belonged in Austin. And the something that had happened to drive her here still bugged him, especially in light of her calling what they had a relationship. And her drunken admission of love.

She woke as he bumped into her driveway, holding her head and groaning as he fished her keys from her bag. Damn she had a lot of crap in her bag. Why did women need so much crap? He helped her out of the truck, and once he had the kitchen door opened, she wobbled her way up the steps. Then she wobbled her way through the room and out of sight down the hall.

He locked the door behind them, tossed her purse and his hat to the table, and followed, resigned to tucking her in and going to his parents alone. He found her standing and shivering in the middle of the bathroom, as if she didn't even have it in her to crawl into bed.

"Hey," he said, coming up behind her and placing his hands on her shoulders. "You need sleep. You can come to my folks for Sunday supper another time."

"No." She shook her head, pushed the mess of her hair from her face. "I want to go today. Just give me a minute to remember where I put myself."

"Then, c'mere," he said, sitting on the toilet lid and pulling her between his knees. He'd help her out of her clothes and into the tub then see if she still had the stomach for a day with his folks. "Let's get you in the shower."

"I can undress myself, you know."

"I know, but it's no fun for me that way. And since this is about the only fun I'm going to get for now, just relax. I got this."

She nodded, a shiver running through her when she did, when she laced her fingers behind her head to let him have his way.

He started with her shoes. He couldn't recall ever seeing her wear anything but three-inch stilettos, and couldn't recall seeing anyone else in Crow Hill ever wearing a pair. He liked what they did to her legs. To her ass and her tits. To her height. She never stumbled, and she walked with purpose, and it was hard to imagine her wearing anything else, even here in cow country.

He massaged the soles of her feet as he lowered them to her bath mat, rubbing her ankles, too, then working his way up her calves as he reached for the zipper at her waist and tugged it open, baring the scrap of her thong. He loved the feel of her skin, how smooth it was, and ran his palms over her hips and down her thighs, holding each lower leg in turn while she stepped out of her pants, her hand on his shoulder for balance.

He stood then, his hands between their bodies at the hem of her man's white dress shirt. Oh, he supposed it was a woman's shirt, but it looked like it needed a cummerbund and bow tie. She wore it beneath a shorter black vest, and at least that didn't have any buttons, because the shirt had more than a dozen, placed close together, all too tiny for his fingers to handle with anything resembling dexterity. He knew that because he'd fought only enough of them last night to pull the shirt off over her head.

"I spend all day using my hands," he said. "Nail guns and fence-wire stretchers and posthole diggers. I saddle my horse, get her bridle on and off without so much as a nip. I vaccinate cattle, treat calves for pinkeye. And I can't work these buttons worth a damn."

"I can do it," she said, covering his hands with hers.

"I know you can. But I want to. Consider it my personal holy grail." Since his ever getting through a set without giving in to frustration was pretty much impossible. "Though why you have this thing for buttons, I'll never understand."

Her grin, for all her feeling like she'd been strapped for twelve hours on the back of a buckin' bronc, was tender, gentle, as soft as her skin. And then she cupped his cheek with her palm. "You are a sweet man, Boone Mitchell. Why aren't you settled down with a half dozen little ranchers at your feet and a wife to take care of who treats you like you deserve?"

He frowned as he busied himself up the line of her buttons, wondering if he'd scare her off by admitting that was exactly what he wanted. A family. A brood of his own. His sons and daughters with him on horseback, all of them working the Mitchell spread. A woman at his side, and yeah, in his kitchen. He liked the idea of eating a woman's cooking, helping her clean up after, tucking in the little ones while she waited in their bed. He wanted a woman to sleep with, to love with, to be his mate and his equal partner.

"Haven't had the time," is what he finally said, though that simple excuse encompassed a whole lot of complications he wasn't sure he wanted to talk about, or could make her understand. Not that she needed to, or would want to, but his life was a hard one, and he didn't feel right asking a woman to share what he sometimes found too much to take. If that made him sexist, fine, but he couldn't bring himself to put someone he loved through the same hell that had him thinking of throwing in the towel.

"Time? To do what?" she insisted after letting his comment settle. "Find a woman to court? Do the courting? Does ranching take up that much of your life?"

He grunted. "Enough that I had to bring you home with me last night because I had chores this morning that couldn't wait."

"You didn't have to bring me home with you. I would've been fine here alone. You should've told Dax or Casper to drop me off. You shouldn't even have come to town."

"I didn't want you to stay alone. I wanted to make sure you were okay."

"I've lived here alone for four years. Why wouldn't I be okay?"

He really didn't have an answer for that, so just continued his way up the row of the tiniest buttons man had ever seen fit to make.

"This is why you'll make some lucky woman the perfect husband one day."

He grunted again, wondering if in her head she'd added the words *it just won't be me* as he finished with the buttons and pushed her blouse off her shoulders, following with her bra. She stood naked, disheveled, still a little bit drunk, and absolutely beautiful. Something sharp hitched in his midsection, like he'd taken a hit steer wrestling, or walked behind the business end of a horse.

Stupid, letting her comment about him being sweet send him off down this road. It was nearing lunch, and he was not missing the day with his family. He'd like Everly to share it with him, but either way, he was done wasting time. He reached into the tub enclosure and turned on the water, adjusting the temperature before switching the flow to the shower head.

Then he leaned against the counter to tug off his boots. The first one hit the tile floor, followed by the second and earning him a wide-eyed look from the woman standing naked, doing nothing else, but giving him hell all the same.

"What're you doing?" she asked, her gaze drifting to the front of his shirt along with his hands, her whole body flinching when he jerked at the snaps, then dropped the shirt to the floor.

"I'm going to give you a bath," he said, losing his jeans, shorts, and socks in rapid order, then pulling aside the curtain and gesturing for her to get in.

"You know I feel like crap," she said, looking much the same, her makeup smeared, dark circles hugging her eyes, her hair a cape of tangles and gorgeous all the same.

"I know," he said, nudging her to step into the tub, holding her upper arm as she did, as she shivered when the water first hit her back, as she huddled beneath the spray and shook.

"That means no sex," she told him, her eyes closing as he

stepped in, too, pulling the curtain closed, bringing her bare body against his for added warmth.

"This isn't about sex," he told her, holding her until she stopped trembling. "Not everything has to be."

"Then what?"

Did she really think there was only one outcome to their being naked together? "It's about me taking care of you for once. Just for a little while. Do you think you can let me do that?"

She shook her head against his chest, her hair wet where it fell over his hands on her back, her hands clenched tightly between them. "I can try."

"Good girl," he said, reaching for the sponge she kept on a shelf, and the bottle of bath gel beneath it, working up a lather, then turning them both so his back was beneath the spray.

She lifted her arms when he pushed for her to, stacking them on top of her head. The motion lifted her tits, too, and he told his dick not to look. But she was beautiful, pale with dark centers, and it was hard not to bend down and taste her, to toy with her and tongue her, to use his teeth until she moaned.

Instead, he soaped her shoulders and her throat and her armpits, bathed her breasts and her ribs and her arms, turning her again so he could wash her back, and then so he could wash her ass. Again he had to tell his dick this was one of those times it had to bide, that better times would be found down the road, but having had such a good time with this woman, none of his words took.

He began to thicken, and he bent to wash her feet and her legs, and she turned while he was down there, giving him her front, his face pussy-level, as if testing him, and damn if he was going to fail. Not this time. Not when his honor was out there.

His promise. And her need to be able to trust that he could keep his word.

Instead of the sponge, he used the soap in his hand to wash her there, sliding the long side of his fingers along the crease of both thighs, then parting her gently. He swallowed hard when she gasped, but he didn't linger, reaching for the shampoo as he stood. She stepped beneath the shower to rinse, wetting her hair again, then lifting her chin and leaning her head back toward him.

Watching as a kid when his mother had scrubbed Faith's in the sink was the only thing he knew about washing long hair, but he did his best, massaging her scalp, working the suds through the long, ropy strands. She rolled her head on her shoulders, to the left, to the right, shuddered as if from the pleasure of his hands, melting against him, her skin hot and slick and comforting.

The words *I could get used to this* came tumbling down along with the flow from the shower as she rinsed her hair, and he reached for her soap to wash up. They beat against him, making him weak when he was here to be strong, because that's what she needed right now. This wasn't the time nor the place for these feelings, these needs he kept buried to start reaching up, giving new life to dreams he was on the verge of letting go.

Moving around him to the rear of the tub, she twisted the water from her hair, then pulled open the curtain, the rings rattling on the rod as she did. She wrapped the first towel she grabbed around her head, the second around her body, then stepped out, and offered him the third.

The moment ticked, and he stayed where he was, watching confusion play out in her expression, until she lowered her hand and asked, "Boone?"

"I'm just going to . . . finish up in here."

He saw the moment the truth clicked on, her eyes going hooded and dark. "I can bathe you, you know."

He shook his head. "Not a good idea."

"Because of this?" she asked, reaching for his hard cock and stroking.

He closed his eyes, groaned and grimaced, trying to remember the assurances he'd made, the words he'd said to her, his code. "Because of this not being about sex."

"It can be."

"No. It can't."

"I want it to be."

"Not this time.

But she wasn't listening. Or she felt she owed him or something, and she dropped both of her towels, returning to the tub, closing the curtain, and bending over, her hands on the tub's corners, her ass pressed into his groin. "You did for me. Now let me do for you."

"Everly—"

She ground against him. "Please," she said, looking back at him over her shoulder, her eyes pleading, filled with a strange sense of urgency, as if his refusal would hurt her feelings, which didn't make any kind of sense.

He bent his knees, fisted his cock, and aligned their bodies, pushing into her, then grabbing her hips and rocking against her. He pounded hard. He pounded fast. Set a rhythm designed to do him in, the shower beating his back.

Water and soap slicked their skin as their thighs slipped and slid. Her moans filled the small enclosure; each time he hit bottom, she cried out. The sounds tore at his gut, driving him harder, making him angry because this was not what he wanted.

He loved it. He ached, and she felt so goddamn good, gripping him, tightening around him, squeezing him as if she could catch him and keep him from pulling away. He wanted to believe she was getting off, but knowing how sick she'd been, it was hard. He didn't want to be the only one here having fun, and he didn't want a tit-for-tat exchange.

But it was too late for much of anything but blowing his wad, and he slammed into her, bounced against her, his balls slapping her ass. His thighs were burning when he surged forward, his fingers digging into her hips as he came. He held her, squeezed her, shuddered as he shot all he had into her, nearly taking her feet off the tub's bottom, and knowing he was bruising her as he did.

Something about marking her left him feeling all kinds of caveman and he tightened his hold for one long moment before letting her go. She stood, stretching, turning into him and wrapping her arms around his neck and tugging his mouth to hers.

She kissed him, a soft press of lips, an even softer slide of her tongue, lifting up on her tiptoes, then using her hands on the back of his head to urge him down. He followed her lead, keeping the kiss tender, falling into it, into her, a deep connection he wasn't sure he understood.

This was supposed to be sex. No emotions. Yet the pull he felt told him he'd need to be bound in barbed wire instead of silk scarves for any such agreement to stick.

# TWENTY-ONE

BOONE WAS SILENT on the drive to his parent's home. Everly was silent, too. She still felt like crap, for one thing, but she was also dealing with the certainty that she'd done something wrong. That begging him for sex, *giving* him sex, insisting he use her body instead of his hand had changed things between them. And that was the strangest thing of all. That sex had been the very thing to bring emotions into play.

She wasn't used to this, having a man do for her, take care of her, see to her needs. Everything with Toby had been about him. His hunger came before anything else, determined everything else. With Boone, she initiated as many of their encounters as he did. He came along willingly, but it was almost as if he didn't want to suggest anything improper. That he didn't mind sharing a quiet picnic and back-porch beer.

That as much as he enjoyed the sex, he wanted to be with

her for reasons having nothing to do with her body, and he had to keep his emotions out of the equation because of it.

So here they were, enjoying one another physically, but neither one willing to invest anything else. Everly because she wanted less. Boone because he wanted more.

How had things become such a mess?

She knew how. Toby. She'd let him get into her head and push Boone out. And yet Toby was not the man she'd grown up dreaming about. The man she wanted to build a life with. The man she wanted for a partner. The way her parents were partners. The way Boone's parents were, too.

Her childhood had been perfect. She was the eldest sibling of four. Her parents never raised their voices to their children or to one another, and only raised their hands in fair discipline, not wanting to spoil the child by sparing the rod. There had been food on the table, clothes in the closets, bikes in the driveway, cars in the garage. She'd wanted for nothing. And because her parents' social circle consisted of couples with children who attended the same church, she'd thought all families were the same.

It wasn't until college that she'd realized how sheltered she'd been. She'd been loved. No question. But she'd known nothing about, well, anything. Hollywood, politics, philosophy, theology, war. Not that she needed an education in those subjects to get by in the world, but it would've been nice to have an idea of what went on across the planet she called home.

Oh, and sex. No one in her family ever talked about sex. Her mother had explained menstruation and conception, though very little about the latter, and absolutely nothing about orgasms. She'd learned about those herself, masturbating in the dark of her bedroom, going still when footsteps sounded in the hallway, feigning sleep when her door opened, finishing herself off when it closed.

She didn't know, for example, that couples squabbled and made up. She thought arguments were a bad thing, since her parents never disagreed or raised their voices, and had spent most of her life avoiding conflict. And yet when she'd been ready for a relationship, she'd gone looking for a bad boy to give her the wild, heated sex her body longed for, never once considering how the rest of Toby's makeup would pour havoc like honey over her life until the sting of trouble had her running far, far away.

"You okay?" Boone asked from beside her. She nodded, then gave him a soft, "Yes," so he wouldn't have to take his eyes off the road. He was sweet. So very sweet. Always thinking of her. Always caring.

He navigated the narrower streets of old Crow Hill to a neighborhood nearer the schools. Large ranch-style homes sat on large fenced lots, trees providing privacy for backyard patios and pools. The Mitchells' house reminded her a lot of the house she'd grown up in. A family home, sprawling, the yard never quite as well kept as those of childless families.

Everly could well imagine the chores of mowing and raking and skimming detritus from the pool falling to a teenage Boone. The same chores had fallen to her younger brother. But between playing baseball and football and tumbling through the grass, running with the family dog through the sprinkler, their yard had always looked lived-in, as did most of the houses they passed.

Casper's truck was parked in the Mitchells' driveway, so Boone pulled up to the curb, helping Everly out through the driver's door, and holding her elbow as they walked up the sidewalk. Faith met them in the foyer that emptied into a big family room. She reached up to kiss Boone's cheek, then gave Everly a thorough once-over. "You look about as bad as I feel."

"Same to you, sister," Everly said weakly.

"Wanna head to the powder room and spend some time with a tube of concealer?"

Everly lifted her bag with both hands. "I'm not sure I brought enough for all the time I'll need to spend."

Faith hooked her elbow through Everly's, as Boone pushed by the both of them with a grunt. "C'mon. We'll give it a go."

"It won't do any good," Everly said, mostly because it hurt to open her eyes. "Your mother's too observant and your father's too smart."

"Oh, I'm not trying to fool them," Faith said, hauling her toward the long hall off the entryway. "I just want Casper off my ass. And Boone, too."

"That's right. You've got two to deal with," Everly said, leaning over the pedestal sink to examine her eye baggage in the mirror.

"Boone, I ignore. Casper's the only one who really gets any say. And only then if I let him." Faith pressed a hand to her own cheek, turned her head this way and that. "Good lord does my skin look like candle drippings or what?"

Everly cut her eyes to the side and met Faith's in the mirror. "Maybe this is a good time to remind you whose idea it was to drink like we'd spent yesterday crawling our way out of a desert."

"Hey, I got Arwen to bring nachos."

That reminder had Everly bringing her fingers to her lips. "Please. Don't speak of nachos. Ever again. I'm going to have enough trouble with pot roast."

Giving up on her face, Faith backed up and sat on the toilet lid, her elbows on her knees, her chin in her hands. "How did Boone talk you into coming over today of all days?"

"It wasn't hard," Everly said, dabbing her ring finger on the concealer, then getting as close as she could to the mirror. "It was either stay at the ranch—"

"Wait." Faith's head came up. "What were you doing at the ranch?"

"That's where Boone took me last night," she said, meeting the other woman's reflected gaze.

"Wow. Do you know you're the first woman he's ever taken to the ranch? As far as I know, anyhow, and this being Crow Hill—"

"You know all."

"This makes me so happy," she said, standing and pulling Everly into a hug. "You are perfect for Boone."

After this morning, waking in his bed where they'd slept without touching, then showering in her bathroom where they'd done nothing but touch, hearing those words from his sister brought confusion raining down like wet confetti. "Why do you say that? I mean, how exactly am I perfect? What makes me perfect for him? I don't understand why—"

"Ev, chill. I'm not dragging the two of you to the altar. I'm just happy to see him with someone who's such a good fit. And," she added, when Everly urged her on with a desperate wave of her hand, "you're a good fit because whether or not either of you know it, you both want the same things."

"The same things. Like Camembert with artisan bread, and a closet full of Loubies, and three hours in the stylist's chair every three weeks?"

"Not those kind of things. Things that matter."

"My hair matters."

"And I'll bet Boone loves getting all tangled up in your hair, but I'm talking about real things. Balls-to-the-wall honesty. Tenderness. Friends and family. No secrets. Everything front and center. And let me tell you, it's not easy . . ."

Were those the things she wanted? Everly mused as Faith went on about her relationship with Casper. Were those the things Faith thought important to her? Family and friends, yes. And she could never again have anything but an honest relationship. But tenderness? Where did that fit in? Where had it come from?

And what about the biggest secret of all that she was keeping from Boone? He'd told her about his history with Penny Upton and her parents. But she hadn't been able to tell him about Toby. Granted, the circumstances were not the same, but while Boone had moved on after the trial, she was letting Toby keep her tied to the past.

Unless things were as similar as they were different, Boone's encounter with Les Upton defining the things he wanted now as fully as her history with Toby defined her.

A loud knuckle rap on the door followed by Boone's bellowed, "Get your asses out here," had both women giggling and Faith opening the door.

"Hold your horses, big boy," she said, patting the center of his chest. "I'm giving your woman here the lowdown on all your peccadilloes."

"My pecca— What the hell did you say?"

Her head spinning, Everly dropped to sit on the toilet lid. "I may need to vomit before I eat," she said, drawing a long string of curses from Boone.

Faith slammed the door, cutting him off, and wetting a

cloth in the sink as he grumbled on the other side. "Are you going to be sick? Because you don't have to be here. I'm happy to drive you home so you can get some sleep."

"No. I'm fine." She pressed the cold cloth to her forehead, then to her throat and her nape. "And I slept. For hours. I had no idea where I was when I woke up."

"So you two didn't . . ." Faith stopped, made some sort of obscene gesture with the fingers of both hands.

Everly shook her head, then puffed out her cheeks to steady the dizzying motion. "I don't even remember Boone and the others coming to the bookstore. Do you?"

"Hmm. I guess I don't. But I do remember later, in bed with Casper, thinking I was dreaming about an elephant, then—"

"Oh my God, Faith! I do not need to hear that."

"I don't need to hear it either," Boone said from outside the door.

"Oops," Faith said. "Are we good to go here?"

"One more thing," Everly said, leaning forward to whisper. "I think, when I was drunk, I told him I loved him."

"What?" Faith nearly yelled the question, falling against the door, and the door falling open.

Boone was leaning against the wall on the opposite side of the hallway, his boots crossed at the ankles, his arms crossed over his chest, his brow in a deep frowning angry V. "You two done now? Mom's waiting."

"Yes, Grumpy. We're done."

"You better hope she didn't hear you."

"Oh, c'mon. You think Momma doesn't know we talk about men's—"

"Criminy, Faith, shut the hell up," he said, following behind them as Faith took Everly's arm and steered her through the house. She cast a look over her shoulder, mouthed an apology. Boone just rolled his eyes and shooed her toward her seat in the dining room.

"Everly, I'm so pleased you could join us today." Catherine Mitchell leaned to set the gravy boat in the center of the table before taking her chair opposite her husband at the end. "I know we met at the anniversary party, but for all the years you've known Faith, you and I should've spent more time together by now."

"Thank you for including me," Everly said. "Everything looks and smells wonderful, though I have to admit I'm a bit worse for wear today."

"You and me both," Faith said, the concealer doing nothing to help her look anything other than queasy.

"Something tells me you two girls got into the same trouble last night." This from Curtis Mitchell, Boone's father.

"'Trouble's' not quite a big enough word," Casper said, reaching for the bowl of carrots Curtis handed him.

"And trouble's going to be exactly what you're in if you don't keep your big mouth shut. Especially since this is all your fault."

"Faith! That's no way to talk to Casper," Catherine said, starting the basket of hot rolls around the table.

"Yes ma'am," she said, earning a chuckle from Clay, who sat between Everly and his soon-to-be father, as he scooped up a helping of mashed potatoes.

Casper reached over to bop him playfully on the head. "And no laughter from the peanut gallery."

"Yes sir," Clay said, adding a slice of pot roast to his plate, his head down, his mouth tight against another laugh.

Everly took a roll when the basket came by, thinking she could probably handle bread, sparing a glance across the table at Boone whose gaze was all for his food. There wasn't a hint that he was fighting a grin. Or a scowl to prove that he wasn't. There was nothing. Much as there'd been nothing earlier on the drive over.

"Well, now I want to know how all of *this*," Curtis said, nodding his head at Everly on his right, at Faith sitting to his wife's, "is Casper's fault."

"No, Daddy," Faith said, glaring at Casper. "I'm pretty sure you don't."

But Curtis, letting his grin take over his face, looked from his daughter to her man. "Casper? What did you do now?"

Everly couldn't let anyone else take the blame. "It's more my fault, Mr. Mitchell—"

"Curtis, please."

"Curtis," she said, then continued. "I was at the house on Mulberry Street Friday night to interview Casper for a story."

"A story? On Casper?"

"I told you about it, Curt." This from Catherine. "Whitey at the *Reporter* is having Everly do a human interest piece on our boys," she said, the word obviously meant to include the absent Dax.

"That's right. How's that all going?"

Everly added a spoonful of mashed potatoes to her plate, then a bite of roast beef and a carrot. "I've talked some to Casper, and I'll be talking to Dax next week. I've tried to talk to Boone but things keep coming up," she said, the words earning her a grunt, "so I don't have a lot yet from him. But I'm also talking to some of the townsfolk. I want to tell stories from as many sources as I can."

"This piece . . ." Catherine paused, frowning down as she buttered her roll. "It's not going to be a hatchet job, is it? You're not planning to make the boys look bad."

"It's not a hatchet job, no." As to whether or not the *boys* would look bad . . . She pulled apart her roll, breathed deeply of the warm yeasty smell, decided her stomach was going to be okay. "I'm looking for bits and pieces from the past as well as the present, and even some of what went on with each man during their years away. I want a complete picture. And I'm also hoping to find out more than I know about Tess and Dave Dalton."

"Well, Boone can certainly help you with that. As can Catherine and I," Curt said, pointing with his fork toward his son and then his wife. "The Daltons were one of the first couples we met after moving to Crow Hill. They made sure we settled in and felt right at home."

"I've told her a lot about working for Dave," Boone put in, his gaze coming up to meet hers.

"Have you told her about playing football?" Catherine asked in a mother-proud tone. "Making the tackle that guaranteed the Hurricanes' win your junior year when y'all went to State?"

"I'm pretty sure she doesn't want to hear about that," he said, his attention returning to his pot roast as, Everly swore, his cheeks took on a tinge of pink beneath his tan.

"Of course I want to hear about it," she said, because he was so adorably cute when he blushed.

While his mother told the story, Boone held her gaze, not looking away once, not reacting. The reactions came from everyone sharing the table with them. And the chatter kept Everly from having to comment, or do more than smile, which was extremely difficult considering the only thing she could think about was showering with Boone this morning.

Sitting as he was at his mother's Sunday table, wearing

clean and pressed blue jeans, a pair of polished boots she'd never seen, and a crisply starched white shirt with mother-of-pearl snaps, it was hard to believe this same man, so courteous to his mother, so respectful of his father, so devoted to his family, and so . . . mannerly, was the same man who'd taken her apart.

How much he must have missed this company while away for half his life. How had he been able to stand it, knowing he wasn't here to celebrate birthdays and cheer his father's football team and wash his mother's dishes with his sister?

Had they argued as children? The one washing filling the sink so full that the one rinsing had no room to run water? None of the dishes ever really getting clean because the hated chore was a battle?

"Everly? You're awfully quiet," Boone's mother said, reaching a hand toward her, her eyes narrowed with concern. "Are you feeling poorly? Could I get you some hot tea?"

"Oh, Mrs. Mitchell, Catherine, I apologize." Everly shook her head, smiling at the older woman who was so incredibly lovely and kind. "I didn't get much sleep last night. Or should I say, I got sleep but since I'd spent the evening with several pitchers of margaritas, it wasn't the sleep I needed."

Curtis chuckled and sliced the side of his fork through a chunk of carrot. "I guess that explains Faith's looking rather green around the gills."

"They had a girls' night out," Casper said. "At the bookstore."

Another chuckle from Boone's father. "Huh. Never knew reading books to cause morning-after regret."

Everly dropped her gaze to her food, regret the last thing she was feeling. Too bad she couldn't put a name to what the emotion was. Too bad she couldn't give this meal and the members of Boone's family the attention they deserved. Too bad she was so confused about what she and Boone were doing that she'd let Casper get to her.

Too bad what she'd told Boone in the truck last night while drunk was probably the truest thing she would ever say.

# TWENTY-TWO

MONDAY AT NOON, Everly reached for her iced tea, sipping while she scanned the notes she'd made while talking to Nora Stokes and her daughter Teri Gregor. Nora's husband Gavin owned the Blackbird Diner, and Teri, married to a deployed Navy SEAL, had been running the place for them since moving back to Crow Hill. Teri had gone to school with the Dalton Gang, and had spoke kindly of all three—though her reticence to talk about Dax left Everly certain the two had been more than classmates.

That wouldn't go into her story, of course. No speculation on her part would. Only stories told by those who'd known them, whether since their return or in the past, belonged. And for all his talk of wanting a celebrity exposé, she knew what Whitey really wanted was exactly what he would be getting—his fully fleshed-out and as-true-as-she-knew-it-to-be human interest piece.

Or he would be if she could make sense of all of her notes. She'd recorded her conversation with Teri and Nora, but she'd jotted additional thoughts as they'd talked. She'd done that with everyone she'd spoken to. It was how she worked. And it also meant she needed to get things typed up before she forgot the possible angles the random words and phrases were supposed to help her recall.

Working on the story while the interview was fresh would also keep her mind off yesterday's meal with the Mitchells. Thinking back to that disaster would have her running to Boone to apologize. Or else crawling under her covers and staying there. What must he be thinking of her? Why had she insisted on going with him? How in the world was she going to face his parents again?

It was bad enough to throw up in one's own home, but to get sick in front of Boone's parents had made it a thousand times worse. He'd been so sweet to hold back her hair, getting in Faith's way when she'd tried. He'd brought her water, and a cold rag, and given her regrets to his parents so she didn't have to see them again. Then he'd taken her home, tucked her in, sat with her until she'd fallen asleep.

She'd woke hours later alone, more water and more aspirin on her bedside table, a clean bowl and pop-top can of chicken noodle soup waiting with a sleeve of saltines next to her microwave, along with another bottle of water. She'd stood there wrapped in the worn chenille robe she'd owned since high school, her hair, her face, everything about her a mess, stared at the note he'd left that simply said *Eat. Drink. Feel better.* and cried.

Enough. Work first. Fixing things with Boone later. If there was anything left to fix. If her wanting to be with him instead of staying home hadn't ruined the best thing to ever happen to her.

Why hadn't she just stayed home?

She'd just tucked her notebook and pen into her purse, when a man appeared in her peripheral vision and stopped beside her. "I hear you're looking for dirt on the Dalton Gang. Boone Mitchell in particular."

It took a second for the words to register, but then her head came up, her heart thumping. "I'm sorry. Who are you?" she asked, even though she knew. The monogrammed patch on his shirt told her, though the nastiness in his tone, and the specific mention of Boone, had been her first clue.

"Les Upton." The man who'd spoken, his nearly bald pate as greasy as the long strands of combed-over hair, spread out his hands on the table, supporting himself as he took the seat across from her. He was tall, gaunt, nearly skeletal, though his ropy forearms spoke the truth of his strength. "I run a towing service and garage out past Fever Tree. Lived here all my life. Know things you might like hearing about the three members of the Dalton Gang. My girl Penny went to school with them."

She wanted to tell him she hadn't asked him to sit, or invited him to join her, or even said, yes, she was looking for dirt on Boone. But some sort of anticipation in his expression told her she wanted to hear him out. And it wasn't the thought of Whitey Simmons canning her if she didn't.

Neither was it knowing what she already did about what had happened between this man and Boone. She didn't need to hear his side of that particular story. Boone had told her plenty, yet her professional curiosity kicked in and she heard herself saying, "I'm not exactly looking for dirt, Mr. Upton. I'm gathering background for a story I'm writing for the *Crow Hill Reporter*. A human interest piece."

"I know who you are. I know what you're doing, and who you're doing it for." He leaned forward, bringing with him the smell of diesel fuel and grease. "I also imagine all you're getting from folks is a whitewashed version of what went on around here back in the day."

So, this man, one she hadn't met during her four years in Crow Hill, was going to give her what no one else could? Or what no one else so far had? Or was it that he was going to give her what no one else wanted to, because whatever crimes the boys—Boone in particular—had committed weren't ones he'd learned to laugh about with time?

She changed her mind. She didn't want to hear anything he had to say. "Actually, I know about your run-in with Boone. He told me about it himself."

"Run-in, huh. Is that what he's calling it?"

"No, that was my word."

"And what words did he use? Huh? Did he tell you about the drugs he sold? The money he made supplying weed to the kids at school? You ever wonder why he didn't go to college, considering how smart he was, and the schools that wanted him to play ball ready to pay his way?"

She wanted to shake off what he was saying. She didn't believe a word of it. She knew Boone, the man he was, the family he'd come from. Knew, too, the trouble he'd caused, the pranks he'd played, the sins he'd committed. His choosing to not attend school had nothing to do with drugs.

Why was she still sitting here listening to him? "Mr. Upton—"

Les leaned closer. "Did he tell you he got my Penny pregnant?"

Everly's gaze whipped up, her heart ricocheting like a pinball in her chest.

"She didn't keep it, of course," he said, his mouth twisted, his whiskers gray and dirty, his eyes like bottomless black holes. "Penny never could be bothered with anything where there wasn't something in it for her. Now if the kid had belonged to Dax Campbell, that would've been a different story. But the Mitchells didn't have enough money—"

Without thinking, Everly reached across the table and slapped the rest of his words into silence. Her palm stung, sweat blossomed at her nape. Her stomach clenched as nausea rose. Les took several long seconds to turn back to her, to rub at the bright red print she'd left on his face. And then he slid out of the booth and got to his feet.

But he didn't walk away. He dug his keys from his coveralls pocket, then used the end of one to pick dirt from beneath a nail, moving to the next, wiping the grime on his thigh, finally lifting his gaze to hers and saying, "I guess he didn't mention it. Feel free to ask him what he said to Penny when he found out."

Everly's hands were shaking when she reached for her glass of iced tea, and she held on tight to keep from spilling the contents, even while thinking of tossing it all into Upton's face. She came close, but was saved from that particular embarrassment by an unexpected white knight.

"Let's go, Upton," Greg Barrett said, stepping between Everly and the other man and putting a hand on his shoulder to push him away. "I don't think the lady's in the mood for any more of your company."

"You don't know what the lady wants—"

"Actually, I do. Her handprint on your face is telling me." Greg pushed harder. "And Trevon Greene in the kitchen is more than ready to escort you to your truck if you can't get there under your own steam. You remember Trevon. Crow Hill High defensive end. Six-four. Two-ninety."

Upton turned, shrugging off Greg's hand as he did, sauntering down the length of the diner as if taking his time proved he was leaving because he wanted to, not because of Greg's threats.

Everly didn't even realize he'd left the building until Greg took the seat across from her, pushing his glasses up the bridge of his nose. "Are you okay? Did he hurt you? Do you need me to call the sheriff?"

"I'm fine, thank you. He wasn't particularly pleasant, but he didn't hurt me. He didn't even really frighten me. It was just the things he was saying . . ." She smiled when Greg reached across and squeezed her wrist. "I appreciate your getting rid of him. I didn't want to make more of a scene than I already had, but he was about to get a free glass of iced tea somewhere he probably wouldn't have wanted it."

"That man's a nuisance," he said as he let her go. "I'm all for freezing his balls off."

That wasn't exactly how she would've put it, but it did make her laugh. "Again. Thank you."

"Again. You're welcome. Highlight of my day. Highlight of my month, to tell you the truth. I don't get out much."

"You and me both." Upton's slow-moving tow truck crept past her window, taunting her. She took a sip of her tea, her stomach almost too tight for the little bit she swallowed, then to get her mind off what had just happened, she reached for the closest distraction. "Could I ask you a few questions while you're here?"

"Sure. I guess so."

"It's for a story I'm doing," she said, digging for her note-book and pen. "So it's not just random."

"What's the story?"

"It's a human interest piece on the Dalton Gang."

He arched a brow. "And you want the bastard half brother's take on things?"

"Do you mind?" she asked, flipping open her notebook.

"Why not." He leaned back in the booth, spread out his arms along the banquette. "Not sure what I can tell you since I don't know Mitchell at all, can't discuss my relationship with Casper, and Dax and I barely manage to exchange hellos in passing."

She'd take what she could get. "Has it been hard? With everyone knowing you're Wallace Campbell's son?"

He shrugged. "I came here expecting it to be hard."

"But you were here for quite a while before anyone knew the truth."

"It was bound to come out. Secrets always do."

The supposed secret of Boone getting Penny Upton pregnant hadn't. In the four years Everly had lived here, she hadn't heard a bit of speculation. Then again, she hadn't heard anything about Boone having to testify at Les Upton's trial until hearing it from him. Some secrets, it seemed, didn't have to come out. Which didn't explain why it was getting so hard to live with hers . . .

"You and Darcy though. You've become friends?"

He nodded toward the empty page of her notebook. "You sure this is for your story?"

Smart man, Greg Barrett. "Part of the hook is the Dalton Gang's return, and what brings people to Crow Hill."

"People like me."

"And like me," she said without thinking where such an admission might lead.

"I came for a job. And, yes, it happened to be a job with my father. I thought I might get to know my half siblings. So in my case, it was family, too. What about you?"

"I came for a job—"

"You know a lot of folks wonder about that, you leaving KXAN for the *Reporter*."

That stopped her in her tracks. Though why she should be surprised she was the subject of speculation . . . "None of the Dalton Gang men came back because they had family here. They came back for an inheritance."

"That doesn't answer my question about why you left KXAN."

"You didn't ask me a question." Though now she was wondering if he knew of her past with Toby. Had he lived in Austin before coming here to work for the man Darcy called The Campbell?

"You're right," he said, then leaned forward in the booth, his forearms on the tabletop, his hands laced. "Do you think coming back for an inheritance rather than for their kin says something about them? Besides Casper, that is, since he didn't have anyone here."

"I don't think it was the inheritance as much as it was the Daltons. The faith they put in the three by willing them the ranch. They could've sold it, and I know Tess needed the money, especially toward the end, but she didn't. I'm sure the older couple believing in them, giving them a reason to believe in themselves maybe?" She thought back to what Casper had said about the Daltons equipping them with what they needed to straighten themselves out. "If coming home because of the inheritance says anything, I can't imagine it's more than that."

"Makes one wonder what truly kept them away."

Had Casper not wanted to face the horrors he'd lived on Mulberry Street, until he'd had Faith at his side while he did? Had Dax's disinheritance left him feeling he no longer belonged, and only Arwen had been able to convince him otherwise?

Had Boone stayed away because of what Les Upton said? That he'd gotten Penny pregnant and she hadn't want his child?

"Listen," Greg said, getting to his feet, "Teri's got my lunch ready, so I need to get back to the office. If you need anything more specific for your piece, just give me a call."

"I will. Thanks. And thanks again for playing the part of the white knight."

"A lot more fun than playing the part of the bastard," he said, leaving her with a wave.

# TWENTY-THREE

AS SHE TURNED off the county highway onto the Dalton Ranch road, Everly wondered if her showing up unannounced made Boone uncomfortable at all. Other than his not being thrilled with the newspaper piece, he'd given her no indication that her visits were disruptive. Quite the opposite, in fact.

Still, she worried. For as much as he was one of a trio, he was a solitary man. He lived alone, and worked alone long after his partners had returned to their homes in town. It made sense he wouldn't want his life on display in the paper. Or have his work interrupted by visitors unannounced.

If she could've reached him on his cell, she would've called instead of making the drive. Though she wasn't sure that was the truth. She wanted to tell him about seeing Les Upton. And she didn't want to do that over the phone.

Plus, she wanted to see him, even though she'd seen him

yesterday, had sex with him yesterday. Even though she'd be seeing him again to finish their interview that had never really started.

A part of her was beginning to wonder if her questioning him had become a MacGuffin. If the story was her way to spend time with him, and not about the assignment at all.

She had no doubt he appreciated their sex life, but on more than one occasion she'd sensed he wanted more. Was he keeping that wish to himself because she'd been very clear in what she wanted? Did that make her selfish? Coming in here and stirring up his past, then allowing him the pleasure of her body on her terms?

Yes, she had her reasons for keeping emotions at bay, but he didn't know what they were. He knew she'd had a bad breakup, but that was all. How fair was she being to him when he'd been so open with her? Was her showing up like this feeding into his dreams when that wasn't what she wanted to happen?

Unless she was fooling herself in that regard. Unless their being together had seeds of hope taking root and flowering. Hope. It had been so long since she'd allowed herself to feel anything close to that particular emotion. Since she'd had reason to. And yet Boone had given her that.

Of course none of that explained her drunken admission of love . . .

Since she'd passed both Casper and Dax on their way back to town not long after leaving Crow Hill, she assumed she'd find Boone at the house or the barn and not out riding the range, or visiting his oil well, or herding cattle, or . . . whatever kept him so busy. She had so much to learn about a rancher's life.

No. She didn't. This was Boone's life, not hers. Hers she had down pat. She knew all she needed to about sitting behind a desk and manipulating the English language into cleverly compelling stories. She also knew all she needed to about her favorite cheeses and wines, the shoes she loved, how to keep her hair from drying out, her makeup from running.

*Face it, Grant. As much as you love your life, you have none.*

She'd left Austin and time had frozen. Her days passed in a bubble that had no relevance to the life she'd lived before. Boone was right. She was wasting a big fat something, and enough was enough. Once this story was done, she'd take his advice and parlay her connections and her talent into the high-profile position she deserved.

Except that wasn't what she wanted. It wasn't what she wanted at all.

Could she possibly be any more confused? she thought, parking, letting the dust settle, getting out of her SUV and shading her eyes to look for him, hoping he was around.

She found him near the barn, standing at the back of the ranch's flatbed, though it wasn't until she got closer, stumbling once when a heel hit what looked like a dried rat carcass—a sight that had her skittering—that she could see the tools he'd laid out, the oil he was using to clean them, the rags.

"What's up?" he asked, giving her a brief glance before returning to his chore.

She sidled up to the truck's door and out of the way of his grime. "I wasn't sure when I'd see you again, and something came up today that I thought you might want to know."

"You could've called."

And left a message. Because he wasn't around during the day to pick up. "I can go. If I'm bothering you. It can wait. I guess."

"You're not bothering me." He looked up at her, looked

down at her, taking in her shoes and her buttons and the mane of her hair. A tic beat in his jaw. "Are you feeling better?"

She nodded. "I hope I didn't embarrass you." Because she had embarrassed herself in so many ways.

"Nah, I have Faith for that," he said, snorting, and that let her smile.

"You were pretty quiet on Sunday. After . . ." She waved her hand instead of finishing the sentence. He knew what she meant, that he'd had nothing to say about what they'd done in her shower. "I love your family. Your parents are wonderful."

"Yeah. They're good people," he said, and got back to work. "So what's up?"

Fine. Done with the small talk. Out with it. "I was at the Blackbird Diner today, talking to Nora and Teri for my story. I ran into Greg Barrett, too, so had a chance to talk to him."

"Yeah?" he asked, but he didn't look over, just kept wiping down the tools and returning them to the toolbox attached to the cab. "How's the dirt digging going?"

"I'm not digging for dirt," she said with a roll of her eyes he was too busy to see. "We've been over that."

"Whatever."

She shaded her forehead with both hands to see him better, but it didn't really help. The setting sun cast him in shadow. His hat brim added another. She could see his frown, and that shadow, too, but little more. "Boone, talk to me. What's the matter?"

He stopped what he was doing, a blade of some sort in one hand, a squeeze can of oil in the other, staring at both, not looking at her. " 'What's the matter' is seeing my mother so excited about the story coming out, and hating what's going to happen when she reads it."

She flinched at the words, but not fast enough. They flew

into her face to beat her like angry wings. "What's that supposed to mean?"

"You know what it means."

Really? "You think I'm out to crucify the Dalton Gang? Seriously?"

"I don't know, Everly," he said, spinning on her. "You're talking to Nora and Teri. You're talking to Casper. You're talking to Greg. But you're not talking to me."

That's what this was about? The fact that she'd yet to ask him questions? And that was her fault? When neither one of them could keep their hands to themselves?

Grabbing a calming breath, she stacked her hands behind her and leaned against the truck door. Then she glanced over. "Are you hungry?"

"It's almost seven," he said with a nod. "I'm starving."

"Why don't I go see about supper while you finish up . . . whatever this is with your tools?"

A smile tugged. A dimple appeared. "You know supper for me means cooking. Not bread and cheese and grapes."

"I didn't bring anything with me. I'll have to use what you have on hand."

He turned back to his shop rags and oil can. No smile. No dimple. "Yeah. Good luck with that."

Good luck indeed, she mused minutes later, staring at the contents of his refrigerator, or the decided lack thereof. His freezer offered more, but all of that more was frozen.

She glanced around the kitchen, saw what looked like a fairly new microwave, wondered if Casper had bought it for Clay to use while those two had lived here. If she recalled correctly, Clay had been really good about cooking up extra batches of chili and stew.

She moved aside butcher-wrapped packages of ground beef

and found a plastic potato salad container with the words *taco meat* scrawled on the side. She popped off the lid, found the expected icy crystals, but freezer burn or not, it would have to do. The pantry didn't yield much more, but she grabbed a can of corn, another of Ranch Style Beans, and one of RO*TEL tomatoes.

Back at the fridge, she pulled open the crisper drawer, and lo and behold, two onions. She chose the larger of the two and then went in search of a knife. The meat was on thaw in the microwave, the onion frying in a spoonful of shortening, since there hadn't been enough butter and no olive oil at all, when Boone came inside.

He hung his hat on a peg by the door, washed his hands up to his forearms in the sink. Then turned and leaned against the counter, watching her work. "Smells good."

"It's just onions," she said as she stirred. "And Crisco."

"Yeah, sorry. Running low on butter."

He was running low on everything considered a staple. "Listen, I'm sorry if I caught you at a bad time. I shouldn't have come."

"No, I'm glad you did. I've been a crabby asshole all day. Dax and Casper will tell you."

"What's wrong? I mean, what specifically?" she asked, the microwave buzzer sounding.

"Nothing," he said as she retrieved the meat and added it to the stockpot. "I'm just pissed about the auction coming up this weekend."

"Already?" She tossed the plastic container into the sink and glanced over. "Nora moves fast."

"Nora's got connections. Nora knows we need the money."

"She's a nice woman. Her and Teri both." She scanned the three lengths of countertops. "Where's your can opener?"

He crossed to the drawer beneath the coffeemaker and handed it to her. "You were talking to her for the story?"

Right. That's what she'd come here to tell him. She opened the corn, dumped the contents, juice and all, on top of the meat. The soup was a whole lot better when slow-cooked all day, but this would have to do. "I was. And after we finished up, Les Upton stopped at my table."

"What? You're fucking kidding me. You're *not* fucking kidding me." He scrubbed his hands down his face, then back through his hair. "Criminy. That son of a bitch."

"I didn't know who he was. At least not right away, though the name on his coveralls registered at the same time he told me." She opened the tomatoes and the beans, stirred the soup while adding both of those, then turned up the flame on the burner.

"What did he say? What happened? Did he give you a hard time? Did he follow you? Do we need to call the sheriff?"

*We.* She liked that he'd said we. "He got mouthy and rude, and I slapped him. He wouldn't leave. Greg Barrett saw the whole thing." The soup came to a boil and she continued to stir, then set the heat at a high simmer. "He got him out of there, and that was the end of it. But I thought since the story will no doubt get around, that I should be the one to tell you."

He was smiling, his mouth twisted, his eyes twinkling. "You slapped him. You slapped Les Upton."

"I did. Then I went to the kitchen and had Teri bleach my hand," she said, because that's what she'd felt like doing. "Not really, of course, but yeah. He's a pretty despicable man, isn't he?"

"He always was. I can't imagine that's changed."

"It hasn't. Trust me."

"Shit, woman. Good for you," he said, leaning forward for a kiss, taking one then lingering for another.

"You really look tired today," she said, when he let her go, scraping her nails through his beard stubble. "More so than usual."

He held her hand to his face, closed his eyes. His weariness spilled from his pores like sweat, soaking him. Soaking her. "This is so far off the record," he said, opening his eyes, "that if I see it hit print you will have no peace in this life and I will haunt you in the next."

If she'd thought for a moment he meant it, she wouldn't have laughed, but she did to lighten the mood. She knew from his threat he was hurting, and she took back her hand to give him space. "I promise. Not a word."

"I feel like I'm losing it, like I'm falling apart. I can't figure out why. I came back to Crow Hill thinking I had it made. It would be a lot of work, but I'd be here with my family, with my boys, Tess and Dave's memory. Everything was set."

"Except it wasn't," she said.

"We got here to find the ranch . . . I don't even know how to describe what bad condition it's in. We're running the flatbed on used tires, and because the roads around the place are such crap, we ruin at least one a week. Same with the horse tack. I'm forever repairing what's there, and we can't replace it. We're lucky Arwen and Faith feed us as much as they do since all our food money goes for the animals."

"Boone. I didn't know. I'm so sorry." She stared at the pot of soup, guilty. "And here I used your food without asking you."

"I've gotta eat. Don't even think about it. That's what it's for."

"I'll bring you out some groceries tomorrow."

"No. You won't—"

"Yes. I will. At least to replace what I used."

"Everly, you're feeding me. You're using the same food I would've used. But you're keeping me from having to cook."

She wanted to cry. Stupid, but that's what she was feeling. A hurt she didn't understand. "I just don't like the idea that you're barely getting by."

"I'm fine. Or I was fine. Getting by." He shoved both hands through his overly long hair, held it to the back of his head, breathed deep. "Then I went to that damn library fund-raiser, and I met you. Nothing's been the same since, and my head's all fucked up."

"In a good way, I hope." Though why she said that after her earlier thoughts . . . Confused wasn't the half of it.

"In the best of ways, I promise. And I thought I had a handle on that. I knew you wanted a no-strings affair. And I was dealing with that just fine." He closed his eyes, scrubbed both hands down his faced. "But then, Friday night . . ."

Friday night. The sex where he'd torn and cut off her clothes. When her world had been upended. When she'd wondered what the rest of her life would be like without him. When she'd realized how much trouble she was in. "What about it?"

"I didn't use a condom."

He was upset about not using a condom? "I told you the first time that I'm clean, and I'm not going to get pregnant . . ." She let the sentence trail, her face heating. The pregnancy Les Upton had hinted at. Penny's pregnancy. Boone had insisted on using a condom even as their relationship—was it a relationship?—advanced because of Penny's pregnancy. Les hadn't been lying at all.

Boone crossed the kitchen, fetched two bowls from a cabinet, two spoons from a drawer, set them on the table. "Until Friday night, I'd used a condom every time I'd had sex since high school. I know you're on the pill, but I know accidents can happen. I let down my guard. I don't like that I let down my guard."

"Because you let it down with me?" she asked, fearing the answer.

"No, because I learned my . . . Because I learned a long time ago about responsibility. I want a family. I want a big family." He found a pot holder, hefted the soup from the stove, set it on a trivet he'd tossed to the table. "I want to see my kids playing hide-and-seek on horseback. I want to play hide-and-seek upstairs with my wife. But I can't afford to take care of myself right now, much less a family. And if things don't get better, I won't be able to afford the life I want. I'll be stuck with this one."

"No you won't," she said, joining him at the table when he motioned her to come. "You'll find something else to do. Some way to dissolve your partnership, or sell the ranch and hire on as a hand elsewhere, or you'll go to school, get your degree, coach football with your father. I promise. It's not that hopeless."

His gaze took her in, searching her face, looking for something she wasn't sure she had in her to give. "It's felt less hopeless since you've been here, and that's probably the worst part because you won't be here forever."

"Boone—"

"I know," he said, holding up both hands, then pulling out her chair and his. "No room in the bed for all that touchy-feely crap."

She closed her eyes, took a deep breath. Should she tell him all the things going on with her? How every day she thought about spending the rest of her life with him? How Crow Hill had become her home in ways Austin never had been? Even though earlier on the drive she'd decided he was right? That she was wasting her talent and connections? That it was time to move beyond the past that had driven her here?

She sat. She ate her soup. She didn't say anything at all.

# TWENTY-FOUR

THE LOOK EVERLY got from Arwen as she passed the bar on her way to see Dax didn't bode well for his interview. Hardly a surprise this appointment would start off on the wrong foot considering how things had gone down with Casper. At least for that one Faith had been on her side.

Since getting the assignment, Everly thought she'd made it clear to her girlfriends that she wasn't out to ruin their men. Seemed she still needed to win over Arwen.

Dax had hardly had it easy since his return to Crow Hill. A lot of that was his fault; she'd heard him referred to as a douche, or worse, more than once. But those people didn't know the man he was. All they saw was what he wanted people to see. The asshole shields he threw up to protect himself from a re-peat of his past hurts were high and wide and did their job well.

And that was the point of her story. To let people see who

Dax really was. The brother who'd been there for the teenage Darcy when their parents weren't. The partner who'd challenged Arwen to reconnect with her father, who'd given her the strength to do so when she could no longer put it off. The man who fought daily beside his two best friends to save a near worthless inheritance because of their love for the Daltons.

This was the Dax she knew. The Dax who'd raised hell of the sort most boys couldn't imagine. But he'd come home and faced his naysayers, made his place in Crow Hill. And he'd proved himself worthy of the very real gift of Tess and Dave's love. That, more than anything, is what she wanted to show.

He was already digging into a plate of Hellcat Saloon enchiladas when she sat opposite in the corner booth near the bar. And she hadn't even had time to say hello before Arwen arrived. "I told him the polite thing to do would be wait for you and see if you'd like to eat with him."

"That's okay," Everly said, reaching into her bag for her notebook and pen. "Boone wouldn't have waited either. I've never seen any man with the appetite of a rancher."

Dax raised just his eyes as he shoveled another bite into his mouth, holding her gaze as he chewed. Once finished, his fork in his hand like a tool, he smiled. "Arwen, bring Ms. Grant here a margarita and a plate of tomatillo enchiladas. On the house." As if he, and not Arwen, who was heading for the margarita machine, owned the place.

"I'm fine," Everly said, her stomach rumbling. "Really—"

"I insist. Any woman who can get Boone Mitchell riled up enough to stop bitching about the money we don't have, deserves a free meal."

Hearing about Boone being *riled up* fit with his admitting the same about himself yesterday, but she was curious to get Dax's take. "He bitches about money a lot?"

"He bitches about money every day, but that's hardly a surprise." He cut into his enchiladas, scraped up a bite. "We haven't even been back six months and the way it's looking, we probably should've sold the place and never tried to resurrect the Dalton Gang."

Is that what they'd done? The reason they'd all returned? To take another run at what all of them claimed were the best years of their lives? "Then it's the state of the ranch to blame for his being—"

"An asshole?"

"I was going to say a grump."

"Oh, it's you making him a grump, but that's a whole 'nother subject," he said, a brow going up as he reached for his beer.

No way was she going to open up her personal life with Boone to this man's speculation. Casper butting in had been bad enough. And the subject at hand was the interview . . . "Were the Daltons responsible for you bucking generations of Campbell tradition? Or had you already decided you didn't want to be a lawyer before you went to work for them?"

"Is that what you really want to ask me?" he asked, his frown on his food, his fork making shreds of his tortilla. "Everyone in town knows that story. My old man has made sure of it."

"But everyone in town doesn't know your side of things."

"Lady, no one in town gives a fuck about my side of things."

"Dax!" Arwen slid Everly's enchiladas in front of her, looking at her man as she did. "What did I say to you about playing nice?"

Dax went back to mangling his food. "You said if I didn't, I'd be sleeping on the couch while you slept naked in the bed."

Arwen rubbed at her forehead. "Good lord, man. I did not mean for you to repeat that to Everly."

Everly was caught between laughing and a budding frustration that she couldn't get anywhere with Boone's partners. She didn't think it was her, but more the threesome's loyalty, and under other circumstances, she'd be fine with that.

But this was her job, and she was not fine at all, so since she wasn't making progress tonight . . . "We can always do this another time. When you're in more of a mood to talk."

"He's never going to be in a mood to talk," Arwen said, heading for the bar and another beer. "Might as well get it over with now."

*Get it over with.* Like she'd be pulling out the bamboo to shove under his fingernails any minute. Or performing a root canal with her fork. Maybe she should just give her interview notes to Whitey, let him finish the story.

Except the moment she had the thought, she remembered Catherine Mitchell's excitement. Then she remembered Boone fearing she would let his momma down.

"Okay," she said, forcing a cheer she didn't feel and clicking the end of her pen. "Where were we?"

Dax set down his beer, wiped his mouth on his cuff. "I'm pretty sure we were talking about what's been making Boone mean."

Before Everly could tell Dax to back off, Arwen, leaning against the booth's tall back, said, "I know the answer to that. Les Upton coming out of the woodwork after all this time."

And now Everly's antennae were twitching. "Have you seen him, too? Or am I the only one to be so lucky?"

"I'm not talking to you about Les Upton," Dax said, his tone reminding Everly way too much of Casper's when he'd accused her of talking Boone for a ride. "That son of a bitch is Boone's business. And I don't share Boone's business with anyone."

Okay. Enough was enough was enough. "First of all, I was speaking to Arwen, not to you. And secondly, I'm not expecting you to talk to me about Les Upton. Or even asking you to." She reached for his beer, slammed the bottle against the tabletop. "I came here to talk about you, not about Casper or Boone or anyone else. But if doing this interview later suits you better, then it suits me, too."

Dax blinked, looked up at a still-hovering Arwen. "You going to let her talk to me like that?"

"Dax, sweetie, not only are you going to be sleeping on the couch, Crush is going to be sleeping there with you. Think about cuddling with twenty pounds of orange tabby with feta cheese breath next time Everly asks you a question." Arwen looked from one to the other and shook her head. "And now neither one of you are eating. You're going to give Myna a complex if she sees her enchiladas come back."

"Hard to eat," Dax said, "you bringing up Upton, and thinking about all the shit that family put Boone through, especially that goddamn Penny."

"Oh, I meant to tell you." Arwen slid onto the booth next to him. "Remember a week or so ago when you came home and asked if I'd ever heard where she ended up? Penny?"

Dax nodded, dug back into his enchiladas. Everly did the same so it didn't look like she was eavesdropping. Which she totally was.

"Well, yesterday I heard Amy and Callie in the kitchen say something about Penny. After Justin Walker, Callie's boyfriend"—Arwen looked at both of them as she added the explanation— "sold his construction company to John Massey? He went to work for Len Tunstall at the slaughterhouse. Dean Blaylock works there. Turns out he married Penny Upton. They live over in Southwest Crow Hill."

"No shit," Dax said.

"No shit," Arwen answered.

And now this evening wasn't looking like the total bust Everly had thought it would be.

If she was going to find out the truth of what had gone on with Boone and Penny Upton, she was going to have to get it herself from the source.

SINCE BOONE'S RETURN to Crow Hill, he had yet to visit his dad at work. Kinda funny that, considering he'd ridden to school with both parents every day his last four years of living here. That meant he was more than familiar with where to find the Coach this afternoon. It was late October. Football season was in full swing. And after-school practice, JV and varsity both, lasted till supper time.

He drove through the high school's small parking lot to the equally small stadium behind the small campus. Calling the field and the metal bleachers a stadium was probably a stretch, though in the last sixteen years a second set of bleachers had been erected, he saw, giving the visiting team their own side instead of forcing them to share one end of Crow Hill's stand of cold metal seats.

After parking in front of the field house, he made his way down the sidewalk and through the open gate to the track that circled the field. His father stood at the fifty-yard line, consulting a clipboard and talking to his assistant coach while the boys on the field ran drills. Boone headed that direction, a flood of memories coming back, all of them unbelievably good.

He'd played defensive end for the Hurricanes, two years on varsity, two years on JV. Dax had been the team's first-string quarterback, Casper a wide receiver. Cory Mallory, the center, had been team captain. He'd also been their graduating class's valedictorian, winning a football scholarship to Texas A&M. Last Boone had heard, Cory had been drafted by the Denver Broncos. Could be something to never having raised anything like the Dalton Gang's hell.

"Dad," Boone said, lifting a hand in greeting as his father looked over, caught by his approach.

Curtis Mitchell finished giving his assistant instructions, then clipboard in hand, walked to where Boone had stopped, grabbing him for a quick back-patting hug. "What're you doing off the ranch this time of the day?"

"Dax and Casper both took off early. Hell if I was going to be the only one working my fingers to the bone," he added, grunting.

His dad turned to face the field, cutting his gaze to the side. "I guess they're doing a lot of that now that they're living in town."

"Yeah." Though it wasn't the living in town but their new living conditions getting to him. Mostly because his living conditions hadn't changed. "I guess having a woman waiting at home has them looking for any excuse to cut out."

"Well, it's like that sometimes. Or most of the time." His dad chuckled. "Which I hope you get to find out for yourself one of these days."

"Maybe."

"Your mother really enjoyed visiting with Everly," he said, hugging the clipboard to his chest. "You should bring her around again sometime."

"We'll see." Nothing like being thirty-four years old and made to feel like a teenager by the man who'd explained the birds and the bees. "Everly's kinda why I'm here. I've got a problem."

"Yeah? Something I can help you with?"

"I don't know. I don't think so. I mean, I need to handle it. I'm just not sure I'm handling it right." *Criminy.* He wasn't handling it at all. "Or the best way *to* handle it. I guess that's why I'm here."

His father nodded, his eyes on the field and the players. "What's the problem?"

"Les Upton."

"Ahh." The single word spoke volumes.

"He's causing trouble. Not for me, though it's about me, but he's bugging Everly."

"Hmm. Well, first off, is it anything the law can help with?"

Boone shook his head. "Darcy asked if I'd thought about a restraining order. At the time, he was just being a pain in *my* ass, following me, lurking like some sort of stalker creep."

"But now that he's bothering your girl, you're thinking Darcy might be right?"

Was Everly his girl? Boone looked up at the sound of blown whistles, felt a pang at the memory of the violations he'd been called for on this very field. "I don't want to bring in the law and stir up all of our history again."

"I can understand that. Those were some dark days."

And his father didn't know everything. "He hasn't threatened her," Boone said, rubbing a hand over his nape. "But I know he's making her uneasy."

"I suppose you could try ignoring him, but he's never struck me as the type to grasp, much less notice, a subtle response."

His dad. Such a kidder. "Subtle's the last word I'd use to describe Les Upton."

"You might try making him uneasy in return," the Coach said after a minute spent focused on the field. "Do some stalker-creep lurking of your own."

He snorted at that. "Could be fun, driving by his garage, showing up wherever he happens to be."

"Then again," the older man said, gesturing with the clipboard, "I'm not sure the two of you being in the same place at the same time he's bothering Everly would be a good thing."

The understatement of the century. "She slapped him."

"What?" his dad asked, looking over.

Boone pushed up on his hat brim and nodded, smiling as something big and prideful swelled in his chest. "He stopped at her table at the Blackbird the other day. She'd been talking to Teri and Nora for her story. Upton got nasty with her, and she slapped him."

Curtis Mitchell chuckled, took a minute to step forward and call some instructions to the assistant coaching the defensive line, then stepped back. Still chuckling. "Your mother's right. You need to bring that one by more often."

"I'll see what I can do," Boone said, meaning it. And realizing that his father was right. Without Upton crossing a legal line, there wasn't much to be done. Everly was a strong woman, able to do a lot toward taking care of herself. That didn't mean he wouldn't be watching to take care of her, too.

# TWENTY-FIVE

THE SMALL HOUSE sat in the part of town that would've been considered the wrong side of the tracks if the railroad had run through Crow Hill. In the four years since Everly had moved here, she'd only ventured southwest of Main Street a handful of times, and it usually had to do with repairs to her SUV.

The neighborhood had seen better days. A lot of them. Many of the houses were rentals, some leased by the extended families of the hands who bunked on the area's ranches, others no more than a source of extra income for the owners, and cared for little by those barely able to afford them.

Everly parked on the street, there being no curb and no sidewalk, only a grassy ditch to separate the city's property from the private. It was the middle of the day, sunny and warm, and most of the blue-collar residents at work. At least she hoped they were at work, and not waiting for luxury SUVs to park on the street. That, of course, was the city girl side of her she tried hard to keep locked away.

She walked on the balls of her feet until she reached the broken sidewalk, not trusting her heels wouldn't sink into the clay of the yard and snap off. Even then, she stepped gently, the sidewalk a mess of broken pieces seemingly glued together by the weeds growing up through the cracks.

The cement steps rocked a bit when she climbed to the porch, but she made it, knocking, then smoothing down the front of her blouse, smoothing back her hair, pulling off her sunglasses and searching for a smile to hide her strange case of nerves.

The woman who answered the door was both unexpected and not. She was the right age, though worn and ragged, the state of her skin easily blamed on cigarettes. One burned between two fingers of the hand she'd braced against the door. But she was also quite beautiful, her bone structure, her build, the care she'd taken with her chunky hair cut and highlights, reminding Everly that she was overdue for both.

"Penny Upton?"

"Yes? Well, it's Penny Blaylock now."

She knew that. Penny's marriage to Dean Blaylock had come up in Everly's fact-finding. She was just stuck on Upton being the name from Boone's past. "My name is Everly Grant. I work for the *Crow Hill Reporter*."

"Yeah? And?" the other woman asked, a phone ringing in the room behind her, then going silent.

"I was wondering if I could talk to you for a story I'm doing."

"For the *Reporter*?" When Everly nodded, Penny frowned and shook her head. "I don't know what I can tell you about anything in town. I do all my shopping in Luling. I homeschool my kids. My dad served his time. My mom moved on. Dean, that's my husband, he works at Len Tunstall's slaughterhouse. And that's pretty much the history of my life right there. Now, if you think any of that can help you . . ."

"The story's a human interest piece about the return of the Dalton Gang to Crow Hill."

"The Dalton Gang . . . Wait a minute. Are you here to ask me about Boone Mitchell?" Her eyes widened, and a big smile took over her face, making her look ten years younger. "You are, aren't you? Well, sugar, come on in. I'm happy to talk about Boone. And just look at me. I've been so busy today I haven't even had a chance to put on my face."

"You look fine," Everly said, stepping into the doorway.

"I look like crap, but it's been one of those days. Lord, I haven't thought about Boone Mitchell in years—"

"Mom! Grammy B's coming to take me and Joel to Dairy Barn for supper."

"Then you'd best finish your geography assignment, kiddo," Penny said, ruffling the sandy blond hair of the boy, no more than eight or nine, who came running into the room. "Jacob, this is Ms. Grant. She works at the newspaper in town. Ms. Grant, this is Jacob, my oldest."

"Please to meet you, ma'am," the boy said, offering his hand, then running off to presumably do the schoolwork standing in the way of him and his burger basket.

Penny smiled after him. "And thank God that lets me off the hook for cooking. Dean can throw a steak on the grill when he gets home. I can toss a salad. Add a bottle of wine, and my night is complete."

The inside of Penny and Dean Blaylock's home was surprisingly neat. Everly didn't know why she'd been expecting anything different. Except she had. She was being a snob, thinking the interior of a house in Southwest Crow Hill would look as sad and rundown as it did out.

She followed Penny to the kitchen, taking one of the four chairs at the smart pine table while the other woman turned on her Keurig machine.

"I've got Emeril's decaf, or Dunkin' Donuts original."

Considering the state of her nerves . . . "The decaf would be great, thanks."

"So you're writing about Boone and the boys," Penny said, reaching into the cabinet for matching ceramic mugs. "Cream and sugar? Black?"

"Cream and sweetener, if you have it."

"I've got the pink stuff, sure," she said, bringing a holder of packets to the table along with Everly's cup, going back for a small carton of half-and-half and her own. "So what do you want to know? What kind of story are you doing?"

Everly stirred her coffee, thinking about what Les Upton had told her, having a hard time picturing this woman being raised by that man. "Lots of folks are interested in where they've been, and what it's been like to come back after so many years. You went to school with them, am I right?"

"I did," she said, lifting her cup and blowing across the top, her cigarette smoldering in the ashtray at her elbow. "But I didn't know Dax or Casper well at all. Only Boone. That boy . . ." She shook her head, sipped. "He was such a sweetheart. And to have gone through what he did with my family. I guess you know about all of that."

"He told me about the night your father . . ."

"Came home and beat my mother half to death?" she asked, her voice almost a whisper, her perfectly arched brows rising.

Everly nodded. She'd wanted information on Boone. Less

for her story than herself. But she hadn't thought what she'd be putting Penny through by coming here. She didn't know the woman, but that didn't let her off the hook for invading her privacy.

Listen to her. Since when had she cared about invading someone's privacy? And yet, having her own privacy invaded at the end of her years with Toby had given her the perspective she'd lacked as a journalist. The fact that she was letting that lesson fall by the wayside for personal gain . . . God, what was she doing here?

"Yeah, that was not one of my finer moments. I had a lot of not-so-fine ones in high school, but wow did I ever let things get out of hand that night. I've always wondered if I hadn't been such a slut," she said, holding up a hand at Everly's gasp, "if that night wouldn't have been totally different. And before you argue that I wasn't, you only have Boone's version of what happened."

"That's not quite true."

"How so?"

"I was talking to some other friends of the Dalton Gang recently. At the Blackbird Diner. Your father stopped by my table."

"Lucky you," she said, rolling her eyes. "Did he tell you it was my fault the way things happened?"

"No, and please don't blame yourself. Abuse is never the victim's fault," she said, and the words hung there so long she actually looked up, seeing her history, her face in Penny's. She hadn't thought she blamed herself for inciting Toby's wrath, but maybe she had, yet in that moment, she knew she never would again.

And then she thought about Boone, not the boy he'd been

who'd known this woman as a girl, but the man he was now. The man who carried just as much baggage as she did, but seemed to never let it weigh him down. Like Penny, he'd moved beyond what had happened. Everly was the one stuck in the past.

"I heard that a lot growing up. From my mother, of all people. She knew it wasn't her fault that my dad beat her. He didn't always, just later, when their lives got so pathetic. I think she was looking for an easy way to check out. Rather than suicide by cop, suicide by husband."

Her hand shook as she brought her cigarette to her mouth. "What gets to me when I think back is how happy she is now. She met a new guy in Corpus Christi. He was a widower, had two kids. I think she's more mom to them than she ever was to me, but I can't hate her for that. My dad really fucked her over. She got through it the only way she thought she could. As bad as it was, it worked out in the end."

"Can I ask you something personal? Totally off-the-record. It has nothing to do with the story, but after meeting your father, I'm curious."

"Shoot."

"With everything that happened, why did you come back here to live?"

Penny's smile, as she reached for another cigarette and lit it, left Everly somewhat unbalanced. She'd expected to find a bitter, broken woman. Penny was anything but. She was a bit frazzled maybe, but she was responsible for the care and feeding and schooling of two young boys. Frazzled was hardly a character flaw with all she had on her plate.

"I'd been born here. I grew up here. Crow Hill, for being a nothing spot on any map, is my home. I left for a while with my mom. I spent a few months in Corpus with her at her sister's while she got over the physical damage. But all that time I was away, I missed my life here. I missed my friends."

"Your father was still in prison when you came back, yes?"

"He was. I stayed with my bestie, Missy Fowler. I got a job at the Dairy Barn. And that's where I met Dean. Or rather, met him again. He'd been two years ahead of me in school, and he'd played football so I knew who he was. But I had no idea he knew who I was," she said, a blush creeping up her extraordinarily long neck to stain her cheeks.

None of this was what Everly had expected to learn when she came here today. She'd thought, for no reason other than prejudice, that she'd find a chip off the Les Upton block. But Penny was delightful, leaving her lost as to what to think about where this woman fit into Boone's past.

"Obviously he did know," Everly said, a smile spreading easily over her face as she lifted her coffee to drink.

"I can't even tell you what it was like, being courted by a man like Dean. He was already working for Len Tunstall. He's been there all this time, actually. He's *such* a good provider for me and the boys. He was so quiet and so strong. I'd always thought strength meant brute force. And a lot of yelling."

"Because that's what you'd seen with your father."

She nodded, tapped the ashes off the end of her cigarette. "Dean won't let my father in the house. He won't let him know the boys. I mean, they know he's their grandfather. And Dean will take them to the garage on Daddy's birthday and at Christmas to give him cards, but that's all. He stays with them every minute. I never go, but Jacob and Joel tell me about it. I don't think they particularly like the visits, but they don't hate them either. They're more curious than anything. Daddy is nothing like their PopPop, Dean's dad."

"Sounds like coming back to Crow Hill turned out for the best."

Penny looked down, her eyes going damp, then red as she struggled not to cry. "When I was a little girl, I thought my daddy hung the moon. He was so sweet to my momma. We did things together as a family, some of the same things Dean and I do with our boys now. I couldn't imagine my life being any better than it was."

"What happened? How did he . . ."

"Become an abusive pig?"

"Yeah.

"I don't know." She turned in her chair to cross her legs, and lean her head against the wall. "He drank more than he should have, for one thing, and he screwed up on a couple of rebuild jobs because of it. He couldn't keep good help. Folks moved to Skeet Bandy's garage."

"So his business declined."

She nodded. "Momma had been a beauty when they got married. Just gorgeous," Penny said, and Everly didn't doubt for a minute that the daughter took after the mother. "I guess she'd put on a few pounds, I mean, hello. They'd been married twenty years. It wasn't like he hadn't lost most of his hair and gained a gut. Maybe she didn't get the attention she wanted from him, so she looked elsewhere. Not saying I know for a fact that she cheated, but I heard talk. Most of it from him. And since she ignored me and he doted, well, it was easy to believe him. Funny, because he turned out to be such a god-damn liar."

"He told me Boone sold drugs to the kids at school."

"Oh my god, he did not," she said, then pressed her fingers to her mouth as if doing so would help her lower her voice. "He's a liar. That's such a lie. Boone Mitchell wouldn't have come within a hundred feet of drugs. Beer, yeah. That boy liked his beer. But he was too smart to mess with things that would mess with him. No, Daddy hated Boone because he stood up to him. Momma quit because he broke her down. She couldn't deal with the ugliness anymore. She just gave in," she said. "But not Boone. Never Boone." Then she picked up her mug, frowning when she realized it was empty, going silent instead of brewing another cup, or reaching for a third cigarette.

Everly went quiet, too. She understood the ugliness. She understood the giving in. She'd managed to get out from under Toby's rule before she'd reached the point Lucinda Upton had, but she understood. She'd been lucky she had the money, and the contacts, and the friends who'd helped her escape.

"I'm sorry to drag you through all of this," Everly said, realizing how deeply she meant it. "I really only intended to ask you about Boone."

"That's okay. It's good to talk about it occasionally. My friends have heard it all a thousand times, and I try not to let it build up, but it happens." She toyed with a wisp of hair that had fallen out of her rooster tail. "Dean always knows when I'm down about it, and with me never having to say a word. I don't know what I'd do without him. He is the best man. The best father and husband. If I hadn't come back here . . . I can't imagine having missed out on knowing him, and loving him."

Thoughts of Arwen and Dax, Casper and Faith came to mind. How often had Everly heard her best girlfriends say the same things about their men? Penny wasn't any different. She didn't have the money Faith did, or the business Arwen did, or the connections Everly did, but she was a woman in love. And in that regard, she had things Everly had only dreamed about.

"You know, I owe Boone a big apology."

"How so?"

She shrugged, tapped the end of her cigarette box on the table. "I was so screwed up in high school. Obviously, right? Judging by my behavior. I got him into such a big mess, knowing how both my folks would react at catching me with him."

Everly frowned. "You knew your father would go after your mother?"

Another shrug. "That part I can't say for sure. Maybe." She paused, flipped the top of the box open and shut. "It was like a keg of gunpowder inside our house. I couldn't deal with it anymore, the wait, and I used Boone for the fuse. And that was really shitty of me."

It was, but shitty things were part of being teenagers. "It was a long time ago."

"Not so long that I don't need to make things right."

Everly left after that, turning over everything Penny had said, wondering about the one thing she hadn't: having been pregnant with Boone's baby.

# TWENTY-SIX

BOONE WAS IN a mood and had been since seeing Everly Monday night. Three days now, and he was still regretting the confession he'd made. What the hell had he been thinking, telling her he'd been falling apart, that he was losing it. Bellyaching about the conditions on the ranch, none of which were her concern. All of which had been building to a worse head of steam than he'd realized.

And then she'd been worried about using his food stores, when what she should've been worried about was his *not* using a condom Friday night *or* Sunday morning. By Sunday, the horse was out of the barn, but Friday . . . He'd torn off her clothes, cut open her clothes, ruined them, and buried himself so deeply inside her he'd disappeared. All without a goddamn condom. But, no.

She'd been worried about him.

She'd stood there in Tess's kitchen, in *his* kitchen, listening and fitting right in, wearing her heels and her buttons as if that's what anyone wore to stand at the stove. She'd cooked for him, stirred the soup and soothed him and calmed him and cared for him. And she'd done it all without once telling him to buck up and get over himself. But she hadn't spent the night. She'd gone home. And since then, she hadn't called.

First thing he'd done the last three nights after walking into the house was check the log on the phone. No messages. No missed connections. He'd stretched out the soup, finishing it last night, but he hadn't called her back. He hadn't even called her tonight, knowing he was coming to town.

What in the hell was wrong with him that he couldn't pick up the goddamn phone and call?

So what if she didn't answer? Her not answering would hardly be the end—

"I thought you did most of your drinking at home," Faith said, climbing onto the stool beside him where he sat nursing his sorrows at the Hellcat Saloon bar. "On the back porch. With your cooler of beer."

His cooler of beer was empty. His wallet would be when he left here tonight. "Had to come to town to sign some papers for Nora about the furniture going up for sale. Wasn't in the mood to go home."

"Because of the auction?" she asked as he drank. "Letting go of Tess's things?"

"That. And . . . other stuff."

"Everly?"

He shrugged. Made no sense that he had a hard time going home because of a woman who didn't even live there. But she'd been there enough that he missed her when she wasn't. He lifted his beer with a grunt, let that serve as his answer.

His sister reached over to rub his shoulder, making him feel even worse because her being there helped. He shouldn't need her to be there. His having next to nothing to his name was his problem, not hers. But it did help, having her, having his dad, his mom.

He should've come home to stay a long time ago. Except if he'd done that, he might've settled down too soon, worked a spread that wasn't his own, married the wrong woman. Missed out on knowing the one he couldn't get out of his mind. She was unforgettable, Everly Grant.

And she was making his life pure hell.

"Do you want to come over for supper? Clay's cooking tonight. Not sure *what* he's cooking, but it really doesn't matter because it'll be better than anything Casper or I could whip up."

"Thanks," he said, shaking off his thoughts of moments ago. "But I'm going to sit here awhile."

"You can't drink your supper, Boone."

"Watch me," he said, emptying the first bottle of the night.

Faith pulled her phone from her purse, typed out a text while saying, "Then order food. My treat. Have a burger. Have a steak. Just do more than drink."

"I don't want you spending your money on me," he said, but he knew his sister and it was no use. She was already signaling for Arwen.

"Boone wants a twelve-ounce rib eye, medium rare, a baked potato, loaded, and a side of squash casserole. That and the beers go on my tab."

"You don't have a tab," Arwen said, jotting the order on a green ticket and tearing it off. "But I've got your credit card number saved," she added, waving the paper as she headed through the kitchen's swinging doors.

"See?" Faith said, patting Boone's shoulder. "Problem solved."

The problem of his empty stomach. Which, come twelve hours from now, would just be empty again. "What're you doing here anyway?"

"I was on my way home. Saw your truck and stopped."

"Home from where?" It wasn't his business, but it kept her from digging into his. And him from doing more whining. He was damn sick of hearing himself cry like a baby.

"From the high school. I've been helping Momma with the holiday carnival planning," she said, and when he groaned, added, "I was glad to see your name on the list of volunteers."

Yeah. That's how it had happened. "Trust me. I did not volunteer."

"You didn't have to. Momma volunteered for you." When he grunted again, she got back to patting and rubbing. "It'll be fun."

He took back his earlier thoughts about being glad he had his family close. But only long enough to order a second beer. "No. It won't."

"C'mon. You've been gone sixteen years. You've missed a lot of holiday carnivals."

"Nope. Haven't missed them at all."

"Then think of it as doing community service to make up for all the shit you caused at the last one you were around for."

She had him there, though he was pretty sure it was Dax who'd started the fire in the hay bales used for the hay ride. "At least the trailer'd been unloaded and the tractor unhitched. We weren't total heathens."

"Yeah, you were," she said, glancing over his head toward the door. She took a swig from his fresh beer bottle, then said,

"I'm going to head home. Don't you move until you've finished the dinner my saved credit card number is paying for."

"Yeah, yeah," he said, waving her on her way, but not before she'd planted a big sloppy kiss on his cheek.

He started to wipe it off, decided against it. Decided he could use all the good karma he could get. Then, less than ten seconds later, Everly climbed onto the stool beside him. "Want some company?"

"What're you doing here?"

"I was hungry. And I'm all out of grapes."

He signaled to Adelita, tonight's bartender, for a third beer since this one was going fast.

"Make it two," Everly called to the other woman, causing Boone to look over and frown.

"Since when do you drink beer?"

She turned on the stool to face him, cocked her head, smiled. "Since you're drinking beer."

"Huh," he said, wondering what she had to smile about. He couldn't imagine it was being here with him. He didn't even want to be here with him. "Surprised to see you. Thought you'd moved back to Austin or something and just didn't want to tell me."

Her smile picked up steam. "I've been working, silly. I have a story to write. And it's hard to concentrate on work with you around. I was going to call you tomorrow. I should have my first draft done by then. Except for the holes I've left to plug in what I learn from *your* interview."

He grunted. He'd been grunting a lot tonight.

"C'mon. Let's move to a booth. I'll order some supper."

"I'm not in the mood—"

"I am," she said, grabbing both beers and giving him no choice. "And I know Faith already ordered for you."

"How do you . . . She texted you, didn't she? Told you to come babysit."

"So, you *are* acting like a baby," she said, wiggling both bottles as she did, as she turned away, laughing.

He grunted, but he got up and followed her, the click of her heels and the swing of her ass doing a lot to cheer him up. The swing of her hair, too. He loved how it fell down her back, the blond waves skimming just below her bra strap. Her pants tonight were black, her shoes black and white zebra stripes, her blouse, with its too many buttons, zebra striped, too.

She made him happy, the way *she* was happy, the way she knew herself, how she refused to be anyone else, or change to fit in. She fit in just fine. And she fit with him. That's what he was having hell with tonight, having signed the papers earlier to sell Tess's antiques. He had to sell what he had to keep what he had. What kind of life was that to offer a woman like this?

"Come with me to the football game tomorrow night," he heard himself asking once they'd settled at a booth near the bar.

"Really?" she asked, her eyes lighting up. "Your dad's team? The high school game?"

"Only one I know of in Crow Hill."

"I'd love to go. Faith and I were actually just texting about my helping out with the holiday carnival. It's like my childhood all over again."

"You had a good one?" he asked, because this felt like safe territory and it was one they hadn't covered before. As grounded as she was, he didn't doubt she'd had a solid upbringing.

"I did," she said, nodding as Luck Summerlin slid his plate in front of him, avoiding his gaze as she did.

She avoided Everly's, too, as she asked, "Can I get you something? Do you need a menu?"

"Hmm. A bacon cheeseburger with jalapenos, medium well."

"Fries? Onion rings?"

"Just the burger," Everly said, reaching for her beer.

Boone watched Luck go, wondering if it was a touch of schadenfreude tugging at the corner of Everly's mouth. "I'm not sharing my potato."

"The burger will fill me up," she said, sticking out her tongue and sitting forward. "Anyway, yes. I had a wonderful childhood. I grew up in Austin. I'm the oldest of four, and our parents were the best. They remind me a lot of yours, actually. Very involved. Very . . . parental in that they were always there for help with homework and school programs and extracurricular stuff, the cheerleading and gymnastics and dance and piano, but they didn't spoil or indulge or skimp on the discipline."

"Did your mother ever sign you up for the dunking booth at her holiday carnival?"

"Oh, no. Seriously? She roped you in, too?"

"All three of us," he said, picking up his knife and fork. "We're supposed to wave the white flag or some community bullshit."

"I love this," she said, sitting back in the booth, crossing her legs, holding her longneck on her knee. "It's going to be so much fun. I can't remember ever being so excited about an invitation to get kissed by a bunch of strangers."

*Wait a minute.* His knife and fork stilled. "Get what?"

"Kissed," she said, and waggled both brows. "I'm going to work the kissing booth while you work the dunking booth."

"I thought Faith was doing the kissing."

"She was, but I guess Casper objected."

Huh. "But my objecting to you doing the kissing doesn't rate?"

"Are you objecting?" she asked after a long moment searching for something in his eyes.

"I don't know. Is that too close to hovering?"

"Why would you ask me that?" she asked then brought the beer to her mouth.

He waited while Luck set Everly's burger on the table, shook his head when she asked if either of them needed another beer. "The night we danced. You mentioned you didn't like men hovering."

"I did?"

"It's stuck with me all this time, and I'm pretty sure I didn't make it up."

"Huh. If I knew the context—"

He sawed through his steak, thinking back. "It was about what Faith and Arwen were wearing. You liked their costumes. But you didn't like Casper and Dax hovering."

"I remember now," she said, her smile fading, the laughter like fireflies in her eyes vanishing. "My objection was because of my ex."

*Calf nuts on a motherfucking cracker.* He'd done that, made her sad, and he wanted to kick the shit outta himself. "He didn't like other men looking at you, so he hovered."

"No," she said, her expression wry. "He wanted to show me off, so his hovering was about making sure I dressed so men *would* look."

"That's fucked-up," he said, his wrists on the edge of the table, his appetite gone.

"A lot of things about him were," she said with a shrug, as if what she'd gone through was nothing.

What he'd gone through with Les Upton was nothing compared to what he sensed she'd endured. "You don't talk much about him."

"There's not much to talk about," she said, pulling a strip of bacon from her burger, popping it into her mouth. "He's not a part of my life anymore."

"But he is the something that happened, isn't he? The something that brought you to Crow Hill?"

She looked down at her plate, as if she'd find an answer, like another slice of tomato, inside her burger's bun. Or a reason to get out of answering him altogether. "He is. Our breakup was rather ugly."

"Ugly enough that you had to go into hiding?"

"That's closer to the truth than you know. I don't like to talk about it. Or him," she said, wrapping her hands around her burger and bringing it to her mouth so she wouldn't have to.

And it frustrated him that she didn't. Because he knew the something that had happened was the very thing in the way of their moving forward.

"So," he said, back to sawing at his steak. "Friday night. The football game. You still want to go?"

"Of course I want to go. None of this changes anything. Trust me."

"I'll pick you up at six thirty?"

"Sure. I can't wait," she said, and he hoped to hell she was telling the truth.

# TWENTY-SEVEN

EVERLY HADN'T BEEN to a high school football game since her years leading cheers, and the two after graduation when she'd watched her brother Ethan play. Those days, she'd been to them all, at home, away, but saw more of the spectators in the stands than the plays on the field.

Tonight, the Crow Hill Hurricanes were playing the Hope Springs Bulldogs, obviously hoping to blow them away. Judging by the section where she found herself sitting, that could very likely happen. The volume of breath used by the fans' voices and the air stirred by their waving arms was enormous.

Boone sat to her right, and in front of them were Casper, Faith, and Catherine Mitchell. Coach Mitchell was on the field, and Clay, only a freshman and too new to the semester to play, had been shown a little nepotism by his future adoptive grandfather and put to work as water boy.

In the two weeks she and Boone had been together, she'd

never seen him so animated, jumping up, yelling encouragement to the players, whistling like it was his kid on the field, not his father calling plays, nor Casper's son dispensing water on the sidelines. Faith was just as loud, as was Catherine.

Casper was a bit more reserved, and Everly couldn't help but wonder if he was thinking about next year, when Clay would officially be his, and no doubt want to be more than a water boy. Casper had played on this very field, along with Dax and Boone. He knew the score of being a Hurricane, and she wasn't talking about the numbers on the ramshackle board in the end zone.

She also understood what high school football meant to the families of everyone involved—the players, the cheerleaders, the drill team and band members and pep squad. Even the concession stand and ticket window were staffed by the booster club, security provided by off-duty sheriffs for free.

The television show had it right. During the school year's fall semester, Friday nights in small Texas towns saw the entire community pitching in for one goal—supporting the boys on the field to a win.

Outside the city limits, away from the cars and trucks honking up and down Main Street, the sounds of the band playing and the crowd cheering carried through the night, along with the lowing of cattle. The stadium lights shone like beacons, and the smell of popcorn and hot dogs permeated the air.

Everly couldn't believe how much she'd missed this. And how experiencing it with the Mitchell family made it brand new.

"Does this bring back memories?" Boone asked into her musings.

"Oh, yeah," she said, hooking her arm through his and leaning close. "Though the view's all wrong. I'm used to being down there, and looking up here."

"But you're having a good time?"

"I am," she said, giving him a smile and a rapid nod of her head.

"You're awfully quiet," he said, his gaze narrowed and making sure.

"I'm having a good time. Especially watching you."

"You're supposed to be watching the game."

"I'm doing that, too."

He pulled off his hat, ran his hand through his hair, then looked to the field as he settled it back in place. "Except for the equipment being a whole lot better than what we had, this could almost pass for a night when the boys and I were on the field. The band's a little better. The cheerleaders a little hotter—"

"Boone!"

He gave her a wink, flicked the tip of her nose with one finger. "Even the waxy plastic cheese on the nachos smells the same. Those were some good times."

"The games? Or just high school in general?"

"Being part of the team. Lots of perks came with being part of the team."

He was talking about girls. Everly was sure of it, and reached up to clear away the hair blowing in her face. "What was it like playing for your father?"

He shrugged. "He did a good job of keeping things fair. Not being harder on me than on anyone else, or being more lenient."

"How was he with Dax and Casper?"

"He was a slave driver," Casper leaned back into their conversation to say.

Boone snorted. "He didn't drive you any harder than he did me."

"You forget the week he made me walk home from practice.

Drove behind me all the way to make sure I didn't hitch a ride."

Faith turned toward him. "And whose fault was that?"

"Your brother's. He's the one who switched out the liquid detergent with the bleach and ruined a whole wash load of jockstraps."

At that, Catherine looked back over her shoulder, an authoritative arch to her brow. "Is that so?"

Boone waved them all off. "It was a long time ago. I don't remember who did what."

"That's because you weren't the one walking," Casper said, swinging back around as the crowd surged to its feet.

Everly stood along with everyone else, watching the Crow Hill wide receiver outrun the two Hope Springs defensive backs and score. Even Casper jumped up at that, grabbing Faith at the same time Boone's arms came around Everly. He lifted her feet from the bleachers. She held on to his shoulders, screeching with surprise, the sound swallowed up by the screeches of others.

She'd really *had* missed this, she realized, as he lowered her, slinging his arm around her shoulders as the crowd remained standing for the extra point. She'd been in Crow Hill four years, but had spent very little of her time away from work doing more than having lunch with her girlfriends. She'd stayed home alone and read books and watched movies and drank way too much wine.

It hadn't been a purposeful thing, keeping herself apart. She'd wanted to make friends, have as active a social life as Crow Hill could provide, and she was certain that meant more than a weekly girlfriend lunch. But she didn't have relatives here, so she didn't have nephews playing football or nieces leading cheers. She didn't attend the First Baptist Church services, so she didn't serve on youth or food service committees.

She didn't volunteer at Coleman Medical Center, so she didn't spend time reading to patients or delivering flowers to brighten their days. And now that she'd taken the time to enumerate all the things she didn't do, it sounded a lot like the only thing keeping her from the social life she wanted was herself.

So why in four years had she not gotten involved? Was she that afraid of getting hurt again? Did she actually think forming friendships outside of those she'd made with her girlfriends was going to put her in harm's way? Had she really let one incident from her past prevent her from leaving it behind?

Another cheer erupted, bringing her back to the present, and she took in the small group that had claimed her as one of their own, even while remaining an active part of the very large surrounding whole.

In fact, she mused, her gaze roaming the filled bleachers, she'd had no idea this many people lived in Crow Hill to come out for Friday night football. Then again, how could she, holed up in her tiny piece of the tiny town with her books and her movies and her wine?

"Hey," Boone said beside her as they sat. "You're back to being quiet again."

"How would you know? Can you actually hear anything in all this noise?"

"Do you want to leave?" he asked, frowning. "Is it too loud?"

She laughed, took hold of his arm and squeezed. "No, it's not too loud and I don't want to leave. I'm having a great time."

"I wasn't sure. I know the football thing can be overwhelming if you never played. Or your dad's not the coach."

"You played and your dad's the coach, so it's fun watching you."

"You're supposed to be watching the game," he said, dimples pulling at his cheeks when he smiled. "We're winning."

*We're* winning. Because this was his home, his town. This was where he belonged. This was his world. The world he felt he was losing because the ranch, the reason he'd come back, was falling down around him. Yet as bad as all of that was, he hadn't allowed the incident with Les Upton that had left so many scarred keep him away, or keep him from moving forward.

In fact, he did his best to blow off Les Upton completely. She was the one giving importance to that night, wanting to know why it hadn't defined Boone the way Toby's abuse had defined her. Or maybe it had, but he'd made the choice to move on while she hadn't.

One thing was certain: She would never be able to create a life with Boone if she kept living in the past.


"BRR," EVERLY SAID, rubbing her hands up and down her arms as she walked through her kitchen, leaving Boone to close and lock the door. He didn't bother locking his own, but ever since she'd mentioned the need to feel safe, he'd made sure her doors were bolted. "I think I need some hot cocoa or coffee or tea or something. I'd forgotten how cold icy metal bleachers could be."

Silly woman. Cute silly woman. "There was no ice. The temperature's only just in the forties. And if you'd sat closer to me instead of keeping a respectable distance between us, I would've made sure you were warm."

She turned from the living room entrance and gave him a

look. "Your mother was sitting in front of us. After last Sunday's hangover lunch, I thought respectable was a good idea."

He could buy that, he decided, tossing his hat to her table. "Now that it's just you and me, can we ditch it?"

He'd been aching to get his hands on her all night, and the reasons were making a mess of his head. Everly being a part of his extended family shouldn't be a turn-on. Her tits were a turn-on. Her buttons, her hair, her ass when she walked in those stupid high heels. Those things were turn-ons.

So the idea of her belonging to his clan, being a Mitchell, wearing his name as her own . . . He wanted her out of her clothes. He wanted to bury himself inside of her, to claim her and brand her. To make her so fully his, she would never feel frightened again.

"We can, but I'm still cold, so . . ." She glanced down the hallway, and took a step that direction. "Maybe we ditch respectable and warm me up in the shower at the same time?"

He took a step toward her. "I like that plan." Then she took another, and he did the same, until Everly was running, kicking out of her heels, and he was chasing her, his boots thundering against the hardwood floor, the sound echoing through the small house.

She beat him to the bathroom, and stood there breathing hard and waiting, her eyes wide, her hair a tangled mess, her skin covered in goose bumps. She'd worn a long-sleeve blouse with her skinny black pants beneath a coat that reached her knees.

The coat was gone, as were her shoes, and her fingers and toes looked nearly blue. She wasn't kidding about being cold. But *calf nuts on a cracker*, if this blouse didn't have as many buttons as all of the others.

He popped the snaps at his cuffs, then the ones down the

front of his shirt and nodded to hers. "I'm not touching those. Unless you don't want to be wearing that blouse again either."

Her fingers moved to the button holding the collar closed and freed it. Then she said, "Watch," and opened the placket to show him the zipper behind. "Magic," she said, and slid it down, her top falling open like a windbreaker.

"Clever," he said, hopping from foot to foot to tug off his boots before stripping out of his jeans and his socks, and standing in front of her with tented drawers.

"Nice," she said, getting rid of her pants and her bra, and standing in front of him wearing a sheer lace thong. "Your turn."

He came toward her, leaned past her, turned on the water, then stood toe-to-toe with her as the room filled with steam. They breathed together, their gazes locked, and when their skin was damp he slid his fingers into the elastic holding the scrap of fabric at her hips, opening his mouth over her throat, kissing his way down her body as he pulled her thong down.

Once she'd stepped out of the panties, he stood, waiting for her to do the same. Instead, she flattened her palms on his abs, pushed her way inside his briefs, holding his cock in one hand, digging lower to hold his balls with the other. She worked him until he hardened, until his balls ached, until fluid seeped from the slit in the tip of his head. Until he found himself clenching his ass to keep his cum from rumbling free.

Then she dropped to one knee and took him in her mouth, and that was just about the end of things. The room was a sauna, her tongue was rough like a rag and hot. Her lips ringed him, holding him like two fingers, her mouth sucking him like his cock was a teat.

He stood there, his hands on top of his head to keep from reaching for her and pulling her up. He wasn't ready for this to be over with, but it was fixin' to be just that. And then things got more dicey, Everly slipping her way between his cheeks and one finger going up his ass. He squeezed against her, and she gave him a wicked-sounding laugh he wasn't sure he would ever be able to shake.

Then she stood, dragging the flat of her tongue in a line up his body to his mouth. "I want to watch," she whispered, rubbing her palm over his cock's head with purpose, then stepping into the tub and beneath the spray, fastening her hair to the top of her head with a clip.

He followed, facing her, crowding her, needing her. "You want to watch what?"

"You," she said, drawing the tip of a finger around the tip of his cock, then stepping around him and out of the spray. "Touching yourself."

He raised one foot to the tub's edge, reached for her bath gel and worked up a lather in his palm. Then he planted his free hand on the enclosure's wall beside her head, gripped his shaft with his soapy hand, and began to stroke.

He did all of it while holding her gaze, hers finally falling to watch the motion of his fist on his cock. She chewed at her lower lip, reached for her nipples and squeezed, shuddering as he rolled over the head again and again, his cock bobbing.

She blinked, sluicing the water from her face to clear her eyes, her tongue darting out, her chest rising and falling. He slicked the cup of his palm over his head faster. Faster, faster, faster. The rhythm of his hand and the heat of the water and the smell of Everly's lust drawing his balls tight.

Her tits were high, the nipples in peaks. Then she slid a hand down her chest and her belly to toy with her clit. Just tiny little touches over the tip, pulling up on the hood with one finger, then using one on either side to pull harder.

Lifting her foot to the tub so that her toes touched his, she pushed a finger into her cunt, pulled it out and brought it to her mouth, sucking it free of her cream. Then she did it again, but this time she offered her taste to him. He took it, sucked it, held her finger by the knuckle with the barest edges of his teeth while he stroked.

Enough. She could watch some other time. Right now, he was the one who'd gone cold and who needed her to warm him. He moved close, into her body, palmed the backs of her thighs and lifted her. Her legs went around his waist, her arms around his neck. Her head fell back against the tiles, and he dipped his knees, aligned his cock with her cunt, pushed deep and pushed hard and pinned her to the wall.

Then he stood there, sheathed, buried so far inside of her he had nothing left of himself to give. She had all of him. She had everything. He was gone.

He leaned into her, buried his face in the crook of her neck, pumped his hips, his thighs aching. He was fucked and it had nothing to do with where he was or what he was doing, but everything to do with this woman and his heart. She owned him. Body and soul. And she wanted nothing from him but this. How the hell was he supposed to live with that?

He couldn't, but right now was not the time for a conversation, much less an ultimatum, and he didn't know whether either one would do any good. He shut off his mind, turned the moment over to his cock, and began to move. He thrust hard because that's what he was feeling. Desperation, frustration. Anger with himself for letting things get so out of hand.

Because that's what they were. He wanted what he couldn't have, and he was fucked. That didn't stop him from finishing her, grinding against her clit until she nearly climbed up his body getting off. Then he came, the powerful bursts of cum making his knees shake and almost leveling him.

They calmed together slowly, making suds of her bath gel and playing, finally rinsing, and drying, and scurrying from the bathroom to her bed, Everly shaking until the cocoon of her blankets and their shared body heat warmed her where she lay curled against his side, his arm around her.

"Good thing you don't have to saddle up before dawn and ride out in temps below freezing."

"It's a very good thing," she said, her hand beneath his chin, one finger rubbing against the scruff of his beard. "And I'm sorry you do. Except I know how much you love ranching."

"Now you're just being mean."

"Are you saying you don't love ranching?"

"I don't love freezing my ass off while doing it, but yeah. I do."

"So it's worth whatever you have to do?"

"Pretty much."

"No matter how bad it sucks?"

"Yeah, because as cold as my ass gets? There's nothing like Sunshine's breath frosting when she snorts, and the crunch of cold grass beneath her hooves, and the sun coming up to melt everything and getting so suddenly hot I'm sweating in my gloves. And everything smells new, even in winter when it's all dead. Because the dirt that gets turned up has all kinds of promises tucked down inside, and you just have to believe things are going to change come spring. All that green sprouting up and coming to life. All those calves dropping, wobbling when they stand. There's nothing like it in the world. Absolutely nothing."

They both let that settle, and he wondered if he'd painted a bright enough picture that she could see what he saw even in the dark. He wanted her to see it, to know the beauty of his life, to understand the hardships would never be hard enough to drive him off the land. Right then, right there, he made the pledge to himself. He'd work the land until his dying day, no matter what it took out of him. No matter what it took from him. Even if it took his dream of this woman as his wife.

"You going to be okay tomorrow?" she asked as she snuggled against his side.

What was tomorrow? Oh, right. The auction. He'd been thinking about it all day, dreading it all day, until the last few hours when Everly had been with him and on his mind instead. "Sure. No problem. It's going to be great to have half the furniture Tess left us sold off."

She threaded her fingers into the hair in the center of his chest, tugging lightly on the strands. "You told me Dax and Casper were okay with it."

"They are."

"But you're not."

He shrugged. "Doesn't matter. It's a done deal. Nora's got guaranteed initial bids, or some shit."

"That's good. That means you'll be getting a nice infusion of cash."

He covered her hand, held it against his heart, wished that everything that money changed could be limited to the good. The bad was giving him hell.

# TWENTY-EIGHT

EVERLY ARRIVED LATE to the auction. She'd thought long and hard about not coming, but couldn't convince herself to stay away. Faith would be there, and Arwen, and all three of the Dalton Gang members, plus family and friends. Dozens of potential buyers would be in attendance as well. Buyers with deep pockets and a love of antiques. Nora Stokes had seen to that.

In the end, she'd come for Boone. She wasn't interested in the pieces up for sale. And except for how much the boys needed it, she didn't care about the money. All that mattered today was that, even with his sister and his parents and his boys at his side, Boone was alone. She couldn't leave him that way. Not when he'd come back for the life he'd wanted, and was now having to watch much of it being taken away.

She parked a quarter mile down the main ranch road, behind the long line of cars belonging to the browsers and buyers who'd arrived for the show. Up ahead, the main ranch yard resembled a parking lot. Boone had to hate that. He was a private man. A quiet man. Intensely so, and she loved that about him. When he shared with her the pieces of his life, she felt honored, and humbled that she'd been able to give him something he needed, a place to unload his burdens. A place to lay his head.

And there she went again, being all poetic, but there was something about him that turned her thoughts to mush. He made her happy. He filled her with joy. She laughed because of him, and with him, and he'd taught her the truth of what it meant to have a man in her bed.

He was also, she realized as she slowed her steps, parked for some strange reason in the line of vehicles up ahead, sitting behind the wheel, half a football field away from his house.

He must've heard her fighting the gravelly road, because he glanced into his side mirror, met her gaze, and seconds later opened his door and climbed from his seat.

"What are you doing sitting all the way out here?"

"What are you doing just now getting here?" he asked, his frown both desperate and relieved.

Aww. Poor baby. "Were you waiting?"

He nodded. "I was. I didn't think you were coming."

"I couldn't stay away," she said, then bravely added, "I thought you could use a friend."

He looked beyond where she stood into the distance, swallowed, gathered himself before he looked back and opened the door to the extended cab of his truck. "Get in," he said, boosting her up onto the bench and climbing in behind her. Once the door was shut, he reached for her, lifting her off the seat to straddle his lap, facing him.

She liked this Boone, the way he needed her, and even the

fact that he didn't ask caused no alarm. He would stop if she told him to. She knew that with all of her heart. It was a comforting bit of knowledge, but one she doubted she'd ever have use for. She needed him just as much.

"You and your damn buttons," he grumbled. His fingers were large, her buttons tiny. She started to push his hands away to take care of the task herself, but she didn't. Instead, she placed her palms on his knees behind her and leaned back.

"I thought you liked my buttons."

"I like getting under your buttons. I don't like what it takes to get there."

"Patience is a virtue."

"Patience can go fuck itself. My hands are too big for this shit."

"I like your big hands. I love your big hands. Do you know what I think about when I look at them? When one is doing something as simple as resting on your thigh while the other is on your steering wheel? Or when one is holding your fork while the other grips your knife?"

His hands slowed. His fingers came to a complete stop. "I'm not sure I want to know."

She flexed her fingers into the muscles above his knees. "I think about how thick your fingers are. How they feel when they slide deep into my body. How you always know when to crook just the one, and where to crook it, and how you rub that spot that makes it so hard to stop shaking. You do that and I want to come and I don't want anything else but an orgasm. An orgasm from you. And your hand. And your thumb on my clit, pushing to the left the way you know I like."

"Goddammit, woman." He let go of her blouse and reached for her hands, pulling them around to his fly. His cock bulged behind the denim, thick and full and anxious. "This is what you do to me. All of the time. I'm out riding herd, I think about you, and this happens. I'm in the shower, I think about you, and this happens. I'm in the kitchen waiting on the coffee, I think about you, and this happens."

She squeezed, loving his girth even more than his very impressive length. "I'm glad I make this happen. I'm even more glad when I'm around to appreciate it."

"Then get to appreciating," he said, reaching for his belt buckle, her hands following and working free the buttons of his fly. He closed his eyes and groaned, and she reached for him, lowering the elastic of his boxer briefs to expose his cock and his balls.

She cupped him, and stroked him, and thumbed the slit in the tip, loving how much he wanted her, that he was already so hard, so ready. She tossed her head back and laughed, feeling caught up by a rush of emotion she couldn't contain, she didn't understand, she never wanted to lose. At this moment, it didn't matter that she'd told herself there could be nothing but sex between them. At this moment, her heart was full of him, and all she wanted was to make the hurt he was feeling stop.

Beneath her, Boone groaned, the vibration a rumble she felt between her legs. It aroused her, overwhelmed her, made her wish she was wearing anything but skinny black pants. She wanted him inside of her, but even in his truck's backseat, there was little room to move; he took up more than his share with just his shoulders.

But he was so big and so hard and so terribly lonely and sad. Nothing mattered but healing the parts of him that were breaking. She let him go, kicked off her shoes, reached back to unzip her pants. He lifted a brow, then helped her, holding her hips as she worked one leg free, wiggling as he pushed his jeans and shorts down his thighs.

His cock stood bold and full, and she didn't even wait, but rose over him and pushed down, taking him slowly, taking him deep. He filled her completely, throbbed there, grew harder and thicker and made her ache at her very core. It was an ache that tore at her resolve not to feel more than lust, a resolve that she'd known for days now, weeks even, was folly.

She loved him. To her very soul, she loved him. He was what she'd never known a man could be, and he gave her things she hadn't known missing in her life, a completeness she thought she'd reached on her own. How could she? He took better care of her than she did of herself, seeing to her needs when she was unaware of them, anticipating them before she did.

How had she let this happen? This was not what she wanted, this feeling of belonging, this loss of the independence she'd worked so hard to gain. And yet . . . Those things weren't what she was feeling at all. She and Boone were sharing, giving and taking, becoming the mythical mated *one* she'd never believed in.

Dear lord, she was believing now. The thought of not having Boone in her life—

"Everly?"

Blinking the moisture from her eyes, she returned, biting down on the words that wanted to escape, saying instead, "I'm here," as she reached up and cupped his face in her hand, as she kissed him. As she rode him, a slow up and down gyration of her hips, squeezing to catch the head of his cock and pull.

He groaned beneath her, his hands on her hips guiding her, pushing up into her, pumping. Through it all, her mouth hovered above his, their breath mingling, his whiskers scraping her cheek and her chin, his lips catching hers, his teeth, too.

The intimacy brought tears to her eyes. Never in her life had she known such closeness, such honesty, such complete involvement. It was as if nothing existed in the world but the two of them, their bodies made one, their needing each other more than sexual desire.

She came because she loved him. She was so overwhelmed with that reality, she couldn't wait, or linger, or draw out the glorious anticipation. She exploded, and he followed, bits and pieces of who she'd been falling around her as she convulsed and barely stayed conscious, so happy he was as large as he was, and caught her as she collapsed.

"Wow," she said, and that was all.

"Yeah. Wow," he echoed, waiting only until they could both breathe before extracting himself from her, helping her with her clothes, tucking himself back inside his and zipping up.

The sound was like teeth on a chalkboard, bring her back to the present where real life existed, and where a lot of truths were waiting to be aired. Her truths, even though they starred him.

"Listen," she said, sliding off his lap and into the seat beside him. "I'm meeting an old friend in Austin tomorrow to see a movie, but Monday night. Can we please sit down for our interview?" It wasn't the interview she needed to have. It was all the things she needed to ask him, and to tell him. About Les. And about Penny. About what she'd done behind his back. About what she owed him. "The Hellcat Saloon? Eight o'clock? Dinner on me? I really need to finish up the story and get it to Whitey before he fires me."

"Like that would be such a bad thing if it happened?" he asked, reaching over to toy with the buttons between her breasts.

"Considering the *Reporter* is the only game in town, yeah. It would be," she said, holding his fingers still.

"You could write a cookbook," he said, lifting his gaze to hers, searching, frowning, wanting something she couldn't see. "You and Clay. Because I hate to say this, but I'm pretty sure the two of you could make me forget how much I love my mother's pot roast."

"Oh, please." She leaned over his lap to fetch her shoes from the floor. "I opened some cans and thawed ground beef Clay had already seasoned."

"It was damn good soup. Best soup I've had in forever."

"You didn't have to cook it. That's what made it the best."

"You made it for me. That's what made it the best."

She waited until both shoes were on her feet before saying, "Boone—"

"I know. It didn't mean anything." He reached behind her for the door handle, shoved open the door, letting in a gust of air that swept through the cab's tension. "It's what friends do. But I gotta say I'm getting tired of being friends."

"You want me to go?" she asked, the knot of nerves in her stomach beginning to burn.

He shook his head, leaned it against the seat back, and, eyes closed, said, "I want you never to go."

She swallowed, so close to telling him that she loved him. So afraid it was the wrong thing and still too soon. "But you'll let me go until Monday night at least?"

"Yeah," he said after a long moment she spent holding her breath. "Dinner's on you. Eight o'clock."

# TWENTY-NINE

"ARE YOU FEELING better?" Everly asked, opening her back door to Boone's knock. He wondered what she'd think if he asked for a key, if she'd be as accommodating as she had when he'd called to see if they could do the interview here instead of at Arwen's. "Now that the auction's behind you?"

He kissed her before he answered her, a sweet brush of lips that became something potent when he lingered. "You know Nora didn't even take a penny? Except paying out the cost of the auctioneer and the advertising, and that wasn't much since it was such short notice. No commission. No nothing."

"She did it because she knows even that small amount could make a difference," she said, her arms looped around his neck.

"She did it because she's good friends with my mother," he said, his hands making their way down her back to her bottom.

She wiggled, squirmed out of reach. "No, Boone. You've got to accept people doing nice things just for you."

"You're the only one I want doing nice things for me."

"No nice things until I get my interview," she said, waggling a schoolmarm finger.

He grumbled beneath his breath, words about bossy women and history belonging in the past. Words he'd already said to her and didn't feel the need to repeat. "So. The interview. We're really going to do this."

"We really are," she said, pulling a chair from beneath the table and motioning for him to sit.

He did, hooking his hat over the chair at his side and raking his hands through his hair. "I've told you pretty much everything you might want to know. And I've done a lot of it while I was naked. Why don't you just write it all down? Except the naked part."

"Because I need a record of everything you say," she said as she sat across from him. "My memory doesn't count. If you ever come back and want proof you said something, I'll need to have it."

"Why would I want proof when I know what I've said?"

"You wouldn't be asking me that question if you'd spent even a month doing my job."

"Huh. People really forget what they've said?"

"They really do. Now . . ." She hit the button on her digital recorder, clicked the end of her pen, and jotted the time and date on her notepad. And then she just sat there, her mouth twisted to one side, as if she wasn't sure where to start. As if she knew him better than she'd thought. As if she wasn't so keen after all on telling the world his story.

Interesting. "Not going to be much of an interview if you don't ask me some questions."

She laid down the pen, shut off the recorder. "I need to ask you something."

Even more interesting. "Shoot."

"You probably won't like it."

Yeah, he'd figured that when she'd turned off the recorder. "Shoot anyway."

"It's about something Les Upton said."

Like he'd thought. "What did he say?"

"He said a couple of things, actually," she said, scribbling circles on her notepad. "And I don't really believe either of them—"

"But you need to hear it from me to know."

"I don't need to, but I want to."

"Same thing."

She held his gaze, weighing his answer against whatever scale of expectations she was holding in her head. "He said you sold drugs to the kids at school."

"Well that's a steaming pile of bullshit." And funny enough to have him pushing away from the table and looking for wine in her fridge.

"And he said you got Penny pregnant."

He swallowed, let the cold air wash the heat from his face, grabbing the bottle of CapRock Roussanne, then going in search of a corkscrew. "When was this?"

"That day at the diner."

"And you're just now mentioning this."

"I should've told you—"

"Yeah. You should have," he said, opening the bottle, returning to the table to fill the two glasses he grabbed on the way, but it wasn't enough. She was waiting for an answer. One to explain the connection she'd been more than smart enough to make between that night and the next sixteen years when he hadn't once had sex without a condom.

Even now he couldn't believe he'd been that dumb. Condoms were a Dalton Gang rule. Had been since day one. The thought of bringing a kid who would be Les Upton's grandchild into the world . . . "No. I did not get Penny pregnant. But that night with her was the last time, until you, I rode bareback."

She pulled her wineglass closer, looked into it as she asked, "What happened?"

He'd told her everything he'd done, just not what had gone on in his head after that night, but they'd reached the point in this relationship, and that's what it was, a relationship, when he had to trust her as much as he expected her to trust him.

"I knew I was going to want a family one day. And that day wasn't necessarily it, but all I could think about after the trial was what if I had gotten her pregnant? What if we brought a kid into all the shit that had happened?" He emptied his wineglass, refilled it, talking while he poured. "Can you imagine a child finding out he was conceived the night his grandfather nearly beat his grandmother to death? And if we hadn't worked out as a couple, and Penny had custody of the kid? Raising him in that environment?"

He started to down his second glass of wine, stopped when Everly reached for it and took it out of his hand, holding him, stroking her thumb over the back of his, then his wrist, then the heel of his palm. "Do you know how rare it is for an eighteen-year-old to think beyond the moment? How amazing you are for knowing what you wanted and making sure you didn't screw it up?"

"Yeah. So amazing I was unzipping my pants when I walked through her front door."

It sounded stupid as he said it, stupid enough that he grabbed his wine and left the room. He'd been the one to let that night with Penny into his head. He'd never spoken of it to anyone, not his family, not his boys. He may have talked to Dave about the trouble getting Penny pregnant would've caused, but only in the most casual way he could. Picking the older man's brain, filing away the results, pulling them out and looking them over when the idea of starting a family came around.

He collapsed on Everly's couch, falling into a mountain of black-and-white pillows. She had the most comfortable pillows. On her couch. On her bed. He could sit here and not move for hours. He could sit here and sleep for days. He was that goddamn tired. That monstrously beat. Between the ranch, and the boys, and the oil well, and the antiques, and now Everly's story and Les Upton showing his sorry face around town . . .

This was not Boone's idea of making a go of anything. This was not the life he'd wanted, and yet there were parts of it he wouldn't trade for the world. And the woman he sensed walking into the living room was the biggest part of all. He wanted her in his life. Permanently. But until he could find a way to straighten out about a billion messes . . .

She sat on the couch beside him, sat facing him, tucked her crossed legs beneath her, her closest knee pushing into his ribs. Leaning forward, she placed her hand along his cheek, waited until he looked into her eyes. Hers were damp, and sad, but broadcast a whole lot of hopeful emotion, and those were the things he reached for, what he clung to.

"You have to know I would never put anything in my story that would hurt you. You have to know that. Digging for dirt's not my style. That's not why I asked you what happened. I asked that for me. I wanted to know that for me."

"Did Whitey give you this assignment knowing that?" he

asked, reaching for the wineglass he'd set on the lamp table, leaving it there to have something besides touching her to do with his hand. "Because I can't imagine he'd be too happy finding it out after the fact."

"What Whitey doesn't know, Whitey doesn't know, and that's just how it is. I'm the one writing the story. And he will never hear anything about Penny from me in any context. Neither will anyone else. Please know that Boone. Tell me you know I would never do anything to add to your pain."

"It's not so painful anymore."

"But it was."

"Yeah. It was," he said, dropping his head back on the couch. He hadn't brought out the story to look at it closely in a very long time, and wouldn't have done so if Everly hadn't pushed. Except she hadn't pushed. She'd asked. And she'd only done that because Penny's goddamn father couldn't keep his fucking mouth shut. Boone wasn't big on hating other men, but what he felt for Les Upton . . .

"I left town because of that son of a bitch," he heard himself admitting out loud for the very first time. "Yeah, I wanted to cowboy. Yeah, the boys were gone, I couldn't make a go of it with Dave, I had no interest in school. But it was goddamn Les Upton that I couldn't deal with. He was in prison, but his shop was still out on the highway, and his house was still over behind the high school, and I had a feeling he'd be coming back here when he got out.

"I shouldn't have let him get to me, but it was hard, seeing another man beat the shit out of two women he was supposed to love. And I could've fathered a kid who'd have carried his blood as well as mine. That was a bigger wake-up call than any of my folks' punishments, or any of the nights I spent in a jail cell, or any of the lessons I learned working for Dave. I let something that never even happened fuck me up. And that is just goddamn crap."

"I'm so sorry, Boone," she said, her voice breaking softly. "I want to say something smart, like life isn't fair, and that night had a one-in-a-million chance of happening, but platitudes never help." She pressed his hand between both of hers, brought it to her face, kissing him, then to her chest where he felt the beat of her heart like a drum leading him home. "What can I do? How can I make things better? I know I can't, not really, but for now, please tell me."

"You being here is all I need."

"That sounds like a platitude to me."

"Maybe so," he said with a smile. "But it doesn't mean it's not true. Things are always better when you're around."

"Are they?" she asked, her voice so quiet and uncertain, he frowned and sat straighter, looking for a hint of what was going on with her.

"You don't believe me?"

"I want to believe you. It's just . . . I've always thought the way to a man's heart was through his open fly. I've never had anyone just want me around without wanting me naked."

That settled it. No sex tonight. Not that he'd been making plans, but they always ended up in bed, or on her sofa, or in his truck, and out of their clothes. "There's something to be said for getting a woman out of her clothes. Not the ones who'll strip for anyone, but the ones who put that kind of trust in a particular man."

"What kind of trust is that?" she asked, and he couldn't tell if she was playing with him, or wasn't sure what he meant, or a combination of both.

He decided to lay it on the line. "That he'll do right by her, and in more ways than making her come."

"Such as?"

"That he won't go talking about what they've done together. That he'll keep her secrets close. That'll he value what she's given him, and take care of that gift, because that's what it is, that privilege. Sharing something like that with one woman only and no one else ever again . . ."

"You want that."

He nodded. "Most men do. Those who recognize all the things a woman can offer. Things that aren't between her legs."

The moment hung there, both of them lost in separate places, Boone wishing he could tell her that he loved her, because those were the words hanging on the tip of his tongue. They were wine flavored and slipping quickly toward his lips, and he was wondering if it was time to put them out there, let the damn chips fall—

"There's something else."

"What's that?" he asked, glad she'd kept him from being more stupid than he'd already managed.

"When I was interviewing Dax," she said, toying with the snaps of his shirt, "Arwen mentioned having heard two of her Kittens talking about Penny's husband."

"Penny's married." He made the statement without really knowing what he felt.

"To a man named Dean Blaylock."

"Yeah. He was in school a couple of years ahead of us."

"I guess he works for Len Tunstall. They live over in Southwest Crow Hill."

"Don't tell me." He closed his eyes, rubbed the grit of exhaustion from them. "You went to see her."

"I had to."

"Why the hell for?"

"Because of what her father told me."

"That I got her pregnant?" When she nodded, he added, "What did she say?"

"About that? Nothing. About the night of the assault? A lot. Most of it what you'd already told me. But a lot of it was about her life now, and the guilt she still carries over what happened in high school."

"I'll just bet—"

"No. Trust me," she said, her hand on his cheek forcing him to hold her gaze. "I know the sort of emotional baggage she's juggling. It's very real." She rubbed her thumb along his cheekbone. "She's not what I expected at all. She's not—"

"Her father?"

"Yeah, but she's also a very nice woman. And I think she'd like to see you."

"I don't know why," he said, blowing out a long breath full of resignation.

And then Everly smiled. "But you're going to find out."

Yeah. He was.

# THIRTY

EVERLY SPENT A long, sleepless night thinking of the things Boone had said. It had been strange doing so with him in bed beside her, either curled around her, or an arm thrown over her, or a foot tucked between hers. She remembered the first night he'd slept in her house, how she'd thought sleeping with him without touching him would be difficult. She'd been right.

He never stopped touching her during the night. Every time she woke his hand was somewhere, as if making sure she hadn't left him, as if wanting her to know he was there, and she was safe, and nothing was going to happen to her. And anyone who tried to hurt her would have to go through him.

Toby had wanted to be with her because of what she offered him: visibility. Her career came with a lot of perks that Toby craved—invitations to society functions, chances to mix and mingle with political figures, with celebrities, with philanthro-

pists, with all the movers and shakers a man with his aspirations
could want.

Boone wanted to be with her. Period. For all the same reasons she wanted to be with him. And yet so much stood between them, their pasts huge, hulking obstacles. Or at least
hers was hulking. He'd pretty much stomped his flat. And listening to him now in the shower, that wasn't hard to imagine.
When the man threw his weight around, things bent to his will.

She glanced at the bedside clock, forcing herself not to
grumble at the time. This was ranching time, Boone's time. If
he could get going at this hour, so could she, though coffee
would help. And she was back with two cups by the time Boone
came out of her bathroom completely dressed save for his
bare feet.

"Wow," she said, handing him his cup, then giving him a
once-over while he drank. "I feel like such a slacker. Not to
mention I was hoping you might come back to bed for a while."

"Can't," he said, placing the cup on her dresser while he sat
in the plush club chair beside it. "Sun's on the way up. Need to
beat it to the ranch." He said it without looking at her, shaking
out his socks and pulling them on, taking another long swallow of his coffee before he reached for his boots.

"Do you want another cup?" she asked, climbing into the
center of the bed, tucking the covers around her waist, feeling
strange. "The pot's still half-full."

"I'll grab one on the way out," he said, standing, the hem of
one pants leg tucked into the top of his boot. "Thanks for
brewing it. You didn't have to."

"I didn't want you on the road this early without *some* caf-
feine," she said, her own mug hot in her nervous hands. Was
this how he was so early in the morning? All business? No time
for fun? "I've got a travel mug in the cabinet above the ma-

chine. And your hat's hanging on the back of the chair where you left it."

"Yeah. I'll get it. Thanks." He headed for the bedroom door, stopped with his hands at his hips, and hung his head before he looked back. "Everly—"

"Just say it," she said, her heart doing its best to jump out of her chest. "Something's wrong. Just tell me."

He met her gaze, held her gaze, breathed in and let his fall to the floor. "I can't do this anymore."

"Do what?" she asked, slowly reaching over to set her mug on the bedside table. Her hand was shaking, her sheets were clean. She spilled anyway, but just a drop. It soaked into the pristine white cotton, staining it. Marking it. A reminder of the moment her life imploded.

"This," he said, waving his arm to encompass the room. "With you."

"What with me?" Because he couldn't mean what she thought he meant. He couldn't.

"The sex."

"You don't want to have sex?"

"I damn well do want to have sex."

She pressed a fist to the center of her chest. "Then what—"

"We're going to have a relationship, a real relationship, or we're done having sex."

*What?* "Boone, wait—"

"No, you wait. Here's the thing." He came back to the bed, gripped the footboard with both hands and leaned forward. "I want what Dax has with Arwen. I want what Casper has with Faith. Hell, I want what my parents have. I want what Dave Dalton had with Tess," he said, pushing to stand. "And I want it with you."

"We have—"

"We have sex. Most of the time when you want it. Where you want it. The way you want it."

What was he saying? She didn't know what he was saying. "I thought you liked having sex."

"I do like having sex. I goddamn love having sex. But there is a hell of a lot more to a relationship than a pussy and a cock, and if you don't know that—"

"Of course I know that," she nearly screamed, her voice breaking, tears spilling before she could stop them.

"Then what's the problem?"

"We agreed—"

"No. We never agreed. I knew you didn't want a relationship, but we never agreed."

"So this is it? We're done? I'm never going to see you again?" How could she go through the rest of her life and never see him again?

"It's Crow Hill. We'll see each other. And we can date, hang out, whatever, but I can't keep doing this,"—he nodded toward her bed, her rumpled sheets that smelled of the both of them, toward her— "losing myself in you, without knowing we're going somewhere. I'm not your ex, Ev. I'm me. I'm Coach Mitchell's son, and Faith Mitchell's brother. I'm a one-third owner of the broke-down Dalton Ranch."

"I know all of that—"

"Every day . . ." He dropped his gaze to the floor, rubbed a hand over his eyes before jamming his hands to his waist and staring at her, red eyed, wet eyed. "You're all I think about. I live for you and I breathe for you and I'm pretty sure you have no idea of any of that."

Her heart stopped beating. Just for a moment, just long enough to let his words sink in. Just long enough for all of what he was saying to find room in her chest to settle. All of it. Every tiny bit. And then she made fists in the covers and pulled them to her breasts, hiding. "You deserve better than me, Boone. I'm . . ."

"Don't tell me you're damaged goods. Don't even say that."

"I don't know if I can give you what you want. What you need." She blinked to clear her eyes, sniffed to clear her nose and her throat, thought nothing Toby had ever done to her hurt as much as this. "I locked so much of myself away after . . . Austin. Self-defense, I guess."

"I get self-defense, Everly. I'm not a stupid man. But have you once needed those walls with me? Have I ever given you a reason to feel afraid?"

She nodded, and she could tell by the vein at his temple, the tic in his jaw that she had pissed him off, but he waited, letting her have her say. "I'm afraid of disappointing you. Of hurting you. Of not living up to this image of who you think I am, or who you want me to be. Of not being able to give you what you want. Those half-dozen little ranchers—"

"I don't have to have that—"

"But you want that. Who am I to take away what you want?" She pulled the covers higher, tighter, used them to catch her tears. "I love you, Boone. I could never take away what you want."

"I want you, Everly. I want *you*."

But nothing about loving her when she'd laid her heart on the line. "And I want to believe that. I *do* believe that. But I don't think you're ready for me. For us. As much as you think that you are."

"What kind of bullshit excuse—"

"He hit me."

He stilled, stared at her, didn't so much as blink as anger rushed from his core to deepen the color of the surface of his skin. "What? When?"

She hadn't want to tell him like this. She hadn't wanted to tell him at all. "My ex. He hit me. It's why I left Austin. It's why I came to Crow Hill. Faith came to my rescue. Found me the house and the job."

"Everly—"

"This," she said while she still had the nerve, showing him the scar on her wrist. "I didn't slip on a melted ice cube and grab for the stove. This was from the prong of his belt buckle."

"Fucking hell. Everly. I didn't know."

"Of course not." It was called hiding out for a reason. "I didn't tell you."

"Why not?" he asked, moving to her bedside and reaching for her hands. "Why didn't you?"

"Because that's not the worst of it."

He closed his eyes, ground his jaw. "What happened?"

She dropped her gaze to his knee where their fingers were wound together. "He liked his sex rough. It was the only way he could get off. And his getting off was all that mattered. If he hurt me while doing it, that was just the price of sex. At least to his way of thinking."

"Who was this guy? Who the fuck was this guy?"

She shook her head. "It doesn't matter. He doesn't matter."

"He hurt you. That matters. It matters to me."

"I love that you want to defend my honor," she said, and felt the stirrings of a smile.

"I want to fucking beat his head into the ground. Nothing about that's honorable."

She squeezed her fingers around his. "Please know I'm fine. I need you to know I'm fine."

"The day in bed when I got rough . . . *Criminy.* You said you liked it."

"I did like it."

"How could you like it when—"

"I liked it because it was you," she said, pulling her hand from his to cup his face, to stroke her thumb over his cheekbone. "But I shouldn't have put you in that position. To worry—"

"The scarves," he said, shaking his head. "They weren't about you getting off, were they? You needed to be sure I wouldn't hurt you."

"I'm sorry."

"Everly—"

"I want to be with you, Boone. I want so much to be with you. I'm just afraid of the next step."

He cupped the back of her head, brought her close, his lips pressed to her forehead as he held her, his heart racing, her heart racing, too. "I really gotta go. I've got an ass chewing waiting at the ranch for being late."

"Go. I'm fine."

He was shaking his head when he got to his feet. "You're not fine, but I have to. We'll talk later."

"Yeah," she said, wondering as he left her there if they'd ever talk again.

# THIRTY-ONE

EVERLY SAT IN the corner booth nearest the bar and the Hellcat Saloon's kitchen, her laptop open, her notes spread out on the table. She sat there, looking like she was working, pretending like she was working, but doing the same thing she'd been doing all day. Thinking about Boone's bottom line. About her confession. About his walking out yesterday morning after she'd opened up and bared her soul. That, more than anything, was what she hadn't been able to reconcile.

Had she expected him to skip work and spend his day with her because of something that had happened over four years ago? Had she expected her revelation to have him changing his mind about the relationship he wanted? Had she expected him to give up his dreams because she'd told him about Toby's abuse?

What *had* she thought would happen once she'd revealed

the big secret of her past? What? What? *What*? That they'd continue to have sex? No complications? No commitment? Years and years of what they had now? Of course he'd walked out. He had a life. One he'd said he wanted to share with her.

So why no reaction when she'd told him she loved him? And why in the world had she picked that moment, of all the ones they'd spent together, to tell him how she felt when even now she wasn't sure the words were true, or a desperate attempt to keep him with her? And how pathetic was that?

"How much time is Whitey giving you on your Dalton Gang piece?" Arwen asked, replacing Everly's empty wineglass with a full one, her third of the night. "And this is it, or Dax will be driving you home."

She didn't want to go home. It was too quiet at home. Too empty. Like the pit of her stomach. Like the center of her chest. "Thanks," she said, leaving the wine where it was.

"Hey," Arwen said, sliding into the seat opposite her. "You okay?"

"No."

"Is it the story?"

Did Boone's being part of the story count? "No."

"Is it Boone?"

Because those were the only two choices? Work and her sex life? Lordy, but she needed to get over herself. One of her best friends was worried about her, and she was being wretched.

She reached for her wine, took a swallow, then met Arwen's concerned gaze. "Can we talk?"

"I thought that's what we were doing," the other woman said, tugging at her ponytail to tighten it.

Everly shook her head. "I mean about something I'm having a problem with."

"Of course, sweetie. Though I'm going to guess your something is really a someone. And since it's just you and me here and not Faith, I'm going to guess your someone is Boone."

"I think I screwed up," she said, and downed more wine.

"With Boone?" When she nodded, Arwen pressed. "How so?"

"He gave me an ultimatum. He doesn't want to be with me anymore, unless it's on his terms."

Arwen sat back, crossed her arms. "That sounds ominous, except knowing Boone, I can't imagine him having any evil intent."

"He wants a relationship. Not just sex." Everly propped her elbows on the table and her head in her hands, rubbing at the ache in her temples. "And if that's not what I want, then we're through. Basically, he's done wasting his time."

"Is that what he said?" Arwen asked, after Everly's statement had settled. "Were those his words?"

"No, but they might as well have been," she said, reaching over to close her laptop and gather her notes.

"Huh. Are you sure he didn't say he wanted to be with you because he loves you?"

Oh, the irony. "He definitely did not say that."

Arwen turned in her seat, crossed one leg, swung her foot. "Did you want him to say that? Is that what's wrong? His terms don't include him loving you?"

"He didn't say it," she said, stacking the papers before clipping them, "but everything else he said makes me think he does. And I'm not sure I'm ready for that."

"Do you love him?"

"I don't know," she said, ready to collapse. "I think so."

"Sweetie, either you do or you don't."

She made it sound so simple. "How did you know you loved Dax?"

"How does anyone know they love anyone? You just do. It's like, even with all the grief they cause you, and grief is a given with the Dalton Gang boys, you'd rather deal with that than deal with the hurt of not having them."

"I don't know if what I'm feeling is hurt as much as, well, confusion. I don't know what he wants from me. But that's not true either. He wants what Dax has with you. What Casper has with Faith."

Arwen smiled, a soft, knowing smile that stirred all of what Everly was feeling into a befuddling fog. "That's about as close to an admission of love as I've ever heard the man make."

"Then why the ultimatum? Why not wait until I'm ready? Why would he want me if I'm not?" Except even as the words left her mouth, she knew that she was. Boone had given her that, allowed her to see that she loved her life, that she loved him, that it was foolish to give her mistake with Toby any more due.

"Let me ask you this," Arwen said. "Are you using your ex to judge him? Boone? Are you letting some kind of clock tick, tick, tick, thinking he's going to strike out?"

"No. Oh no." She shook her head vehemently. "I don't for a minute think Boone would hurt me. I'm more worried about hurting him by holding back. I trust him completely, but I don't trust me. I'm afraid I'll always be waiting for the other shoe to fall."

"Maybe that's what Boone's sensing. Maybe he's in whole hog and knows, even without you saying anything, that you're not."

"How am I supposed to make him understand?" she asked, pulling her wineglass close.

"You can't. It's just like love. Either he does or he doesn't. There is no 'make.'"

Everly groaned. "Since when did you start dispensing *Star Wars* philosophy?"

"Look at it this way," Arwen said, ignoring her. "He's told you about what happened with Penny Upton, right?"

"So you do know—"

"Yeah, I do. I lived here at the time. Do you understand what happened to him?"

"Do I understand that he was having sex with her when her father came in and tried to beat her mother to death? What's to understand?"

Arwen waited a moment, then asked, "Do you understand what the fallout did to him?"

She nodded, thinking back to Boone sharing his fears about bringing a child into Penny's family.

"Does that change how you feel about him?"

"No, but his past—"

"Don't say it's different than what you went through. I know it's different. But it's damage, nonetheless."

Arwen was right, and Everly should've realized that the moment Boone trusted her with his fears. Of course he was damaged. Of course that incident had left its mark on him. He was kind and tender, a vulnerable man, an unforgettable man, no matter how intimidating his size and bearing.

Yet he'd made love with her and not used a condom. Her. No other woman. Her. If she needed a sign that he loved her, he'd given it to her that night, even before she'd known she loved him.

"Thank you," she said, taking the first full breath she'd managed in hours. "I may have just figured this out."

"There is no figure," Arwen said, smoothing her Hellcat Saloon T-shirt as she got to her feet, and adding with a wink, "there only is."

# THIRTY-TWO

BOONE PULLED TO a stop at the edge of the grassy ditch in front of the frame house belonging to Dean Blaylock, hoping the other man wasn't home. It was hard to tell from the number of cars parked in the driveway and yard who was. For all he knew, the entire Blaylock clan might be inside with shotguns. There had to be at least a half-dozen vehicles, and none on blocks or with their hoods popped for repairs.

That left Boone wondering, as he walked by, if he was walking into a Blaylock ambush, or if they all belonged to Dean. And that took his wondering all the way to what kind of salary Len Tunstall paid. The slaughterhouse might be a good place to apply if the ranch went belly-up, because if that happened, Boone would need work.

As he headed up the driveway, winding his way through the cars, two boys, blond-haired and both under ten, came running from the back of the house, shooting at each other with big colorful water cannons. Not quite the ambush he'd been imagining, but close enough.

They dodged this way and that, one turning down the path where Boone stood, the other coming after the first—and shooting. Since the smaller boy had ducked, Boone took the hit from the taller, a splatter of cold water soaking his midsection and spreading out across the lower front of his shirt.

The boy who'd pulled the trigger stopped, his big blue eyes going calf wide. "Sorry, sir. I'm really sorry. I didn't see you there. Joel, go get Mom." The younger boy scampered off toward the back of the house, yelling, "Mom! Mom!" while Boone pulled the tails of his shirt from his belt and tried to wring out some of the moisture.

"Don't worry about it. A little water never killed a man."

The boy's cheeks were bright pink, and Boone was pretty sure it wasn't from the sun or the exertion. "I was looking at Joel, and he ducked right when I was shooting, and there you were. I'm really sorry."

"You and your brother out of school for some reason?" Seemed strange to find kids running around in the middle of the day.

"Mom homeschools us. We're on our recess break," he said, just as the other boy came running back to say, "She's coming," then, "Here," as he handed Boone a clean hand towel.

Penny Upton having kids was one thing; why shouldn't she have moved on and done just that? But homeschooling them? Hard to believe the girl he'd known would've had the initiative, not to mention the smarts to educate these two boys.

"Thanks, kid," he said to the little one who looked just as guilty as the older. Boone started to say more, but just then the front door opened, and Penny stepped out on the porch.

She looked good. That was the first thing that came to

mind. A strange thing to come to mind, but she did. With the part of town she lived in, and the front yard used for auto storage, and Dean working at the slaughterhouse . . . He hadn't expected her to look good. He'd expected worn and haggard and down on her luck. But those were the things he associated with her father, and she was none of them.

"Why, Boone Mitchell," she said, one hand going to her cocked hip, a smile lighting up her face as he walked closer, drying his stomach with her towel. "As I live and breathe. And don't you look like a walking advertisement for Wrangler jeans."

"Penny," he said, pulling off his hat when he reached her, not quite sure what to do with her comment. "Good to see you, too."

"Is it? Because you're the last person I'd have ever thought would think seeing me was a good thing," she said, her laugh unexpectedly nervous. "Jacob. Joel. Did you apologize to Mr. Mitchell for getting him all wet?"

The boys nodded, their mother's arched brow getting both to mumble another, "Sorry, sir."

"Okay then," she said. "Recess is over. Go put on dry shirts, then it's thirty minutes of Harry Potter. I'll be in to talk about what you've read when you're done."

"Yes, ma'am," they said in unison before running back into the house. Tickled, Boone found himself unable to stop the pull of a smile at their obvious love and respect for their mother.

This woman, as much if not more than Tess and Dave Dalton, had determined what he'd done with and how he'd lived his life. And here he was, caught off guard by what she'd done with hers. He hadn't expected any of this. He wasn't sure what he was supposed to feel.

Penny let the screen door slam shut behind her sons, and stayed on the porch with him. "I do apologize. I have to let them run off some of the wild several times during the day, or Dean comes home and all three of us are ready to pull out our hair from being cooped up."

He didn't want to hear about her life with Dean Blaylock. He'd already seen and learned too much, and he wasn't sure what he thought about how happily settled the other man was. "Could we talk?"

"Well, now, I don't know," she said, nervous again, pushing at the bangs falling into her eyes. "Dean's due home and I need to get supper started. Not sure he'd be happy to find me having a little tête-à-tête on his front porch with another man who used to share my bed. Except *sharing* may not be the best word since you were only there that once, and not for long."

He stepped off the porch and down the cement steps that wobbled to the sidewalk, which was cracked and held together by weeds. "This won't take but a minute. Or I can come back when it's more convenient for you."

He didn't want to come back. He wanted to get this over with. Coming here today had taken more guts than he could ever have imagined it would, with what they had between them. But he didn't want to crowd her, or make her uncomfortable, or cause her trouble when her life looked to be pretty damn good.

"Okay then," she said, stepping inside the house for a box of cigarettes and a lighter, then coming back out and pulling the door all the way shut. She moved to sit on the top step, tapping the box against her palm as she did, then lighting up. "What's on your mind?" she finally asked after inhaling, then blowing a stream of smoke off to the side.

He jammed his hat back to his head. "I know our history's pretty fucked-up, but I wondered if you might call off your old man. He's . . . bothering a friend of mine."

"Bothering? A friend?" she asked, taking another drag, then chuckling. "Does your *friend* happen to work for the *Reporter*?"

"She does."

"She the one doing a story on the Dalton Gang? The one who came by because she wanted to know some of our history?"

"I told her our history. He told her I sold drugs."

"Yeah. She mentioned that."

"He also told her I got you pregnant," he said, and jammed his hands to his hips.

"He would've liked that," she said, shaking her head. "Me being pregnant by you instead of . . . Crap." She bit off the word, cringing.

Frowning, he took a step closer, but then he had to stop so he could breathe. "You were pregnant?"

She nodded. "I'd found out that day, actually. It's kinda why I brought you home with me," she said, punctuating the admission with a shrug.

"What?" This wasn't making any sense at all.

"Oh, Boone." She pushed her bangs off her forehead and held them there, sadness creeping into the spot where cockiness had been. "You had the best family in the world. Mine had gone to shit. I wasn't about to bring a baby into that. I thought if I told you it was yours, maybe your family would take me in." She laughed a laugh with no humor, picked a speck of tobacco from the end of her tongue. "Nice of me, wasn't it? Trying to use you to get me a better life."

*Whoa. Talk about out of the blue.* "What changed your mind?"

"You did," she said, her bottom lip quivering with the break in her voice. "Saving my life and my mother's. I couldn't ruin your life, when you'd saved mine."

His heart was pounding. His heart was aching. "Did you have the baby?"

"I did." She wrapped her arms around herself, her eyes going bright red and damp. "When I was in Corpus with my mom. I stayed there eight months, had the baby, gave her up for adoption."

*Criminy.* "But it wasn't mine."

"*She* wasn't yours," she said, finally looking up, tears spilling over, dripping from the tips of her long lower lashes to wash down her cheeks. "But she was mine. My daughter. Until she wasn't anymore."

"Penny . . ." His gut was in knots, good ones, bad ones, all the hateful thoughts he'd had of her tossing themselves into the fire of his rage. It burned fiercely, consuming itself, leaving almost no ash as a memory, leaving him free. "I don't know what to say."

"Don't say anything, Boone." She brought up her hand, pressed her fingers to her mouth, looked off over the yard of cars, blinking hard. "Don't say anything."

He waited a long moment, pulling off his hat to worry the brim, giving her time to settle. Giving himself the same. "I didn't come here to hurt you, or make you feel bad. I just thought you could help me with Les."

"If I could, I would, but I don't talk to my father, Boone. I can't help you," she said. "My best advice would be not to engage him. It's worked for me."

"Okay," he said, and it was all he had. His problems with Les seemed like nothing in light of what this woman had gone through. "Thank you. For telling me the truth."

"I should've done it sooner. When I came back. I should've looked you up and told you then. I don't know why I didn't, except I was embarrassed. And I was sad. I thought letting you off the hook for your grief, even though you had nothing to grieve, would buy me some good karma." She waited a moment, added, "I think it worked."

"It's okay, Penny. Really—"

"No, Boone. It's not. I've lived with this for so long. This one thing has been the reason I've made so many of the choices I have. Don't get me wrong. I love my life. I love Dean and the boys. I wouldn't trade what I have for anything. But if I'd told you sooner, I might've been just a little bit happier all this time, you know?"

He didn't know if she would have, but the ways *his* life would've been different . . . "You had your reasons, and yeah. I wish you would've come clean a long time ago. But you doing so now means a lot to me."

"You going to marry that girl?" she finally asked when he'd run out of things to say.

"I don't know."

"She loves you."

"I don't know that either," he said, Everly's voice saying those very words filling him with hope.

"She does. I could tell. Give her some time to realize it. Or, you know, tell her first. That you love her. She might need to hear it. And it might do you a whole lot of good to say it."

As he drove away, he decided Penny Upton Blaylock was a whole lot smarter than he'd ever given her credit for.

# THIRTY-THREE

UNTIL BOONE HAD walked out of her bedroom three mornings ago, Everly had been thrilled about participating in the holiday carnival. Now that the evening was here, she and Kendall Sheppard manning the kissing booth as promised, she was having to feign excitement.

She did not want to be here. She did not want to kiss dozens of strangers. She did not want to help out friends who were as close as family.

And she certainly didn't want to do so under the watchful gaze of Boone Mitchell.

That was the worst part of the night. The proximity of his booth to hers. She wouldn't have been as out of sorts if he'd been farther down the midway, but no. Directly across from where she stood beneath a banner painted with dozens of kissing lips, Boone sat on the seat in the dunking booth, completely dry, glaring at everyone who dared take a shot.

Between shots, he glared at everyone who leaned across the stand to buss her on the cheek. She wanted to glare at them, too, but mostly in warning. Like they didn't know who they were messing with, getting on Boone Mitchell's bad side. Then again, they weren't a couple, were they? He'd said they would talk. They hadn't. Exactly as she'd predicted three mornings ago when he'd walked out of her room.

Yet none of this would be happening if she'd been brave enough to tell him she wanted the very things he did: a relationship that was more than sex, a life lived on the land, a family. And all of it with him. She needed to tell him she wanted all of it with him. Her telling him that was the only thing keeping them apart.

Well, that and him telling her he loved her, too.

"Hey, Ms. Grant. Kendall."

"Clay Whitman," Kendall said, giving the teen a playful glare when she saw the strip of tickets he held. "Does your father-to-be know you're here?"

Clay gestured over his shoulder to where Casper waited his turn in the dunking booth. "He dared me to come. He gave me the tickets."

"Sounds just like Casper Jayne to me," Everly said, taking Clay's tickets. The Dalton Gang weren't called boys for nothin'.

Kendall crooked a finger. "Bring your cute self closer." Clay's whole face went red as she reached for his chin, giving Everly a wink and a nod. Both women leaned toward him at the same time, planting their lips on his cheeks. The photographer behind them snapped the shot with a huge flash that lit up their booth brighter than the midway's rides.

Clay was still grinning when he pulled away, matching lipstick prints on his cheeks. "That was pretty cool," he said, then ran off to a group of similarly gawky boys to brag and stroll down the midway like God's gift.

Definitely a Dalton Gang member in the making.

"Sometimes I wonder if that kid is the real deal," Kendall said, "or if Casper conjured him up somehow, because he's going to break some hearts."

"Time will tell." Though Everly agreed. "In another year, he could be a regular hell-raiser."

"And that would serve Casper right," Kendall said, adding a sharp, "Oh, my," under her breath that had Everly glancing over—just in time to see Greg Barrett approaching their booth. He looked like he'd just come from the office, dressed in black pants and Italian loafers, and a crisp white shirt with a sharp designer tie.

Tucking his glasses in the pocket of his shirt, he nodded toward Everly, but handed his ticket to Kendall. She took it, stared at it, rubbed it between her forefinger and thumb, her gaze finally coming up to meet Greg's bright blue one, her cheeks going hot pink beneath the booth's strings of twinkling lights.

The rules for the kissing booth included no touching, but Greg broke them, sliding his hand into Kendall's hair to cup the back of her head. She kept her hands flat on the stand, a divider between her and Greg's bodies, but as Everly watched she curled her fingers, making fists, slanting her head beneath Greg's kiss.

It was beautiful, the want in both of them, the kiss simple and nearly chaste, but only on the surface. Everly knew that because of her own reaction, her gaze searching out Boone across the midway, her heart turning flips in her chest, her stomach tied in knots of longing.

Greg was the one to finally break the contact, but only that of his mouth. His hand lingered, stroking through Kendall's hair until neither she nor Everly could breathe. Then he let her go and stepped back, hesitating briefly as if he had something to say before turning and walking away.

The tension in the booth as thick as fresh cream, Everly sidled up to the other woman and grabbed her arm. "What was *that*?"

"I don't know," she said, an anxious squeak of a laugh escaping with the words, "but God, my knees are knocking, and can I please have another?"

No kidding. "Have you and Greg—"

"No," Kendall said, shaking her head. "Never. We've hardly even had occasion to talk. At least not about anything that wasn't business."

"I'm pretty sure that wasn't business," Everly said, her gaze still on Greg, the sound of a loud splash and even louder cheer rising to snag her attention.

She looked toward the dunking booth in time to see Boone grab for his hat and go under, a group of teens high-fiving their member who'd sent him down. He came up sputtering, slamming a battered mess of wet straw on his head as he climbed from the tank.

But rather than taking his seat, he kept climbing, jumping from the platform to the ground, ignoring Dax and Casper as they motioned him back. The group of teens skedaddled, boots scooting in the midway dirt as they got out of the way of what looked like an imminent explosion.

It was when Everly realized he only had eyes for her that her own heart began to race, her breathing going shallow and short, her feet telling her to run. But she couldn't move. She was rooted to the ground. Stuck there by the fire burning in his eyes, his nostrils flaring like a big bad bull's.

He was soaked to the skin, his clothes plastered to his body, his boots turning the dirt of the midway to mud behind him, but still he came, the crowd parting like the Red Sea to make way.

"Ev?" Kendall asked beside her, reaching over to squeeze her hand. "Are you okay? You're shaking like a leaf."

She nodded, squeezing back before Kendall let her go. "I think so," she said, then gave a desperate laugh. "I hope so," she added, because she couldn't be sure. "I guess I'd better be," she finished with, because the time had come. Boone was there, rounding the booth as he came for her.

Without saying a word, he grabbed her wrist, spun her into his body, bent her backwards, and leaned over her. She held tight to his shoulders, her eyes wide as she looked into his, his stern mouth breaking into a smile just before it covered hers.

He kissed her like no one was watching, like she was the only woman in the world, like he'd die if he didn't, like he loved her. She clenched her fingers, digging into the balls of his muscles, arching her body into his and kissing him back the same. Because she loved him. More than she'd thought possible. And she couldn't imagine living her life without him there every day.

When he began to ease away, the crowd who'd gathered erupted into whoops and hollers and applause, but Everly had eyes for no one but Boone. He was her whole world. He was her whole existence. She'd lived her whole life waiting for him, and she'd never even known.

"Can we go someplace and talk?" he asked as he set her back to rights, his arm still around her back, her hands still on his shoulders. But he didn't wait for an answer, taking her by the hand and tugging her beside him until they reached the parking lot and his truck.

He let down the tailgate, lifted her up to sit, and frowned. "You're wearing boots."

She straightened her legs to show him. The vamps were brown leather, the shafts embroidered with a Southwest design in gold and purple and brick red. "I am."

"You're wearing them with a skirt."

She was that, too, a flowered Laura Ashley number that matched her off-the-shoulder lavender peasant blouse. "I'm not sure I'll ever be a jeans person. But I can do boots."

"I like the boots. I like the skirt." And then he started pacing, as if what he liked had no bearing on whatever it was consuming him.

"Boone? What's going on?"

"About the other morning," he said, and stopped. "I'm sorry. So sorry. About everything you told me. About everything I said." He voice caught, choked back by all the things he was feeling. "I know I'm doing this all wrong, but I love you, Everly. I goddamn love you. I want to spend the rest of my life with you. Just tell me we've got a chance. Down the road. When the time is right."

"We've got a chance," she said, adding because she knew in the deepest part of her heart it was true, "And the time *is* right. I love you, Boone Mitchell. I love you so very much."

He came to her then, but instead of holding her, or kissing her, or even sitting beside her on the tailgate, he went back to pacing, making her wonder if he'd even heard what she'd said. His expression was conflicted, dark when it should've been bursting with light, harsh when it should've softened.

"I don't have anything to offer you," he said. "I'm so broke there's not enough duct tape in the world to fix me."

"Oh, Boone." Could he be any sweeter, worrying like this? "I don't need money—"

"It's not just money. It's the life. Asking you to share in all of what I go through . . . I shouldn't ask that of you." He stopped, dragged a hand over his jaw. "Except having you with me these last few weeks, everything has seemed so much easier."

"I can help with the money, you know."

"I don't want you to help with the money."

"But I do. Whitey doesn't pay me much, but I can sell my shoes—"

That brought his gaze to hers. He came closer, his hands at his hips as he took in her boots. "No. You're not selling your shoes. I like your shoes. I love your shoes."

*Oh, poor misguided man.* "Do you know my shoe collection is worth as much as a couple of Tess's antiques?"

"Okay." He nodded, and his head came up. "You can sell your shoes," he said, and she laughed.

"And about those little ranchers—"

"I want you," he said, closing in on her to stand between her legs, his hands possessively at her waist. "That's all that matters. Well, and you wanting me."

She did, so very much, in so very many ways. "What if the little ranchers are my idea?"

"Then I'd have to say I like the way you think." He looked at her feet again, arched a brow. 'You'll need better boots though. Real boots."

"These are real boots," she said, straightening her legs and pointing her toes and turning her feet right and left.

"Those are city-slicker boots. First time you step in a cow pie wearing those—"

"Wait a minute." *Eww.* "No one said anything about stepping in cow pies."

He laughed. A deep, glorious burst of rumbling noise. "If you're going to ranch with me, you'll be doing more than stepping."

"Hmm. Then I'll have to tell Kendall I changed my mind about her renting my house. Because cow pies are a deal breaker."

He wasn't laughing now. "You talked to Kendall about renting your house?"

Fighting a grin, she shrugged. "Just in case."

"Just in case what?"

"Just in case you wanted a roommate."

He leaned in, pressed his forehead to hers, breathed deep as if he couldn't get enough of her. "I don't want a roommate. I want a partner."

"You already have two," she said, because he was so cute when teased.

"Not that kind of partner," he said, kissing his way across her brow. "I want a partner to share my bed and my life and all my stupid dreams."

Reaching for him, she took his face in her hands, her thumbs rubbing the dampness from the corner of his eyes. "Your dreams are not stupid, Boone. And I would love to share them with you."

"I don't know why."

These were the simplest words she would ever say. "I love you."

"Good, because I love you," he said, grabbing her off the tailgate, swinging her around until she felt the evening breeze beneath her skirt, then holding her head as he brought his mouth to hers, kissing her as the spinning slowed.

He held her close, his wet clothes making hers damp, his tongue sliding into her mouth, one hand sliding into her hair while the other made its way down her back to her bottom. He squeezed and she wiggled and he chuckled into her mouth. She grinned against his, loving him. *Loving him.*

When he finally set her away, he yanked at the snaps of his shirt and peeled it off, tossing it into the bed of his truck before heading for the cab. There he found two T-shirts, pulling on both of them against the cold. But his hair was wet, and his pants were wet, and he was shivering when he walked back to where she waited.

She rubbed her hands over his bare arms, warming him with the friction. "Hey, buddy. You owe me a ticket for that kiss, you know. Carnival kisses are not free."

His eyes soft, his smile equally so, he dug into his front pocket and came up with the handful of tickets Faith had given him earlier. They were wet, worthless, but he found two not quite as mushy as the rest in the center of the strip and smoothed them out on the tailgate. He folded them in half lengthwise, then again, the layers strengthening the whole.

Then he took Everly's left hand in his and wrapped the narrow strip of purple paper around her ring finger.

"It's beautiful," she said, spreading out her fingers as if he'd slipped her Liz Taylor's diamond. "I'll cherish this forever."

"You damn well better," he said, and then he kissed her again.

And she knew without a doubt that she'd found her man, her love, her life.

Though she really was going to miss her shoes.

READ ON FOR A SNEAK PEEK AT
ALISON KENT'S NEW NOVELLA

# THE GUNSLINGER'S HEIRESS

APPEARING IN THE ANTHOLOGY
BOOTS UNDER HER BED BY JODI THOMAS,
JO GOODMAN, ALISON KENT AND KAKI WARNER.
AVAILABLE JANUARY 2014 FROM BERKLEY BOOKS

SAN ANTONIO, TEXAS, 1895

IT WASN'T ANY of Maeve Daugherty's business how Miss Fannie paid her girls, but these disbursement amounts hardly seemed fair. Annie received twice as much for entertaining the odious Mr. Reed as Etta received for her time spent with Mr. Jackson, who was young and spry and smelled delightfully of lavender and bergamot.

Not that Maeve knew the particulars of what occurred upstairs; she rarely ventured beyond her room into the grand parlor, and only then on her way to the kitchen for breakfast or midmorning for tea (when the girls still slept and few visitors lingered), but the set of ciphers Miss Porter used had been easy enough to discern.

Never before had Maeve been so thankful to her father's accountant, who'd indulged her fascination with numbers. Her father hadn't known; he refused to have his daughter involved in the unseemly pursuit of sums. And only the charity work her mother approved was allowed, not that which called to Maeve's sense of compassion.

Of course should Mr. Feagan see exactly *how* she was putting her instruction in profits and losses to use, he would no doubt regret having defied his employer. Fannie Porter's boardinghouse, while highly thought of and generous with donations and current on all licenses and fees, was still a brothel.

Demure whispers, delicate laughter, and skirts swishing like the wings of large hawks filtered through the door she'd left partially open while she worked. There were the payments to the girls to tabulate, as well as the proceeds from the gentlemen callers. But there were also charitable contributions, revenue due to the community for taxes, and that paid in dubious fines to police officers Maeve found equally dubious.

Then there was the recording of the transactions with the vendors supplying alcohol, and the profit made selling the drinks by the glass. Miss Fannie did stock some of the best liquor Maeve had ever seen. Until arriving, she'd never imagined such comforts had found their way to Texas. After all, Uncle Mick had made the trip sound like a Grand Adventure into the Wild Wild West where savages and buffalo roamed the plains.

Plush carpets, fine crystal, silk sheets . . . though only on the beds upstairs, not the one Maeve herself slept on. Her room was a far cry from the luxury she'd known at home. It was no more than serviceable, in fact, she being the help. But having expected dirt floors, not rooms redolent with the smoke of choice cigars and the warmth of bonded bourbon, she was quite comfortable in her newfound employment.

Fannie Porter's girls certainly had it better than the families living in Manhattan's Mulberry Bend and Bone Alley. And though her own conditions were plain and austere, she did, too.

More of the girls' hushed chatter reached her ears.

"Who is he?"

"I have never seen him before."

"Look at his eyes."

"Look at his hands. I would like very much to meet those hands."

Feeling a bit warm, Maeve slipped a finger behind the tie at her blouse collar, tugging slightly as she breathed in. What silliness. Meeting a man's hands. Hands were hands were hands, and the fact that a certain pair came to mind, a pair with broad palms, long, well-shaped fingers, and a dusting of dark hair along the edges meant nothing. Even if said pair bore frighteningly harsh scars.

The twittering continued, leaving Maeve curious. Miss Fannie's girls rarely engaged in gossip about men, and why would they? They saw so many in the course of a day, and there was nothing new under the sun. What about this latest arrival could possibly be of interest?

On the other hand, Maeve kept to herself, to the corner of the office where she worked, to the small storage room where she slept. Since the Day of the Disaster with Uncle Mick, she'd rarely done more than cross South San Saba Street to the druggist for Miss Fannie's medicinal supplies. Or to the butcher and grocer for the steaks and the cream and cheeses the boardinghouse chef required.

She would be the last of the women living in the house to understand the appeal of one man over another. Though, to be honest, that wasn't true. She did understand. She'd made a fool of herself because of that understanding.

"There's company in the parlor, girls."

Miss Fannie's words tumbled through the room down the hall from Maeve's open door, and the piano notes of Charles

K. Harris's "After the Ball" followed. It was fairly early in the afternoon, but she had learned that men's needs were not confined to the hours after dark. Or perhaps such was only the case here in the Wild Wild West where she recognized very little of the propriety she'd grown up with.

Whomever had arrived, the girls were certainly keen to gain his favor. The hushed chatter and twittering had been replaced by much boisterous laughter. She picked out Annie's and Etta's, if those were the girls names anymore than Mr. Reed and Mr. Jackson were who they claimed to be. Maeve had no right to presume. She'd been going by the name Mae Hill since the Day of the Disaster with Uncle Mick.

"I'm looking for a young woman," said the company in the parlor, the deep voice a resonant bass which was easily heard above the din.

Maeve's head came up, her hands stilled, and her heart nearly stilled, too, before it began beating in her chest like the drums in the Sousa band.

"I have several young women whose companionship I'm sure you would enjoy."

"No, ma'am, I mean, I'm looking for a particular young woman. Her name is Maeve Daugherty. She stands close to your height, and her hair's like that of a chestnut horse. Last I saw her, it was about to her waist. I was told someone of her description was in your employ."

"And when did you last see her?"

"It would've been last month," he was saying, and Maeve pictured him pulling off his hat, using his large hand to rake back his hair. "I work for her father. She left New York with her uncle and hasn't been heard from. Her family's worried."

Maeve closed her eyes, shook her head. Why would her parents not leave her to her life? She was twenty-two years old. She knew her own mind. And why in the world, if they'd had to send somebody to fetch her home, did it have to be Zebulon Crow?

"I don't believe I know a Maeve Daugherty," Miss Fannie was saying, but her words were hesitant.

Maeve imagined her frowning and casting a glance toward the hallway which led to the rear of the first floor and to the office. Zeb would follow the direction of her gaze, because nothing slipped his notice, and almost as the thought entered her mind, heavy footsteps thudded closer, leaving her no time to hide.

She pushed back her chair and stood, smoothing her blouse and her skirt, doing the same to her coiffure. She'd had no idea Zebulon Crow had ever noticed the color of her hair, though of course she wasn't seeing to her appearance for him. She only wanted him to realize she was in good health and good spirits and not homesick at all.

Yes, that was it. That was all the time she had. The door opened, and there he stood. Tall and broad-shouldered, his dark hair hanging to his collar, his dark beard emphasizing the strength of his jaw, his blue eyes like sapphires shining from the bottom of a flute of champagne. The dusting of dark hair along the edges of his hands making her knees inexplicably weak.

"Miss Daugherty." His voice was deep, almost rough, and nearly angry.

"Mr. Crow." The formalities. Oh, how ridiculous they were. "What are you doing here?"

"The night I found you in your father's library, drunk on his brandy, you asked me a question." He pushed the door almost all the way closed, though Miss Fannie would certainly be able to hear her should she cry out, then he moved toward her. "I came to answer it."

# ABOUT THE AUTHOR

A native Texan, **Alison Kent** loves her cowboys and is thrilled to be writing about them for Berkley Heat. She is also the author of more than forty contemporary and action adventure romances, and *The Complete Idiot's Guide to Writing Erotic Romance*. If there's a better career to be had, she doesn't want to know about it, as writing from her backyard is the best way she's found to convince her pack of rescue dogs they have her full attention. Alison lives near Houston with her petroleum geologist husband, where every year she fights the heat to grow tomatoes, and spends way too much time managing a feral cat colony. You can find her online at alisonkent.com, on Twitter at twitter.com/alisonkent, and on Facebook at facebook.com/author.alisonkent.